Awards, Reviews & Read...

BRITFIELD & THE ...

One of the most awarded books in fiction, best-selling adventure novel *Britfield & the Lost Crown* will be made into a live-action, feature-length **movie**, globally released in the fall of 2023.

Gold Medals: *Parents' Choice Foundation Awards*, Book and Audiobook

Gold Medal: *Children's Literary Classics International Book Awards*, Middle Grade Chapter Book

Gold Medal: *Mom's Choice Awards*, Best In Family Friendly Media

First Place: *CIBA Gertrude Warner Award*, Middle Grade Fiction

First Place: *Purple Dragonfly Book Award*, Middle Grade Fiction

First Place: *CIPA EVVY Awards*, Juvenile Fiction

Winner: *Book Excellence Awards*, Pre-Teen Fiction

Winner: *Indie Reader Discovery Awards*, Y/A Fiction

Winner: *American Fiction Awards*, Best Cover Design

Winner: *Next Generation Indie Book Awards*, Children's/Juvenile Fiction

Winner: *San Diego Book Awards*, Children's Fiction

Winner: *National Indie Excellence Awards*, Pre-Teen Fiction

IndieB.R.A.G. Medallion: Award-Winning Middle Grade Books

Blue Ribbons: *Old Schoolhouse Magazine*, Favorite Middle Grade & Y/A Book and Teens' Choice Award

First Runner-Up: *Eric Hoffer Award*, Young Adult

Silver Medal: *Global Ebook Awards*, Children's Literary Fiction

Silver Medal: *Moonbeam Children's Book Awards*, Preteen Fiction

Second Place: *Readers Views Reader's Choice Awards*, Teens

Bronze Medal: *The Wishing Shelf Book Awards UK*, Fiction Ages 9-12

Grand Prize Short List: *Eric Hoffer Award*

Award-Winning Finalist: *Eric Hoffer First Horizon Award*, Superior Work by a Debut Author

Award-Winning Finalist: *International Book Awards*, Children's Fiction

Award-Winning Finalist: *American Fiction Awards*, Pre-Teen Fiction

Award-Winning Finalist: *Best Book Awards*, Children's Fiction

Award-Winning Finalist: *CIBA Dante Rossetti Award*, Young Adult Fiction

Award-Winning Long List: *Shelf Ubound Magazine*, Best Indie Book

"Such a thrilling book filled with so much awesome history about England, crazy mysteries, and truly amazing characters. It had me hooked every second of reading it! I can't wait for the sequel."

– Hannah, *Kids' Book Buzz* - **5 Stars!**

"A perfect mixture of fast-paced excitement, heart-stopping surprises, fascinating history, and endearing characters with historical references scattered along the way. Tom and Sarah's devotion to each other provides an excellent backdrop to the many mishaps and dangers in which they find themselves. I could see this book being used in a classroom setting both as a literature piece and as a geographical and historical resource. Stewart's clever narrative draws you in and doesn't let you go till the end!"

– Dawn Weaver, *Reader's Favorite Book Reviews* - **5 Stars!**

"An intriguing first-in-series read that is sure to capture the attention of the middle grade and young adult crowds. Readers journey through English cities and countryside beautifully rendered in the narrative. The book also includes maps and intelligent background information about the setting and history with access to online illustrations and commentaries. Britfield *weaves plot, texture, storytelling, and fascinating characters into a winning combination and enriching experience."*

– Chanticleer Book Review - **5 Stars!**

"In this series opener, Stewart offers nearly nonstop action, with escapades both perilous and amusing, and exhilarating hairsbreadth escapes. The conspiracy is bold and compelling while the plot folds in intriguing facts about British culture, history, and famous sites."

– Kirkus Reviews

"Along with its relentless action and suspense, Stewart's novel provides young readers with a wealth of information about British culture (with frequent references to literary classics) and the history of the Monarchy and the Anglican Church. Highly recommended, Britfield and the Lost Crown *will appeal to both young readers and their parents."*

– *Parents' Choice Awards* - **Gold Medal Award**

"Author C.R. Stewart's Britfield & The Lost Crown *is a thrilling tale with loads of adventure and unexpected twists that will captivate youth audiences. Recommended for home and school libraries, this book earns the Literary Classics Seal of Approval."*

– *Children's Literary Classics* - **Approved!**

"A joy to read to the very last page, Britfield & The Lost Crown *is a high-spirited saga, enthusiastically recommended for personal and public library young adult fiction collections."*

– *Midwest Book Review*

"This is a far-flung adventure story that will readily interest the target audience. Stewart writes in clear, descriptive prose and integrates alluring and novel details that at times harkens back to an earlier era, an effect that offers an element of timelessness to the storytelling."

– *The Booklife Prize*

"Recognizing & honoring accomplished authors in the field of children's literature that inspire, inform, teach & entertain."

Award-Winning *Story Monsters Ink Magazine* - **Approved!**

"As a middle school English teacher of 28 years and a multiple bestselling author for middle grade books, I can honestly say Britfield and the Lost Crown *has all the right stuff. Intriguing characters, foreshadowing, and suspense will draw readers in deep and have them gasping for breath for the next chapter and the next."*

– Wayne Thomas Batson, bestselling author of *The Door Within Trilogy*

C. R. Stewart

Devonfield Publishing
"A Home for Exceptional Writers"
www.DevonfieldPublishing.com

ISBN: 978-1-7329612-1-0

Cover Design by Silvertoons.com / Art by Daren Bader

Make sure to explore The World of Britfield
www.Britfield.com

BRITFIELD

&

THE LOST CROWN

BOOK 1

C. R. Stewart

Devonfield Publishing
"A Home for Exceptional Writers"
www.DevonfieldPublishing.com

This book is dedicated to
Sarah Jane Fellows
In perpetuum diemque unum

Arte et marte
By skill and valor

Consilio et animis
By wisdom and courage

Fide et Amore
By Faith and Love

*"If you're reading this book, then you'll know
of my extraordinary story."* - Tom

CONTENTS

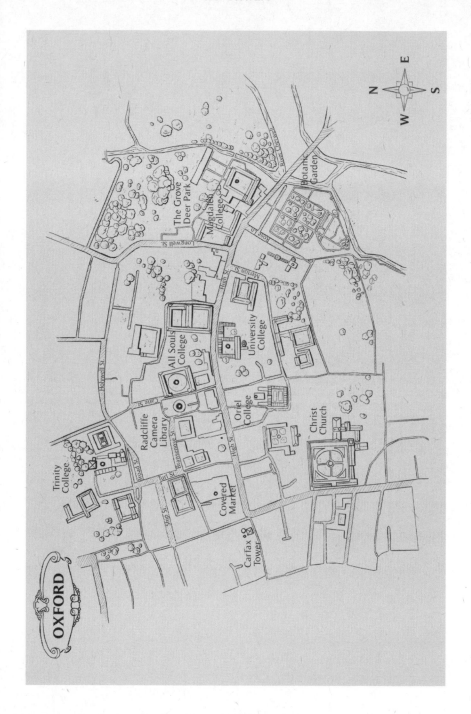

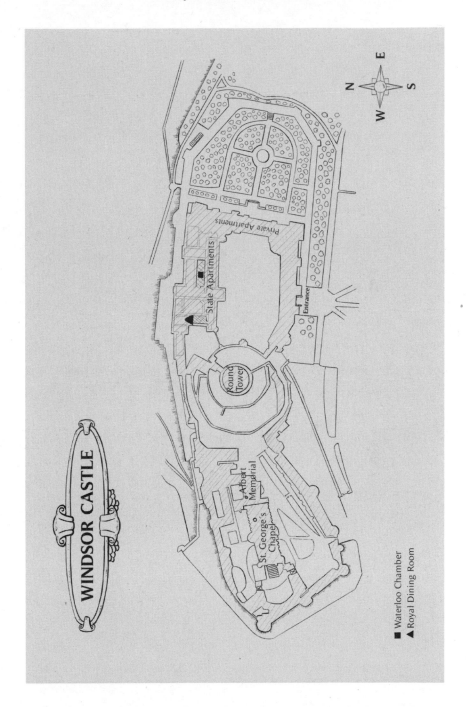

WINDSOR CASTLE

■ Waterloo Chamber
▲ Royal Dining Room

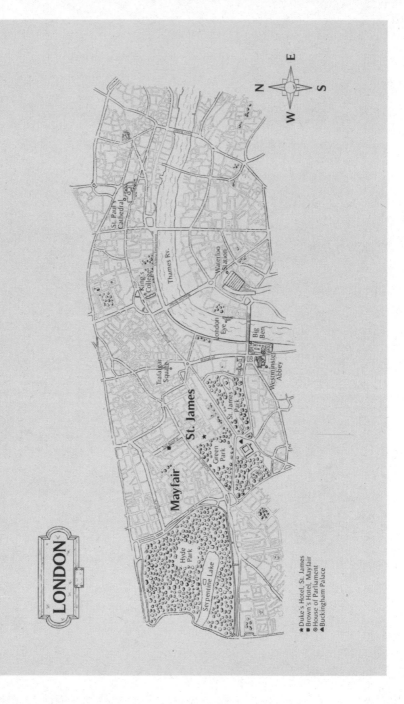

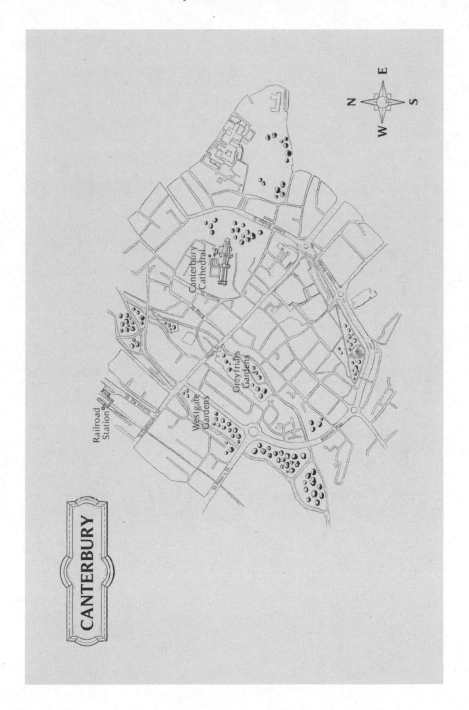

1
WEATHERLY

"Number forty-seven! Stop chattering to thirty-four and get back to work, immediately!" Speckle shouted from across the room.

"Yes sir . . . back to work . . . right away," replied Tom instinctively, pretending to be a dutiful servant.

He knew too well that talking violated the sacred Weatherly Rule Book, a seventy-five-page document of laws and regulations all orphans had to memorize when they arrived. Any violation of these rules resulted in punishment, the penalties varying in length and severity. However, some rules were made to be broken; it was the orphans' only way to survive here. They did what they were told and got away with what they could.

Just then Speckle closed his laptop, walked over to Tom, and slammed his stick on the table. Everyone froze at the loud crack; the room went silent.

"One more word out of you, and I'll send you outside!" hollered Speckle, looking around for other violators. No one moved an inch.

Speckle, the new supervisor, had arrived nine months ago. Over six feet tall with wavy grey hair, he had a deep, scratchy voice and a grip like a vice. He also managed Brewster and Sludge, two henchmen who helped keep order and discipline. These burly yet feeble-minded bullies followed his every command.

Tom grabbed a large piece of lumber, walked over to a table saw and ran it through the blade with ease. He then placed the wood on a workbench and started sanding the rough edges.

Every morning at 6:00, each orphan marched straight to this work area, referred to as "The Factory" because it was managed like an industrial plant. Their jobs consisted of putting together an assortment of handcrafted items: the girls made wicker baskets, and the boys built wooden chairs and tables. All these objects were hauled off in a large truck and sold by Brewster and Sludge in the local villages.

Glancing around the room, Tom quickly made eye contact with Sarah, who smiled and made a silly face. He began to laugh but stopped when Speckle trudged over.

"Is something funny, Tom?" he snapped, ready to strike with his stick.

"Ah . . . no sir, nothing at —"

"Perhaps you'd like to stand outside in the cold for five or six hours! Would that be funny?" he thundered in a threatening manner.

"N-no, it wouldn't."

Speckle lowered his gaze, closely examining Tom for any insincerity. Once again, the entire room went quiet.

Unconvinced by his answer, Speckle grabbed Tom's arm, yanked him from his bench and dragged him outside. The door slammed behind them. The weather was frigid, a strong Yorkshire wind chilling the barren landscape. December was always a deadly time of the year.

"Don't move!" ordered Speckle, his tone displaying a combination of contempt and indifference.

Tom nodded resentfully, his wiry twelve-year-old body shivering in the cold.

Speckle angrily marched back inside, glaring at the other children as he hovered around their workstations. He randomly picked up an item, inspected it and tossed it back down. Every day he would find some flaw, tearing up a basket or smashing a chair. Speckle observed everything and missed nothing. No one dared to question him or make direct eye contact. But even Speckle could be outfoxed. The orphans feared his strengths and did whatever they could to exploit his weaknesses.

Peering in from the window, his blue eyes glistening, and brown hair dampened by frost, Tom stood motionless. He'd been locked up at Weatherly for six miserable years, and this was the year he planned to escape.

* * * *

Located in Aysgarth, Yorkshire, in Northern England, Weatherly was about three hundred miles northwest of London. Although it was the 21st century, the orphanage looked medieval. The main building was an enormous sixteenth-century Elizabethan castle constructed from bluestone. Towering seven stories high, it had four massive turrets, one in each corner. The entire estate was enclosed by a twelve-foot high granite wall, with a massive wrought iron gate at the entrance. About fifteen years ago, the property was purchased by the Grievouses and turned into an orphanage, which the British government helped pay for as long as it was run privately. Although the Grievouses were supposed to provide each child with new clothing, healthy food, heated rooms, and schooling, they kept the money for themselves.

Like many of the other orphans, Tom didn't know anything about his parents, who they were or what had happened to them. But he hoped to find out someday.

* * * *

After missing lunch, Tom was let back inside. He cautiously walked over to a workbench and sat down by Patrick, number thirty-four.

Known as *the teacher*, Patrick, at sixteen, was the oldest and wisest orphan, with nine hard Weatherly years behind him. If anyone needed to know something, he was the best resource.

"Got the book?" whispered Tom, scanning the room for Speckle.

"Yeah . . . you ready for the mission?" asked Patrick assertively, his eyes intense and focused.

Tom gave him a confident nod. "Of course. I've been planning for it all week."

"Good. See if you can find anything by Dickens or Hardy — and no more Shakespeare," he said adamantly, leaning in closer. "Now remember, be extra careful. They've moved Wind to the east side of the house."

"Got it," replied Tom, ready to carry out his perilous assignment.

Patrick carefully removed *The Count of Monte Cristo* from behind his jacket and skillfully handed it to Tom under the table. It was a flawless transition, and Tom hastily stuffed the book in his shirt.

Speckle turned, mumbled something under his breath and continued to pace the room, searching for any sign of disobedience.

Tom returned to his work and started building another chair, his heart racing with nervous excitement.

If the orphans ever had a spare moment, they loved to read — it was their only way of escaping into another world. They had a total of eight books in their library, which consisted of a small dusty storage closet in the cellar. They had read each one probably twenty times, including a dictionary, an encyclopedia, and the history of the British Empire. But with so few books, they needed to come up with a strategy to get more, so they invented an exchange system. Each month, one orphan sneaked out at night, ran across the field, outmaneuvered a vicious dog named Wind and climbed in a small window at the Grievouses' beautiful Victorian mansion located close by. They borrowed one of the books from a well-stocked shelf in the study and exchanged it for one of their own.

When the clock finally struck 7:00 p.m., the orphans diligently put away their tools and cleaned up their workstations.

They filed out of The Factory two-by-two and down a long dark corridor. This was one of the brief moments they weren't monitored or supervised by any Deviants, a codeword the orphans used when describing authority figures.

Sarah ran up behind Tom and gave his shirt a swift tug. "So are you going tonight?" she whispered enthusiastically.

"I'll head out in a few hours," he replied nonchalantly, trying to mask his anxiety.

"You scared?" she inquired. "I'd be scared . . . especially of Wind."

"A little bit . . . but it's got to be done, right?"

"Right," she acknowledged, then hesitated for a second. "I wish I was going with you."

"It's always been a one-person mission — too risky for more."

"Fine," she said with a hint of disappointment.

"Although I wish you were coming," he added earnestly.

Sarah smiled, then reached in her pocket and handed Tom a small golden locket.

"What's this for?" he wondered, examining the delicate object.

"It's for good luck. You'll need it tonight."

"I can't take this."

"Sure you can," she said graciously. "Just keep it on you at all times."

"But it's the only valuable thing you have."

"There's more to life than just objects, Tom," she added philosophically.

Sarah Wallace, age twelve, had arrived two years earlier from Edinburgh, Scotland. Coming from a wealthy family, she had led a privileged life before her parents died in a suspicious automobile accident. She didn't have any relatives, except for a greedy uncle who only wanted the money, so she was shipped around to a few places and finally ended up at Weatherly. She had long, sandy-blond hair, hypnotic hazel eyes and an infectious laugh.

Just as they reached the stairwell, Mrs. Grievous appeared from behind a wall and advanced toward Tom. A cold chill suddenly came over him.

"What — do — you — have — there?" she snapped, her dark sinister eyes honing in for the kill.

Tom quickly switched the locket to his other hand and slid it into his pocket. Sarah faded back and watched intently, hoping her prized possession wouldn't be confiscated.

"Nothing. Nothing at all," he replied in mock puzzlement. "By the way," he interjected, quickly changing the subject, "I made two chairs in the workshop —"

"Open your fingers!" she demanded, grabbing his hands and yanking them forward.

They were empty.

"See . . . nothing," he retorted, playing innocent like a seasoned actor.

"Hmm, well they're filthy." She gave his hands a slap and pushed him aside. "I've got my eye on you, forty-seven. One misstep and you've had it. Now get to bed!"

"Yes, Mrs. Grievous," he muttered coldly, wondering why this awful woman was ever born.

Mrs. Grievous always seemed to appear whenever an orphan did something wrong. She had ghostly pale skin, kept her bright red hair compressed into a bun, and always wore grey flannel suits. Continually on edge, she had an explosive temper and made an unsettling clicking noise with her jaw. It was best to avoid her at all costs.

The children marched up the stairs and hastily retreated to their rooms. Speckle followed closely behind, making sure everyone was locked in and the lights were turned off. Standing by each door, he listened for any talking or movement. The orphans knew this, so they would wait about twenty minutes before they started exchanging stories and discussing the day.

There were fifty-six children at Weatherly, thirty boys and twenty-six girls, ages ranging from six to sixteen. If the number ever dropped below fifty-six, the facilities would be taken over by the government. The orphans hoped this would happen, because they couldn't imagine anyone else allowing what went on there. As far as they were concerned, anything was better than the Grievouses.

The boys and girls were kept in separate rooms with the bunk beds spaced two feet apart. These cramped quarters had water-stained walls and plaster crumbling from the ceilings. When it rained, the roof leaked and flooded most of the castle. The summers were hot and humid. The winters were chilly and bleak, with the cold creeping in through loose stones and broken windows.

Their garments were tattered and sparse: the girls wore dark brown dresses, with their hair usually pulled back; the boys wore brown trousers, long sleeve shirts and at times, overalls. Their shabby attire felt more like prison uniforms than normal clothing. Most orphans hated these outfits more than the dilapidated rooms or horrible food.

After everyone was asleep, Tom patiently rested on his bottom bunk bed and watched the clock on the wall.

The minutes slowly ticked away until it finally read 11:00 p.m., the perfect time to leave, for the Deviants were usually asleep by then.

Tom quietly slid off his wafer-thin mattress, got dressed, and snatched the book from under his pillow. As he tucked it in his shirt, the bedroom door slammed open. It was Speckle shining a flashlight directly in Tom's face.

2
THE BOOK EXCHANGE

Tom hastily ducked under his sheets, strategically placing the book in his pillow. He knew that if he was caught, especially with an illegal item, he was finished. Thoughts flashed through his head about the different forms of punishment: no food; standing in the freezing rain for hours; twice the workload for a couple of months; banished to The Dungeon, a musky and decrepit room in the cellar; the dreaded kitchen duty; solitude in the attic; or worst of all, something he could never mention or think about.

Just as Speckle approached, his stick tightly clenched in his fist, Richie, ten years old, knocked over a chair on the other side of the room.

Speckle stopped and shined the flashlight in the opposite direction.

This was a typical diversion tactic that the orphans had mastered. Whenever another child was in trouble, they would do anything to distract the attention of the Deviant. Dropping an object, knocking something over, or even yelling out usually did the trick. Although they risked retribution, it defused the situation and helped the other in need.

"What's that ridiculous racket over there?" Speckle yelled, his temper flaring.

"N-nothing, sir. I'm s-sorry," Richie stammered. "I was just g-getting up to ah . . . get my b-blanket and —"

"Stop that muttering and shut your mouth," he grumbled in an icy tone. "Now pick up that chair and get back to sleep!"

Flustered, Speckle pulled out the "dreaded notepad" and noisily flipped through the pages. This little book listed every mistake made and incident caused by an orphan. Speckle recorded everything and forgot nothing.

"Twenty-seven, Molly, thirty-one, Nickolas, thirty-four, Patrick, there it is, number thirty-nine, Richie. Yes, the stutterer. Another infraction for thirty-nine," he sneered, scribbling a few notes in his book. "I'll deal with you in the morning."

He suspiciously scanned the room again, then hastily left, slamming the door behind him.

Distressed, Tom knew that the mission was even more dangerous than before, but he had to go through with it. Everyone counted on a new book each month. It was the only way to be inspired and learn at Weatherly.

He waited until 11:30 p.m. and got up, throwing on his tattered jacket and gathering what he needed. He stuffed the book in his shirt and tiptoed toward the door, taking every step with caution.

"Good luck, Tom," whispered Richie, suddenly awakened and wiping sleep from his eyes. "Be careful."

"Thanks. I owe you one."

Tom pulled out a safety pin tucked beneath his collar and jiggled the lock. After a few moments, it clicked open. Unfortunately, these bedroom doors were the only place this technique worked. It was a valuable trade secret passed on by Patrick.

When Tom opened the door, it was pitch black, except for a sliver of moonlight shining through a cracked window. "It's now or never," he murmured to himself, leaving the secluded protection of the bedroom.

The floorboards creaked as Tom walked into the damp hallway and towards the staircase. Half-blinded by the darkness, he used the wall to guide him, running his hand along the rough surface. He slowly maneuvered down the stairs, taking each step with care and avoiding the middle section where it made the most noise. He paused and surveyed the different rooms. No sign of anyone.

He continued through the main foyer and approached the back door. It was locked. This was normal, but the orphans knew that the key was hidden on top of the doorframe, out of their reach, unless you stood on a solid object.

Tom quietly glided across the room, grabbed a chair, and carefully positioned it. He climbed up, snatched the key and unbolted the lock. After meticulously putting the chair back, he opened the door and crept out.

The freezing air caught him off guard: his teeth chattered, and his breath crackled. The moonlight illuminated the ground, silhouetting the landscape; it also made it more dangerous, for the brighter the moon, the easier he could be spotted. Although the Grievouses' mansion was only a hundred yards away, it seemed like miles.

Tom courageously started toward their house, hiding among the dormant bushes and lifeless trees, their branches surrendered to the cruel winter. One of the most important things to remember was finding the exact location of Wind — the dog's hearing was legendary, and his chain was long.

Tom scampered across the grass towards the mansion and quickly ducked behind a Mulberry tree situated twenty feet from the back of the house. This was always the best entry point, for it was dark and rarely occupied. *But where was Wind?* he wondered. Not knowing this critical information only added to his fear.

Just then he heard a faint growl coming from behind. It started with a subdued rumble, slowly growing deeper and louder. Tom twisted his head. Standing ten feet away was Wind, his white fangs glistening, and eyes focused on his victim.

Nicknamed *Wind* because no one ever saw him coming, this huge, unsightly dog terrorized everyone. If it weren't for the twenty-foot chain that kept him anchored to a metal post, there wouldn't be any children left. Sometimes the Grievouses just let him wander the grounds, barking at anything and chasing everything — those were the best times to stay inside or run for shelter.

Scared but undaunted, Tom steadily reached in his jacket and pulled out a piece of salami. It was a regrettable waste of food, but the only safeguard each orphan carried on these monthly excursions. Instantly Wind's eyes lit up and his mouth closed; he was transfixed by the object.

Tom tossed the salami about thirty feet behind Wind and bolted for the house. While the dog devoured the tasty treat, Tom made it to the Grievouses' back window. *Perhaps Sarah's locket did bring me luck*, he thought fondly.

Standing by the glass, he peered inside. It was unoccupied. He removed a skinny metal ruler from his pocket and slid it between the double-hung windows, unlatching the brass lock. As Tom gently opened the window, it squeaked against the wooden frame. He stopped and looked around. No one heard. Pushing it up, he climbed in and landed softly on the floor.

The room was dark except for a hint of light coming from the hallway. The walls were lined with mahogany cabinets and hundreds of leather-bound books. Everything from Geoffrey Chaucer and William Shakespeare to Jane Austen and George Eliot inhabited the neglected shelves.

Tom quietly closed the window and silently walked over to this treasure trove of knowledge, diligently surveying each book.

After searching through the first three rows, he couldn't find any Dickens or Hardy, so he climbed up and checked the fourth level. Tom held on with one hand and looked through the books with the other. After several minutes, he spotted *The Lion, The Witch, and The Wardrobe* nestled in the middle of the fifth shelf.

"Perfect," he said softly.

As he reached up and grabbed it, the bookshelf tilted forward. He held on tightly as it rocked back and forth. The creaking noise was dreadful, echoing throughout the room. *Perhaps they're not meant to be climbed on,* he quickly surmised. Tom desperately tried to balance himself, visualizing the impending disaster.

A few fretful moments later, the swaying slowed and the shelf settled back into place. Tom's forehead was dripping with sweat, his shirt soaked. He let out a long sigh of relief.

"Who's in there?" Mr. Grievous bellowed from another room.

Hanging on by one arm, Tom quickly removed the old book from under his shirt and slid it into the vacant space.

Footsteps approached from the hallway.

Tom hastily maneuvered down and hid behind a leather chair in the far corner of the study.

The door swung open. A desk lamp flicked on. Mr. Grievous entered, looking around and breathing heavily.

"What's that noise?" he muttered, holding a cigar in one hand and a wineglass in the other.

A heavyset man with blond curly hair, Mr. Grievous wore a bright red riding coat and tall black boots and carried a horse crop he often used for striking orphans. An unscrupulous wretch, he liked to think of himself as an English gentleman; English he was, a gentleman he was not. Puffing like a chimney, he constantly reeked of cigars and waddled more than walked.

Mr. Grievous shuffled around until he stood right over the chair. Tom remained motionless — not a sound escaped from his lips.

Looking puzzled, Mr. Grievous continued to examine the room, making sure everything was in its proper place: the desk was untouched, no chairs moved, windows were shut. He then looked at the bookshelves and did a mental count.

"Nothing's missing," he mumbled, scratching his head.

"I know I heard something."

Exhausted from his sudden excitement, he plopped down on the leather seat and continued puffing his cigar, a bluish haze lingering in the air. The smoke drifted over the chair and engulfed Tom, penetrating his eyes and nose. He wanted to cough and sneeze, but silence was crucial. Desperate to breathe, he covered his face; the smell was nauseating and unbearable. His legs began to cramp, and his head felt dizzy.

After enduring twenty agonizing minutes, Tom watched with relief as Mr. Grievous finally extinguished his cigar in a nearby ashtray, took one last sip of wine and fell asleep. The loud snoring vibrated through the room.

Anxiously looking for an exit, Tom silently crawled back to the window, knowing freedom was only inches away. He nudged it open just enough, climbed through, and closed it quietly. Using his ruler, he resecured the brass lock.

Now aware of the exact location of Wind and the length of his chain, Tom kept to the far south side of the estate, outflanking the dog's last position. Strategically dashing from tree to bush, he made it back to the castle door and twisted the knob. It was locked.

"Impossible," he stammered, his hands trembling. "Who could've locked it?"

Remaining calm, Tom remembered the emergency back-up plan: if an orphan was ever locked out, there was a slim chance the kitchen door was unlocked. Mr. Picketers, the cook, often forgot to secure it when he left. But it was directly under Speckle's bedroom.

Tom had no choice. He carefully ran around the building and stopped by the kitchen entrance. He tried the door. The knob turned slowly. Relieved, he pushed his way in and firmly closed it.

The kitchen was pitch-black, creating an obstacle course of rusty stoves and outdated equipment. The smell of stale bread and spoiled soup permeated the congested space.

Tom moved stealthily around, reaching out for unseen objects as he tried to find his way to the other side. He occasionally knocked his head on a copper pot dangling from the ceiling but quickly rubbed away the stinging sensation. Following a few more jabs to his side from sharp corners, he found the exit and stepped softly into the dining hall.

Gingerly walking across the hardwood floor, he entered a corridor and stopped. Passed out by the fireplace were Brewster and Sludge, snoring in unison.

Tom gently tiptoed past and started for the stairs when he heard someone coming. He jumped behind an antique cabinet and knelt.

In staggered a dark figure carrying a candle and reeking of alcohol. It was the groundskeeper, Mr. Crowley, better known as "the Badger," because he was small, but mean and nasty. Although he oversaw maintenance, no one was sure what he fixed or repaired, trimmed or cut, raked or cleaned, but he certainly drank a lot. A short stocky man, Crowley had skin like leather, a few sprouts of hair and a pudgy nose.

Tom remained stationary while Crowley stumbled

into the kitchen, probably heading for a late-night snack.

Tom cautiously made his way up the stairs and back to his room. Once the book was securely hidden, he crawled into bed, closed his eyes and instantly drifted off to sleep. The mission was accomplished.

Early the next morning, Tom was violently awakened by the shaking of his bed.

"Get up!" yelled Speckle, towering over him. "You're coming with me!"

3
THE SECRET FILE

Speckle jerked Tom from his bed and searched under the mattress, yanking off the sheets and ripping through the pillow. The other orphans stirred from their rest, observing the commotion: this early morning search-and-seizure was a common practice, and they were usually prepared for it.

"What's the problem?" asked Tom, nodding to Patrick that everything was safe.

"Quiet!" shrieked Speckle as he finished rummaging around.

Fortunately, the book was hidden under a small floorboard in the corner of the room. This was the orphans' *secret vault* where a cache of books, pencils and other illegal goods were stored. They guarded it with their lives.

"*Someone* was outside last night and in the kitchen!" Speckle stated. "I suspect it was you!"

Tom remained silent.

"I see, nothing to say — typical," grunted Speckle, dragging Tom from the room. "Mr. Grievous wants to speak with you."

* * * *

Tom stood in the main office, better known as "the interrogation room." It was a demoralizing experience, but every orphan had gone through it. Either Mr. or Mrs. Grievous would storm in, yell some type of accusation, question them mercilessly and finally dispense a fitting punishment. It was like a well-acted Shakespearean play filled with unnecessary drama and too much oratory. The ritual was supposed to spread fear among the orphans, keep them in line and break their spirits. However, it had the opposite effect: everyone just resented Weatherly and the Grievouses even more.

While Tom stood, Mr. Grievous strutted into the room, holding a riding crop and sucking on his cigar. Speckle remained by the door just to add a flavor of intimidation.

Mr. Grievous slammed his crop on the desk, dispersing his papers. "Who was out last night?" he yelled, confident in his show of force and false grandeur.

"What do you mean . . . sir?" Tom asked curiously, a blank expression on his face.

"Don't play stupid with me, number forty-seven!" roared Mr. Grievous, whacking his crop again. "I want information, and information is what I'll get! I need to know what's going on around here!"

He paused for effect and then paced the room, trying to frighten Tom with a menacing glare. To Mr. Grievous, Tom was different from the rest: he was well-liked among the orphans. If Mr. Grievous could manipulate him, he could influence the others. And Mr. Grievous did have one secret that Tom wasn't expecting.

"Someone was outside last night. I want to know who it was and how they unlocked the door!" he demanded, raising his eyebrows and staring at Tom with disdain.

Tom looked away, nervously fidgeting with his hands.

Mr. Grievous marched over, scratching his head and wheezing with every breath. "I know things go on here, behind my back! What're you kids up to?"

"I don't know what you're talking about, sir," Tom replied, a queasy, unsettling feeling in his stomach.

"You don't, do you?" asked Mr. Grievous, inhaling his cigar and blowing the smoke into Tom's face. "Mr. Speckle found the back door unlocked last night. I also heard some kind of noise in my house!"

"I-I have no idea —"

"There's more! Just the other day, we confiscated an illegal pencil from number eleven. How did she get a pencil into Weatherly, and what was she doing with it?" continued Mr. Grievous, circling Tom like a wolf. "We also found an apple core in one of the trashcans behind the dining hall. Fruit is forbidden at Weatherly, so how did it get here? Whose was it? I — want — answers!"

Tom remained still, an innocent look etched on his face. It was the orphans' best defense against the Deviants' constant belittling and ridicule; it usually worked. If the orphans ever said anything, they would simply be condemned for either revealing a secret or talking back to an authority. It was like a boxing match. You stood firm, kept your guard up, selected your moves carefully and always looked for the best shot. In this case, silence was the greatest weapon. It was wise to let them ramble on for a few minutes, take the punishment and leave — *but this time it was different.*

After bullying Tom, Mr. Grievous walked over to a

cabinet, pulled out a file and sat down at his desk. He whipped it open and started browsing the pages.

"We have all your information in here," Mr. Grievous said cunningly. "Know everything about you, even your past."

He glanced at Tom for a reaction but found nothing.

"Been here for six years; thirty-four infractions; talked back to an authority eighteen times; solitude nine times; cellar four times; caught with one piece of cheese, resulting in kitchen duty for a month," Mr. Grievous read out loud.

Speckle smiled, pleased that he kept such accurate records of all the orphans' violations.

"You never did tell us where you got that cheese. Did it just magically appear one day?" he asked mockingly. "Found outside twice. And it seems your best friend is Sarah . . ."

This last comment caught Tom by surprise, but he remained composed and continued to stare at a random object on the wall, knowing never to make eye contact or divulge any emotion.

Mr. Grievous continued shuffling through the pages. "It says you came from Southern England. You spent time at Edmundbyers, Westerville and Crumpbury before you came here."

Determined to break Tom's spirit, Mr. Grievous pulled out a manila envelope and closely examined the contents.

"Hum, that's interesting, most interesting," he mumbled in a devious tone, hoping to entice Tom.

"W-what's that, sir?" asked Tom, wondering what was so remarkable about his past.

"According to my file, there's some fascinating information here. Life-changing, if you ask me."

Although Tom was used to these clever tactics and fanciful wordplay, there was something different about Mr. Grievous's attitude.

"Tell him!" said Speckle loudly.

Tom's interest was now thoroughly sparked.

"It says your parents are still *alive*. Isn't that odd?" scoffed Mr. Grievous with a flair of indifference.

This revelation hung in the air as Tom tried to grasp its full meaning. He was completely stunned and felt like a huge object had just hit him from the side. Suddenly everything he believed about his past came into question. Mr. Grievous's well-placed remark had worked, bringing Tom's guard down and undermining his confidence — *round one clearly went to Mr. Grievous.*

"M-my, my, parents . . . still alive? Y-you know where they are? Are they okay? Do they know I'm here? C-can I contact them?" inquired Tom with mounting anticipation.

"Ah, I see I finally have your attention," he began, grinning with satisfaction. "I'll tell you what, Tom. I'll make a deal with you."

Mr. Grievous smirked at Speckle, then glanced back at Tom with a malevolent scowl.

"I want to know *everything* that goes on at Weatherly. All your secrets. What you kids do when we're not around. Who's to blame? Who you get things from? Where do you hide them? I — mean — everything!" he thundered. "You tell me this, and perhaps I can help you find your parents."

Feeling the trap was set and the bait taken, he comfortably leaned back in his chair.

Tom was filled with indignation. He tried to compose his thoughts but was caught up in the moment.

"How long have you known this?" he demanded fiercely, his voice rising. "Why didn't you tell me?"

"Watch your tone with me!" snapped Mr. Grievous, pulling forward and grabbing his riding crop.

Speckle walked over and stood by Tom, adding further pressure.

"I'm going to give you two days to think about this and gather all the information I need," continued Mr. Grievous. "I want everyone turned in. If you don't, you can forget about ever finding your parents. And most importantly, I'll make sure your next six years are a living nightmare."

Tom gulped. "Worse than now?"

"Much worse . . ."

Tom's eyes started to well up, but he remained stoic. After everything he'd gone through, he never expected this. Not just the threat, but that his parents might still be alive.

"We'll meet back in this office at six o'clock Tuesday morning. Now, get him out of here and back to the workshop!" Mr. Grievous commanded Speckle.

Tom stood immobile, his body slouched and his spirit broken.

Speckle firmly clutched Tom's arm and pulled him to the doorway.

"You have two days, Tom! Two days!" repeated Mr. Grievous, motioning Speckle to stay for a moment.

"Wait here and don't move," Speckle warned Tom, leaving him in the hallway and shutting the door.

"Do you think he'll talk?" asked Speckle.

"It's hard to say with that one. He's stubborn. Keep a close eye on him and report back to me," ordered Mr. Grievous.

"Yes sir."

"There's one other thing we could try."

"What?"

Mr. Grievous laughed to himself. "I'll let you know when the time comes. Now go."

4
CAUGHT

Tom stood in the workshop like a statue, his strength gone. He stared off into space, thinking about what had been revealed: *Is it possible that my parents are alive? Do they know that I'm in this miserable place? Or is Mr. Grievous just bluffing to get information?*

Seeking his attention, Sarah waved from across the room, but Tom was in a daze, drifting in and out of thought. She sulked, frustrated that her attempts went unnoticed. However, she knew something was wrong and anxiously waited to speak with him.

The time dragged on until the bell rang at 1:00 p.m. Stopping their projects, the orphans eagerly marched to the dining hall, starving for their first meal of the day. Working from morning until night, they usually ate once a day, twice if they were lucky. Their only ally here was the cook, Mr. Picketers, a kind, elderly man who did his best to sneak them extra food. Usually when he came back from the weekend, he brought some cheese, salami or even fruit. The kids cherished these additional rations and did their best to distribute them fairly.

The eating area consisted of four long tables, two on each side of the room: the girls sat on the left and the boys on the right. The ceiling hovered fifteen feet overhead, its massive wooden arches covered in cobwebs. The stone walls had slender Gothic windows, which were a patchwork of broken glass and makeshift repairs.

Sarah followed closely behind Tom, tapping his shoulder.

"Hey, what's wrong with you?" she asked impatiently, interrupting his train of thought. "You look as though you've seen a ghost."

"I have . . ." he answered in a monotone voice, a vacant expression on his face.

"Is everything all right? What happened last night? Did you get the book? I heard you were pulled into the office this morning. What'd they want?" she asked in rapid-fire succession.

Mrs. Grievous entered the dining hall and looked directly at Tom.

"I can't talk now," he murmured. "Let's meet later tonight."

"Okay," she whispered back. "Where?"

Just then Mrs. Grievous rushed over. "You two! Stop — your — talking —and — sit — down!"

Sarah looked up angrily and grimaced at Mrs. Grievous.

"How *dare* you make eye contact!" snarled Mrs. Grievous, her pale face turning bright red. "Keep your head down, forty-four, and don't test me today!"

Sarah recoiled and went off to her table.

After everyone was seated, Mr. Picketers strolled in and placed steaming pots of soup on the tables. He was followed by Danika and Daylen, both thirteen years old. Daylen grudgingly placed pitchers of water next to them, annoyed by the dreadful never-ending kitchen duty. Danika skillfully tossed stale bread to the hungry orphans.

When Speckle wasn't looking, Mr. Picketers pulled out some biscuits and apples from under his apron and quickly handed them to Bertie, who cautiously distributed the goods among the orphans, passing them under the table and down the rows. This little bit of extra food made a big difference. There was always great anticipation for what might come, and immense disappointment when there was nothing left.

Sarah pulled out a small crumpled piece of paper and a tiny pencil and quickly scribbled a message. After making sure no one was looking, she sent it down the row and over to Tom.

Still in a daze, he opened it:

Hi. I hate this awful soup.
Let's sneak out later.
I want to hear everything!!!
Where and what time?
– Sarah

Tom promptly destroyed the note. He looked over at Sarah, and pointed a finger to the ceiling, indicating *The View*.

The View was at the highest part of the roof. Orphans would risk getting caught just to look at the beautiful countryside or watch a sunset. They could see for miles, the green rolling hills, towns and villages, and even other castles, such as Middleham Castle, once the strongest fortress in the north; Bolton Castle, where Mary Queen of Scots was held prisoner in 1568; and Rosedale, a village in the North York Moors, with stone cottages and a towering medieval church. Being up there gave them a sense of freedom and reminded them that there were other places beyond the orphanage, that there was more to life than what surrounded them each day. It was a place where they could truly dream.

Sarah glanced back with a displeased frown but nodded yes. She loathed going to the roof. Anything over a few feet off the ground made her nervous. It hadn't always been like that. When she was younger, she loved high places and climbing trees until she fell one day and broke her arm. Since then, just looking out a second-floor window made her queasy. Nevertheless, she knew the roof was the best place to meet and usually safe from discovery.

Tom held up his fingers indicating 11:00. She nodded.

It was a well-known fact among the orphans that it was always better to meet at a prearranged location than go together. If one was ever captured en route, the other could get away.

As night fell and everyone was securely locked into their rooms, Tom got up and made his way to the door. Sneaking out two nights in a row was crazy, but he had to speak with Sarah, and this was the only way they could safely communicate. Although he was upset about what happened in the office, he would never tell on another orphan or expose their secrets. He would rather take the blame for everything than turn anyone in.

"Sarah will know what to do. She always does," he whispered to himself as he left the room and made his way toward the roof.

Sarah dressed quickly, unlocked the bedroom door with a hairclip and crept into the hallway. It was hard to see, but like the others, she was used to getting around at night. She kept close to the walls and felt her way down a narrow corridor, through an empty storage room and up a steep set of circular stairs leading to the rooftop. Fearful of being near the roof, her heart raced and her hands quivered, but she knew Tom needed her.

Opening a small window, Sarah leaped up on the ledge and warily crawled out.

The best location to meet was behind an enormous brick chimney at the highest point, a perfect hiding spot. The slate tiles were slippery, so each step had to be carefully placed. A few iron exhaust pipes protruded along the surface and were essential for grabbing onto. The air was freezing, and the wind was reckless.

Step by step, Sarah vigilantly made her way over the slick surface, remembering to look down and concentrate on the next move. She slowly inched across the steep slope to the chimney where Tom was waiting.

Seven stories above the ground, there was a 360-degree view of the entire countryside. The moon cast a subdued glow across the rooftop, and the stars brightened the midnight sky. Lights from the surrounding villages were shrouded in a layer of fog.

Sarah sat down, relieved not to be moving. The weather was damp and chilly, so she quickly buttoned her jacket and crossed her arms for warmth.

"I couldn't wait to see you," she exclaimed with excitement. "What happened today?"

"It was horrible."

"Tell me."

"This morning I was jerked out of bed by Speckle, brought to the interrogation room and questioned by Mr. Grievous," he answered glumly.

"Why? Did he know you went out last night?"

"He knew someone went out . . . but not who."

"Did anyone find the book?"

"The book is safe. I hid it in our vault last night."

"That's good . . ." She leaned back with a sense of relief. "I thought for sure they found it."

"No, but he knows things are going on here and wants me to tell him all of our secrets: the sneaking out — the illegal food — who's involved — *everything.*"

"You're kidding," she snapped indignantly, her fiery Scottish temper flaring up.

"I wish I was."

"What a load of rubbish. Who does he think he is?" she hissed. "As if things weren't bad enough, the Deviants always find a way to make them worse."

"Yep."

"And if you don't tell him what he wants to hear?"

"Then my next six years at Weatherly will be a living nightmare," he replied despondently, dropping his voice in defeat.

"You mean more than now?" she scoffed. "I couldn't imagine."

"Neither could I." Tom turned and looked at her. "What am I going to do?"

"We have to come up with something . . . a plan. You know, fight back," she exclaimed valiantly.

Tom gazed at the distant landscape, lost in his thoughts. "I . . . I agree," he mumbled unconvincingly.

"What else did he say?" she demanded, suspecting there was more.

Tom let out a heavy sigh. "Mr. Grievous said that . . . that my parents are still alive," he answered with a hint of suspicion. "He has some *file* in his office."

"Are you serious? But I thought —"

"I know."

"Well that's great. That's incredible." Her voice grew louder with enthusiasm. "Maybe you could finally get out of this dreadful place. See the world. Do something with your life —"

"I'd never leave here without you," he interjected, looking directly into her eyes. "If I go, you go. That's our deal, remember?"

"Yeah, but —"

"That's our deal."

She smiled and grabbed his hand. "Do you think he's telling the truth?"

"I don't know. He lies about everything else."

"So he's using this as leverage to get you to talk?"

"Exactly." Tom kicked the chimney in frustration.

"That little *swine*," she snapped again, shaking her head.

"I can't take another six years here. Not even six days."

Just then they heard a noise coming from the other side of the roof. It sounded like footsteps crackling on the slate tiles.

They hastily moved around the chimney, ducking out of sight.

"Someone's out here," whispered Tom, spotting a distant figure. "We'll have to go down the other way."

Although it was risky to hurry, they had no choice. They rushed over the rooftop and hid behind a large dormer, pausing to catch their breath.

The figure still approached.

"Who is it?" she asked quietly.

"I don't know."

"Do you think anyone saw you come here?"

"No. And you?"

"I don't think so."

"Let's keep moving."

He grabbed her hand and continued to the other side.

As they scurried over a steep incline, Sarah's hand slipped free from Tom's grip. She fell flat on her stomach and slid down the roof. The shock of the moment was heightened by the rapid pace of her descent.

"Sarah!" yelled Tom, unaware that he was shouting.

"Help!" she shrieked.

Consumed with disbelief, Tom felt powerless as he watched her disappear.

Sarah reached her arms out, desperately seeking anything to grip, her body scraping along the surface.

"Grab something, Sarah! Anything!" he hollered, frantic to help but unsure what to do.

Moving her hands outward, she clutched an iron exhaust pipe. The impact jolted her body but stopped her fall.

Tom sighed with relief. "Stay there and I'll . . ."

Suddenly the pipe snapped off and sent her swiftly downward. Sarah scratched her fingers along the tiles as she flew over the edge.

Tom's jaw dropped open, paralyzed with shock.

"Sarah!" he gasped.

Just managing to grab the gutter, she dangled eighty feet in the air. The iron pipe whipped past her head and hurtled to the ground making a loud *THUMP!*

"T-tom . . . h-help me," she pleaded, her voice shaking with fear.

"I'm coming," he whispered loudly, now aware of the noise they must have made.

Holding on tightly, her head twitched back and forth, examining the deathly drop below, her long blond hair shifting in the wind. *I'm too young to die,* she thought.

Searching for a solution, Tom grabbed a thick electrical cable lying on the roof and scaled down towards her.

Sarah's hands began to slip as the gutter pulled free.

"I'm losing my grip!"

"Don't — let — go!" he cried frantically.

"I can't hold on."

"I'm almost there."

"Hurry!"

She closed her eyes, preparing for the fall.

Tom rapidly approached the edge and seized her arm, both their lives now depending on the strength of the weathered cable.

"I've got you," he exclaimed.

She twisted and grappled until, with all his strength, he was able to pull her up.

"D-don't let me go," she gasped. "Please."

"I won't."

She clutched him firmly, hanging on for dear life. Her face was pale; her eyes were filled with trepidation.

The cable started to stretch and fray.

"It's going to snap!" she screeched.

"No . . . it won't," he assured her, hoping he was right. "Just hold on to me."

As they steadily climbed back up, he could feel her trembling, her breathing erratic. All she could think about was how close she came to death, how short life could be.

They found a secure area behind another chimney and collapsed.

Sarah hugged him tightly, feeling both terrified and grateful.

"Y-you saved me."

He gently pulled her head toward his shoulder. "Everything's fine."

"I-I've never been so scared."

"Neither have I," he confessed.

After collecting her thoughts, she grasped the front of Tom's jacket and yanked him forward.

"I told you I hate heights!" she scolded him.

"I . . . I know. I'm sorry."

"You better be."

Wondering if they'd been seen, Tom scanned the area. The figure continued moving toward them.

"Someone's still coming," he exclaimed. "Are you okay to move?"

She nodded reluctantly. "Y-yeah."

He helped her up and they cautiously maneuvered toward the other side of the roof. Desperate to escape, Tom pointed to a window a short distance away.

"If we can make it over there, we should be able to get back inside. Let me go ahead and see if it's safe."

"Okay," she said hesitantly, rubbing her sore knees and elbows, her clothes covered in muck.

"Stay here and rest for a minute."

"Be careful."

Tom descended a narrow gulley to a small four-foot drop-off onto another section. He jumped down and looked around. It appeared safe. As he glanced back to Sarah, she was gone.

"There you are!" growled Speckle, holding her firmly. "Where's the other one?"

Sarah struggled in his grasp, trying to pull free. "I-it's just me."

"You're lying!"

"N-no . . . I'm not."

"I don't believe you!" he said sharply. "I know I saw someone with you."

"I'm up here alone," she insisted. "There's no one else."

He suspiciously surveyed the roof again, looking for any movement.

"Very well," he grunted. "Let's go."

"Where?"

"Where do you think?"

"Please . . . not the attic!"

"You should have thought of that before you came out here."

Before Tom could do anything, Speckle whisked her up and made his way off the roof.

After sneaking back to his bed, Tom had a sleepless night. He tossed and turned, thinking about Sarah: did Speckle just threaten her and send her back to her room, or was she in real trouble? They probably didn't know about her fall or the broken roof pipe, just that she was outside. It couldn't be a serious punishment. Considering all the trouble the orphans caused, Sarah was kind of a saint, except for a few misdemeanors, like occasionally talking back to a Deviant.

Tom continued to think about the day as he stared at the peeling paint on the ceiling. He thought about Mr. Grievous's threat, the file about his parents locked in the office, six more years at this miserable place and his friend Sarah. It was a long night, but Tom knew at that moment it was time to leave Weatherly.

5
A WELL-CRAFTED PLAN

When morning arrived, Tom was the first one up. He shot out of bed and quickly dressed, anxious to get to the workshop and make sure Sarah was safe.

Wearing their raggedy, dark brown uniforms, the orphans entered The Factory in pairs and returned to their projects.

The weather outside was stormy; icy rain fell as gusts of wind violently shook the windows. The deteriorating roof continually leaked, forming puddles of water on the floor and benches.

Tom eagerly searched for Sarah, observing every face and counting each orphan: Helen, Andrew, Nathan, Calvin, Hope, Charlie, Kate, Trevor, Malory, Rob, Shelley, Weston, Melisa, Bertie, Jane, Branik, Cathy, Richie, Amber, Patrick, Elizabeth and so on . . .

All the orphans were present, all but one.

Tom looked at Sarah's table again, but her seat was empty. Perhaps she was running late or not feeling well. No, they always made you work even when you were sick. He knew something was wrong.

As Tom stood by his bench scanning the room, Speckle approached.

"Looking for your friend?" he muttered, an intimidating grin on his face.

Tom turned swiftly. He felt a strong urge to strike him

but remained calm. He couldn't afford another infraction or the brutal retaliation that would follow.

"You won't be seeing her for a while. She's in solitude — thirty days," Speckle announced with delirious pleasure.

"Thirty days," he repeated angrily. "That's crazy. No one goes into solitude for thirty days."

"Are you *questioning* me? There are plenty more attics. Maybe you'd like to see one again," he threatened.

Tom backed down, clenching his fists. "No . . . I wouldn't."

"Perhaps you can get her out early," he suggested, pulling Tom aside. "You have until tomorrow morning to give us the information we need. If not, you won't be seeing your friend for a long time."

Just then, Helen accidentally slipped on a puddle of water and sent her basket flying in the air. She screamed as it landed on one of the table saws and was instantly obliterated; shredded wicker fragments scattered everywhere. Mouths dropped open, and silence seized the room. The orphans were speechless.

Speckle glared.

"What've you done, you stupid little girl? Half a day's work gone!" he yelled furiously, then rushed over and grabbed her. "You'll pay for that. All of it. Now come with me." And off they went, disappearing from the room.

Mr. Crowley was summoned to clean up the mutilated basket. While some of the kids helped sweep the floor, others picked wicker from their hair.

Seeing the coast was clear, Patrick approached Tom.

"Backed you into a corner, has he?" inquired Patrick.

"He's trying to get information from you, right?"

"Yeah. How'd you know?" asked Tom, surprised.

"Because they've tried that on me before."

"Did it work?"

"No, of course not," he answered matter-of-factly, and put his arm on Tom's shoulder. "What do they have on you?"

Tom hesitated. "Mr. Grievous has some kind of file in his office. He says my parents are still alive."

"Really?" he questioned skeptically. "Could just be a trick, but it's worth looking into. I'll see what I can find out."

"He's also got Sarah locked up for a month."

"I heard."

"It's ridiculous. No one deserves thirty days!"

"I've seen some pretty bad things here, but lately this place has gotten out of control."

"What can I do?"

The two stood quietly, pondering the situation. Patrick's mind was like a tactical database of well-crafted plans never executed.

"When are you supposed to confess what you know?" asked Patrick.

"Tomorrow morning . . . but I'm not going to tell them anything."

"They'll make it really hard for you. Probably keep Sarah locked up."

"Then it's time to take action."

"What're you thinking?"

"Something I should have done a long time ago."

Perceiving his meaning, Patrick walked closer and whispered, "A breakout?"

"Exactly."

"You're going to need help."

"I know."

"Count me in. Let's talk at lunch, and I'll see what I can do."

* * * *

There had been many breakout attempts since Tom arrived at Weatherly, none of them successful. There was Eddie, age fourteen, who simply tried to escape out the front door, climb the front gate and run a mile to the main road. Regrettably, Mrs. Grievous quickly apprehended him and put him in "solitude" for a week; he was never the same after that. Then there was Branik, age thirteen, who was slightly more inventive. One Friday night he slipped into the trunk of the Grievouses' car, hoping to get out when they drove to York the next morning. Not a bad plan, but they never left that weekend. He was found by Speckle and punished severely.

There were the twins, Danika and Daylen, who had the most ambitious plan. Their idea was to dig a tunnel from an unused storage shed, out seventy feet to the stonewall surrounding the orphanage and climb over it with a rope they had found. They worked in shifts. Each week one of them would sneak out and dig a few more inches. They had dug about eight feet when Mr. Grievous discovered the small hole next to a pile of dirt. Consequently, both the girls had been on kitchen duty ever since. Everyone dreaded kitchen duty, and thanks to Danika and Daylen, none of them would have to worry about it for a long time.

And finally, there was Patrick. He had made nine elaborate escape attempts during his time at Weatherly. Every one was painstakingly planned, and all were enormous failures. The first one was when he was eight; the last one was six months ago. In his first attempt, he fell off the roof at night while trying to climb down; almost crippled, he laid in bed for three weeks, which he made up for by working overtime in the Factory. In his last attempt, he had made it to the front gate, but while trying to pick the lock, he was cornered by Wind and nearly eaten alive. Although undaunted, Patrick had become much more cautious.

* * * *

At lunch, the dining hall was ghostly quiet: it was as if a moment of mourning was taking place. Everyone was aware of Sarah's capture and the length of her solitude. Regardless of how bad Weatherly was, no one liked to be alone, especially for thirty days. The orphans were a tightly knit family, each one looking out for the other and helping each other when they could. Whenever someone was in trouble, everyone felt it. Sarah was admired, always optimistic and cheerful. She had a way of lighting up a room whenever she entered and making a bad situation better. It was obvious that she was already missed.

Tom and Patrick sat across from each other eating their rations and hashing out a plan.

"We've got to get her out of there," declared Tom.

"I agree," said Patrick, surveying the room and making sure no one was watching. "But we've got to be careful. The Deviants will be watching you closely."

"Then what's our best tactic?"

"I heard they have Sarah in the East Wing, above the storage facility. It's one of the larger attics, but it's close to the main office. It's way too dangerous during the day, so the only time to get her out would be at night, but the door . . ."

"What about it?"

"It's a massive double-bolted oak panel, probably six inches thick, with large metal hinges. The lock is impossible to pick. I know . . . I've tried before."

"So how can we get her?"

Patrick leaned back, devising a strategy.

A few other orphans looked over, knowing something was brewing and desperately wanting in.

Patrick snapped back to attention, a new idea taking shape. "There's a small leaded-glass window at the end of the gable. If we could somehow reach it, you could help her climb out."

"How in the world are we going to . . ."

Speckle entered the dining room followed by Brewster and Sludge. Like two unruly bulldogs hungry for attack, they lurked around the tables searching for any disturbance.

"Quiet. Deviants," warned Patrick, lowering his head.

Tom returned to slurping his soup, and Patrick chewed on some bread.

Sitting at another table, Trevor, age eleven, sensed the need for a diversion. Patrick made eye contact and gave him a nod.

Trevor waited until Speckle strolled by, then dropped his bowl on the floor. It made a loud crashing sound.

Furious, Speckle pounced on the disruption. "You thoughtless child!" he blurted. "Pick that up immediately!"

"Y-yes, s-sir," stuttered Trevor.

"What's wrong with you kids today?"

To add further confusion to the situation, Trevor began to cry.

"Stop that! Stop that blubbering!" declared Speckle. "Grow up, you whining little fool!"

Trevor rubbed his eyes as he picked up the shattered pieces, throwing Patrick a secret wink.

"Perfect, Deviant distracted," acknowledged Patrick. "Now, the best way to get to the window is for someone to tie a rope around the roof peak and throw it over the side. I can do that."

"Good." Tom sighed with relief.

"You climb up from the outside, scaling the wall and using the stones as footing. I'll make sure the rope is knotted so you have something to grab onto."

"But where are you going to find a rope that long?" he questioned, still trying to digest the boldness of their plan.

"I hid one behind a wall panel in the workshop. Found it a while ago in Mr. Grievous's shed. Knew it would be handy someday."

"Okay, but once I get Sarah . . ." Tom paused, internalizing what he was about to propose.

"What?"

"We're leaving this place — forever."

"I understand," he nodded, unfazed. "It's the only way. After the rescue, you'll have to leave."

Speckle looked over. The two instantly stopped talking and gazed straight ahead, continuing to eat.

When no one was looking, Tom stood up. "I need to show you something. Cover for me."

Patrick jumped from his seat and intercepted Speckle, engaging him in a pointless and distracting conversation.

"Mr. Speckle."

"What?" he snapped as he observed Tom leaving. "Where's number forty-seven going?"

"Bathroom. He'll be back in a second."

Speckle glanced at his watch, timing Tom's absence.

"I've been meaning to ask you," Patrick continued, "are there any other ways to speed up production in the workshop? You know, be able to produce more chairs and tables in a single day? I've been thinking about efficiency lately and wanted to get your opinion."

Like a cow caught up in a swirling tornado, Speckle was sucked in.

* * * *

Tom ran up to his room and over to the secret vault. He undid a screw, removed a wooden plank and grabbed a piece of paper wrapped in plastic. After putting everything back in its place, he raced downstairs and sneaked back into the dining hall.

* * * *

Speckle was busy complaining to Patrick about the lack of enthusiasm among the orphans and their inability to work harder. He blamed their attitude and the need for more discipline.

"That's a good point, Mr. Speckle," conceded Patrick, noticing Tom re-enter. "I'll think about what you've said." He then turned on the spot and joined Tom at their table.

When no one was looking, Tom unfolded a perfectly drawn diagram of Weatherly and the surrounding areas. It was magnificently sketched with details of distances, roads, streams, towns and, most importantly, the train station.

It had always been an accepted strategy among the orphans that a train to London would be the best way to escape. Once in the city, they could blend in, have some fun and maybe even find a family to live with. Basically, start enjoying a relatively normal life. It wasn't much of a plan, but it offered far more than they had. If they remained nearby, they would probably be found by the Grievouses or the local police, who took great pleasure in rounding up orphans. But up until now, no one truly knew the details of what was beyond that twelve-foot wall. Tom's drawing was a revelation.

"This is incredible," Patrick marveled, transfixed by the intricate details. "You've shown the entire estate and neighboring areas."

"I've been working on this for a while," said Tom with pride. "Using a map I found when I first got here and surveying the surrounding landscape from The View, I've figured out an escape plan."

"Proceed, my friend," he whispered as he eagerly studied the map.

"There's a damaged section of the wall about three hundred feet from the Grievouses' house. Many of the stones have fallen down, so we could easily squeeze through the opening."

"Sure, that could work."

Tracing the map with his finger, Tom continued. "Once we're free, we could follow this ditch down to the road, hurry along the path, across this field and over to Leyburn — there's bound to be a train to Harrogate. And from there . . . London." he exclaimed.

"The rest of your plan makes sense," interjected Patrick, "but that's a long distance to go from the castle to the wall, especially if the Deviants are alerted to a breakout. It's almost a full moon tonight — it's like a spotlight shining on the grounds. And if they unhook Wind from his chain, you'll never make it."

Feeling deflated, Tom slumped down.

"But there may be another way to get to the wall," Patrick announced with a burst of inspiration.

"How?"

Mrs. Grievous entered the dining hall and spotted them talking. Her eyes locked on Patrick as she marched over.

"Deviant," warned Bertie.

Tom quickly folded his map and sat on it.

"We can't talk now," said Patrick softly. "Let's go

over it later. I'll sneak the rope out before we leave the workshop."

"We've got to go *tonight*," insisted Tom. "Who knows what will happen tomorrow morning?"

Mrs. Grievous hurried to their table, anxious to condemn those who strayed from the rules.

"You there!" she shouted, her scrawny arm gesturing to Patrick. "Stop your chattering! I can see your lips moving from here! Lunch is over! Get back to work!"

"Yes, madam," grunted Patrick.

The orphans finished their meal and returned to the workshop.

Tom was only too aware of the essence of time: it was already 2:00 p.m. He was expected in Mr. Grievous's office the next morning at six. Meanwhile, Sarah was locked in the attic, facing thirty miserable days of solitude. This was one of the lowest times of his life. Hopefully Patrick had some more tricks up his sleeve, or their plan would surely fail.

Towards the end of the workday, Patrick slipped away. He was intrigued by what Tom had mentioned about his parents. Every Weatherly orphan wished for a family, so if there was even an ounce of truth to what Mr. Grievous said, Patrick had to find out.

He dashed down a hallway and up a set of backstairs, knowing the office was empty. By now the Grievouses would be enjoying their evening cocktails at their mansion.

Patrick tried the main door, but it was locked. Undeterred, he pulled out a leather pouch filled with an array of metal objects, all specifically designed for picking locks, unlatching doors and opening cabinets. In his nine long years at Weatherly, he had accumulated quite a collection of tools.

He grabbed a slender wire, jiggled the lock and popped it open.

"Perfect," he mumbled to himself.

Entering the room, Patrick went directly for the file cabinet. He had gone through it before, but there was never anything interesting or information he didn't already know.

He anxiously fingered through countless folders and found Tom's file, not under T or even the number 47, which is usually how the files were organized, but under B. This struck him as odd. *Maybe there was some truth to what Mr. Grievous had said,* he wondered.

Opening the cabinet, Patrick reviewed the usual information until he noticed a manila envelope. He had just opened it and looked down when a noise came from the hallway, possibly Crowley heading for the kitchen.

Hastily examining the first page, Patrick scribbled something on a piece of paper and put everything neatly back.

He then crept out of the office and firmly shut the door behind him. He still needed to get back to the workshop before Speckle noticed he was missing. There was one more important item required for tonight.

When all the orphans were locked in their rooms that night and the lights shut off, Tom sat on the edge of his bed anxiously waiting. Although everything in the last few days had happened so fast, he was ready.

Patrick, who had the only working flashlight, turned it on and sat next to Tom.

"Take a look at this," he whispered, opening an ancient piece of parchment.

"What is it?" asked Tom, puzzled.

"It's an old architectural drawing of the foundations and underground caverns at Weatherly. I found it in the cellar when I was locked down there a few months ago."

"There are underground passages?"

"Yeah, but no one is supposed to know about them. I'm not even sure if the Grievouses know."

Patrick placed the sketch on the bed.

"Incredible," gasped Tom, his hope revived.

Trevor and Richie watched breathlessly, as though Christmas presents were being opened.

"This is the main cellar," said Patrick, skimming his finger along the surface. "And here's the outlying foundation. It looks like there's a false wall *here*, made of wooden planks and hiding a small tunnel behind it. The passageway supposedly leads under Weatherly and out to this shed, close to the wall. It's probably only thirty feet from the section you said is damaged."

"*Small tunnel*," repeated Tom nervously.

"Yes, why?" asked Patrick with a shrug.

"I ah . . . have a problem about being in small places," Tom answered warily, his face showing a trace of panic.

"Small places?"

"Yep."

"Well, you'll have to get over it."

"Right."

"I'm serious. We have only one chance. You've got to overcome your fear."

"I will. I promise."

It's not uncommon for castles to have caverns under their foundations. If one of these dwellings were ever conquered in a battle, the occupants could escape through an underground tunnel. In other circumstances, some residents practiced religious beliefs that opposed the government's laws. These groups would gather together to hold secret meetings. If discovered by the local authorities, the people could flee through a passageway, avoiding capture and persecution.

Tom continued surveying the diagram, then turned to Patrick. "You've had this map for a couple of months?"

"Yeah, but I haven't been able to check it out. I'm not even sure if it's accurate."

Tom looked at him decisively. "It's a chance we'll have to take."

6
THE RESCUE

Trevor, Richie, Bertie and Tom eagerly followed Patrick to his bed, where he reached under the mattress and pulled out a large knotted rope.

"I'll climb onto the roof, right over the east attic where Sarah is being held. I'll tie this rope around a secure object and throw it over the edge. You climb up and pry open the window with this," explained Patrick, handing Tom an old rusty screwdriver.

"Where'd you get it?" inquired Tom, now realizing the extent of Patrick's supply of illegal goods. He had always known Patrick was resourceful, but this was borderline amazing.

"Where else? I snagged it from the workshop. Now, once you wedge the window open, climb inside and get Sarah. You two can scale down the rope and make your way to the cellar door," he said nonchalantly, somehow implying that the task was easy. "Remember, the entrance is on the west side of the castle, so you'll have to hurry."

Tom nodded in agreement, still trying to envision getting Sarah down the rope.

"Trevor," Patrick whispered with emphasis, "it's vital that you unlock the cellar door from inside and have it ready for Tom and Sarah."

"No problem," he replied willingly.

"Richie, you're in charge of lookout. You know the signal if you see a Deviant?"

"Of course," he answered confidently. "I've got what I need."

"Make sure you find a secure location outside where you can observe everything," continued Patrick. "And keep a close eye out for Wind."

"Got it."

"Bertie, let the girls know what we're planning so they're ready."

"Yep, will do."

The rest of the boys gathered around, knowing that their role in this heroic endeavor was to cause a loud diversion, if needed. They would quietly remain in their rooms, but if signaled by Richie, they would run throughout the castle and make as much noise as possible — *chaos* and *total confusion* were their goals. Bertie would remain at the window, ready to alert the boys and girls in their separate bedrooms.

"Tom, once you're in the cellar, use the flashlight to guide your way, find the false wall and force it open with whatever you can." Patrick paused, taking a deep breath. "If the map is accurate, that tunnel should lead to the shed and finally out."

"And if it's not?" asked Tom tensely.

"Then you'll have to improvise," he added firmly. "But whatever you do, get past that stone wall and away from Weatherly!"

Rubbing his forehead, Tom processed the information. This was by far the greatest breakout attempt in the history of Weatherly. Never had a plot been so brilliantly organized or coordinated.

The air was electric with excitement. Each orphan felt included, knowing his or her involvement would help in this grand endeavor.

Tom sprang to his feet and paced the room. Wanting to leave the orphanage was one thing; actually doing it was another. *What if the map was wrong? What if they were caught? And what would happen to the other orphans?*

"Don't worry, Tom," said Bertie. "We've got your back."

"You can count on us," added Trevor boldly. "We'll manage."

"It's now or never," insisted Patrick.

Tom looked over. "All right, let's do it."

"Brilliant. Get your things together," said Patrick, firmly shaking Tom's hand. "And good luck, my friend."

"You're not coming with us?" asked Tom.

"It's too dangerous for anyone else to go. Anyway, by the time I get down from the roof, you and Sarah should already be in the tunnel."

There was a solemn pause while Tom thought about what everyone else was doing. He was overwhelmed by their sacrifice.

"Thank you. All of you," he acknowledged. "I'm grateful."

The other orphans nodded, excited for Tom, yet sad they had to stay. Nonetheless, if just one of them escaped, it would be a victory for everyone.

Tom walked over to the hidden vault and grabbed his map, a pocket knife and a compass: all these items had been collected for just such an occasion. He also removed Sarah's locket and stuffed it in his pocket. If he ever needed luck, it was tonight.

The four of them moved to the door.

Patrick put his hand on Tom's shoulder and gave him the flashlight.

"Once you've escaped, don't forget about us. Tell everyone how we're treated. You're our *only* hope of ever getting out of here."

"You can count on me," Tom assured him, his voice sharp with sincerity. "I know someday we'll all be together again."

Patrick handed Tom a folded piece of paper. "Put this in your pocket and read it later."

"What is it?" he asked as he tucked it away.

"I'm not sure. I got it from the office cabinet. Perhaps it will help you find the truth."

Trevor, Richie, Patrick and Tom silently drifted into the hallway, glided down the stairs and melted away in opposite directions, confident in their mission, yet terrified of being caught.

* * * *

Carrying a rope slung over his shoulder, Patrick swiftly made his way down a long corridor and up a narrow set of stairs. He exited through a small stained-glass window onto the roof and headed toward the east gable where Sarah was being held.

Covered in frost, the slate was slippery, and it was almost impossible to find solid footing. Patrick took each step slowly, knowing that if he fell, it wouldn't just be the rope going over the edge. He was also close to Mr. Crowley's bedroom, so silence was essential.

* * * *

Richie cautiously made his way outside and found a perfect observation point where he could view the east side of the castle yet still see the orphans' second-story bedroom window. If any Deviants appeared, he would notify Bertie with a hand signal, and their diversion plan would be put into action. Richie also had one self-lighting match he swiped from the kitchen, which he would strike and slowly move back and forth in case of trouble. Hopefully either Tom or Patrick would see the glow and know something was wrong. The third precaution was an oddly shaped, hollowed out piece of wood. When he blew into it, it made a low-pitched sound, like a swallow. Although not a common bird in the north, especially this time of year, it was all they had.

Richie knelt behind some thorny bushes and gave Bertie a thumbs-up, acknowledging that he was in place and all was well.

Looking through the bedroom window, Bertie returned the signal. Everyone was ready.

* * * *

Trevor went to the basement door and unlocked it using the hidden key from above the doorframe. The floor was fourteen feet below, with twenty-seven unstable and awkward steps leading down. Although it was pitch-black, it was too risky to flip on a light switch because the glare would be seen from underneath the door. He hesitated for a moment, then closed the door behind him. In preparation for Tom and Sarah, he was supposed to navigate his way to the exterior bulkhead door and unlock it.

As he slowly descended, total blindness overwhelmed him. He moved his arms back and forth, clumsily trying to find his way. Somewhere between the fourth or fifth step, Trevor misjudged the distance, lunged forward and tumbled head first down the stairs. By the time he reached the bottom, he had been knocked unconscious.

* * * *

Tom hurried out the backdoor and around the castle to the other side. He knew that timing was everything. Although caution was necessary, speed was vital.

As he maneuvered from one bush to another, the bright moonlight made him a moving target. He crouched down behind a thick shrub, his hands nervously trembling. The air was brisk, the mood tense. This was the most daring thing he had ever done, and he was scared out of his wits.

Tom looked around, making sure everything was clear before continuing to the east side of the castle. Approaching his destination, he noticed an odd figure in the distance. It was Wind. Someone had unchained him.

* * * *

Patrick climbed to the top of the gable and carefully scooted along the ridge, his pants soaked from the dampness. He shook off the cold and made his way toward the end, the attic directly beneath him.

While Patrick was removing the rope from his shoulder, a few of the slates broke free and caused him to lose his balance. The rope slipped from his hand and skated down the roof, hitting a television antenna and snapping it off. Tangled in the twisted aluminum, the rope made an awful screeching noise as it continued to slide.

Horrified, Patrick stared in disbelief.

After a moment, the object slowed, stopping close to the edge.

"Oh, thank goodness," he gasped, grateful for Divine intervention, but realizing that if he didn't retrieve the rope, their mission was over.

* * * *

Awakened by the outside noise, Mr. Crowley sprang from his bed and flipped on a light.

"What the heck was that dreadful racket?" he blurted out, rubbing his face and trying to rouse his groggy brain. "Those stupid kids! What're they up to now?" he complained to himself.

Crowley quickly dressed and left his room. He staggered to the end of the hallway and banged on Speckle's door.

"Mr. Speckle! Mr. Speckle! Get up!" he yelled. "I heard a strange noise on the roof!"

A light switched on. The door swung open. A figure appeared.

"Did you, you decrepit old drunk?!" snapped Speckle, unamused. "Sure you're not just hearing things again?"

"I know what I heard," he grumbled. "I think something's going on!"

Speckle let out an exasperated sigh, too tired to squabble. "This better not be another wild goose chase," he said irritably, grabbing his flashlight.

"No, no. I'm positive this time."

"I'll check it out."

* * * *

Frozen with fear, Tom watched Wind aimlessly roam the grounds. Although he hadn't been seen, he couldn't risk any sudden movements or noises.

Reaching into his pocket, Tom pulled out a carrot; regrettably, it was all the orphans could find — no more salami. He wasn't even sure if Wind liked carrots. He seemed like a dog that only thrived on meat, preferably fresh.

Tom squeezed the carrot tightly in his palm and continued around the castle, each motion methodical and unhurried.

After a few minutes, he stood under the attic window and looked up. No rope — something was wrong.

* * * *

Patrick slithered down the roof toward the edge. He tightly grasped an exhaust pipe and tried to hook the rope with his foot, the cold penetrating his inadequate layer of clothing.

"What a nightmare," he mumbled.

After countless efforts, he finally snagged the rope and pulled it up, untangling the knotted mess. He gently placed the antenna behind a chimney and climbed back to the ridge, securing one end of the rope around a gigantic copper weathervane and tossing the other over the side.

* * * *

Speckle angrily stomped through the hallways, plodded down one flight of stairs, up another, and over to the orphans' bedrooms.

He checked each door to make sure it was locked. Everything seemed in order.

Leaning down by the keyholes, he listened for any talking or suspicious sounds. It was silent.

Speckle then looked out the hallway window and surveyed the outside property. No one in sight.

Frustrated that he had been summoned from his rest, he marched downstairs to investigate further. He closely examined the different rooms, focusing on each object and looking for any movement.

"That's odd," he muttered, noticing the cellar door slightly ajar.

He hastily walked over and opened it, switching on the light.

* * * *

The rope tumbled down and made a loud thump. Tom's heart leaped as Wind looked over but remained motionless. *Now's my chance*, he thought.

Grabbing the rope, he yanked himself up and used the uneven wall stones for footing.

Patrick popped his head over the peak and whispered, "Keep going, Tom. That's it . . . you're doing great."

Tom swayed back and forth, pulling himself closer to the fourth-story window. It was harder than he imagined; his muscles burned and his arms grew tired.

After only three stories, he glanced to the ground: the distance was staggering. *Not a good idea to look down*, he concluded, closing his eyes and taking a deep breath.

"I've got to keep going," he encouraged himself as he climbed.

Each second felt like an eternity, his momentum slowing. Wind curiously watched from the distance.

With tremendous effort, he finally reached the attic window and lightly tapped on the glass. The large A-framed room was dimly lit by the moonlight. Scattered throughout the space were an assortment of damaged furniture, moldy fixtures and a makeshift bed built out of wooden crates.

Sarah was shivering in the corner, covered by a moth-eaten blanket. Her eyes lit up when she saw him.

"What are you doing?" she inquired in a dry, scratchy voice. "Are you crazy?"

"I've come to rescue you," he gasped, clinging to the rope.

Stupefied by his courage, she hurried over. She tried to lift the double-hung window, but it was sealed shut.

"It won't budge," she said, flustered.

Tom pulled out his screwdriver and started scrapping off layers of old paint. Tiny flakes drifted downward as he hacked and chipped from all angles.

"Can you open it now?" he asked urgently, feeling his arms starting to give.

"I'm trying," she huffed, pushing upward with all her weight.

The window finally popped loose, and she shoved it open.

"Thank goodness," he said breathlessly. "Now help me in!"

Reaching out, she grabbed his shirt and pulled him inside. He gave her a weary hug then dropped to the floor, exhausted.

"Are you all right?"

"Just . . . give . . . me . . . a . . . second," he wheezed, sweat covering his face as he mentally prepared for the coming descent.

"I can't believe you climbed all that way," she exclaimed with admiration.

He hesitated for a moment. "Well, unfortunately, we'll have to go back down that way."

"What?"

* * * *

Speckle gazed down the stairwell and around the cellar. "Hmm . . . nothing," he grumbled, flipping off the light and locking the door.

When Trevor had fallen, his body had been thrown into a pile of boxes. It not only made for a softer landing, but it also provided the perfect camouflage.

Hunting for any indications of trouble, Speckle continued searching the other rooms. Crowley now followed close behind, more of a burden than a help.

After thoroughly investigating downstairs, Speckle decided to go outside and check the grounds.

"Stay here and see if you find any of them wandering about," ordered Speckle.

"And if I find one?"

"You know what to do."

* * * *

Realizing there was only one way to escape, Sarah apprehensively peeped out the window.

"Y-you want me to . . . to g-go down that?" she asked timidly, pointing at the dangling rope. "Especially after what happened last night?"

"It's the only way," he answered candidly.

She stood motionless, never more afraid of heights.

"I . . . I can't, Tom," she stammered, her voice quivering.

"You'll be okay. It's easier than it looks."

"What about the attic door?"

"It's bolted shut. There's no way to get it open."

He grabbed the rope and brought it towards her. She stared at it with a vacant expression.

"Remember how you used to love climbing trees," he encouraged her, motioning to the windowsill. "It's no different. Just grip the rope confidently and lower yourself down, one knot at a time."

She looked at him with trusting eyes. "Okay . . . I'll go," she said reluctantly, her voice jittery.

Although Sarah was afraid, she had a bit of fearlessness that seemed to flourish when truly challenged. She seized the rope and prepared for the descent.

"Keep your eyes on the wall. Don't look down," he cautioned her.

Sarah grasped it firmly and pulled herself through the window, her feet resting on the knot below. Hand under hand, one length at a time, she crept down.

Tom waited until she was about halfway and followed behind.

Just then Patrick noticed that the added weight was causing the weathervane to bend. He hastily grabbed the rope, hoping to stabilize it.

* * * *

Meanwhile, Richie had been watching everything from his hidden spot, excited to see the mission going well.

But as he continued his vigil, he suddenly noticed someone walking outside the castle. He leaned forward and watched the figure emerging from the shadows — it was Speckle.

Richie hastily fumbled for his match and lit it. He held it high and slowly moved it back and forth, but it burned out before anyone saw it.

Next, he clutched the wooden object in his hand and blew: a low, humming sound vibrated into the air.

* * * *

Patrick heard the noise and glanced over.

"Tom. There's someone coming," he called down as quietly as possible. "Hurry up."

Tom rushed down the rope. "Sarah, we've got to move."

"I-I'm going as fast as I can," she grumbled, steadily inching her way down.

The further strain added more tension to the weathervane, jerking Patrick's arms forward and pulling him toward the edge.

Sarah hastened to the bottom, grateful for solid ground.

Tom jumped the last few feet, making a loud thud on the lawn. The sound echoed into the field.

Wind growled and began to run in their direction.

Patrick frantically pulled up the rope and started to make his way off the roof.

As Speckle rounded the corner, he spotted Tom and Sarah standing in the distance. He was stunned.

In a fit of rage, he pulled out a whistle attached to his neck and blew. Its deafening shrill pierced the night and woke every living soul.

7
THE GREAT ESCAPE

Hearing the ear-splitting whistle, Crowley hurried to the electrical panel and flipped a switch; searchlights flooded the estate. Panic set in as the whole place exploded with chaotic activity. Now everyone was aware of the breakout.

* * * *

Upon hearing the noise, Mr. Grievous dashed to his bedroom window. He stuck his hands against the glass and peered out, his eyes bulging as he watched Speckle chase two orphans.

"What the . . . oh my gosh! We've got a problem. A real problem," he said hysterically, scratching his head and glaring at Mrs. Grievous.

With alarming intensity, Mrs. Grievous flew to the window.

"Those miserable little brats!" she exclaimed, stomping her foot. "How *dare* they disobey us?"

"Y-yes, you're right, my dear. . . quite right!"

She turned to Mr. Grievous, busy guzzling a glass of brandy to calm his nerves. "I want you to drive over there immediately and apprehend them," she demanded sternly.

"Yes, yes, right away," he spouted back, fumbling for his keys. "I'll get the car."

"I'll cover the rest of the property on foot."

"Good idea."

"I don't care what you have to do, just get them!" She grabbed a large bamboo stick and charged to the doorway. "Once they're caught, we'll make an example out of them!"

"Y-yes, my dear, of course."

She stormed down the stairs and off into the bleak night.

* * * *

"STOP — RIGHT — THERE!" screamed Speckle, astonished by the orphans' rebellious nature and useless attempts to escape.

Ignoring his order, Tom and Sarah sprinted toward the bulkhead door fifty yards away.

"Where're we going?" asked Sarah anxiously.

"The cellar . . . just around the corner."

"We're going back inside?" she gasped.

"We have to! It's part of the plan!"

"What plan?"

"Just trust me!"

She closely shadowed him until they reached the basement entrance.

Tom eagerly grabbed the bulkhead handle and yanked hard. It didn't open. He pulled again, and again, and again . . .

"Trevor!" he cried out. "Open the door!"

Wind dashed across the field, barking frantically as he closed in on his victims.

* * * *

Bertie witnessed all the commotion outside and gave the thumbs-up signal: *Operation Chaos* was in motion.

The boys hastily dressed and made their way to the door. This was their moment to shine and make a stand.

"All right, boys," said Bertie, unlocking the latch, "you know what to do."

As they scurried downstairs, Bertie approached the girls' door and gave it three knocks — the code for *chaos*.

It instantly opened.

Danika and Daylen stood at the entrance, never more ready to cause some trouble. Two long months of kitchen duty had taken their toll, and now it was payback time.

"Okay girls!" yelled Danika. "Let's move it out!"

"Come on everybody, quickly, quickly," added Daylen in a commanding tone.

Excitement seized the room. The floors trembled and walls shuddered as a stampede of girls descended the stairs. The orphans were about to conquer Weatherly.

* * * *

"Tom!" screamed Sarah. "Look!"

He glanced up and saw Wind about twenty feet away, his eyes glowing with demonic rage.

"Trevor! Open the door!" he repeated frantically.

They were boxed into a corner, Wind and Speckle rushing towards them. Sarah nervously clung to Tom.

"What's taking so long?" she asked desperately.

"I don't know!" Tom feverishly jerked the handle again.

71

* * * *

A hand tenderly shook Trevor. His eyes sprung open.

"I thought you could use some assistance," whispered Mr. Picketers as he pulled Trevor from a pile of boxes and brushed him off.

"W-what . . . how did you know I was down here?" he asked, shocked and disoriented.

"I knew you guys were hatching something."

"Really?"

"I haven't worked here for eight years without learning a few things," he replied with a smile. "I'm here to help."

"Fantastic."

Frantic screams continued outside the bulkhead. "Trevor!" yelled Tom. "GET — THIS — THING — OPEN!"

"Coming!" he shouted back, then led Mr. Picketers around the cellar looking for the exterior door. Traces of light beamed through the basement windows, illuminating their way.

"It's over here, Trevor," exclaimed Mr. Picketers. "Give me a hand!"

They tugged on the lock, but it was rusted shut. They pushed and pulled, but it wouldn't budge.

"Hurry," pleaded Tom, his voice cracking with despair.

"I'm trying," Trevor replied loudly, scouring the ground for anything that would assist him.

Outside, Speckle paused ten feet away, leaning over and wheezing, a turbulent storm brewing in his soul.

"Give up, you two!" he demanded, his body shaking and his temper flaring. "You have nowhere to go!"

Click! The bulkhead unlocked, forced free by a brick Mr. Picketers had smashed against the fastener bolt. Trevor nodded to him as if to say *well done.*

The door sprang open.

"Come on, get in!" urged Trevor, motioning with his hands.

Just as Sarah and Tom ducked into the basement, Wind's snout appeared behind them, his teeth snapping and his foul breath filling the air.

"Close the door!" gasped Tom, perspiration pouring from his forehead.

While Trevor was shutting the bulkhead, Speckle grabbed the handle and yanked. An intense tug-of-war ensued.

"Help!" panted Trevor as he was lifted from the ground.

Tom and Sarah leaped over. With the help of Mr. Picketers, they all jerked with one swift motion and pulled the door shut. Trevor hastily locked it.

"OPEN THIS DOOR — NOW!" roared Speckle, desperately trying to force his way in.

They all stood back, watching the metal frame violently shake. Tom glanced over.

"Mr. Picketers?" he wondered aloud.

"He helped me open the door," interjected Trevor. "And ah . . . woke me up."

"Thanks . . . for the help," said Tom, a bit confused but grateful.

"Happy to lend a hand," Mr. Picketers acknowledged.

Sarah stood in bewilderment, trying to process everything that was transpiring.

"I'd better get back," said Mr. Picketers. "If they know I'm here, I'll be fired."

"Which means no extra food," said Trevor in a somber voice.

"Exactly," he affirmed, giving them a heartfelt smile. "Good luck, kids, and Godspeed." He turned and hurried up the basement stairs.

Mr. Picketers would have liked to do more, but he couldn't risk it. If he was removed from Weatherly, the children would suffer. Along with providing them additional food, he would add extra meat or vegetables to their soup for nutrition. He would sneak them a pencil here, a book there, and occasionally even some chocolate. Always confined to the kitchen, he could assist them in these small but meaningful ways.

The bulkhead door continued to rattle as Speckle slammed something against it.

"What's the plan?" asked Sarah restlessly.

Tom quickly took out the old map and held it to the light.

"There's supposed to be a secret passageway that runs underground and out toward the wall. Once we're through, we can escape and get a train to London," he replied with a determined spirit.

"Escape?" she questioned, finding the very thought exhilarating.

"Yes. We're not spending another minute here!"

"How do you know about the tunnel?"

"Patrick gave me a map."

"Is it accurate?"

"It better be . . . or we're in real trouble."

"That's not very reassuring."

"I know. But it's all we've got, so let's find it."

* * * *

Most of the orphans made their way downstairs. Some went towards the kitchen to raid the pantry and refrigerators, while others ran down prohibited hallways or up forbidden staircases. A few strolled outside, gallivanting around and exploring the estate. Chairs were knocked over, rules broken and independence regained — it was total pandemonium. All this chaos would hopefully buy Sarah and Tom some time; even a few minutes would help. With so much disorder, the Deviants' attention would hopefully be diverted.

Overwhelmed by the oncoming stampede of children, Crowley was clueless. Dealing with orphans one-by-one was never a problem; ten-on-one was a big problem.

He stepped into their path and squealed, "STOP THIS INSTANT! GET BACK TO YOUR ROOMS!"

The kids were unfazed, now filled with the liberating sense of freedom and rebellion. They pushed past Crowley, knocking him down and continuing on their way.

He cowered helplessly on the ground, beleaguered by the force of so many. After a moment, he crawled over to the telephone and called the local police department. Although he was forbidden to dial for outside assistance, this catastrophic event was beyond his control.

Once he got through, all he mumbled was, "Emergency . . . Weatherly . . . Hurry!"

As the orphans rushed into the other rooms, Crowley leaned back against the wall, panting. In all his years, he had never been so shocked or surprised. He fixed his overalls and slowly got to his feet.

"Must . . . wake . . . Brewster . . . and . . . Sludge," he whimpered as he limped off to their bedrooms.

* * * *

Carefully studying the map, Tom flashed his light around the damp, musty cellar. Cluttered with centuries of worthless junk, it was an enormous space running the length and breadth of Weatherly.

Sarah and Trevor carefully investigated every wall, nook and closet but were soon discouraged.

"I can't find anything," confessed Trevor, tapping the stone foundation and surrounding areas.

"It's got to be here somewhere," said Tom worriedly.

"Are you sure there's not another basement?" asked Sarah.

"I . . . I hope not."

"Great . . ." she mumbled sarcastically.

"Just keep searching. We'll find it."

Trevor and Sarah split up while Tom tried to coordinate his location on the drawing. The thundering stampede of orphans rumbled overhead, their takeover of Weatherly thoroughly in motion.

"Sarah, try that area behind the broken furnace," suggested Tom, pointing to a corner.

"All right," she said, clawing her way through a barrage of cobwebs and low hanging pipes.

"Trevor, why don't you look —"

"Over here!" yelled Sarah confidently. "I think I found something!"

Tom and Trevor rushed over and examined a section of wood paneling. As Sarah tapped it, the wall echoed.

"See," she said, encouraged. "It's hollow on the other side."

"Find a heavy object to smash it with!" Tom urged, knowing their time was running out.

Grabbing the first thing she found, Sarah handed him a lead pipe. "Will this work?"

"Most definitely." He held it firmly. "Stand back! Both of you!"

Without a moment to spare, he hammered the wall, shattering the dry brittle planks into pieces. A cloud of dust engulfed them.

"It's working!" exclaimed Sarah, jumping in and pulling away the debris.

Little by little the wall disappeared, exposing a small opening.

"We found it!" said Trevor triumphantly.

Tom flashed the light inside, revealing a long tunnel that led into a dark abyss.

* * * *

Mr. Grievous frantically drove his car to the castle and skidded to a stop at the front entrance. He grabbed his riding crop and got out.

Noticing him waddling toward the front door, Patrick hurried over the roof and hurled his tightly wound rope into the air. It flew downward like a guided missile and struck Mr. Grievous. He was instantly knocked on his back and out cold.

"Brilliant," exclaimed Patrick with a renewed sense of satisfaction. "I've been wanting to do that for nine years."

Taking full advantage of the situation, he climbed over the copper gutter and shinnied down a waterspout. He then stared at the beautiful car: a sporty, silver, two-door Mercedes-Benz, the Grievouses' pride and joy.

"Interesting," he said deviously, reflecting back three years earlier when he had "borrowed" the Grievouses' truck and driven it around the yard.

Watchfully approaching the body, Patrick leaned down and grabbed the car keys from Mr. Grievous's pocket.

"You won't need these tonight," he said mockingly, then opened the car door and hopped in.

"Oh yeah," he exclaimed happily, sinking into the leather seat.

He started it up and revved the engine — *it purred*. Shifting into drive, he hit the gas.

The car jolted forward.

Patrick turned toward the front gate, an enormous structure of wrought iron towering twelve feet high. He aimed right for the middle and floored it. He swerved from side to side trying to steady the vehicle.

The car gained speed.

SMASH! He burst through the gate, forcing it wide open. The front window shattered into a web of cracked glass.

"Yahoo!" he yelled, sensing freedom was finally at hand.

* * * *

Danika and Daylen made their way to the kitchen, trailed by Branik for backup. Each one walked over to a separate refrigerator.

"Y-you know, we really shouldn't be in here," stuttered Branik.

"Oh grow up," Danika scoffed. "It's time we had a decent meal."

As they opened the doors, the inside lights flipped on: it was a vision of delights. The shelves were packed with meats, cheeses, fruits and everything else forbidden. Their mouths watered as they gazed in astonishment. *Why was all this food kept from us*, they wondered?

Without hesitation, they grabbed whatever they could.

"Start handing this out to the others," ordered Danika.

"Sure thing, sis," replied Daylen, munching on a pear.

Branik feverishly devoured an apple, then seized a hoard of tasty treats and followed the girls.

One by one, each orphan was given a variety of food. It was as if Christmas had finally arrived at Weatherly.

* * * *

Speckle bolted around the corner, frantic to get inside and down to the cellar. He simply couldn't figure out what Tom and Sarah hoped to accomplish by locking themselves in the basement.

"WHAT — THE — HECK'S — GOING — ON — HERE?" yelled Mrs. Grievous, running up behind him.

"Don't worry, madam," said Speckle decisively. "I'll take care of this."

"You better!" she snapped. "I want those two kids captured at once!"

"Yes, madam. They're trapped in the cellar. Nowhere to go," he assured her.

They marched to the backdoor and opened it. Their eyes lit up, startled beyond belief. The orphans were immersed in a whirlwind of anarchy. Furniture was knocked over, curtains were pulled down and food was scattered everywhere.

Boiling with rage, Mrs. Grievous let her mouth drop open.

Speckle was speechless, his fists tightening.

"SPECKLE!" she hollered at the top of her lungs.

* * * *

While Tom stared down the mysterious passageway, Sarah noticed his anxiety.

"What's wrong?" she asked tensely.

His voiced trembled. "I — don't — like — small — places."

"You're telling me this now," she said bluntly, a slight frown crease on on her forehead. "It's our only way out!"

"I know . . . just give me a second," he grumbled irritably.

"Good luck," said Trevor, a hint of sadness in his voice. "I'll miss you guys."

Sarah wrapped her arms around him. "You're the best," she said fondly. "Thanks for everything."

His face turned beet red. "Ah ... yeah ... no problem," he mumbled, not sure how to react to being hugged by a *girl.*

"We should get going," said Sarah, nudging Tom toward the hole.

"Yeah ... of course." He turned to Trevor. "Make sure to cover the entrance with something when we leave."

"Absolutely."

Not knowing if the passageway would lead to the outer wall, Tom and Sarah apprehensively stepped in.

Built out of brick, the inside was about five feet high and arched at the top. Roots sprang through the loose mortar and spider webs canopied the ceiling. Water trickled down, making the ground muddy — the smell was putrid.

The farther they went in, the more uncomfortable Tom became, his palms clammy and eyes wide open.

"It's okay, Tom," said Sarah, taking hold of his arm. "You'll be fine."

"Easy for you to say. Y-you're not claustrophobic."

"And you're not afraid of heights."

"Point taken."

As they continued onward, the ground soon filled with shadowy objects scurrying around. Tom curiously shined his light to the floor.

"Yikes!" he exclaimed, jolting backwards.

"They're just rats, Tom," she said calmly, kicking a few out of the way. "Weatherly's filled with them."

"Sorry. They, uh ... startled me."

Sarah grabbed the flashlight. "Why don't I lead the way?"

"Good idea."

Meanwhile, Trevor found an old cabinet and shoved it in front of the opening. He quickly picked up the broken planks and threw them into a dark corner. As he was leaving, he heard footsteps approaching the basement door.

* * * *

Andrew watched all the activities in bewilderment. Being new at Weatherly, he wasn't sure if this was typical behavior or just a special occasion, but he enjoyed it — he too was a veteran of the "Orphanage Club."

Bertie walked over and handed him a chicken leg. "Eat up, my friend. It may be a while before you have another chance."

"Thanks," said Andrew, partaking of the snack and enjoying his freedom.

Tonight, each orphan had his or her own agenda, whether it was raiding the kitchen or just seeing part of the castle they'd been forbidden to enter.

Calvin and Nathan made their way up one of the turrets, longing to take in the views they'd only heard about. The two sat on a wall and gazed at the vast landscape: the wind blowing, the bright stars, the distant lights — it was amazing. If only for one stolen moment, they realized that there was another world beyond Weatherly.

Rebel by nature, Eddie was in his element. He had been waiting a long time for such a splendid opportunity. He grabbed a blanket, stuffed it with supplies, and made his way to a window. Escape attempt number two was under way.

* * * *

"Get in there and take care of this!" insisted Mrs. Grievous, pushing Speckle forward like a human shield.

Crowley emerged from a hallway, still shaken by the upheaval. "B-Brewster and Sludge are on their way and I . . . I . . ."

"You what?" asked Mrs. Grievous sharply.

"I called the police."

"You idiot!" she howled. "I told you NEVER to call the police!"

"I had no choice — it's complete chaos!"

Mrs. Grievous threw up her hands. "You fool! You know we don't want *them* here!"

"What should I do now?" He quivered, cowering like a wounded animal.

"Round them up and lock them in the attics!" she replied contemptuously. "All of them!"

"Mrs. Grievous, I must get to the basement and deal with those two orphans," interrupted Speckle.

"Go! Find those despicable little monsters and bring them to me!" she ordered, her face twitching and jaw clicking in nervous succession.

Speckle dashed off, determined to apprehend Tom and Sarah.

The Deviants did their best to counter the uprising and capture all the orphans. Before Eddie got to a window, he was intercepted by Sludge and carted off to an attic. Crowley nabbed two kids trying to escape out the kitchen door. Brewster ran through the rooms waving his arms and scaring everyone upstairs. Mrs. Grievous swung her bamboo stick back and forth, swatting at anything and occasionally making contact.

* * * *

The cellar door banged open. The lights burst on.

Speckle thundered down the stairs and searched the entire basement, throwing open closet doors and looking in every conceivable spot. It was deserted.

"Impossible," he said out loud.

Then he heard someone panting. Crouched under an empty oil tank, Trevor was shaking with fright. Slithering by, Speckle reached down and seized him.

"Where are they?" he demanded, dangling Trevor in the air.

"Huh, ah . . . who, sir?" he muttered, mouth dry and throat parched.

"You know *darn* well who I'm talking about!" shrieked Speckle, pulling Trevor up to his face. "Where are they?"

Even though Trevor was terrified, he would never betray his friends — it was the *Weatherly Creed*. He simply hung there, limp, staring into Speckle's soulless eyes.

"Doesn't matter!" roared Speckle. "I'll find them myself!"

He locked Trevor in an antique wardrobe and continued his search.

＊＊＊＊

Splashing along the water-soaked floor, Sarah and Tom hurried through the subterranean tunnel. Strategically dodging puddles, Sarah accidently slipped and tumbled face-first into the mud.

"Blimey!" she cried out, now covered in muck.

Tom quickly stopped and pulled her up. "You okay?"

"What do you think?" she snapped, fuming and obviously embarrassed.

"I . . . I think it actually looks pretty good on you," he replied, chuckling to himself.

"Oh really?!" she said in a threatening manner, then wiped her face and smeared it on his cheeks.

"What're you doing?"

"Since you said it looked so good."

"Well . . . maybe no one will recognize us," he grinned.

"Maybe."

They both laughed, feeling the need to ease the tension. Sarah then used Tom's jacket to clean her hands.

"Do you mind?" he inquired, perturbed.

She gave him a frosty look. "You're supposed to be a gentleman."

"Use your own jacket . . ."

Suddenly they heard a distant sound of someone shoving the cabinet aside.

"Clever little kids," said Speckle, entering the opening. "How'd they ever find this?"

"The hole has been discovered!" exclaimed Sarah, her smile abruptly vanishing.

Tom checked behind him and saw a faint light dancing on the walls. "Let's move!"

Speckle tried to increase his speed but kept banging his head on the low-vaulted ceiling. "Bloody tunnel," he cursed, crouching lower.

"How far is it?" Sarah asked, becoming increasingly concerned.

Tom studied the map. "It looks like about a hundred feet before it stops."

"What's at the end?"

"I don't know."

The passageway twisted and turned until the light finally hit an oncoming barrier.

"I think we're here," announced Sarah. Frantically searching for an exit, she spotted an old wooden ladder shooting up about twenty feet. "Look! This must lead out!"

Hearing the oncoming footsteps, Tom quickly helped her up then followed close behind.

Sarah scrambled to the top only to find it covered by a heavy object. She pressed on it, but it wouldn't budge.

"It's blocked."

"Let me see."

Tom climbed next to her, and they both pushed. The object moved slightly, scraping along the overhead floor and showering them with dirt.

"Keep pushing," he urged her.

The hatch cracked opened just wide enough for Sarah to squeeze through. As she reached up, the flashlight tumbled to the ground.

"Don't worry about it," said Tom. "Just get through the opening."

She gripped the moist ground above and pulled herself out.

"What's up there?" he asked, trying to peek around.

"I'm inside some kind of shed," she answered, inspecting the cramped space.

"Good. We're in the right place. Now help me up!"

Kneeling, Sarah clutched Tom's hands and pulled. He was about halfway through when someone grabbed his foot.

"Gotcha!" declared Speckle victoriously.

* * * *

The wind roared through the car as Patrick accelerated down a long curving driveway. He was shaken by the crash but energized by his newfound freedom. Only fifty more yards and he'd hit the main road. From there he could go north to Scotland or south to London, but it didn't really matter, he would finally be out of Weatherly.

When he approached the main road, Patrick was horror-struck by the sight of a police car racing towards him, lights flashing and sirens blaring.

"Darn — the coppers!" he shouted discouragingly.

He looked for another way off the road, but it was impossible. The oak trees were thickly nestled together, forming an impenetrable wall on both sides.

As the two vehicles raced toward a collision course, the police car made a sharp turn, blocking the entire path.

Patrick slammed on the brakes and slid, smashing into one of the trees and destroying the car. Although he was stunned by the impact, he was still conscious, his face and hands cut in several places.

Two officers quickly ran over to the vehicle.

"Get out of there!" one of them yelled, forcing the door open and yanking him free.

Patrick struggled, but it was useless. His dazzling moment of glory was over.

* * * *

Mrs. Grievous continued chasing the orphans, aided by Brewster and Sludge. Each child was systematically captured and handed over to Crowley, who carted them away to different attics. When Weatherly was finally cleared of children, it appeared as though a tornado had swept through.

Crowley shook his head in despair. "I can't believe it," he huffed, exasperated. "What a disaster."

"Start cleaning up!" Mrs. Grievous hissed. "I'm going to find those two missing brats!"

"Yes, madam."

She went outside and whistled for Wind. "Come here, boy! Come on!" she shouted.

The dog obediently galloped over and stood at attention.

"Good boy," she said, tying a leash around his neck. "Let's go find ourselves some orphans."

* * * *

Feeling an iron grip secure his ankle, Tom was immobilized.

"Going somewhere, number forty-seven?" said Speckle with a sinister laugh. "You can't leave Weatherly. Not now!"

Sarah pulled harder, but Tom was slipping from her hands.

"No!" she cried out in desperation. "You can't take him back!"

With that, Tom kicked Speckle squarely in the face and knocked him down the ladder. Tom then sprang forward, tumbling over Sarah.

"Quick!" he hollered, getting to his feet. "Cover the opening!"

They shoved the concrete object back into place and searched the room for heavy objects. Sarah pointed to a mound of bricks stacked nearby.

"Over here," she motioned. "Get as many as you can!"

One by one, they frantically piled them on top.

Tom gasped, wiping dirt from his face. "That was close."

"Too close."

Regaining their senses, they examined the room: it was the water shed with a rusty pump sitting in the middle. Tom walked to the door and cracked it open. He saw the stone wall about thirty feet away and a small area where the rocks had fallen out.

"I see it," he said excitedly. "There's an opening not far from here."

"What do you think?" she asked anxiously. "Should we run for it?"

Tom surveyed the surrounding field. It seemed clear.

"Yeah . . . let's go."

He grabbed her hand, and they bolted from the shed. Everything seemed to happen in slow motion: their feet gliding across the grass, their hearts pounding with anticipation.

Standing fifty feet away, Mrs. Grievous watched the two figures run by. She bent down and unhooked Wind's leash.

"Go get'em, boy!" she cried. With the speed of a leopard, the dog shot across the lawn.

Tom and Sarah were about ten feet from the wall when they heard a familiar bark.

Sarah's heart sank as she glanced back. "Tom!" she shrieked, crestfallen.

"I see him!" he exclaimed, his adrenalin pumping and legs cramping. "Just keep running."

Sarah reached the opening and climbed up about four feet, using the dislodged stones as steps. She wedged through the gap and fell out onto the other side.

With Wind right behind, Tom leaped for the opening. He slipped on the rocks but managed to wedge himself through and tumbled next to Sarah.

Wind popped his head in the hole, snapping his fangs. His claws scraped the stones but failed to get enough footing to continue. Collapsing on the frosty ground, they both stared at the dog, its mouth foaming and eyes glaring.

Tom hastily grabbed Sarah and hurried across a dirt road, jumping into a ditch covered by wild overgrowth.

"You all right?" he asked, his head still spinning.

"Yeah, I . . . I think so," she wheezed, shuddering with exhaustion.

Tom looked up. Wind had vanished.

"He's gone?"

"Good, I always hated that dog!"

"Me too."

Covered in mud, rattled and weary, Tom still managed to smile.

"We're out!" he declared proudly. "We've escaped from Weatherly!"

Grateful for his gallantry and courage, Sarah inched closer.

"Thanks for rescuing me tonight," she said warmly, "and getting me out of that horrible place."

"You're welcome," he said cautiously, a concerned look in his eyes.

"What's wrong?"

"It's not over yet."

* * * *

Enraged, Mrs. Grievous marched back to the castle. She knew Tom and Sarah couldn't get very far, but she had to act fast. While crossing the estate, she discovered Richie hiding in the bushes. She clutched his shirt and dragged him out.

"Something tells me you know exactly what's going

on here," she said ominously, veins popping from her forehead.

"I-I don't know anything," he mumbled.

"You're going to tell me *everything*!" she stated matter-of-factly, then dragged him to the orphanage.

Crowley stood by the door as Mrs. Grievous tramped in, temporarily locking Richie in a cubbyhole.

"Since you've already called the police, inform them that two orphans have escaped," she ordered, incensed. "They got through the southside wall."

"Right away, madam," he said obediently and walked to the phone.

"And where on earth is *Speckle*?" she inquired sharply, her voice shaking with anger. "Why do I have to do everything?"

"I haven't seen him for about . . ."

At that moment Mr. Grievous came barreling in, swinging his crop from side to side.

"Where are they?" he asked, disoriented. "Where are those two kids?"

"You're a bit late!" rebuked Mrs. Grievous, giving him a piercing glare. "And what the heck happened to you?"

"One of those brats knocked me out and stole my car."

"What?" she gasped. "Our beautiful Mercedes? It better not be scratched!"

* * * *

Meanwhile Patrick sat in the back of the police car, his hands securely cuffed.

One of the officers got off the radio and turned to his partner. "Two kids got away, southside wall."

"Contact headquarters for back-up," instructed the other officer. "Have them circle the outside perimeter and neighboring areas."

Hearing the news, Patrick said triumphantly, "They made it!"

The police car then drove up to Weatherly, where Patrick was handed over to Brewster and Sludge. They hauled him up to one of the attics and securely bolted him in for the night.

As Patrick sat there on the filthy floor, he reflected on everything that had happened. Although his future looked grave, the last few hours had been the most exhilarating time of his life. He was amazed at how someone could live so much in such a short amount of time.

He smiled and laughed to himself. "Way to go, Tom. Way to go."

* * * *

The plan had worked, and the orphans knew it. Although they had risked everything, each child realized that a rebellion of this magnitude wouldn't necessarily result in dire punishment. What were the Grievouses going to do, lock everyone in solitude or the dungeon? Make them all stand outside for days? How would any work get done, baskets woven or chairs built? The Grievouses' valuable little profit center would come to a halt, and they all understood that production for this place was crucial. No, there was power in numbers. Whatever penalty befell them, in one way or another, the orphans had succeeded.

For Tom and Sarah, it was only the beginning of their journey, but so far, it had been the longest night of their lives.

8
THE ILLUSTRIOUS DETECTIVE GOWERSTONE

Tom and Sarah had run about two miles from Weatherly, ducking behind bushes when police cars raced by.

Uncertain about her future, Sarah was still excited. The last thing she remembered was being condemned to the attic. Now she had escaped from Weatherly and was experiencing her first feelings of independence and hope. Wherever the road might lead, she was certain it would be better than the one she had left behind.

Their destination was Leyburn, a small village southeast of Weatherly. From there they could get a train to Harrogate, then to Leeds, and finally to London. Although they didn't have any money, they were confident they could sneak on the train when it started moving and even sleep for a while as they traveled to their destination about three hundred miles to the south.

Tom carefully studied the map he'd drawn and looked at his compass.

"Leyburn is about four miles away," he told Sarah, pointing to the location. "If we stay off the main roads, follow this path, and walk across a couple of farms, we could get there in a few hours."

"I'm ready, whatever we have to do," she assured him. "But let's rest for a minute?"

"Sure," he agreed, tucking the map safely in his pocket.

They found a secure hiding place behind a massive oak tree, its leafless branches casting shadows on the frigid ground. Finally, able to relax, Tom reclined against the trunk. Sarah sat close by for warmth. The night was getting colder.

Trying to forget their hunger and tiredness, they closed their eyes and thought about what the future might bring.

* * * *

Back at Weatherly, all the orphans were taken from the different attics and led back to their bedrooms. Crowley started installing new locks on the bedroom doors, hoping to prevent any future breakouts. While Brewster remained in the orphans' hallway, Sludge commanded a spot at the bottom of the stairs. The place was thoroughly locked up for the night. There would be no more missteps or carelessness at Weatherly.

The shared theory among the Grievouses was that there were just too many orphans to punish. Any reprimand would delay production in the factory and disrupt the well-structured routine. The Grievouses would just have to accept what happened tonight and never speak of it again. First thing in the morning they would go through the entire orphanage, double all the locks, repair the stone wall and replace the front gate. Yes, they'd give all the children a long lecture, have them clean up the entire castle and threaten all kinds of punishment, but the threat alone was enough. Patrick would be working double-shifts for quite a while to pay for the Grievouses' wrecked car, but he too would survive this event.

The Grievouses only had one thing on their mind: getting Tom and Sarah back. If word of the breakout got out past the local police, Weatherly could be shut down or taken over by the government. Once the authorities started sniffing around, interviewing the orphans and investigating the last fifteen years, they'd uncover all kinds of despicable and fraudulent activities. The Grievouses' corrupt little system would be exposed, and they would lose everything — even go to jail. For them, the situation was dire.

Mr. and Mrs. Grievous sat in their office, discussing their options. Speckle stood close by, caked in mud and rubbing the red welt on his face.

"We must get those two orphans back!" demanded Mrs. Grievous. "We can't afford to have them missing!"

"The entire local police force is searching the area. They'll find them," Mr. Grievous assured her, half flustered and half infuriated about his car.

"That's not good enough!" she refuted impatiently. "We can't take that risk!"

"Then what do you propose?" he asked, clearly distressed.

Speckle stepped forward. "I could go after them, madam —"

"No! We need you here, keeping a close eye on the orphans," she interrupted abrasively. "They've tasted the power of *freedom* tonight and will be twice as hard to control tomorrow."

There was a moment of silence while they contemplated the situation.

"There is someone," suggested Mrs. Grievous hesitantly. "He's profoundly gifted and extremely proficient. He's also quite . . . discreet."

Mr. Grievous read her mind. "Yes, of course, Detective Gowerstone," he blurted out. "That's an excellent idea!"

"I know it is," she said in a dismissive tone.

Detective Arthur Gowerstone was a legend. Although he travelled throughout Britain and Europe solving different criminal cases, his specialty was missing children and runaway orphans. He was unsurpassed in his field. Educated at Eton and Oxford, he had his choice of any profession, yet he had selected law enforcement: it was the pursuit, the chase, the task of figuring out his adversaries' next move, outthinking them and finally capturing them. He *loved* the hunt. Gowerstone stood six feet tall with dark brown hair and an athletic build. He was brilliant, cool and unpredictable. He had never lost a case in his entire career, never failed to capture a villain or find a child. Never that is, except once. However, that had happened a decade ago, under circumstances that still haunted him. Needless to say, Tom and Sarah would be up against the best there was.

"Make the call," ordered Mrs. Grievous. "Let's get him over here, now!"

* * * *

Tom had fallen asleep under the tree but was suddenly awakened by a police siren racing by. He glanced at Sarah and gave her a gentle nudge.

"Wake up," he whispered softly. "We've got to go."

She slowly stirred, desperate for a few more hours of rest.

"I'm so tired," she mumbled, her clothes dampened by a thin layer of frost.

"I know . . . but we *must* keep moving," he insisted, then stood up and brushed the dirt from his pants. "The trains stop running at one a.m."

"How do you know?"

"Patrick told me."

"It figures. He's a wealth of knowledge," she laughed half-heartedly as she got to her feet. "I hope the other orphans are okay."

"So do I, but we need to stay focused on getting to that train station." Tom pulled out his compass again and examined the direction needle. "We should head southeast," he motioned.

"Okay. I'll follow your lead."

As they walked through the desolate landscape, clouds rolled in, threatening rain. The temperature continued to drop.

"We can stay on this trail until we get to Leyburn, hop a train to Harrogate, then to Leeds, and finally to London."

"What about the police?"

"They'll be on the main roads," he answered unsurely, his voice dropping. "Or at least I hope so."

"And if they're not? What if they search the whole countryside?"

"Then we run — we hide — we do whatever we have to. But we don't get caught!"

Sarah nodded in agreement, encouraged by Tom's enthusiasm and her own nervous excitement.

They took a deep breath and bravely embarked on their three-mile hike.

* * * *

A few hours later, Detective Gowerstone calmly walked into the Weatherly office, followed by two police officers. He was a portrait of refinement and elegance: fresh from Savile Row, he wore a perfectly fitted Gieves & Hawkes pinstriped suit, a crisp white Turnbull & Asser shirt, a light blue Thomas Pink tie and highly polished Church shoes. He also had a slight scent of Floris Number 89. He looked more like a movie star than a public servant.

"Thank you for coming so quickly," said Mr. Grievous, a bit apprehensive.

"You're fortunate I was in the area working on a case. Who's missing?" asked Detective Gowerstone in an authoritative manner.

Mr. Grievous quickly fumbled through his file cabinet and handed over Sarah and Tom's folders. "These two," he replied, feeling intimidated by Gowerstone's threatening presence. "They broke out about three hours ago."

"I see."

"I can't tell you the amount of trouble —"

"Save it. I'm not interested," said the detective coldly, grabbing the folders.

He pulled out a small leather notepad and meticulously wrote down every detail. After methodically reviewing Sarah's information, he started on Tom's file.

"Hmm, very interesting," Gowerstone whispered to himself, examining a recent photo.

"You know him?" inquired Mr. Grievous, desperate for insight.

Gowerstone remained silent, lost in his thoughts. "Fascinating . . ." he continued, digesting the picture.

Mrs. Grievous stood quickly, overwhelmed with anticipation. "What is it?" she wondered. "I must know."

"You wouldn't understand, so I won't waste your time," he answered abruptly.

Defeated, she sank back into her chair.

Gowerstone took a few more notes, then removed the manila envelope. Before he could open it, Mr. Grievous tried to snatch it from his hand.

"Oh, that's, ah . . . nothing important," he said nervously, tripping over his words. "I don't know how that g-got in there."

With a piercing stare, the detective studied Mr. Grievous's worried eyes. "You're not hiding anything from me, are you?" asked Gowerstone suspiciously.

"N-no," he stuttered. "W-why would I do —"

"Because if you are, or if you hinder this case in any way, I'll find out," he threatened.

"Y-yes, I understand. I understand completely," mumbled Mr. Grievous, sweat glistening on his forehead.

When Gowerstone opened the envelope and read through the contents, his eyes brightened. "This explains a great deal," he stated straightforwardly, then carefully placed the papers back in the envelope and turned to Mr. Grievous. "How long have you had this information?" he asked directly.

"Not long, not long at all. I just received it," he responded unpersuasively.

"I'll be keeping these documents," the detective informed him.

Mr. and Mrs. Grievous exchanged concerned looks but said nothing.

Gowerstone then walked to a local map posted on the wall and studied it, perusing the immediate areas and calculating distances.

"That's where they'll be," he declared, pointing to an exact location.

"Where?" asked Speckle, making eye contact with Gowerstone. The two shared a moment of silence.

"No need for you to worry," replied Gowerstone coolly. "It's out of your hands now."

"You'll find them, right?" asked Mrs. Grievous anxiously.

"Of course," he answered plainly as he checked the time on his Cartier watch.

"And capture them?" she continued.

"I always do," he confirmed.

Gowerstone walked to the door, carrying the folders under his arm. "It's time for us to leave. We have a great deal of work ahead."

Speckle blocked the entrance. Gowerstone lifted his eyebrows, gesturing him to move. Suddenly feeling the hierarchical subjection of the British class system, Speckle quickly opened the door and slowly melted away.

"Cheers," said Gowerstone as he gracefully sauntered out. The two policemen trailed behind.

* * * *

Tom and Sarah had gone several miles but were exhausted.

"How much farther?" she gasped, struggling to keep up.

"I'm not sure," he replied, sensing her fatigue and discouragement. "But it must be close."

"I'm worn out and starving."

"I know. But you're doing great, and we're almost there."

Tom stopped for a minute and grabbed her hand.

"Just think how exciting it's going to be when we're in London," he encouraged her. "All the great things we'll do together. We'll make it, I promise you."

She smiled, her spirits slightly lifted.

"You're right . . . let's keep going."

They hadn't gone more than a few steps when headlights came barreling down the road they were crossing.

"It's a car!" she exclaimed. "Maybe we could get a ride!"

"We don't know who it is."

"But think how fast we could get to the train."

Suddenly red and blue lights flashed on.

Without hesitation, Tom grasped Sarah's arm. "Quick, over here!" he yelled, gesturing towards a farmhouse.

They raced across the pasture and disappeared into a dormant wheat field.

"Follow me!" he shouted, swinging his arms to clear a path.

They navigated through a maze of tall stalks and exited near a thatched cottage, smoke billowing from the chimney. The police car continued, unaware of their presence.

"They didn't see us," said Tom, bending over to catch his breath. "We'll wait until they're out of sight, then —"

"What're you two doing out here?" a rough voice interrupted as a tall muscular figure approached. The stranger had broad shoulders and a handsome face weathered by time and hard work.

Startled, Tom and Sarah whipped around.

"We, um, are trying to get to Leyburn, sir," replied Tom nervously.

"At this time of night?" asked the man skeptically. "That's over two miles from here."

"I . . . I know," said Tom. "We're trying to catch a train to London."

The man walked closer, scrutinizing their disheveled appearance: dirty faces, clothes covered in mud, shuddering from the cold. He also noticed the familiar outfits only orphans from Weatherly wore, and he immediately understood their predicament.

"That's a long journey for two children." The man's voice softened. "Look, why don't you come inside for a few minutes and get warm. I've got some stew on the stove. I'll fetch a couple of bowls."

Sarah looked at Tom, nodding yes.

"Sure, that'd be great," he answered happily.

"Yes, thank you," added Sarah, her stomach growling at the thought of nourishment.

They followed the man into his modest cottage. Although the home was small, it was paradise: the warmth from a roaring fire and the security of being safely inside. A lone Christmas stocking hung from the mantel, something neither of them had seen for years. A few other handmade holiday decorations were scattered about.

He walked them to a sink where they washed up. Feeling the hot water on their hands and face was a taste of Heaven.

"You must be freezing. Here, put these on," insisted the man, throwing each of them an oversized woolen sweater. "You can keep'em."

"We can't take these," objected Sarah humbly.

"Don't worry, I've got plenty," he replied, indifferent. "My older sister knits me five a year."

Tom and Sarah put them on, pleased to be clothed in something new and warm. They looked at each other and smirked: Tom wearing a gigantic navy blue sweater and Sarah wearing a huge emerald green one.

They sat down at a makeshift table, something their host probably built. The man walked over with two steaming bowls of stew and some freshly baked rolls.

"This looks wonderful," said Sarah, digging in and momentarily forgetting all forms of manners or etiquette.

He then poured them two tall glasses of milk, a rare luxury.

"Thanks," added Tom appreciatively, devouring the tasty stew and taking a long, satisfying gulp of milk.

"The name's Wilbury," he interjected, extending his arm and shaking both their hands.

"I'm Tom, and this is Sarah."

Sarah grinned with a mouthful of stew.

"Pleasure to meet you," he said genuinely.

Wilbury glanced at his watch then looked out the window, the rain sprinkled on the glass.

"Tell you what," Wilbury began with a burst of inspiration. "Let me get both of you another helping of stew, and when you're done, I'll drive you to the train station."

"That'd be great!" they exclaimed, stunned by their sudden good fortune.

* * * *

Although it was dreadfully late at Weatherly, the orphans couldn't contain the exhilaration they felt. Closely huddled around each other, they whispered and laughed about what had transpired that night, the wonderful food they ate, and where their two *escaped* friends might be. In a sense, each orphan now lived vicariously through Tom and Sarah — every day the two remained missing was a silent victory for all of them. Their minds raced with ideas of what Tom and Sarah might be experiencing: the rush of the wind as they traveled on a train, a warm tavern where they might get something to eat, the brilliance of London (*the greatest city in the world*), or maybe even finding a loving family to live with. Reflecting back, they all agreed it was the greatest night in the history of Weatherly, one they would remember for a lifetime.

* * * *

While Wilbury drove along the road, the rain turned into a downpour. Tom sat in the front seat, trying to view the quaint village of Leyburn: ancient cobblestone streets, three-story stone buildings, tiled rooftops and an open pub with lights flashing in the window.

Wilbury pulled up to the train station, the brakes squeaking to a stop.

"Thanks for everything," said Tom, overwhelmed by his kindness.

"We wouldn't have made it without you," Sarah added genuinely.

"It was my pleasure," replied Wilbury, handing Tom a ten-pound note. "Something tells me you could use this."

"I can't take this. It's too much," he protested, not really sure how much ten pounds was worth.

"I insist," Wilbury continued. "And Tom — be careful. Watch after Sarah."

"You can count on it," he assured him, reluctantly pocketing the money.

Wilbury smiled, his eyes glistening with compassion. "Good luck, kids."

Tom and Sarah got out, ducking under a protective awning and waving goodbye as the car drove off.

They hurried to the station platform, excited about finally heading to London. There were a few other people muddling around, impatiently waiting for the last train. A mounted clock read 12:45. Tom and Sarah knew that once the passengers were on and the train started moving, they could carefully sneak on the back.

Viewing the surroundings, Tom noticed a suspicious looking man wearing a midnight blue Burberry trench coat and a stylish Bowler hat. The life suddenly drained from Tom, his instinct warning him something was wrong.

Detective Gowerstone calmly turned around, a relaxed, cool expression on his face.

"Hello, Tom," he said casually.

Sarah cringed, not sure what to think. "You know him?"

"No . . . but I know of him," replied Tom in a downtrodden voice.

Gowerstone nodded to the left and right. Two police officers at opposite ends of the platform emerged from the shadows.

"Tom!" exclaimed Sarah, trying to snap him out of his trance.

"Huh . . ."

"Let's get out of here!" She grabbed his arm, yanking him toward the front of the terminal.

"Yeah . . . let's go," he mumbled, still traumatized by the encounter.

Gowerstone marched after them speaking into his walkie-talkie. "They're heading out to the main entrance. Gently apprehend them."

Police cars screeched to a stop in front of the train station. Six officers exited, forming a line and fanning out in different directions.

"Wait!" Tom cried out. "We're running into a trap!"

They froze in their tracks.

"Are you sure?" questioned Sarah. "How do you know?"

"Because I've heard about this guy."

"Then what're we going to do?"

Noticing a fire alarm mounted on the wall, Tom rushed over and pulled the switch. A deafening bell sounded, striking panic throughout the train station and sending everyone toward the entrance.

Without a minute to lose, Tom and Sarah headed out a side exit and ran toward the village. They pushed their way through an endless forest of bushes, then sprinted down a back alleyway.

Gowerstone saw the side door half-open just as a policeman ran up.

"They didn't come out the front," the officer declared, somewhat confused.

"Intelligent one, this Tom," replied the detective, making a mental note. "We must never underestimate him."

"What should we —"

"Get after them!" he ordered abruptly. "They'll be headed for the village. Set up a perimeter and cautiously move in."

"Yes, sir."

After scurrying across a backyard and over a large fence, Tom and Sarah came upon a vast marshland. It was a massive area surrounded by wild plants and six-foot Norfolk reeds. Instantly drenched from the rain, their sweaters felt twenty pounds heavier.

"Let's go through here," whispered Tom. "It'll be harder for the police to follow us."

"They won't be the only ones having trouble," grumbled Sarah as she stepped into the swampy landscape.

The two sloshed through the thick wetlands, the overgrowth slashing their faces and bodies.

"Who is that guy?" wondered Sarah, looking back to see if they were being followed.

"His name's Detective Gowerstone," answered Tom directly, angered that their plans had been ruined.

"And?" she demanded. "How do you know him?"

"He caught one of my friends about seven years ago. He's a legend in orphanage circles."

"Hmm." She frowned. "You never told me."

"No, I guess I didn't."

"Well, what happened?" she persisted, lagging behind in the thick mire.

"I had been at Crumpbury Orphanage for a while. You know, the one down in Hampshire."

"I've heard of it."

"It wasn't nearly as bad as Weatherly, but it was still miserable. I just wanted to leave."

"What'd you do?"

"Early one morning, my friend Charles and I tried to sneak out through a chain-link fence. Before I was halfway under, I was caught by one of the caretakers, but Charles got away."

The two grudgingly pressed on as they sank deeper in the mud.

"So where'd Charles go?" Sarah questioned.

"He wandered into a small town a couple of hours later. Charles had a few pounds, so he found a bakery and went to get something to eat. As he walked in, Detective Gowerstone patiently sat there sipping his tea."

"No."

"Yep. Gowerstone looked up and said, 'You look hungry, Charles. Let me buy you a sandwich and we'll head back to Crumpbury.'" Tom paused and glanced at Sarah. "Just like that. Of all the places Charles could've gone, how did Gowerstone know he'd be there?"

"I don't know. So, then what happened?"

"He bought Charles a sandwich, a bag of crisps and a soda, and then he drove him back to the orphanage."

"Wow."

"Yeah, tell me about it," grumbled Tom, shaking his head in disbelief. "Gowerstone's very clever, Sarah. I've heard many stories about him. He seems to always know what you're thinking. Like tonight. He knew exactly where we'd be."

"Maybe someone told him?"

"Maybe . . . but I doubt it."

They slogged on through the swamp, waist-deep in freezing water.

"Tom, do you hear that?" Sarah asked, listening to an orchestra of voices growing louder.

"It's the police. They're following us."

9
THE MAGNIFICENT BALLOON

Tom and Sarah finally reached the end of the marsh and climbed onto a seemingly endless field. They were chilled to the bone and ready to collapse, mud dripping from their weary bodies. Kneeling to rest, they could still hear voices behind them.

"They're getting close," said Tom, hastily standing.

"Why can't they just leave us alone?" vented Sarah, incensed.

"I wish it were that simple," he replied, his voice weak with exhaustion. "Let's keep moving."

They sprinted over the wet countryside, not sure which direction to head. After a hundred yards, Tom noticed a huge shadowy object emerging in the distance.

"Look!" he exclaimed.

"What is that?"

"I've no idea."

"Let's head for it. We can rest for a minute — get out of the rain."

As they approached the object, it grew larger and larger. They stopped and tilted their heads back, staring in awe.

Eighty feet high, it just sat there in the middle of the field. A netting of wires draped the sides, attached to a wicker basket four feet tall by six feet wide. It was secured to the ground by ropes. Someone's truck was close by, the engine running and lights on.

"I think it's a . . . balloon," said Tom, bewildered.

"What's it doing here?"

"Don't know."

"Should we investigate?"

"Definitely."

The two ran to the basket.

Tom looked up again and marveled. "It's fantastic."

"I've never seen anything like it."

Looking behind him, Tom saw fifteen figures drawing near, their flashlights searching the area.

"They're still coming!" he exclaimed.

"I can't go on anymore," confessed Sarah. "I've got to rest."

"Let's jump in the basket and hide. Hopefully they won't see us."

Sarah climbed over the side and ducked down. Tom followed and knelt beside her.

There were two large propane tanks secured to a corner. Metal tubing extended from the tanks to a high-powered burner unit suspended under the balloon's opening.

Policemen approached from all directions, lights flickering in the rain.

"Over here!" one of them yelled.

"They've found us!" announced Tom, peeking over the top.

"Now what?" she asked anxiously.

"I'll think of something," he replied swiftly.

Sarah popped up to survey the situation. It looked dire. Swallowing defeat, she bowed her head.

"We've come so far," she said sadly.

"I know," he acknowledged, resting his hand on her shoulder. "But don't give up yet."

The police slowly circled and closed in.

"I can't go back to Weatherly, Tom. I just can't." Her voice was trembling.

Desperately searching for an answer, Tom noticed the two ropes anchoring the balloon.

"Maybe you don't have to."

"What do you mean?"

"I've got another idea."

"What?"

"Trust me," he said reassuringly and started untying one of the ropes.

"What are you doing? Are you nuts?"

"You want to go back to Weatherly?"

"No!"

"Then help me!"

As one of the policemen advanced, Sarah sprang to the other side and wrestled with the second rope.

"The knot's too tight! I can't pry it loose!" she exclaimed.

"Here," said Tom, handing her his pocket knife. "Cut it!"

She started slicing through the thick cord.

The officer flashed his light in the basket. "Okay you two. You've given us enough trouble for one night. Now get out of . . ."

The rope snapped, and the balloon launched into the air like a rocket.

"Well I'll be," mumbled the officer, his mouth open as his flashlight hit the ground.

An elderly man suddenly leaped from his truck. Furious, he ran over, dropping his picnic basket and scattering its contents.

"Hey, my balloon!" he yelled angrily. "What are you doing? Come back here!"

The other policemen gawked as the magnificent object soared hundreds of feet over their heads, shrinking with every passing second.

The elderly man shook his head in disbelief and raised his fist to the air. "You bloody thieves!" he hollered at the top of his lungs. "Bring back my balloon!"

Gowerstone ran up just in time to observe it disappearing.

The dense rain clouds engulfed the balloon in a turbulent whirlwind of fog before releasing it into a clear, cobalt sky.

Tom was exhilarated by the effortless feeling of soaring through the atmosphere. He peered over the side and looked out into the vast unknown. The air was fresh and crisp. Blazing stars ignited the heavens, and the clouds beneath him were washed in a dreamy sea of moonlight.

Meanwhile, realizing they were off the ground, Sarah crouched in a corner, terrified, her eyes shut.

"I can't believe we got away," Tom admitted, feeling confident in their escape. "For a minute, I . . . Sarah? Sarah?"

"I told you! I — hate — heights!"

"Right . . . forgot about that," he sighed, immediately comprehending the predicament. "You know, it's really not that bad. You should see for yourself."

He reached down to help her up. She shook her head.

"You're missing some great scenery."

"I don't care!"

"The stars are so beautiful," he continued, trying to entice her. "Look how close they are."

Finding it impossible to resist, Sarah slowly raised her head. Still safely curled in her corner, she looked around the upper rim of the basket. "I . . . I can see Cassiopeia."

"What?"

"Those five stars that looks like a W. And there's Andromeda," she said, suddenly interested.

"Who are you talking about?"

"The stars, they represent Greek mythology."

"Oh."

"Cassiopeia was a beautiful queen from the Kingdom of Ethiopia. Her daughter Andromeda was chained to a rock —"

"Too much information," interrupted Tom, holding up his hand.

"Fine!" She frowned, dispirited, then smacked his arm.

"Ouch!"

"Serves you right for not listening to my story."

He rubbed his arm, somewhat surprised by her reaction.

"So how do you know all this anyway?" he asked, feeling a bit intimidated.

"I used to go camping with my parents. At night, we'd look at the stars for hours."

"Sounds fun."

"It was," she said reflectively.

Tom reached down again. "Here, stand up so you can see better."

"No!"

"Well, if you're afraid."

That provoked her. She gave him a hard stare and apprehensively pulled herself up. She tried to get her balance, hands firmly clasped on the basket's edge, legs wobbly and arms tense. She timidly looked over, then swiftly drew back, taking a deep breath.

"See how easy it is," he teased her, chuckling to himself.

"It's not funny!" she snapped, annoyed by his sarcasm.

"I'm just trying to help."

"Well, you're not!"

Lost in conversation, neither of them was paying attention to the balloon's quick ascent: 1500 feet — 2000 feet — 2500 feet — 3000 feet — 4000 feet. As it raced upward, frost gathered on the balloon.

"It's getting colder," said Sarah, rubbing her arms.

"That's odd." Tom snapped off a piece of ice. "Look what's forming around the ropes."

Sarah immediately glanced back over the side.

"Tom! The balloon's not stopping!" she shrieked, realizing they could disappear into space, freeze to death, or both. "How do we stop it?"

"I . . . I don't know," he admitted reluctantly, his confidence evaporating.

"Great."

"It seemed like a good idea at the time."

They both peered over the side again and saw the clouds beneath them getting smaller and smaller.

* * * *

Gowerstone observed the sky as the rain hammered down. An officer approached with an umbrella, popping it open and covering the detective's head.

"Cheers," said Gowerstone, removing a handkerchief from his pocket and wiping his face.

"What should we do, sir?" inquired the officer, discouraged from being outfoxed by two children.

"Depending how high they go, most of the currents move southwest, about fifteen knots."

Gowerstone glanced at his watch, then pulled out his pad and did some calculations.

"It's now two a.m. It's too dark to see anything and too dangerous to get an aircraft in the sky until morning. For the moment, we'll dispatch a few men to the neighboring areas and keep a lookout — see if the balloon touches down. Get someone to the local radar station and see if they pick up any objects. If Tom and Sarah continue their course, by 6:00 a.m., sunrise, they should be about fifty miles southwest of here."

"Understood," replied the officer, frantically jotting down notes.

Gowerstone removed a map from his coat and scanned it. "I want you to get a crew of men to Manchester, Sheffield and Doncaster. These will be our three northern bases for now. Locate the highest hill and have a spotter watch for them. Once dawn breaks, report anything they observe. Keep local lines open for any reports of disturbances."

"Sir, pardon me, but isn't this a lot of work for two escaped orphans?"

"Just do it! I've got my reasons."

"Right, sorry."

"Also, ask the owner what type of balloon he has, how much propane is in the tanks and any other relevant details."

Flipping from page to page, the officer continued scribbling instructions. "Got it."

"Finally, contact all the police stations within a hundred-mile radius and let them know what's going on. Give them a description of Tom and Sarah, their clothing, age, height, recent photos and any other pertinent facts. Have them start combing the countryside, towns and villages. I'll alert the local airport and see what's available for the morning. Most importantly, treat those two children with absolute care."

"Yes, sir," nodded the officer. "I understand." He hurried away as another one approached carrying a cup of hot tea.

"Here you go, detective. I thought this might take the chill off."

"Capital. Good thinking, Officer." Gowerstone surveyed the sky and sipped his tea. "Where are you going, Tom?" he wondered aloud. "Where are you going?"

* * * *

Tom quickly scrambled around looking for a button, switch or lever — anything to stop the balloon from rising. Not knowing what to do, Sarah turned on the propane tank valves hoping this might work.

There were two small ropes dangling down with a knot at the ends. Tom grabbed the first one and pulled it, igniting the blast valve pilot light. A flame burst from the burner and shot straight up into the opening. The balloon accelerated faster, throwing them off balance.

"Stop pulling that!" Sarah screamed. "You're making it go higher!"

"It's not like I'm a balloon expert!"

Tom quickly reached for the other rope, the parachute valve cord, and tugged hard. Instantly the ascent slowed. A large circular flap at the top of the canvas opened, letting the gas escape.

"It's working!" she exclaimed.

Tom pulled again and held it. After a moment, the balloon stopped climbing and hovered approximately 5000 feet in the air.

"You did it," she proclaimed, feeling a sense of relief. "Well done."

"I'm not quite sure what I did, but it worked." Baffled, he inspected the upper workings of the balloon. "Any idea how to steer this thing?"

"Sure, I took ballooning classes at Weatherly last fall while everyone else was working," she teased him. "What do you think?"

"I was just asking."

After lowering the balloon a few thousand feet and

drifting for a while, Sarah and Tom decided to examine things more closely. There was a small waterproof storage bench attached to the wicker basket. Sarah opened the lid and looked inside: there was a jug of water, some additional rope, a few tools, four wooden stakes, a pair of binoculars, two large rubber patches and a blanket.

"Maybe we should rest for a bit," he suggested, his eyes heavy.

"What about the balloon?" she asked. "Shouldn't we try to land?"

"It's too soon. They'll only catch up with us. It seems safe enough now that we know how to go up and down. Let's see where it drifts."

"What if we crash?"

"I'll make sure we don't."

"Promise?"

"I promise."

Tom grabbed the blanket. "You sleep first, and I'll keep watch."

"Okay . . . but wake me up if there are any problems."

"Will do."

"And make sure you don't fall asleep."

"I won't."

They sat on the bench, their backs resting against the basket. Tom covered their legs with the blanket and Sarah rested her head on his shoulder. She soon nodded off, breathing deeply. Tom tried to keep his eyes open, his head drifting forward then snapping awake. He blinked a few more times and dozed off.

As morning arrived, the sun illuminated the balloon, now drifting only fifteen hundred feet above the ground.

Tom awoke, realizing he had passed out. He quickly jumped up, nervously looking around and wondering where they were.

"Sarah, wake up," he whispered loudly. "It's morning."

She was startled, deep into her dreams.

"What's wrong?"

"Nothing. You were asleep."

She looked back and forth, completely disoriented, rubbing her eyes and getting her bearings.

"We're in a balloon."

"Yep."

"It wasn't just a dream?"

"Nope."

She warily leaned over the basket to take in the wonderful views and became dizzy. The feeling of being up so high was still overwhelming, but she was gradually getting used to it. It helped having Tom close by. If he wasn't scared, why should she be?

"Were you up all night?" she questioned him suspiciously, noticing he didn't look tired. "That was quite a sacrifice. You should've woken me."

Embarrassed, Tom glanced away, fiddling with the basket. "Oh, it was no bother."

"You fell asleep, didn't you?" she reproached him, her tone changing.

"Right after you."

"Figures," she said, not surprised. Her scowl turned to a smirk. "Well, at least we didn't crash."

"I told you so."

"And you know everything?"

"Almost everything."

"Yeah, right."

The balloon drifted southwest towards Lancaster, a small town with red-tiled roofs, 16th century castles and St. Mary's Abbey perched on a hill. The storm had passed, leaving everything bright and clear.

Tom and Sarah admired the picturesque countryside. They had never seen such vast distances or such a tapestry of colors: emerald fields with sheep-filled pastures, rolling hills and valleys, towns and villages, cottages and churches, roads and railways.

"It's really quite stunning," admitted Sarah, captivated by the 360-degree vista.

"And I thought the roof at Weatherly was high."

Tom took out his map and tried to figure out their location.

"If that's Lancaster," he pointed, "and Liverpool is to the right, then Manchester must be in front of us, and behind us are the Cumbrian Mountains."

Sarah turned, mesmerized. "Look at all those lakes!"

"Wow," he gasped, leaning over the basket.

"They're beautiful." She admired the crystal blue surfaces reflecting the sky.

"We'll have to go swimming there someday."

"I can't swim," she said gravely. "Remember?"

"Oh, that's right. Perhaps we could rent a boat."

"And if I fall in?"

"Then you're on your own," he jested, giggling.

She gave him a sharp look followed by a shove.

"I'm kidding," he said quickly.

"You better be."

Sarah sat down on the bench. "I still can't believe we actually escaped. That we're free."

"I know . . . it's hard to imagine. But we still have a long way to go," he cautioned her.

"And by the way, you were amazing last night. That was very brave."

Tom blushed, taken aback by the compliment. "It had to be done, right?"

"Right."

"I just wish the other orphans could have gotten out," he added regretfully.

"We'll have to figure out a way to help them and let people know what goes on there."

"And get even with the Grievouses."

"Absolutely."

"What about Speckle?"

"Especially Speckle!"

Sarah grabbed the water from the storage bin and shared a drink with Tom.

"Any idea where London is?" she wondered.

"I'm not sure."

Tom examined his compass and map again, trying to estimate the direction and distance. There was a scale in the bottom corner, so he snapped off a piece of woolen thread from his damp sweater and used it to measure.

"If this map is right, we still have about a hundred and fifty miles left to go, but . . ."

"But what?"

"We need to be moving southeast, not southwest," he said worriedly.

"Should we try to land the balloon around Manchester and get a train?"

Tom thought about Sarah's question as he surveyed the passing landscape. The train had always been their initial plan and the easiest means of transportation, but their circumstances had changed drastically.

"What's wrong?" she asked, sensing his frustration.

"I thought once we were out of Weatherly, we'd be safe. If we got to the train fast enough, we'd already be in London," he grumbled loudly. "But now, this Detective Gowerstone, he's a *real* problem. He won't stop until he has us."

"You're sure?"

"Positive."

"Then we'll have to stay one step ahead of him," she interjected with a mischievous flair of confidence.

"That's not easy," he contended, skeptical.

"Yeah, but think what we've done so far," she continued. "You rescued me from the attic, we escaped through the tunnel, we outsmarted the Grievouses and Speckle, and we even got away from the police. I think we're doing pretty well."

"You're right," he acknowledged proudly.

"Gowerstone doesn't even know where we are," she added incisively.

"But *we* don't know where we are."

"Precisely. The English countryside is huge. It's not going to be that easy to locate us."

"Yeah, but he's probably notified every policeman in Britain."

"They'll be looking for us on the roads, in towns and at the train stations," she concluded boldly with a flare of mischief.

"Then the balloon may be our best option," Tom realized. "At least for now."

After a moment, they removed their damp sweaters and draped them over the basket, letting them dry in the morning sunlight. They huddled under the blanket and planned their next move.

* * * *

Gowerstone hastily ran across an airport runway and into a waiting helicopter. He jumped into the passenger seat and attached the headgear. The engines fired up, and the massive blades began to spin, increasing with speed.

The pilot turned to him. "Where are we headed, Detective?"

"South, toward the Midlands."

"What part?"

"All of it."

"All of it?" exclaimed the pilot, still bitter at being awakened so early and rushed to the airport. "But that's over twenty thousand square miles!"

"Then we can't afford to waste time," replied Gowerstone coldly, glaring at the man.

"Y-yes sir," the pilot stammered.

The rotors spun at full velocity as the helicopter lifted

from the ground. The detective read through his notes and reviewed a large map of England.

"Exactly what are we looking for, sir?" inquired the pilot.

"A large balloon."

"A what?!"

* * * *

A strong breeze swiftly moved the balloon over Manchester, a lively city with Victorian buildings, grand cathedrals, old brick factories turned into retail outlets, tightly-packed housing blocks and tall charcoal-stained chimneys reaching into the sky.

Tom and Sarah put on their dry sweaters and examined the different mechanisms of the balloon. Tom inspected the propane tanks, burner unit and all the other attachments and gizmos.

"We need to figure out how to steer this thing," he said curiously.

"Let me help." Sarah stood on the storage bench and fiddled with one of the switches.

"Be careful up there," he warned her.

"Of course," she shot back stubbornly.

While Sarah was busy, Tom watched the metropolis below, captivated by all the sights.

"It's incredible, isn't it? Everything looks so different from up here."

"This is nothing," she commented. "Wait until you see London!"

"Grander than this?"

She laughed. "They don't even compare."

"Really?"

"Really."

As they drifted along, a police officer drinking his morning tea glanced up.

"Bobby," he mumbled, dropping his cup and shattering it.

"What is it now, Charlie?" inquired Bobby, irritated. "Can't I just enjoy a peaceful moment after our long night?"

"B-but . . . Bobby . . . look," he continued, motioning to the passing balloon.

"Get on the radio!" he screamed. "Call Gowerstone! Let him know we've sighted them!"

"Will do, boss."

Charlie sprang from his chair, knocking over the table.

"You idiot!" yelled Bobby. "Can't you do anything right?"

"Sorry, boss. I've got it. I've got it," he repeated, staggering to the police car. He whipped open the door and grabbed the radio. "Detective, Detective Gowerstone, we see them . . . the balloon . . . it's over Manchester!"

* * * *

Gowerstone acknowledged the message and turned to the pilot. "Manchester," he ordered urgently. "Now!"

The helicopter changed direction and raced at seventy-five knots toward the balloon.

* * * *

"Tom, what about this?" asked Sarah, moving a metal funnel around in a circle.

"Hmm," he sighed, closely inspecting the contraption. "Maybe if we switch this valve down, move the funnel in the opposite direction and pull the propane rope, it will push the balloon forward."

"That could work."

"Then again, it could catch the whole balloon on fire," he said hesitantly.

"That's also true."

They spent a few minutes tinkering with the different levers when Sarah heard the slight rumble of an engine. She gazed into the distance and spotted a shimmering black object approaching.

"Tom," she gasped, jerking his arm.

He peeked over. "What?"

"Look!" Her eyes widened. "What is that thing?"

"It looks like a —"

"A plane?"

"No, it's a helicopter! And it's headed right for us!"

* * * *

"Sir," shouted the pilot. "I think I see it!"

Gowerstone stared out the window and observed a tiny floating object on the horizon.

"Yes, that's them. Aim for it." He got on the radio and contacted the local authorities. "This is Gowerstone.

They're over Manchester. Alert the local units and converge on the area."

* * * *

"If we're ever going to figure out how to make this thing move, now's a good time," stated Sarah firmly.

Tom jumped on the bench, flipped a lever on the exhaust funnel and turned it toward the oncoming helicopter. He then leaped down and yanked the rope. Instead of the hot air firing into the balloon, it shot out through the funnel, propelling them forward. They gradually picked up speed as a stream of hot air exited.

"It's working!" she said jubilantly, gripping the side. "Can we make it go any faster?"

Tom looked around the basket. "Open up those valves on the tanks — all the way!" he shouted. "Maybe that'll work!"

Sarah turned both knobs. The coils hissed as gas screamed through the tubes. Suddenly the surge of propane hit the burner and blasted out a bright orange flame.

They abruptly swung backwards as the balloon accelerated.

* * * *

"It's turning, sir," observed the pilot. "And picking up speed."

"So they've figured out how to pilot it," said

Gowerstone, shaking his head in bemusement. "These kids don't miss a trick. All right, increase your speed."

The helicopter continued moving closer: thirty miles — twenty-five miles — twenty miles — fifteen miles.

The chase continued through the Heart of England, over the countryside of Staffordshire and Cheshire, past Stoke-on-Trent, over Birmingham and toward the medieval town of Warwick.

* * * *

"He's closing in on us!" yelled Sarah.

"The helicopter's too fast," said Tom, discouraged.

Sarah glanced ahead and saw the sky dotted with exquisite colors: dazzling blues, radiant reds, bright greens and fluorescent purples.

"Tom, over by the hills. It looks like . . ." she paused, mystified, then grabbed the binoculars. "Balloons . . . hundreds of them."

"Let me see." He quickly grabbed the binoculars from her hands.

"It must be some kind of festival," she surmised.

"In the air?"

"Where else are you going to have a balloon festival?"

"Right . . . good point."

Sarah looked back. The helicopter was getting closer: twenty-five miles — twenty miles — fifteen miles . . .

"He's almost here!"

Reacting fast, Tom slowly released some hot air and lowered the balloon to around 1000 feet. "Let's aim directly for the festival. Maybe we could blend in."

"Good thinking." Sarah jumped back on the bench, trying to turn the funnel. "It's jammed." Frustrated, she grabbed two supporting ropes and climbed on the basket rim.

"Sarah, it's too dangerous," he yelled, more concerned about her than the helicopter.

"I've almost got it —"

She moved the funnel to the proper position and jumped down. "There . . . it's fixed."

Tom pulled the rope, and the balloon gradually accelerated toward the festival. The helicopter banked to the right, following closely behind.

Sprinkled throughout the sky were balloons displaying every conceivable color and design. People from all over the world had gathered for this annual event.

Some of the balloons resembled figures, like a large turtle, Rupert the Bear, The Scottish Piper, a pint of beer and a towering gothic castle. Many of the baskets flaunted their country flags, such as France, Spain, Germany and Austria. The air was filled with music and singing, celebration and laughter.

As Tom and Sarah watched this extravaganza, the sky soon became crowded, like a circus suspended in midair.

"It's unbelievable," Tom articulated, intoxicated by the magical scene. "You ever see anything like this?"

"No, not even in books."

They soon mastered the ropes and funnel unit, maneuvering in and out of the balloons like pros.

"Bonjour! Comment vas-tu?" a Frenchman yelled over.

Tom stared back, perplexed by the foreign language.

"Nous sommes très bien, monsieur," replied Sarah with the finesse of a gifted scholar.

Tom turned to her, dumbfounded. "You speak . . . French?"

"I wasn't always at an orphanage, Tom," she answered abruptly.

"Guten Morgen! Was für ein schöner Tag!" a German woman hollered.

"Ja, es ist spektakulär," responded Sarah in a deep voice.

Tom just shook his head. "You know, there's a lot I don't know about you."

"And you're just now figuring that out," she said dismissively. "The Frenchman said hello and asked how we are. The German woman said good morning and that it is a beautiful day."

"Whatever," he grumbled, feeling a bit outmatched. "It's all gibberish to me."

"Perhaps I'll teach you a few words later," she jested.

"Sure, that would be great," he answered sarcastically.

"I've never seen such young pilots before!" a Scottish man shouted. "Very impressive, lads! That's the way you learn something, start when you're young!"

"That's exactly what we've done," replied Tom, thankful to hear a relatively familiar voice.

The man reached down in his basket and reappeared with freshly baked bread. "You look hungry. Here, eat up," he said, hurling the loaf through the air with the precision of a seasoned cricket player.

Tom reached up and snagged it.

"Nice throw!" Sarah yelled back.

Tom tore off a piece and handed it to Sarah. The two munched away, enjoying a gulp of water with their breakfast.

* * * *

Meanwhile, Gowerstone watched from his binoculars as Tom and Sarah disappeared into the mix of multicolored balloons.

"We've got to get closer," he demanded.

"Sir, we're not allowed within two miles of the balloons," warned the pilot. "The turbulence from the blades disrupts them."

The detective contemplated his options. "Hold your pattern. We'll track them from here."

He watched as hundreds of flying objects hypnotically drifted in every direction; it was an impossible situation. For a brief moment in his long and illustrious career, Detective Gowerstone was stumped. Nevertheless, he was exhilarated by the challenge of what was proving to be two brilliant adversaries.

He got on the radio. "Agent Carlson, what have you found out about the balloon?"

A static reply came back: "Sir, I spoke with the owner. He's furious. Said he had his balloon all prepared for today's festival!"

"And?" asked Gowerstone, agitated.

"It's an A-Type Altastrata, manufactured in Bristol, with a high velocity quad burner unit — very sturdy and well constructed. It's built for long distance travel. The balloon is about 150,000 cubic feet and carries two ST-100 propane tanks, which provide approximately twelve hours' worth of flight time. Depending on the weather, it could be longer."

"Good work, Carlson."

Gowerstone glanced at his watch and turned to the pilot.

"It's almost noon. Depending on how much propane they've used, their fuel will be running out shortly." He then surveyed his map and searched the area. "We're passing over Warwick now. These children are smart. If they're going to land, they'll pick a major area — easier to blend in with the crowd and still get to a train station," he stated, grabbing the radio. "Carlson, get a team of men over to Oxford. I also want some officers dressed in plain clothes. Station them at cafés, bakeries, bus stops and especially train stations."

"Right away, sir."

* * * *

Tom and Sarah were having fun mingling among the different balloons. They laughed, yelled to others and finished their bread.

"Look at that one," Tom voiced, pointing to a large colorful dragon. "How do they do that?"

"I have no idea," Sarah pondered aloud.

"Buon pomeriggio," a group yelled and waved. The balloon canvas had three large stripes: green, white and red.

Sarah waved back, "Buon pomeriggio. Come stai?"

"Here we go again," Tom sighed.

"It's Italian." Sarah was quick to respond.

"How many languages do you know?"

"That's it. Just four."

"You were busy in your youth."

"The best prep school in Scotland, before . . ." her voice faded.

"The car accident?"

"Yeah . . ."

"You don't like talking about it, do you?"

"No." She shook her head coldly. "Maybe another time . . ."

"Sure."

They passed right over Warwick Castle, an ancient citadel with grey sandstone walls, circular towers flanking the corners and a dried-up moat around the perimeter.

"Now that would be a nice place to live," Tom stated.

"Maybe you do, *Lord* Tom," she teased.

"I wish," he laughed. "Think how much fun we'd have."

"I'm having fun now."

"So am I."

Sarah leaned over and examined the mighty fortress. "What would you do with your own castle?"

"I'd move everyone in from Weatherly."

"Everyone?"

"Well, just the orphans. The rest can go to jail."

* * * *

Gowerstone closely observed the festival from the helicopter. He had set up ground crews in the surrounding area with telescopes and professional spotters looking for any sign of the balloon.

"Sir, we're getting complaints from the balloon pilots. We've got to back off and get out of this area!"

"Understood. Let's head to Oxford."

* * * *

A strong breeze shot across the sky as Sarah and Tom followed the pack of balloons over Oxfordshire. Known as the Thames Valley, this lush countryside was a multicolored patchwork of square farmlands crisscrossed by hedgerows and rock walls. The Thames River gracefully snaked through the open fields covered with extravagant mansions built centuries ago.

Although most of the balloons headed toward Canterbury, some floated off in opposite directions. By mid-afternoon, most of them had vanished. Tom and Sarah followed behind a few but soon lost them in the hazy clouds. Every so often, Tom gave the balloon a long blast of hot air to maintain its altitude.

While they drifted southeast toward London, their main concern was Gowerstone. Peering through the binoculars, Tom searched for the helicopter.

"I don't see him."

"Do you think he gave up?"

"No," he replied quickly. "He'll never give up."

"We seem safe for now."

"For the moment," he added with caution.

As Sarah admired the scenery, Tom reached into his pocket to retrieve her locket.

"This really does bring me luck," he concluded, handing it to her. "Thanks for letting me borrow it."

"It's yours, silly," she smiled, pushing it back. "Just promise you'll always keep it with you."

"But —"

"Promise."

"All right . . . it's a deal." Stuffing it back in his pocket, he felt the piece of paper Patrick gave him and removed it.

"What's that?" she inquired curiously.

"Before we left, Patrick broke into the Grievouses' office and looked through my file. He wrote something down."

"Let's see."

Tom opened it. Scribbled across the page was just one word.

"Hmm," he grunted, expecting detailed information.

"What does it say?" she demanded.

"Britfield."

"Britfield? What the heck does that mean?"

"How am I supposed to know?"

"There must be more." She snatched the paper from his hand and thoroughly examined both sides. Dissatisfied, she shook her head. "So Patrick *breaks* into the office, *sneaks* your file out, and writes only *one* word on it — is he mad?"

"I'm sure he was in a hurry," his voice deepened, "given that we were planning to *rescue* you and everything."

"Then it's a clue?"

"It's a name."

"Maybe it's your last name," she suggested encouragingly.

This comment caught Tom off guard. After all these years of having only a first name, it was a lot to digest and felt rather strange.

"Maybe," he shrugged, not sure what to think.

Pacing back and forth, Sarah considered the matter. "What do you really know about your family? You've shared a few things with me, but is there anything else?"

Tom sat on the wicker bench and leaned back, contemplating.

"Well?" she persisted.

"I believe I was at my first orphanage, Edmundbyers, when I was around two? But before that I don't remember much, just vague pictures. I'm not really sure if they're real or just dreams." He rubbed his head a few times. "It was so long ago."

"Interesting," she said, her mind racing a thousand miles an hour. "And they never told you about your parents — nothing?"

"No, it's always been a closed subject," he answered, an unsettling gaze in his eyes. "Whenever I asked or tried to look into it, they just got angry. All they said was, 'They're dead!'"

"That's weird."

"I know."

"Someone must have brought you to the orphanage."

"That's just it . . . those are the memories that seem

distorted," he continued with more intensity. "I remember being happy and playing outside in a big yard . . . it was sunny . . . then suddenly being wrapped in something. It was dark and I felt scared . . . then I awoke on a bed at Edmundbyers."

"That's not much to go on, is it?" she said despondently, her forehead wrinkled in thought.

"That's all I remember."

"So how'd you end up at Weatherly?"

"Rumor has it that someone paid for the exchange, because there was no reason for me to leave Crumpbury . . . the last place I was at."

"Paid!" she snapped loudly. "From one orphanage to another . . . that's ridiculous."

"Not really," he refuted. "Think about it. The Grievouses need to maintain their quota of fifty-six orphans. So, they make a deal with another orphanage that has a surplus of children, pay them a few hundred pounds, and then work the kid to death for the next ten years." His voice rose with indignation. "They end up staying in business and making a ton of money!"

"That makes sense, I guess . . . especially for the Grievouses." Sarah sat next to Tom. "How do you know all this?"

"Patrick told me," he answered matter-of-factly. "But some of it I already knew."

"What a corrupt little enterprise," she said indignantly, her desire for revenge resurfacing.

"To say the least," he added resentfully.

Sarah looked at the paper again. "Britfield," she

thought out loud, searching for a connection. "That's a very interesting name. We'll have to find out more about it."

Another hour crept by as the two discussed the clue, talked about the past and shared stories. The clouds nestled together in large patches of whimsical patterns and soon exploded in a watercolor of bright pinks and reds. The air cooled as dusk settled in.

Although Detective Gowerstone was nowhere in sight, the balloon had been tracked from a distance. While some officers followed it from the ground, others watched from hilltops.

As Tom pulled the rope again, one of the propane tanks suddenly sputtered, gasped for its last breath and went dead.

"What was that?" exclaimed Sarah, staring at the propane tank and hoping her instincts were wrong.

Tom turned the knob back and forth, putting his ear to the gauge and jiggling the tank.

"What's wrong with it?" she continued, anxiety building.

"It's empty."

10
A PILLAR OF KNOWLEDGE

"Empty?" Sarah blurted, leaping up. "I guess we didn't think about that."

"No," exclaimed Tom, lifting the tank then checking the other. "This one's almost out, too!"

Hovering around 800 feet, the balloon started descending.

"We've got to land this thing — now!" Sarah cried out.

"I'm on it!"

Tom leaned over and scouted for a safe place.

Sarah pointed to a nearby city, its tall towers and majestic buildings dominating the skyline.

"What's over there?"

Tom hunted through his map and pinpointed the location. "It's Oxford."

"Let's aim for that open field on the outskirts," she said frantically, her voice filled with nervous tension.

"I'll do my best."

Founded in 1176 and made up of thirty-eight independent colleges, Oxford is Britain's oldest university. Hailed as one of the world's greatest pillars of knowledge, the name of the town evolved from its position on the river meaning "a ford for oxen."

Tom tried to steer the balloon and safely guide it to the ground. He switched the burner lever back and forth, giving one blast of heat up and another one out, hoping to navigate toward their target. The flame became weaker and weaker.

"It's really starting to fall," Sarah expressed despondently, dashing from one side to the other.

Working feverishly, Tom aimed for a farm with animal stalls and a large stone barn.

As the last bit of propane sputtered out and the air inside the canvas cooled, the balloon was at the mercy of the winds and weather. The cold sky coupled with the lack of warm propane exacerbated the problem, pushing the balloon downward.

They hastily descended toward the remote field where police officer Alexeyevich Vinogradov was diligently searching the sky for two orphans and a balloon.

A Russian immigrant, Alexeyevich loved working for the English police force. He was a proud twelve-year veteran, but he struggled to work his way up the administrative ladder and longed for a chance to prove himself.

Munching on his sandwich, he looked up and saw the balloon barreling right for him. He dropped his food and grabbed his walkie-talkie.

"Sir, dees is Alexeyevich! Eyev got'dem en cite . . . Yaa, da valloon!" he stammered excitedly.

"Good. Hold your position and arrest them when they land," Gowerstone ordered. "We'll send backup now, but don't harm them in any way."

"Right, sir."

"And Vinogradov."

"Yez, sir."

"Be careful," he cautioned him. "They're very clever."

Vinogradov pulled his gun and walked to the middle of the pasture, ready for his finest moment.

This successful capture would bring him the long-awaited respect and admiration he so desperately sought. Alexeyevich would soon be treasured by everyone in the force. Maybe he'd be promoted to captain, finally stationed in London, and perhaps receive a prestigious medal from the Queen.

Lost in thoughts of grandeur, Alexeyevich prepared to do his sworn duty and uphold the law.

"I see the field!" yelled Tom.

"I don't think we're going to make it," gasped Sarah, observing the oncoming buildings and cottages.

"Brace yourself!" he warned as they both grabbed the basket.

The balloon quickly dropped, crashing over rooftops and smashing into chimneys: bricks flew, branches cracked, phone lines snapped, and birds scattered everywhere.

Raising his gun, Vinogradov shouted, "STOP — VIGHT — DARE!"

The balloon came crashing through the trees and right toward Vinogradov. His face exploded with surprise. "STOP!" he squealed.

Hovering above the ground, the basket smacked Vinogradov off his feet and sent him flying into the air. He landed with a loud wallop and skidded across the field covered in dirt. He was out cold — his moment of glory over.

"Sorry," hollered Sarah, a perplexed look on her face.

The basket hit the ground and slid toward the stone barn, plowing up the pasture: fifty feet — twenty-five feet — fifteen feet . . .

The balloon shook and rocked, knocking Tom on his back.

Ten feet — nine feet — eight feet . . .

"We're going to hit the barn!" screamed Sarah.

Five feet — four feet — three feet . . .

The balloon slowly slid to a stop, only inches from the structure.

Sarah was momentarily speechless, stunned by the fear of death or at least the thought of being permanently injured.

"We're okay. We didn't hit it," she murmured, grateful for Divine intervention. "All I saw was that wall coming right for us and . . . Tom?"

She turned and noticed him flat on his back, motionless. "Tom? Are you alright?"

The impact of hitting the ground had thrown Tom down and knocked the wind out of him. Sarah rushed to his side, kneeling over and rubbing his forehead.

"Tom . . . wake up! Get up!" she pleaded frantically, giving his body a gentle shake.

No answer.

"This can't be happening. Not to you!"

For a moment Sarah felt the pain of losing her best friend. She shook his body again, but he still didn't move.

Determined, she opened the storage bin and grabbed the jug of water, dumping its entire contents on his face.

"What the . . . who . . . stop!" he yelled out, shocked by the sting. "What — are — you — doing?"

"I'm —"

"Are you out of your mind?"

"Oh, Tom," she said sweetly, dropping the jug. "You're alive!"

"Of course I am," he grumbled, feeling somewhat dazed.

Sarah hugged him tightly.

"What'd you do that for?" he complained, shaking free from her grasp.

She smiled nonchalantly. "No reason."

"Whatever," he said indifferently, not knowing what he had done to warrant such attention.

Tom wearily got up and wiped his face. He wobbled a bit, still dizzy from his fall.

"You okay?" she wondered, bracing his shoulder.

"I feel lightheaded."

"Don't worry, I'll help you," she assured him, clutching his arm for balance.

A blast of static blurted from the walkie-talkie: "Vinogradov . . . what's your status? Do you have them? Vinogradov . . . do you read me?"

Sarah and Tom inspected the surroundings. Lying on the ground about ten feet away was Vinogradov buried underneath a pile of dislodged grass clumps.

"Poor guy," said Tom, feeling slightly guilty. "Nothing I could've done."

"Yeah, but what kind of idiot stands in front of an out-of-control balloon?" she countered dryly.

"Good point."

"You feeling any better?"

"I think so."

"We should get out of here before someone comes."

"First let's secure the balloon, so it doesn't blow away."

They grabbed a hammer, rope and two stakes from the storage bench and leaped over the side.

This was the first time their feet had touched solid ground in almost fifteen hours. The initial sensation was unsettling but soon felt wonderful. Sarah marveled at their journey and how she had overcome her fear of heights.

They worked rapidly, pounding in the stakes and firmly securing the ropes. Just as Tom threw the hammer in the basket, a group of policemen arrived.

"Hey, you two!" shouted an officer. "Don't move!"

Tom and Sarah instantly bolted in the opposite direction, sprinting around the barn and down a dirt road. The policemen quickly pursued.

After navigating through a forest of shrubbery and across an open field, Tom and Sarah stumbled onto Magdalen College.

Sarah glanced back. "I think we lost them."

"I think we lost ourselves."

"Where should we go?"

"Let's hide in one of those buildings, and we'll figure out what to do."

They crossed over the River Cherwell where a flat bottom boat glided by, then entered the university through an enormous iron gate.

As the last remnants of daylight disappeared, lights flickered on throughout the campus. The property was breathtaking with its manicured lawns and impeccably trimmed hedges. The 15th & 16th century buildings were a masterpiece of craftsmanship: slate rooftops, stone chimneys, dormers and gables; large bay windows with leaded glass; and clusters of arched walkways. Scholars and academics raced to their dormitories or the dining hall. There was a distinct aura of privilege and tradition.

Tom and Sarah proceeded past the ivy-covered walls and over towards St. John's Quadrangle, a courtyard with marble statues and wooden benches neatly organized around the outer edges.

Two students in a heated debate hurried by.

"No, no, no . . . the Labor Party's on its way out! They lost the majority in the last election," one student proclaimed. "And they deserved to."

"Give me a break, Thornton," the other student refuted. "They've never been stronger. You're reading too many radical newspapers, and it's twisting your mind."

"Radical! Well at least they're willing to voice their opinions and contribute something of substance," he replied bitterly as they disappeared through a doorway.

"What are we going to do? The balloon's out of fuel and probably surrounded by the police," Sarah inquired downheartedly.

"I still have ten pounds," replied Tom, pulling out his money. "I'm sure there's a train station nearby. Maybe we could buy a couple of tickets and get to London."

"Don't you think they'll be looking for us there — just like last time?"

"Probably," he answered tentatively, "but we've got to risk it. We have nowhere to stay tonight. We'll just be extra careful. Scout the area first and look for any police."

"All right," she agreed apprehensively, unaware of other options.

They wandered past Porter's Lodge and out onto High Street, a busy avenue congested with traffic.

Known as "The High," the road formed a gentle curve through the center of Oxford. Christmas wreaths were attached to lampposts, and colorful lights hung from one side to the other. Students hurried along the walkways carrying heavy backpacks and holiday presents. Nestled among the numerous shops and pubs were Waterfield's Books and Shepherd & Woodward, two well-known landmarks. Other prestigious colleges fronted the street, their grand facades towering over the sidewalks.

Tom and Sarah rushed by Queens' College and down the block.

A red double-decker bus screeched to a stop, loading and unloading passengers. As Tom and Sarah crossed the street, they noticed a policeman walking along the adjacent sidewalk. Fifty feet behind him were two other officers peeking in windows and cafés.

"Here, quick," Tom whispered, grabbing Sarah's hand and ducking into University College, Oxford's oldest school.

Lost in the crowd of students, they worked their way down a corridor and to the Shelley Memorial, a tribute built to the famous Romantic poet who drowned off the coast of Italy.

They stood at the doorway and cautiously peered out.

"I don't think they saw us," said Tom optimistically.

"I'm getting tired of running and hiding."

"So am I. I told you Gowerstone was a nightmare."

"How do you know he's behind this?"

"He's behind it, trust me."

Sarah glanced behind her and examined the circular room, its walls painted in a subdued pastel lilac. She was transfixed by the white marble statue perched on an angel's wings and balanced by two bronze lions.

While Tom searched the hallway, Sarah was drawn to the human-sized replica of Percy Shelley draped across the top, lying solemnly on his side.

"It's beautiful," she said softly, running her hand across the smooth surface.

Tom glimpsed the sculpture from the corner of his eye and turned. He too was mesmerized by the brilliant lights washing over this lost soul captured in time.

"He seems so sad," observed Tom, walking around the outer edge.

"Yet finally at peace," she added astutely.

Briefly forgetting their troubles, they gazed at this hypnotic work of art and enjoyed a stolen moment.

* * * *

Detective Gowerstone had set up his base of operation at Radcliff Camera, an 18th century classical rotunda ninety feet high in the heart of Oxford. Inside were tables filled with computers, phones and busy personnel. A detailed map was pinned to a wall showing where the chase had started and abruptly stopped.

"Sir, incredible piece of deduction today," a sergeant said flatteringly. "Extraordinary luck that you knew exactly where they'd be."

"Deduction isn't luck," Gowerstone retorted sharply, "it's logic. Understand your opponent, analyze the circumstances and mathematically figure out the conclusion."

The dejected officer shrunk back. "Right, I meant —"

"What's the update?"

"We found the balloon and have two policemen guarding it. Vinogradov was taken to the hospital. Nothing too serious, just a —"

"The children, Sergeant!"

"Yes, yes, of course, right. We're searching every street, store, building and college. We've got a net of men slowly closing in."

"And the train station?"

"It's all set."

"Good, let's not fail this time."

* * * *

After finding a town map and asking for directions, Tom and Sarah hurried towards the train station. They passed All Souls College, turned right on Catte Street, and walked by St. Mary the Virgin Church, a glorious cathedral with angelic figures springing from the rooftop. The voices of fifty young men singing Pachelbel's

Christmas Canon filled the chambers and harmonically burst through the open windows.

"Listen," said Sarah, transfixed. "Do you hear that? It's magnificent." Recognizing the tune, she hummed along.

"Oh, brother," complained Tom, more eager to get to London than to listen to a choir.

"Just a minute," she requested, lost in the melody. "It's been so long since I've heard music."

They reached up to a cracked window and gazed in as the soft tranquil voices reminded them of the holiday season.

"Aren't they wonderful," Sarah said admiringly.

Tom watched, somewhat perturbed.

"What do you think?" she asked searchingly.

"I think I've heard enough," Tom griped, antsy to move.

"Just another second, please."

"Good grief," he muttered, enduring a few more minutes.

"They're amazing," she stated as her eyes perused the ensemble. "Such beautiful voices —"

"That's enough. Let's go," Tom grumbled, grabbing her hand and dragging her away.

"Boys . . . no sense of culture," she said under her breath.

After being misdirected three times, they found the train station. Strategically hidden behind a tree, Tom and Sarah peered out. There were several adults and students waiting for the next train but nothing out of the ordinary: no officers, police cars or anything suspicious.

"It seems a bit too easy, doesn't it?" said Tom, unconvinced. "This would be the one place I'd expect to find them."

"Do you think it's a trap?" asked Sarah skeptically.

"Could be."

They stood for a moment, debating their options.

"Let's take a chance," said Tom boldly.

"Agreed. I'll be right behind you."

They cautiously approached the building and searched the crowd, eyeing each individual: a man reading a newspaper, a couple holding hands, a few men casually talking and five students playing hacky-sack. It looked almost too perfect, like a movie set.

Tom and Sarah strolled over to the ticket counter and got in line. One-by-one the people moved forward.

An underpaid, overworked man looked down at Tom through his thick glasses. "Where to?" he asked.

"Oh, um . . . London," Tom mumbled. "Two tickets to London."

"What class?"

Tom grimaced at Sarah then back at the man. "Regular?" he guessed.

"Aren't you a bit young to be buying tickets?" the man squawked. "Where are your parents?"

Thinking quickly, Tom spotted the couple waiting by the platform. They looked over as he waved and smiled.

"Right there," answered Tom smugly. "They're waiting for us."

"Fine! That'll be seventeen pounds, each!" he demanded.

"Thirty-four pounds?" exclaimed Sarah, barely able to contain her temper. "What a rip-off!" She gave the man a harsh frown.

Tom threw her a sharp look communicating silently that this wasn't the time or place to make a scene.

"That's the price. Make up your mind," grunted the man.

"Ah . . . give me a minute," said Tom, moving to the side.

"Now what're we going to do?" Sarah wondered, still outraged by the overpriced tickets.

"Not sure," he sighed. "Ten pounds doesn't seem to get you very far."

"Maybe we could sneak on when it starts moving."

"There are too many people."

"We were going to do it before."

"It was the middle of the night and not as crowded."

As they turned to leave, Sarah noticed the two plainly dressed men staring at her.

"Tom, isn't that strange?" she indicated.

"What?"

"Those guys over there. They keep glancing at me."

Tom looked. One of the men slowly lifted his hand and spoke into a small radio receiver.

"Run, Sarah!" Tom shouted. "Run!"

The men sprang towards them.

Tom and Sarah dashed around the outside ticket counter and back across the main street.

As the men rounded the corner, Tom noticed that the nice-looking couple was also chasing them. The woman flashed a badge and grabbed her X26 Taser Gun: with a range of thirty-five feet, it could shoot two dart-like electrodes, delivering a powerful shock that would immobilize its victim.

"Great... now there are four of them," Tom complained.

Sarah took the lead. "This way," she motioned, pushing through pedestrians and dodging bicyclists.

The two sneaked into the nearest building and ran through the lobby.

Close behind, one of the officers reached out and grabbed Tom's sweater, tugging him backwards. A frantic struggle ensued. Tom wrestled feverishly as the officer held on with a fanatical grip. Trying to break free, Tom banged his elbow against the wall. His arm went numb.

Sarah looked behind her, aware of the intense brawl. As she ran back to help, Tom kicked the man's shin.

The officer wailed, buckling to his knees. "You stinking little brat," he shouted, rubbing his throbbing leg.

Sarah grabbed Tom's hand and quickly rushed out the back door. The other officers were right behind them.

They continued up St. Aldate's Street and across the road to Christ Church.

Filled with Renaissance and Georgian structures, the fable-like campus was buzzing with students rushing to various activities. Known for graduating thirteen prime ministers, it was the most prestigious of all the schools.

"Over there," gestured Tom, desperate for somewhere to hide.

They hurried towards the dining hall where a group of students was waiting in line. They slowed down and tried to blend in.

"That blaggard ripped your sweater," said Sarah, noticing the tear.

"I know," replied Tom, rubbing his sore elbow. "He almost had me."

"Nice kick."

"I would have liked to have done more."

"Shhh, they're coming."

The two plainclothes officers stopped close by, one of them limping. They scanned the campus and examined the students. Seeing nothing suspicious, the officers marched to the library.

"They're gone," said Sarah, relieved.

"Let's wait here for a minute, just to be safe."

Mingling among the scholars, they noticed a tall gangly student, Oliver, who seemed to know everyone. They watched this charismatic young man with interest.

"Kate, Laura, looking good," said Oliver, waving.

The girls politely smiled, then quickly dismissed his comment.

"Paul, see you in the morning," he yelled. "And good luck with the match."

"Party at my place afterwards!"

"I'll be there," affirmed Oliver.

Two drunken students aimlessly wandered by. Sebastian, known for his aristocratic ties more than his academic performance, hollered over.

"Oliver, you dicey little scoundrel! Get your butt over to *The Bear* and join us for a pint!" he shouted, slurring his words.

"Not tonight, Sebastian. I've got an early crew race in the morning."

"Come on — just one pint," he persisted. "I'll play you darts. Winner buys rounds!"

He waved him off. "Tomorrow . . . I promise."

The two students stumbled away.

A distinguished young gentleman dressed conservatively sauntered over. He had neatly combed hair and wandering brown eyes with a serious yet tortured look on his face, often the consequence of having privilege over friends.

"Darcy," Oliver nodded slightly, giving just enough greeting, but not overstepping his ground.

"Oliver," he replied tonelessly.

"What brings you to town tonight?"

Darcy stood there aloof, rudely ignoring the question. There was an uncomfortable moment of silence.

"What do you think of that girl over there?" Darcy asked in a contemplating manner.

Oliver looked across the courtyard and saw an attractive young woman with long brown hair, a pleasant smile, and a spark of wit.

"You mean Elizabeth?"

"Yes."

"She's pretty."

"You think so?"

"I don't think it's disputed. She's quite stunning, Darcy."

They stood for a long second.

"Right, well then, good night," Darcy said coldly and walked off in the opposite direction from where Elizabeth was standing.

Oliver turned and noticed Tom and Sarah hiding among the crowd. "Poor guy had the misfortune of ending up at Cambridge for two years. Comes from too much money; doesn't know how to act properly."

"Cambridge?" Tom questioned.

"Our *rival* school," whispered Oliver, dropping his voice. "We don't usually mention the C-word in public."

"Oh," Tom mumbled, more confused than ever.

"You look lost. Maybe I can help," he offered.

"Uh, no, we're, ah . . . fine, sir," replied Tom nervously.

"Sir . . . I like that. Don't think I've ever been called sir before," he laughed. "The name's Oliver, Oliver Horningbrook, second year."

"Second year?" Sarah inquired, trying to be part of the conversation.

"In college. I'm a sophomore."

"Right," Tom interjected awkwardly and extended his hand in a cordial gesture. "I'm Tom, and this is Sarah."

"Hello," smiled Sarah, her stomach rumbling at the wonderful aromas drifting from the open door.

As Oliver shook their hands, he wondered what was behind their worried faces.

"Nice to meet you," he acknowledged, continuing to observe them. "Well, you couldn't be students, unless you're some kind of geniuses. We have a few of those here."

"Tom's pretty smart," Sarah chuckled, "but I wouldn't call him a genius."

"Thanks," snapped Tom, giving her a disapproving look. She frowned back, taunting him.

"You guys look hungry. Why don't you join me in the dining hall?" offered Oliver, motioning toward the door.

"Oh, we don't, ah . . . really have much money, sir . . . I mean, Oliver," explained Tom.

"But thank you," added Sarah quickly.

Oliver grinned. "Don't worry about it. You'll be my guests."

Tom hesitated. "Well, um —"

"Sure," said Sarah, nudging Tom's side.

"Good, follow me," said Oliver as he guided them through an enormous doorway.

The main dining hall was a beehive of activity: the loud chattering of conversations, the clanging of glasses and the rattling of utensils. Long oak tables were packed with students. The thirty-foot high vaulted ceiling was a marvel of medieval engineering, and stained-glass windows studded the walls. Famous paintings of past presidents and distinguished alumni hung about, their disapproving faces glancing down at the overconfident students. Professors and other faculty, dressed in burgundy robes, sat at a head table.

As Oliver escorted them toward the main serving area, Tom and Sarah's eyes ignited. There were all kinds of food: turkey and roast beef, mashed potatoes with gravy, bowls of salad, fruits, vegetables, breads and pastries — it was a vision of delights.

"Do we grab one item?" asked Tom innocently.

"Take all you want, my friend," encouraged Oliver, patting Tom on the back.

Tom and Sarah smiled, their mouths watering and

stomachs growling. The two felt as if they were at a toy store and could take anything they desired.

They each grabbed a plate, piling it high with everything they saw.

As they got to the end, there was a soft drink machine, along with milk and assorted juices. Tom couldn't remember the last time he had something as simple as a soda. He seized the largest glass available and filled it to the brim, followed by Sarah, who packed hers with ice and topped it off with root beer.

After lugging their heavy trays to a table, they sat down and dug in. It was sheer joy as a variety of flavors exploded in their mouths.

Oliver chatted with Tom and Sarah over dinner. They learned that he was an only child from Richmond, located in the county of Surrey. His father was involved with the government in a powerful position, but Oliver didn't go into any detail and was a bit evasive. His mother was a society woman, whatever that meant. Tom thought it sounded like an excuse for not working. Although Oliver studied hard, he struggled with his grades. He wasn't the natural academic his parents hoped for, but he was protected by a long legacy of relatives who had attended Christ Church, Oxford, going back to his great-great-grandfather, a famous figure in Parliament. Oliver's one redeeming quality was his athletic ability. He was number one on his rowing team and captain of his boat. Sarah and Tom listened intently and shared their own story: where they came from and how they got to Oxford. After hearing of their struggles and adventures, Oliver thought they were the bravest kids he'd ever met.

As students finished their meal, the dining hall slowly cleared. Soon the enormous room was nearly empty.

Sarah leaned over and spoke in Tom's ear, "Where are we going to sleep tonight?"

"We'll find something," he whispered back.

Oliver quickly discerned their dilemma; if there was another thing he was good at, it was reading people. "So where are you staying tonight?" he asked, concerned about their well-being.

"We're um . . . not quite sure," Tom replied clumsily.

"Well then, it's settled. You can stay with me," said Oliver, excited. "I'll say you're my cousins visiting from Kensington. You guys can crash on my couch."

Tom looked at Sarah — she agreed happily.

"That'd be great," replied Tom.

Oliver stood up. "I have to get a few things from the library. Interested in coming?"

"Sure," answered Sarah and Tom together, thrilled at the prospect of exploring something new.

They left the building and walked across the quad. Oliver waved left and right as friends walked by.

"Hey Oliver," a student called over, rushing to the library.

"Hey Winston, good luck on your exam tomorrow!" he yelled through his hands.

"I'll need more than luck!"

Tom and Sarah suddenly became aware that they were once again vulnerable to being seen. They investigated the area but didn't notice any police; nevertheless, they weren't sure what to look for. After seeing some of the officers dressed in normal clothing, how could they recognize them? Those dark blue uniforms were always easy to spot. Now any adult became a suspect. It could be one of the professors or a faculty member, a groundskeeper or store clerk. Even some of the students looked suspicious. Gowerstone had once again raised the bar.

"Just stick close to me," said Oliver confidently, noticing their concern.

"Good idea," they both agreed, moving closer.

"You guys see that big tower over there?" asked Oliver, pointing to a clock as it struck 9:00 p.m.

Tom nodded. "I see it."

"It has a huge bell hanging in the middle. Guess what it's called?"

"No idea," he answered.

"It's called Great Tom," Oliver announced proudly. "What do you think about that?"

Tom and Sarah looked at him skeptically.

"I'm serious, ask anyone," he insisted. "Not sure why it's called that, I just know its name."

"I think it's a brilliant name for a bell," Tom said smugly.

"I'm sure you do," scoffed Sarah, smacking his arm.

"Ouch!"

"Perhaps you were meant to find this campus tonight and bump into me," continued Oliver philosophically, glancing toward the sky. "One never knows how these things work out sometimes. Maybe someone is looking out for you." He smiled as they walked up the library's enormous granite steps.

After getting through the receptionist and turnstile, all three entered the library. Every book imaginable lined the mahogany shelves.

It was paradise: no more sneaking one book at a time, now they had access to all the knowledge in the world.

"You two can grab something to read tonight if you want," Oliver suggested as he rummaged through his notebook.

"Really?!" Tom questioned, knowing the options were limitless.

"Sure. I need to go to the research area, but I'll be back in thirty minutes. Is that cool?" he asked.

"Very cool," Tom replied enthusiastically.

"Yeah . . . take your time," added Sarah, already browsing through one of the shelves.

"Have fun." Oliver sauntered off.

The two marveled at all the different sizes and titles of the leather-bound books. Walking down the endless rows, they studied ancient documents and skimmed various British classics: Jane Austen, Robert Browning, Lewis Carroll, Charles Dickens, Elizabeth Gaskell, Rudyard Kipling, Alfred Lord Tennyson, William Makepeace Thackeray . . . the authors went on and on. They flipped through some geography books half their size, ran down aisles searching for topics and climbed up a wooden ladder to a second level that overlooked the marble floor below. Warned twice to be quiet and once for running, they were simply having fun.

* * * *

Detective Gowerstone was extremely disappointed that his undercover agents had allowed Tom and Sarah to escape. After giving each of them a long-winded reprimand, he decided to take matters into his own hands. Grabbing his trench coat, umbrella and Bowler hat, he walked out the door. Tonight, he would search the streets and campuses alone.

* * * *

By the time Oliver wandered back, Tom had chosen a Dickens novel and Sarah a large art book filled with pictures.

Just as they were checking out, Sarah gasped. Out of the corner of her eye, she spotted one of the plainclothes officers browsing the aisles.

"Ah, Oliver," she murmured fearfully. "We should hurry."

"What is it?"

"That man, by the shelves," she replied, nodding in the general direction.

"I see him."

"He's looking for us."

Tom's eyes opened wide. He anxiously fumbled with his book, dropping it to the ground and making a deafening thud.

Everyone in the library instantly looked over, including the officer.

"Oops!" mumbled Tom, horrified.

"He's seen us," exclaimed Sarah.

"Leave the books," said Oliver impulsively. "Let's get out of here!"

They hurried to the entrance and out the door. The officer rushed after them but got stuck in the turnstile. He groaned as he smacked the metal object.

"Get this thing open!" he demanded. "Now!"

"Sir, you'll have to go around the other way," said the librarian, indifferent.

"Rubbish!" he cursed, kicking the turnstile.

"Quick! Across the quad!" Oliver insisted. "My room isn't far from here!"

All three swiftly headed to his dormitory, running across the campus.

"You weren't kidding," Oliver admitted, a bit disoriented.

"We told you," Sarah interjected dryly.

"It's kind of exciting though, don't you think?" Oliver added, exhilarated by the unexpected adventure.

"Maybe for you," Tom voiced grudgingly.

"You're right," Oliver realized. "It's not much fun for you guys, is it?"

"No!" they responded in unison.

"You'll be safe in my room," Oliver assured them.

"Anywhere's better than out here," said Tom, peering behind him.

They sneaked in the back entrance of the dormitory, a magnificent Romanesque structure on the edge of campus, and climbed up five sets of winding stairs to a large suite.

When Oliver opened the door, Tom and Sarah were surprised by the size of his room; it was more like a luxurious apartment than student housing. A small, lonely Christmas tree sat in the corner, covered with a few makeshift ornaments and an angel on top. The smell of pine was a pleasant reminder of the holidays.

"Wow, this is some room," gasped Tom, studying the enormous surroundings.

"The funny thing is, I don't really need this much space," admitted Oliver humbly. "But it's the same room all my relatives had, four generations' worth."

Sarah waited by the doorway, still shaken and uneasy about entering.

"You guys okay?" asked Oliver, worried.

"I suppose so," Sarah replied halfheartedly.

"We're sort of getting used to it," Tom added reluctantly.

"Just doesn't seem fair," continued Oliver, sympathetic to their plight.

"We just want to be left alone," Sarah maintained.

"Why are they so determined to get you?"

"I have no idea," said Tom, flustered.

Sarah finally strolled in, glancing at the pictures on the wall: Oliver with some friends on top of the Great Wall of China; a black-and-white photo of him rowing on the Thames; Oliver with an attractive young woman sitting at a café in Sydney, Australia; Oliver skiing down a hill somewhere in Switzerland; two friends with Oliver on top of the Eiffel Tower in Paris; Oliver with an older gentleman and an attractive woman standing in front of Buckingham Palace.

"Who are they?" asked Sarah, pointing at the man and woman.

"That's my mum and dad. It was taken two years ago before I came up to college."

"He looks quite serious," she said pointedly, closely studying the picture.

"He is," Oliver mumbled unhappily, his mood becoming melancholy. "We don't always see eye-to-eye on everything."

"What about your mum?" asked Tom.

"Oh, she's great. I get along with her brilliantly."

Tom and Sarah studied the picture, trying to imagine what it would be like to have a family. *Regardless of the circumstances, it must be nice to have parents*, thought Tom.

Feeling the strain of the day, Sarah collapsed on the couch. She glanced out a large bay window and down at the quad, wondering if they'd been followed.

Oliver closed the door and locked it.

"You guys want some hot chocolate?" he asked, perking up as he walked toward the kitchen.

"Sure," they both replied, needing a distraction to calm their nerves.

A moment later, Oliver reappeared with two large mugs and a couple of blankets under his arm.

"You guys can sleep on the couch," Oliver said, handing them their beverages. "I've got to study for an economics test tomorrow. I hate economics," he sighed heavily, accepting the long night ahead. "Then it's lights out; early crew match in the morning."

Oliver noticed their troubled faces.

"They won't check this building," he told them

reassuringly. "It's only accessible to the aristocracy and privileged families."

"Are you sure?" asked Sarah straightforwardly.

"At least not until the morning. They'd have to clear it with the dean, and he dislikes any interfering police. It's one of the advantages we have here."

"Okay," Sarah agreed trustingly. "And Oliver, thanks for everything: the food, a place to stay, all your help."

"Yeah, you're awesome," added Tom, contentedly sipping his hot chocolate.

"You guys have a good rest. Let me know if you need anything else." Oliver lugged a large textbook into his bedroom and closed the door.

Tom joined Sarah on the couch and tried to relax. It was the first night in years they felt somewhat comfortable. They both relished sitting peacefully: no lights out, no freezing bedroom, no harsh discipline and no one crashing through the door in the middle of the night.

As they quietly talked, their eyelids fluttered, their minds drifted, and they fell asleep.

* * * *

The next morning was glorious, the sun beaming through the windows. Outside, students were rushing to breakfast or an early class.

Tom and Sarah woke up around 7:30. Both had slept through the entire night, hopelessly in need of rest. They stumbled off the couch and stretched their arms.

"That felt so good," Sarah yawned, her eyes half open.

"I know what you mean," mumbled Tom, feeling rather displaced. "I could get used to this."

They looked around the room and noticed Oliver's bedroom door was open. Tom glanced down and saw a note left on a table in front of them:

Off to my crew match.
Welcome to come and watch.
Over on the Cherwell by
the boat-house – big race.
Tea in kitchen. Lock door
behind you if you leave.
Perhaps we can figure out
something when I'm back
- Oliver

Moseying into the kitchen, Sarah found the teapot and some biscuits on the counter. They each poured a cup and contemplated their next move.

They surmised the following: taking a train to London was now out of the question, too risky and dangerous. As far as they were concerned, every stop would be under surveillance by the police, some in uniform and others in plain-clothes. The bus stops and other forms of public transportation would also be watched closely, so that wouldn't work. Hiring a taxi was unfeasible, for they didn't have enough money. And walking would be impossible, because it was over sixty miles and would leave them constantly exposed. They couldn't stay where they were, because Gowerstone and his officers were everywhere. It was only a matter of time before someone saw them or a student mentioned their location.

No, the only plausible solution was the balloon, at least to get to London, but it was out of fuel and probably well guarded. Tom still had ten pounds from Wilbury, which may be enough to get propane for the tanks, but how would he fill them or even get close to the balloon?

Sipping their tea, the two looked out the kitchen window and pondered what to do.

11
AN UNLIKELY ALLY

"Perhaps Oliver could help us?" suggested Tom.

"It's possible. He's quite clever," Sarah concurred.

They finished their tea and walked into the other room.

"Hmm . . ." mumbled Tom, pulling the paper from his pocket and reading the word *Britfield* for the hundredth time.

"What?" asked Sarah.

"I was just thinking," he began, pacing the room and developing his idea. "While we're waiting for Oliver, maybe we could find out what this name means. You know, do some research."

"Don't you think it's safer to stay here?"

"Probably."

"And more dangerous if we're out there."

"Most definitely." He smiled at her with a mischievous grin.

"Fine — where?"

"The library we were at last night. I'm sure that's a good place —"

"How are we going to get in?" Sarah interrupted. "We're not students."

"I've got an idea."

"That's reassuring," she said sarcastically.

* * * *

On the other side of campus, huddled in a cramped office, three floors up at Trinity College, Professor Hainsworth was feverishly correcting student papers. Throughout his dimly lit room were desks and tables stacked with never-ending piles of exams and reports. Exhausted and flustered, he read line after line and page after page, scribbling *X's* here and circling words there. He repeated to himself in a melancholy rhythm, *"Hour by hour and day by day, all I do is grade and grade."*

Dr. Randolph Churchill Hainsworth III was a celebrity in the academic community, with doctorate degrees in physics, advanced sciences, mathematics and British literature (the fourth degree was just for fun). Promised a sabbatical three years ago, along with countless other vacations, he still hadn't received any time off. Stressed and overworked, with no help or assistant, he was plagued with endless days of teaching and grading. He longed for a break, for adventure, for freedom, for anywhere in the world but Oxford.

* * * *

The plan was simple: Sarah would cause a distraction as Tom sneaked in.

She walked up to the front library counter and sprawled out a large colorful map of Oxford. With her animated gestures and well-timed sobs, she pretended to be in a frenzy trying to locate one of the colleges.

"C-can you help me, sir?" she cried, desperately trying to elicit tears for a more believable performance. "I-I'm so lost and desperately need to get over to St. John's College and, and . . . find my brother," she sniveled. "I've been searching everywhere and I, I . . ."

The librarian was instantly lured in.

"It's okay," he said sympathetically, leaning over the counter. "Let me help."

"Oh, t-thank you, sir . . . thank you," she continued, wiping her eyes.

While the man was busy pointing to the map, Tom ducked under the turnstile and into the main library. He wasn't sure where to begin, so he asked a female student nearby.

"Hi, I'm trying to find out about a name. Any idea where to start?" he inquired.

"You mean research?"

"Exactly."

"Oh, that's easy," she acknowledged, walking him to a computer. "Just type in what you need, and push enter."

Tom gazed vacantly at the screen. He had never seen a computer before.

"What's the name?" she asked, perceiving his bewilderment. "I'll do it for you."

"Britfield," he replied, handing her the piece of paper.

"That's an odd name," she commented. "Well . . . let's see what we find."

After she entered the data, the computer screen lit up with volumes of references.

"There's quite a bit of information," she said, surprised, reading through several editorials.

As time passed, Tom eagerly watched the student navigate from one article to another. She would stop, examine something, then type more.

"That's strange," she said.

"W-what?"

"It says that the Britfields were an extremely prominent family in England — all kinds of interesting facts, scandals and intrigue, but then it just ends. No more information after 1837," she replied, puzzled.

"Oh," sighed Tom, disheartened.

"Is this for a school project?"

"Sort of."

"I can print some of the information for you, such as timelines and other significant facts," she offered. "It might be helpful."

"That would be great."

The student returned a few minutes later and handed Tom several pages.

"Thanks for the help," said Tom politely, skimming over the data.

"Sure." She turned to leave. "Hey, good luck on your project."

Tom waved goodbye and walked toward the main entrance, more confused than ever. *Nothing after 1837*, he thought, feeling an empty sensation in his stomach. *What does this name have to do with me?*

He approached the front desk to collect Sarah, who was still gazing at the map and engrossed in conversation.

"Oh, there's my brother," she exclaimed reproachfully. "Where have you been?"

"I got lost."

"I've been looking all over for you!"

"Um . . . sorry.

"Thank you, sir," she said graciously, looking at the librarian. "Boys today — what are you going to do?" Sarah sighed and threw up her arms.

The man smiled, satisfied to see her reunited with her family.

After leaving the library, Tom and Sarah moved cautiously across the campus.

"Here, check this out," said Tom, handing her the documents.

"It's actually a last name," she said excitedly.

"Yeah, but everything stops at 1837 — what good is that?" he fired back. "There couldn't possibly be a family connection, given that I wasn't alive over 170 years ago."

Sarah thought for a second, reading the details and searching for a significant link to Tom.

"But why would the Grievouses have this name in your file?" she wondered, shaking her head distrustfully.

"I don't know."

"There must be more. We've got to find out," she persisted. "But for now, let's get back to Oliver's flat. It's not safe out here."

Sarah handed back the information, and they hurried down Oriel Street, hiding whenever they saw someone suspicious. It had become second nature.

They ran across High Street and stopped by Radcliffe Camera, trying to remember where Oliver's dormitory was. Tom observed the building, studying the interesting architecture: towering Corinthian columns, classical pediment windows and a massive leaded dome.

Looking at the windows, he suddenly noticed Detective Gowerstone talking on the phone.

Their eyes met.

"It's him!" exclaimed Tom, tugging on Sarah's sweater.

The detective slammed down the receiver and ran for the door.

"Who?" she asked, alarmed.

"Gowerstone!"

* * * *

Meanwhile back at Weatherly, the situation was dire. It had been almost two days since The Great Escape.

Mr. Grievous was hysterical, frantically tramping around the office and scratching his head. Mrs. Grievous sat on a chair with her face buried in her hands, incensed.

"We're down to fifty-four kids! It's not enough!" he exclaimed, exasperated. "If word gets out, they'll . . . they'll shut us down!"

"I'm aware of that," she responded sharply.

"If those brats fall into the wrong hands . . . start talking . . . tell people about this place," his voice building to a crescendo, "it could mean *real* trouble for us! Real trouble!"

Mrs. Grievous abruptly stood, her face contorted. "Not a word from Detective Gowerstone?" she asked indignantly.

"No . . . nothing! Nothing at all!" he moaned, lighting

a cigar and taking a puff. "Why hasn't he caught them? They're *just* two kids! How hard could it be?"

"We shouldn't have treated them so well!" she scoffed. "What a mess they've created!"

"What are we going to do?"

"There's only one thing left," she replied sternly, a burning look in her eyes. "Take matters into our own hands."

"B-but Gowerstone specifically said that —"

"I don't care what he said! We're running out of time!"

"But –"

"I'm not going to lose this orphanage because of a couple of insignificant children!" she shrieked, trembling with vengeful rage.

"But if Gowerstone finds out that we're interfering —"

"He won't find out anything!" she declared. "Now, I think it's time we start interrogating each orphan individually."

"Yes, yes," Mr. Grievous approved. "One of them must know where those two are headed."

"We'll squeeze the information out of them if we have to."

"I'll start at number one and work my way through the list," said Mr. Grievous with a sinister grin.

"Good. Now get Speckle in here."

* * * *

Gowerstone rushed out of the Radcliffe Camera and watched Tom and Sarah disappear down a street. He quickly called for backup and pursued on foot.

Dashing along Brasenose Lane, Tom and Sarah ran past Lincoln College, its 15th century medieval facade dripping with ivy. Students lingered in front.

They frantically worked their way through the crowd and continued on.

"Where to?" Sarah questioned, fatigued.

"I don't know! Just keep running!"

As they hurried over the uneven cobblestones, Sarah tripped and twisted her ankle. She smacked the ground, screaming in pain.

Tom rushed back and knelt beside her.

"Are you okay?" he asked anxiously.

"Oh Tom . . . it really hurts," she groaned, clutching her foot.

"Can you get up?"

"I don't think so."

With his arm, gently around her waist, he carefully lifted her.

"Try to stand on it," he urged.

She slowly shifted her weight. "I can't. It's too painful."

"Put your arm around my neck. I'll support you."

She hung on securely as they staggered down the road, stopping on Broad Street.

Policemen soon swarmed the area.

"Let's get to that building over there," Tom suggested. "Maybe we can hide inside."

Sarah cringed, the throbbing pain shooting through her body. "I can't go any farther."

"Don't talk like that."

"But —"

"I've got you."

Tom lifted her in his arms and awkwardly hobbled across the street to Trinity College.

Looking for an entrance, he stumbled along the campus walkway and tried each door.

Everything was locked.

Huddled in an entryway, he realized they were surrounded.

Crestfallen, the two exchanged a nervous glance.

"I'm sorry, Sarah," he admitted sadly.

"It's okay, Tom," she whispered with a heavy heart, tears gathering in her eyes. "We did our best."

Just then a door swung out behind them, knocking Tom in the back.

"Pardon me, terribly sorry," Professor Hainsworth apologized. He was dressed in a crisp white shirt, burgundy vest and tweed jacket. His short, grey hair was neatly trimmed. "I was headed out for a bit of fresh air."

"Oh, sir, you've got to help us," Tom pleaded. "You've got to hide us!"

"What's this all about? Who are you?" he questioned abruptly, noticing Sarah nestled in Tom's arms. "What's wrong with her?"

"She twisted her ankle."

"Then get her to a doctor."

"There's no time! It's not that simple!"

Hainsworth looked up and observed the policemen knocking on doors and peering into shop windows.

"Are those officers looking for you?" he asked disapprovingly.

Tom paused for a moment then replied, "Yes, sir."

"Why? What have you done?"

"It's complicated."

"It usually is."

"It's a long story," said Tom, frantic. "We don't have time to explain right now!"

"*Please,* sir," begged Sarah. "Can't you just help us?"

Although Hainsworth was busy with his own problems, he was touched by the sincerity in their voices. Tom's integrity and Sarah's innocence softened his rigid exterior and stern temperament. He felt compelled to help.

"All right," he replied apprehensively. "Get her upstairs quickly and wait for me in my study."

"Thank you, sir," they both exclaimed, grateful.

Tom carried Sarah through the door and disappeared.

A few seconds later, a young officer approached Hainsworth.

"Good morning, Professor. You haven't seen two children run by here, have you?"

"Two children?" he asked, surprised. "What did they look like?"

"A girl and a boy, one blond, the other brown hair," the officer stated. "Each was wearing a colored sweater."

"Well that makes sense."

"What's that?"

"That they were wearing sweaters."

"Why, Professor?" the officer asked impatiently, hoping for a clue.

"Because it's so cold out," replied Hainsworth matter-of-factly.

Unamused by his evasiveness, the officer became frustrated.

"Have you seen them or not?" he demanded angrily.

"Why do you want them?" inquired Hainsworth. "What have they done?"

"I'm not at liberty to discuss that."

"Then I'm not at liberty to tell you anything else," said the professor, then walked back inside and shut the door.

"Pompous academic," the officer huffed as he grudgingly continued his search.

Gowerstone ran up to Broad Street and stared at Trinity College, studying the buildings.

"We've lost them," said an officer despondently.

"I know they're in there," he stated with certainty. "Keep searching."

"Yes, but —"

"I want every building, hallway and room systematically checked!"

"We'll scour the entire campus, sir!"

"And station two policemen at each corner."

As the officer dispatched his orders, Gowerstone surveyed the street and vigilantly examined each detail. He sensed Tom and Sarah were close.

Gazing through the third story window, Tom watched the detective below.

Hainsworth came stomping up the stairs and into his study. Sarah was resting on the couch.

"Well then," he said coldly, "I think you owe me an explanation."

"Sir, I'll explain everything, but can we help Sarah first?"

"Yes, of course," said the professor courteously, calming himself. "I'll get some ice."

Almost an hour had passed. Sarah's foot was wrapped with ice and elevated on a pillow. She had taken an aspirin for the pain and was now sleeping soundly. Hainsworth deduced that it was nothing more than a twisted ankle and should be fine. Tom walked around the room telling Professor Hainsworth everything: his life growing up in the different orphanages; his time at Weatherly and the terrible conditions; the Factory and its grueling work; Mr. and Mrs. Grievous and their vicious dog, Wind; Speckle; rescuing Sarah; all the orphans helping them escape; running through the countryside; Detective Gowerstone; finding the balloon; the continuing chase; and anything else he could think of. Tom had never talked so much in all his life. His throat was parched, and his mouth was exhausted.

"That's incredible, Tom," said the professor sympathetically, trying to process all the information. "The things you've both endured at Weatherly — horrible, just horrible." He shook his head in disgust. "Despicable people, those Grievouses. I can't believe things like that still go on, right here in England of all places. It's just dreadful," he declared.

"Yes, it is."

"And now you'd like to get to London. Start a new life."

"Yes, sir," he answered confidently.

Hainsworth poured a glass of water and handed it to Tom.

"Thank you, sir."

"I suppose if I ever ran away, London is where I would venture. Spectacular city — so much to do, so many places to go." The professor paused in thought, reminiscing. "The author Samuel Johnson once wrote, *'When a man is tired of London, he is tired of life.'*"

"Hmm," sighed Tom, gulping his water and pondering the philosophical quote.

Sarah stirred from her rest.

"Good . . . you're up," said Hainsworth, his mood turning cheerful. "I'll prepare some tea, and we can figure out what to do." He left the room.

The British definitely like their tea. It's their solution to everything, all problems and concerns. If there's ever a major crisis, a cup of tea will help. If there is disturbing news, tea will calm the nerves; a perplexing issue or conflicting situation, a cup of tea will offer an answer; a minor conflict or major war, tea will provide strength and endurance. Whether one is entertaining a guest or villain, friend or foe, tea is the olive branch of hospitality. Whatever the occasion, morning or night, there is never a wrong time for tea. It was the bond that held the British Empire together.

"How do you feel?" asked Tom, turning to Sarah.

"Better, but my ankle still hurts," she responded, rubbing her foot.

"It probably will for a while."

"So is he going to help us, the professor?"

"I'm not sure," he whispered as he walked to the window. Tom pulled the curtain back and looked out. Gowerstone was gone, but several policemen patrolled the area.

"How does it look?"

"They're still out there."

Hainsworth returned with a silver tray containing a china teapot, cups, sugar and a few small cakes. The aroma of Earl Grey filled the room.

After pouring the tea and settling in, the professor found Tom and Sarah captivating. He embraced their company as a diversion from his work. Surrounded by demanding students all day, he enjoyed the refreshing conversation of two honest children and their hopes for the future.

Unfortunately, just as they finished their first round of tea, there was a loud knock at the door.

* * * *

The Grievouses had methodically implemented their plan: one-by-one, each orphan was brought to the office and thoroughly interrogated. They sat down in a small, uncomfortable chair, while Mr. Grievous marched back and forth complaining about the breakout, asking endless questions and trying to intimidate them. He used every tactic he knew: threats, punishment and bullying. However, not one child uttered a word or disclosed a secret. Mr. Grievous was surprised by their resolve, but the orphans remained silent. They were so proud of what Tom and Sarah had accomplished that every passing hour was a victory, every day another triumph.

Nevertheless, Mr. Grievous still had one more trick up his sleeve that he knew could lead him to Tom and Sarah.

As the last orphan left, Mr. Grievous opened the door and motioned to Speckle, who had been waiting outside the office.

"Get in here," snapped Mr. Grievous.

"Yes, sir," replied Speckle obediently.

"You said you might have a lead, a contact that could help us find the children."

"A very reliable one, sir."

"Excellent. I want you to deal with this personally. Find those two brats and bring them back here," he ordered. "Do whatever you have to do. Understand?"

"Yes, sir," replied Speckle, a malicious grin on his face. "Leave it to me."

* * * *

The knock came again, even louder this time.

Everyone was startled by the interruption. Hainsworth mouthed to Tom and Sarah for silence as he got up.

He cautiously crept downstairs and slowly opened the door: all he could see were two short stubby legs and a mountain of papers. It was Professor Chadwick, a scrawny little man wearing thick tortoiseshell glasses and an odd bowl-shaped hat. He abruptly entered the foyer and dumped the documents on the stairs.

"I brought these over from this morning's exam," he hissed. "They need to be graded immediately."

"I still have *hundreds* to do before I can get started on these," complained Hainsworth, letting out a long weary sigh.

"Then get to them," he muttered rudely. "No time to waste!"

"But —"

"No buts. I want them done by the end of the day. As long as I'm chair of this department, I give the orders," exclaimed Chadwick, then turned and marched out.

Professor Hainsworth grabbed the pile of exams and painstakingly climbed back up the stairs, taking each step with greater effort. It seemed that his short break was over.

"No need to worry," he told Tom and Sarah. "It had nothing to do with you."

After setting the stack of papers next to the others, Hainsworth plopped down in his armchair and let out a disheartening groan.

"Is everything all right?" inquired Tom.

"Is there anything we can do?" asked Sarah.

"You both have enough problems of your own," replied the professor, staring at the daunting pile of unfinished work. He then gazed out the window, deep in thought.

Tom and Sarah shared glances, wondering where the professor's zeal had gone. After a long moment, the silence was broken.

"Did you say you had a *balloon*?" inquired Hainsworth, magically revived from his subdued state of depression.

"Yes, just on the outskirts of town," Tom replied.

"That sounds quite adventurous," he continued, enthusiastic.

"That's ah . . . one way to put it."

"Where exactly is it located?" asked the professor, his curiosity growing.

"I'm not sure."

Tom pulled out his map of Oxford. Sarah leaned over to assist.

"We're right here, Trinity College," confirmed Hainsworth, pointing to a small clump of buildings. "Does that help?"

"Not really," answered Tom, still perplexed.

"The problem is, Professor, we've been all over this city," interjected Sarah. "So many of the roads and structures look the same. It's hard to know one from the other."

"Retrace your steps from when you first got here," suggested Hainsworth.

Tom ran his finger along the map, tracing where he thought they had been. He remembered High Street, a large campus, the river and a field with a barn.

"I think it's right around here . . . on this farm . . . by Magdalen College," he said, uncertain.

The professor looked over, encouraged. "Yes, Wesley Field. I know where that is."

"But we're out of propane," said Sarah, dispirited.

"And the balloon is probably surrounded by Gowerstone's men," Tom grumbled.

"It's quite a quandary." Hainsworth leaned back in his chair, thoroughly intrigued by the challenge.

"And it won't be long before Gowerstone searches this building, including your office," warned Tom. "He won't stop until he finds us."

"He's somewhat of a fanatic, isn't he?" commented the professor.

"You think?" Sarah replied poignantly.

"Why would a detective commit so much time and resources to just two orphans?" inquired the professor, pondering the question himself. "It doesn't make any sense."

Sarah threw up her hands. "It's what we've been trying to figure out for the last two days."

Hainsworth looked over at the stacks of papers dominating his office.

"I'll tell you what," he began, inspired by a sudden spark of insight. "I'll make a deal with you."

"Yeah?" Tom responded eagerly.

"Yes?" Sarah questioned suspiciously.

"I'll pay for the propane and get you to your balloon, if . . ."

"If what?" they both exclaimed.

Hainsworth leaped up. "If you let me safely escort both of you to London," he said excitedly, overjoyed by the thought. "It sounds like you could use some help."

Tom and Sarah were surprised. Yet considering their current situation, it was an offer they couldn't refuse.

"Absolutely," Tom stated jubilantly, overwhelmed by the prospect.

"That . . . that would be wonderful," Sarah added, grateful.

"Splendid," said the professor with a sudden burst of vitality. "If what you said about Gowerstone is true, we should leave now."

"Good idea," Tom agreed, restless to get moving. "But before we go, can we take care of Sarah's ankle?"

"Indeed," nodded Hainsworth.

Tom and the professor firmly wrapped her foot in a gauze bandage and helped her up. She was definitely feeling better. Her ankle was still tender, but she could walk on it.

"Sarah, do you think you can manage?" Hainsworth asked candidly.

"I'll manage just fine," she replied stubbornly.

"Excellent," he acknowledged, then grabbed his wallet, raincoat and umbrella.

"That's all you're bringing?" questioned Tom, expecting a small suitcase or at least a duffle bag.

"It's all I need."

Tom helped Sarah downstairs, followed by Hainsworth. No one knew what to expect when the door opened or what the future would bring, but there was an underlying sense of excitement. Although Tom and Sarah had journeyed this far on their own, they now had a trustworthy ally.

"Wait here for a moment," cautioned Hainsworth, opening the front door and walking outside.

He motioned to one of the policemen scouting the area. "Officer, come here! Quickly!"

The officer rushed over. "Yes, Professor, what is it?"

"I was sitting in my office, looking out my window, when I saw two suspicious children, a boy and girl, one brown hair, one blond, run down Giles Street towards Saint John's College."

"Really? That's exactly who we're looking for. Many thanks, Professor," the officer exclaimed then hastily yelled into his radio. "We've got them! They're headed towards St. John's College! Get everyone over there!"

One by one the officers raced by until the area was clear.

Hainsworth walked back to the doorway. "We're all set," he announced, a playful smirk on his face.

"That was quite a story, Professor," said Sarah admiringly, now realizing the depth of his capabilities.

"Yeah, I almost bought it myself," Tom jested.

"Years of lecturing to eager-minded students does have its advantages," he said gracefully.

After making sure no other officers were near, they sneaked down the road until they found a hardware store. With Tom's help, Sarah limped along, her foot slowly improving.

Hainsworth arranged for a propane truck to drive out to Wesley Field. At first, the serviceman obstinately refused to help on such short notice; however, the professor offered the man *three times* what he normally charged. At that price, the problem was resolved.

The serviceman closed his shop, hurried to the back and drove his propane truck to the front. Everyone hopped in and headed toward the balloon.

An optimistic mood overcame the professor. The idea of leaving behind all that schoolwork, helping two fugitives and venturing into the unknown was thrilling. After years of tedious work, he felt like a part of his youth had been regained.

The truck stopped by Wesley Field. The serviceman waited impatiently, wanting to fill the tanks, get his money and leave. Tom, Sarah and Hainsworth investigated the area before they got out.

"We'll just be a minute," Hainsworth told the driver.

"Hurry up," he muttered. "I've got to get back to the shop."

The three of them peered around a corner: two policemen were patrolling by the balloon, each one fully armed and carrying a radio.

"Now what?" asked Tom.

"I've got an idea," declared Hainsworth, bending over and quietly discussing his plan.

A minute later, Hainsworth casually strolled down a gravel road, merrily tapping his umbrella.

"Good day, officers," he said, gesturing with a friendly wave.

"Hello, Professor. What can we do for you?" asked one of the policemen.

"I'm not sure if it's any of my business, but as I was taking my daily stroll, I came across two children hiding in that building over there," he whispered softly, pointing to the stone barn with an enormous wooden door. "It just struck me as a bit strange."

Surprised, the two officers looked at each other, then raced to the building and ran inside. Tom and Sarah sprang from behind a bush and shut the door.

"Quick! Lock it!" yelled Sarah.

Tom slid a massive bolt over the door. "That should do it."

The professor smiled and hastily motioned the truck to back up.

"Look, Tom," exclaimed Sarah, a worried expression on her face.

"Oh no," he mumbled, dismayed.

Although the basket was firmly secured to the ground, the balloon's canvas sprawled across the field like a wounded animal, barely inflated and holding on to its last gasps of air.

"It's all right," said Hainsworth coolly. "We'll fill the tanks and blast hot air inside the canvas."

It had now occurred to Tom and Sarah what a valuable asset Hainsworth was. Having a gifted academic definitely had its advantages, and the possibilities were limitless.

Meanwhile, the two officers realized they had been tricked, and by a professor of all people. They banged on the massive door. It didn't move. As they searched for a heavy object to smash their way out, one of the men called Detective Gowerstone and told him what happened. The entire Oxford police force was on the way.

The serviceman exited his truck, unhooked a hose and filled both propane tanks. Hainsworth paid the man his cash and sent him on his way.

"Okay, you two," exclaimed Hainsworth. "Let's get this balloon filled!"

Sarah jumped in the basket, ignited the blast valve and pulled on the rope. A flame shot out. Tom and Hainsworth held up the canvas opening, trying to capture the hot air. Gradually the balloon started rising and coming back to life.

Nearby, an orchestra of sirens roared as police cars zipped down a dirt road.

"Hurry up!" cried Sarah feverishly.

"Were going as fast as we can!" exclaimed Tom, his face tense.

The two officers inside the barn found a metal beam and started battering the door. The thundering noise echoed into the field.

"We've got to get out of here," urged Sarah, her anxiety building.

"Just another minute!" yelled Tom.

"We don't have a minute!"

"It's almost there!"

The balloon slowly lifted upward, expanding and stretching to its full capacity.

Hainsworth eagerly climbed inside the basket as Tom untied the ropes and pulled up the stakes.

Police cars plowed over the field and headed right for them.

"Get in!" shouted Hainsworth as the balloon lifted off.

The two officers shattered the barn door and ran toward the balloon.

Tom leaped up and pulled himself in, assisted by Hainsworth.

One officer dove for the basket, just managing to grab it. A second later, he looked down to the ground, now fifteen feet below. Panicked, he let go and landed directly on the other policeman.

Enraged, the two officers quickly got to their feet, pulled out their guns, and aimed for the balloon. Part of Britain's Armed Unit, they were well trained at hitting moving targets.

12
A TURN OF EVENTS

"Hold your fire!" yelled Detective Gowerstone, swiftly jumping from one of the vehicles.

The two officers hesitated for a moment, desperately wanting revenge, then lowered their weapons.

The balloon rocketed skyward as Tom, Sarah and Hainsworth gazed over the side and smiled.

Gowerstone closed his eyes and let out a lengthy sigh. *How could they have escaped again*? he contemplated. Tom and Sarah had been surrounded at the train station and cornered at Trinity College, the balloon was guarded, and he had every resource at his disposal. This defeat was a severe blow to his long list of accomplishments.

Just last year, he was hailed as the greatest detective in the country. He had caught the "Illusive Phantom," a sly and clever criminal who had successfully robbed over fifty million pounds' worth of jewelry and artwork from thirty prominent estates. Gowerstone had tracked the thief from the cliffs of Cornwall to the Scottish Highlands, finally springing his trap on the Isle of Skye. While the entire Scotland Yard Police Department thought it was just one man, Gowerstone concluded that it was actually two people: a brother and sister team, ex-circus acrobatics posing as real estate agents. The detective had meticulously put together all the pieces of the puzzle. Two different size shoe prints at the crime scenes; a pink hairclip; Moroccan pipe tobacco; the monthly occurrences of the incidents; and the height of the windows broken into. He baited the two criminals with a luxurious house full of priceless artifacts and patiently waited. When the criminals approached on a moonless night, one of their trademarks, his officers arrested them as they climbed up the exterior wall. The Prime Minister held a press conference to congratulate him, and the Queen offered him a knighthood.

Then there was Lord and Lady Westmoreland's missing daughter, Isabella. She had been missing over two weeks when Gowerstone was finally called. The parents were frantic to get their child back. All they had was a poorly written ransom note demanding one million pounds in cash. After carefully examining the letter, interviewing the staff and thoroughly exploring the estate, the detective knew exactly where Isabella was. One of the newer servants, a German maid, had cleverly hidden the child. Her bedroom was searched and behind a falsely paneled wall was Isabella happily playing with her toys and living on biscuits and milk. The Westmorelands were so ecstatic that they gave Gowerstone a mansion in South Wales, a beautiful property overlooking the shoreline. But he refused it. He said he was simply doing his job.

Yes, this case was becoming more complicated than he imagined. Gowerstone knew that these were no ordinary children. They obviously had resources of their own and were somehow well connected — how else could it be explained. And now there was a third party: a suspicious older man who manipulated two policemen, assisted in the escape and accompanied them in the balloon. Was he a seasoned criminal or a mastermind of the underworld? The detective needed to find out all the facts. He needed to extend his police force, gather more information and take this chase to another level. But he did have one thing going for him: he would now know exactly where Tom and Sarah were headed.

"Sir, we have a few police cars following the balloon, but we'll soon lose them over Stonor Park. There are just too many trees and not enough roads," explained an officer. "And the weather is getting worse. There's a terrible storm brewing."

"Follow the children as far as possible, and let me know of any new developments," ordered Gowerstone. "And find out *everything* you can about that mysterious man. Talk to anyone who saw him. Have our sketch artist draw a picture and take it around to the different campuses to see if someone recognizes him."

"Yes, sir," said the officer, writing down the details. "What about tracking the balloon? Should I call the airport or —"

"I've got that covered," Gowerstone replied calmly. "Just bring me my car."

"Sir." Another policeman handed him a cell phone. "It's an urgent call. It's the Prime Minister."

"Great, just what I need," he complained bitterly.

* * * *

"Marvelous — brilliant — fantastic!" cheered Hainsworth. "Well done, you two! What a remarkable escape!"

The professor was so ecstatic he could hardly contain himself. He moved back and forth, looking over one side then another. He couldn't believe it, that he had left Oxford and was floating through the sky in a balloon. His long-needed vacation had finally arrived because he seized the moment and took it. His spirits soared as he embraced the breathtaking views.

"Without your help, I don't think we would've made it," admitted Tom, moving over to Hainsworth.

"You saved us, Professor," Sarah added with a jubilant grin. "That was some show you put on."

"I did what was necessary," he acknowledged proudly, realizing their fates were now miraculously intertwined.

"We're both grateful," said Sarah humbly.

"And very impressed," added Tom.

"Happy to do it," said Hainsworth. "Now let's get to London."

"That's been our plan all along," mumbled Tom, a trace of frustration in his voice.

"You two can manage this thing, right?" he asked, looking at them confidently.

"Of course," replied Tom, glancing at Sarah apprehensively.

"I'm relying on both of your expert skills to get us there."

"We won't disappoint you, Professor," Sarah assured him.

The balloon caught a southeast breeze at about twenty-five knots. Gauging the altitude, distance and wind current, Hainsworth figured they'd be on the outskirts of London in less than two hours.

As time passed, Tom and Sarah got back into their routine. They diligently worked the ropes and funnel, maneuvering in and out of clouds and heading toward their presumed destination.

"Professor?" inquired Sarah, noticing an enormous property below. "What's that over there?"

"That's Blenheim Palace," he answered matter-of-factly, "the birth place of Sir Winston Churchill."

"Our Churchill?" asked Tom.

"Is there any other?"

"I suppose not, Professor," he replied quietly, aware that he was with a devout Churchill enthusiast.

Constructed from a soft, golden stone, this massive five-story Baroque structure dominated the countryside. There was a beautiful lake in front and thousands of acres of tree-covered hills and parkland. The roof was covered with an assortment of intricate towers and spiraling chimneys.

"It's amazing," said Sarah, overwhelmed by the size.

"Yeah, not a bad place to be born," Tom added.

"Not bad at all," laughed the professor.

"So how does someone get a house like that?"

"You mean a manor," the professor corrected him.

"Yes, a manor."

"When John Churchill, Winston's grandfather, defeated the French and Bavarians at the Battle of Blenheim in 1704, Queen Anne gratefully built him this palatial estate."

"Just for winning a battle?" Tom wondered aloud.

"It wasn't just *any* battle!" stated Hainsworth with

the conviction of a seasoned historian. "The future of England hung in the balance."

"Oh . . ."

"Which means, if you desire a property like this one, you need to save our country from some impending disaster," he jested, patting Tom on his back.

"Sure . . . will do, Professor."

After working the exhaust funnel and giving a few more blasts of propane, Tom pulled out the information from the library.

"Maybe the professor can help us with this," he whispered to Sarah.

"Ask him," she suggested, nudging him on.

"What's that?" inquired Hainsworth, glancing at the documents.

"A few days ago, when I was at Weatherly, Mr. Grievous told me that my parents were still alive."

"Did he? Well, that's incredible news," said the professor, then quickly caught himself. "But why would he do —"

"That's what we're trying to figure out," interrupted Sarah.

"Mr. Grievous had a secret file but wouldn't let me see it, so my friend Patrick sneaked in and wrote down this name." Tom handed Hainsworth the papers.

The professor's eyes opened wide, reading each page with thorough concentration. "That's a name I haven't seen for a long time, a very long time."

"Then you recognize it?" asked Sarah, encouraged.

"Yes," he answered hesitantly.

"But any information I found ends in 1837," continued Tom.

"Of course it does. That's when Princess Victoria became Queen of Great Britain and a new era was born," declared Hainsworth. "Shortly after that, Britfield was spelled with two *t's,* not one, if the name was used at all. Since then, few have spoken of it."

"But why would they change the spelling of the name?" inquired Sarah.

"Because of all the danger associated with it."

As they were getting into the conversation, a strange silence filled the air. The temperature quickly dropped, and the atmosphere darkened, rapidly turning the sky pitch black.

"Look at the clouds," noticed Sarah. "I think it's going to . . ."

Suddenly an explosion of rain showered down, the heavens unleashing their wrath.

Everyone nervously glanced around, completely caught off guard.

"I hate the rain," grumbled Hainsworth, his mood turning from cheerful to disgruntled.

"You live in England and don't like rain?" asked Sarah, surprised.

"One of the unfortunate dispositions of this glorious country," he admitted sadly, as he pulled his coat more tightly around himself.

"What should we do?"

"Let's try to maneuver out of this mess and take the balloon toward the ground."

However, before anyone had a chance to act, a gust of wind swept them upward and into the eye of the storm. They each grabbed the basket as a turbulent gale battered the balloon, knocking it around like a tiny raft in a raging sea. Out of habit, Hainsworth popped open his umbrella, but the wind whipped it from his hand and sucked it into the belly of the tempest.

"We've got to get out of this," yelled Tom, hopelessly tugging on the ropes.

"Hold on tight," shouted Hainsworth, a concerned look creeping over his face.

Lightning bolts sliced through the sky, followed by sharp cracks of thunder. Vibrations shook the air as the balloon was tossed among the clouds. Hail rained down in devastating bursts, landing and ricocheting everywhere. One smacked Sarah on the hand; another hit Tom in the back.

"The balloon's going to be ripped apart!" Sarah screamed.

* * * *

Detective Gowerstone drove up to 10 Downing Street, Westminster, London. He parked his Range Rover in front of the famous brick facade and legendary black door.

This address had been the official office and residence of the British Prime Minister since 1732. Originally three separate Georgian houses, it was consolidated into one home with a Cabinet Room, State Dining Room and a private apartment among the other hundred rooms.

Gowerstone walked to the door, nodded at the guard and went in. Although he'd not been there in a while, he wasn't happy to be back. Gowerstone believed that total autonomy was the only way to get things done. When others interfered, it slowed him down and undermined his progress. He enjoyed the freedom of doing what he wanted and not being questioned.

The Prime Minister, a few inches shorter than Gowerstone, was pacing his office. His slightly grey, balding head glistened in the light.

"You wanted to see me, sir?" inquired Gowerstone, an undercurrent of agitation in his voice as he entered the room.

"Yes . . . brandy?"

"No, thank you."

"Tea . . . coffee?"

"I'm fine."

"Right then, let's get to the point," he said, his manner turning serious. "I felt we needed to talk."

Gowerstone sat down, impatiently staring at his watch.

"I know you have an impeccable record, Detective. You've always succeeded in capturing your adversary." The Prime Minister paused for a moment, correcting himself. "Well, except for —"

"Yes, I know."

There was an awkward silence as Gowerstone became noticeably uncomfortable.

"That was ten years ago," continued the Prime Minister, collecting his thoughts. "It's time that you let that case go."

"It's not that easy."

"Regardless, we're privileged to have you on the force."

"Thank you."

"But this whole thing with the orphans is spinning out of control. I mean all this trouble for just two children?"

The detective was about to interject but the Prime Minister cut him off.

"You've scoured the countryside, used a local airport and have policemen searching half of Britain. This is absurd," he exclaimed, walking toward Gowerstone. "And you *still* haven't caught them!"

"It's more complicated than you can imagine, but I can't discuss it. You'll just have to trust me."

"Detective, we go back a long way, from Eton to Christ Church. You know I'll support you as much as I can."

"I appreciate that."

"However, if this leaks to the press, if things come out in the papers," the Prime Minister said as he marched around, "it will be a political nightmare. Not just for me, but for you."

The Prime Minister poured himself a brandy and guzzled it. Gowerstone waited, knowing that time was a precious commodity he didn't have.

"This is an election year. I don't need to remind you that my public approval ratings are low," declared the Prime Minister in a stern tone. "If the public finds out you're chasing two orphans all through England, it could get ugly. They'd see the children as heroes and us as villains. It's simple things like this that can end careers."

"I understand, sir, just give me more time."

"You've got two days, Gowerstone," he stated firmly. "After that, I can't cover your back. I'll need to look out for my own."

* * * *

While Tom, Sarah and Hainsworth huddled inside the basket, the storm raged on. Rain swept in from all directions. Thunder blasted. Lightning shot across the sky, splintering in the clouds and igniting the darkness. If just one bolt hit the canvas, it would explode.

Sarah repeatedly pulled the descent cord, but the wind wouldn't release the balloon, carelessly tossing it around in an ocean of turbulence. Trapped in a thermal, warm air rushed upward and cold air pushed downward creating a crushing effect.

"It won't descend!" she cried out.

"There must be something we can do!" Tom yelled.

Hail kept flying in and hitting their arms, legs and faces. Suddenly a large piece of ice flew past, ripping a gash in the balloon's canvas; the escaping air hissed loudly.

"We've been hit!" exclaimed Sarah, rushing to the side.

"Let me see," Tom looked up, trying to locate the hole. Without a thought, he opened the storage bench and grabbed a rubber patch.

"I'll take care of it!" he stated boldly.

"Are you out of your mind?" she gasped, grabbing his arm. "Don't even think about it!"

"We've got to do something, or we'll lose all the air."

"Forget it. It's too dangerous!"

"We'll crash if I don't!" he declared, relinquishing her hold and walking to the edge. "It's coming from this side. I can hear it."

"Tom, stay in the basket!" hollered Hainsworth.

Before anyone could react, Tom stuffed the rubber patch in his pants, tied a safety rope around his waist, and climbed up the balloon's netting.

"Come back down!" shouted the professor, trying to seize Tom's leg but missing.

Tom clung to the netting, making his way around the outside of the balloon and toward the tear. As he struggled upward, the rain and ice battered him relentlessly. His hands were frozen.

"What a brave boy," Hainsworth marveled.

"What a stupid kid!" ridiculed Sarah, leaning forward and yelling at the top of her lungs. "Thomas! Get back in here!"

Tom inched his way up until he found a hole about ten inches wide. The hot air blew in his face as he grabbed the rubber patch. It had a strong waterproof epoxy on one side, covered with plastic. He tore off the seal and stuck it over the gap, smoothing it down with his hand; it bonded instantly.

"I think it's working!" he hollered, then lost his grip and tumbled into the open sky.

* * * *

Philip Candor Rothenshire IV was busy coordinating yet another dinner gala at Windsor Castle. This one involved over fifty dignitaries from around the world, a seventy-five-piece orchestra, a twelve-course meal, two hundred bottles of vintage wine and a fireworks display afterwards. The preparations were exhausting. And while the Queen was away at Buckingham Palace, the staff had been reduced to a mere one hundred servants, a small number to handle such an enormous estate.

Philip was a fourth-generation butler and superintendent whose relatives had been associated with the royal family for almost four hundred years, going back to James I and the Stuart dynasty. Often behind the scenes of politics, he had seen everything. Loyal to the end, he was proud of his position and honored to serve the Queen and crown. Unlike most servants, Philip had the privilege of being educated at Trinity College, Oxford. However, those years at the university had been difficult. If it wasn't for the friendship and guidance of his advisor and teacher, he probably would have failed, lost his position at Windsor and drifted into obscurity. He had never forgotten his favorite professor and felt truly indebted. Little did he know he would soon be able to repay that debt.

* * * *

Falling past the basket, Tom tried to yell but was paralyzed with shock. All Sarah and Hainsworth saw was the quick flash of a plummeting body.

Partially fainting, Sarah was skillfully caught by the professor, who gently laid her down on the wicker bench and rushed to the edge.

Dangling twenty feet below, Tom was caught by the rope, swinging back-and-forth with the balloon's erratic movements.

Hainsworth was both stunned and astonished; the sheer bravery Tom had shown was extraordinary. It filled the professor with a heroic energy. He grabbed the rope and tugged with all his force. For that brief moment, the professor had the strength of an entire army.

"Hang in there, my little friend!" Hainsworth yelled down.

Tom felt the tug of the rope gradually pulling him upward. Inch by inch he came closer to the basket until he felt two large hands reach over, clutch his arms and drag him inside.

Tom was shaken. Everything had happened so fast. All he remembered was a quick descent and a hard yank around his waist. His body was sore and his sides ached, but at least he had succeeded in buying some time for the balloon.

"Are you all right?" asked the professor, bending over and untying the rope.

"I . . . I think so," answered Tom, disoriented.

"That was a very foolish thing to do!"

"I'm sorry."

"It was also extremely brave," he added. "I'm proud of you."

"Thanks."

"Are you sure you're all right?"

"I'm fine, Professor."

Sarah, still lightheaded, reached over and grabbed Tom.

"Don't do such stupid things, you idiot," she said sharply. "I thought you died."

"I was just trying to —"

"I know what you were trying to do," Sarah interrupted him, then coldly turned her back. "And you scared the life out of me."

Hainsworth stood, noticing a slight break in the weather.

"We need to find a safe place to land," he said with urgency.

Sarah and Tom quickly rose and snapped into action, tugging on one rope and pulling on another. They shot a blast of hot air into the balloon, then let some out, trying to balance its position and move away from the storm. With the hole temporarily patched, the balloon drifted along and slowly descended.

Tom peered over the basket and saw a vacant meadow with a gigantic structure sitting in the middle.

"We should aim for that clearing over there," he suggested.

"What is it?" asked Sarah, squinting her eyes.

Hainsworth looked out. "That, my dear, is Windsor Castle."

"M-maybe that isn't such a good place to land," Sarah cautioned.

"We don't have a choice," Tom said impatiently. "It's there or nowhere."

"But we'll be arrested."

"Don't worry. It'll be fine," Hainsworth said evenly. "It's time I pay a visit to an old friend."

All three worked feverishly to control the descent as the balloon swiftly skimmed the tree tops and headed up the "Long Walk," a pathway leading directly to Windsor Castle.

The oldest inhabited royal residence in Britain, Windsor Castle represents the pinnacle of majesty. First built in 1070 by William the Conqueror, the original wooden structure was replaced with greyish stone and improved over the centuries. Perched high on a hill and illuminated by lights, it stood as an enormous fortified structure with thirty-foot walls and fifty-foot rectangular towers.

The balloon scraped over the grass and skidded to a stop on the Royal Mews, right next to the main entrance. Tom and Sarah each grabbed a stake and quickly jumped out, firmly securing the balloon.

By the time they finished tightening the ropes, twenty well-armed royal guards had surrounded them: it took no more than sixty seconds from the balloon touching down to a security force being sent out. Make no mistake about these well-trained men: unlike the popular Beefeaters dressed in their colorful red and black suits and carrying long staffs, these men were wearing high-tech army gear and holding M-16 rifles. They would do anything to protect the Royals and Windsor Castle.

Sarah looked up. "Tom . . ." she whispered, her worst fears realized.

He glanced over and froze. "Not the welcome we hoped for," he responded dispassionately. "Professor?"

As the commander aggressively approached the balloon, Hainsworth peacefully surveyed the situation.

"You're trespassing on royal property!" exclaimed the commander. "You will be arrested and held until the local police remove you from these grounds!"

"Perfect," said Tom cynically.

"I told you so," Sarah murmured.

Tom looked at the professor for a reaction but noticed his calm face and what appeared to be a smirk. *Why isn't he worried?* he wondered.

Hainsworth motioned to the guard. "My good man, there's no need for any of that. If you would be so kind as to contact Philip Rothenshire, I'm sure this matter will be cleared up instantly."

The commander was dismayed by the request.

"What does this have to do with Mr. Rothenshire?" he demanded irritably. "He's very busy at the moment."

"As you can see, so are we," retorted Hainsworth.

There was a silent standoff as the two men gazed at each other waiting for the other to flinch.

"Fine!" the commander snapped, annoyed by the request. He pulled a radio from his side belt and spoke into the receiver. "It's Robert, front entrance. Have Mr. Rothenshire come out here immediately."

The mood remained tense. Standing with their rifles carefully aimed, each guard had a stone-cold expression on his face.

Tom and Sarah stayed motionless, afraid that one wrong move might end in their early demise. Hainsworth was the only confident one.

After a few uncomfortable minutes, Philip walked out of the castle and down toward the balloon. Wearing Wellingtons and carrying an umbrella, he pushed through the guards and over to the commander. Tall and muscular, his pale blue eyes glistened intensely, and his blond hair was damp from the recent rain.

"What's this all about?" he asked indignantly. "I don't have time for this. I have only three days to get . . . Professor Hainsworth!" he exclaimed with astonishment. "But what are you doing here?"

"A long story, my good friend," replied the professor.

"I'm sure it is," said Philip, looking up at the towering balloon.

"How about inviting us in and I'll explain everything?"

"Huh . . . oh, right . . . yes," said Philip reluctantly, trying to figure out the proper protocol for something like this. "It would be a privilege, Professor."

"What would you like me to do with these intruders?" asked the commander.

"Escort my personal *guests* inside — now," answered Philip, completely dumbfounded by the incident.

The commander hesitated for a second. "As you wish," he nodded coldly. "Disengage, men!"

The guards lowered their weapons and stood at attention. Tom and Sarah exhaled, unclenching their tightly clasped fists.

"That was a bit awkward," whispered Tom under his breath.

"You think?" said Sarah, rattled.

Hainsworth cheerfully climbed over the basket,

helped by one of the guards. After the initial shock wore off, Philip became engaged in conversation with the professor, walking toward the castle as two lost friends reunited. Tom and Sarah trailed closely behind.

"What's going on?" she asked Tom, still bewildered by what just transpired.

"I'm not quite sure, but I don't think we're going to jail."

"That's a relief."

"To say the least."

The guards returned to their posts as Philip, Hainsworth, Tom and Sarah marched through an arched entryway leading to the main entrance hall.

The inside of Windsor was like a museum, with beautiful paintings, marble statues and priceless artifacts meticulously arranged throughout. The twenty-foot ceilings had colorful motifs and gilded carvings. Positioned by the main stairway was an enormous Christmas tree, carefully decorated with colored bulbs, glass angels and plaid ribbons. White lights covered the tree from top to bottom and presents of every size were neatly stacked underneath. Six-foot wooden nutcrackers dressed in the Royal Stewart tartan stood on either side. The smell of cinnamon and pine overpowered the room.

Dripping wet and shivering, they waited anxiously in the foyer.

"I hope we're not imposing," said Hainsworth sincerely. "I know we've put you in quite a predicament."

Philip turned to his guests. "For you, Professor, I'd be willing to make any sacrifice." He lowered his voice.

"Luckily, the Queen and the Royals are away for a few days, so I can take a few liberties. However, if they were here, well...that would be an entirely different situation."

"I quite understand," nodded the professor. "Please, let me introduce my friends. This is Tom, a very talented and resourceful young man. I expect great things from this lad."

Philip leaned over and firmly shook Tom's hand.

"Your opinion carries great weight, Professor," said Philip flatteringly. "I'm honored to have him as a guest." After shaking his hand, Philip noticed something familiar about Tom but couldn't place it.

"And this delightful young lady is Sarah, a refined and strong-willed young woman," added Hainsworth.

Philip took Sarah's hand and bowed slightly.

"Delighted to have you here," he said, looking back at Tom and trying to place him.

Sarah noticed his odd look but dismissed it.

"We must get you out of those soaked clothes and into something nice," insisted Philip. "After you have eaten, you may stay here tonight."

"Wonderful — then it's settled," Hainsworth declared.

Tom and Sarah grinned at each other, wondering what incredible delights awaited them.

Philip snapped his fingers, summoning the first footman, who quickly came over.

"Yes, sir," replied the servant briskly.

"Take Professor Hainsworth, Tom and Sarah to the state apartments in the east wing. Run a bath for each of them and make sure they have a clean change of clothing," ordered Philip. "When they're ready, bring them down to the Waterloo Chamber."

"Right away, sir," said the first footman, snapping his fingers and summoning two under footmen.

This section of the staff is known as G or "General Branch," and is structured as a pyramid of seniority. Philip held the highest position as head butler and ran the estate; the head housekeeper is responsible for the female staff and supervises the interior cleaning; then there's the chef, usually French; the lady's maid and gentleman's valet; then the first footman, second footman and so on down the ladder.

"I will see you soon, my old friend," said Philip, firmly shaking Hainsworth's hand again. "We have many years to catch up on."

"Indeed," he smiled. "And thank you for your help tonight."

"It's the very least I can do," Philip added respectfully.

The professor, Tom and Sarah followed the footmen down a long corridor and through adjoining rooms. Each section was its own masterpiece: walls covered in velvet or silk, centuries-old tapestries embroidered with scenes of famous battles, crystal chandeliers sparkling from the coffered ceilings, antique furniture from around the world and bronze statues artistically positioned.

Afraid to touch anything, Tom and Sarah walked straight ahead, arms pinned to their sides. They made their way up two marble staircases and into a mahogany hallway with polished teak floors. Each was shown to a bedroom.

Hainsworth disappeared through a door as Sarah looked over at Tom and bid him farewell.

"Adieu, mon ami," she whispered, vanishing into her bedroom.

"Yeah, whatever."

Tom entered a room that could have easily fit half of the Grievouses' house. The ceilings soared above him. There was a four-poster oak bed with enough room for every orphan at Weatherly, a fireplace he could stand in and an array of elegant tables and stylish chairs.

"Your bath is ready, sir," said a footman.

"Ah . . . thanks."

"Will you require anything else, sir?"

"Um, nope," replied Tom clumsily, not really sure what else to ask for.

"Then I will go and retrieve your outfit."

The footman departed as Tom walked into the bathroom. The floor was covered in exotic tiles and the walls were wrapped in marble. Pristine white towels embroidered with the Windsor crest hung neatly on silver racks. He had washed many times in Weatherly's dingy concrete showers, but he had never bathed in a pool-sized bathtub with hot water and an assortment of soaps and shampoos.

Quickly undressing, Tom dove in. The water was the perfect temperature and felt soothing on his tired body. He ducked under one end and shot up at the other. He lathered up with shampoo, tried the different soaps and scattered suds everywhere.

It was about the time he emerged from the tub that an uncontrollable smile crossed his face. The irony of the situation had not entirely slipped his mind. Just three days ago he was sitting in Weatherly's dismal workshop. Now he was bathing in the splendor of Windsor Castle. *Not a bad transition*, he thought. *No, not bad at all.*

Tom worried about the other orphans and wished they could be here. He missed each one. They were his family, his brothers and sisters, perhaps not by birth or bloodline, but certainly by bond and friendship. He was determined to help them and let others know about their situation. The Professor might offer some assistance, but for now he would focus on getting to London.

As Tom finished drying off, he noticed a beautiful set of clothing laid out on the bed. There were a new pair of tailored pants, a crisp blue shirt, a pair of shiny leather shoes and silk undergarments with matching socks. It was the nicest set of clothing he had ever seen, but he didn't question the circumstances or the sudden generosity. He just went with the flow. His other clothes had disappeared, but resting on the nightstand were his ten-pound note, compass, map, papers and Sarah's locket.

He dressed hastily, stuffed the items into his pocket and strolled into the hallway. A footman waited attentively by each door.

"Are you ready to go downstairs, sir?" asked a footman, stepping forward.

"I'll wait for my friends, if you don't mind."

"As you wish," he said, returning to his statue-like position.

Tom sat on the first object he spotted, a priceless French Baroque Louis XIV chair exquisitely hand carved from walnut. He shifted around trying to get comfortable in his new clothes and fiddled with his collar. Tom glanced up at the footman, who gazed into space — no eye contact, not even for a second.

After a few minutes Hainsworth exited his bedroom. He was wearing a pinstripe shirt, dark slacks and a navy blazer. He walked over to Tom.

"Well, don't you look dapper."

"Thanks for whatever you've done, Professor," Tom said earnestly.

"It's Philip who deserves the praise."

"He'll get it," Tom replied eagerly as he stood.

Sarah suddenly appeared from her room wearing a dazzling emerald dress and new shoes. Her hair was done up with a matching ribbon. Tom was speechless — long gone were the worn pants, wet sweater and matted hair.

"What do you think? Not a bad outfit, is it?" she grinned, twirling around to show it off. "I haven't worn a dress in years. Sort of feels nice."

Tom turned to one of the footmen. "Where did you get all this stuff?"

"We buy and stock every type of clothing for just such occasions. We have many guests and countless needs. Our in-house motto is *'always be prepared for anything,'*" he whispered proudly. "You'd be amazed at some of the requests we receive."

All three examined each other's transformed appearance.

"You look beautiful, Sarah," said Hainsworth.

"Thanks, Professor," she nodded then looked at Tom. "Well?"

"Well what?"

"How do I look?" she asked impatiently.

"Yeah, you look kind of . . . nice," he admitted grudgingly.

"Hmm," she said, examining him closely. "Look at you. I almost walked right by," she teased. "You clean up quite well, I suppose."

Tom shook his head, ignoring her comments and mischievous glare.

"I'm just kidding." She gave him a gentle shove. "You look very distinguished."

"Do you think so?"

"Yes, I do," she said admiringly with a playful laugh.

"Are you ready?" asked a footman.

"I believe so," answered Hainsworth.

"Then right this way," he motioned.

They followed the footman through a hallway and down two flights of stairs. A distinct smell of leather and aged wood filled the air.

"I'm still amazed at what's happened, Professor, but I'm afraid to ask," Tom conveyed innocently. "I don't want any of this to disappear."

"Not to worry," Hainsworth assured him. "We should be set for the night. Philip and I go back a long way."

"How do you know him?" asked Sarah.

"He was one of my students at Oxford. And with some guidance, he became an excellent scholar. I'm very proud of him," he said with paternal pride. "Unlike so many, he worked extremely hard. I admire that character trait in people."

"His kindness is overwhelming," said Sarah, sliding her hand along the fine silk dress. "I could get used to a place like this."

"Indeed," nodded Hainsworth, as he looked around. "Of all the places to land, we picked the right one."

"It seemed like a disaster at first," admitted Tom, still fidgeting with his shirt.

"That welcome was a bit daunting," laughed the professor. "But remember Tom, patience and a little faith will get you a long way in this world."

"I'll remember."

"Just this morning I was ready to have a nervous breakdown, overwhelmed by endless work," confessed Hainsworth. "Yet tonight, I'm with a fine young man and an enchanting young woman at Windsor Castle. You two have made me *very* happy."

"What about your job, Professor?" Sarah questioned apprehensively.

"I'll worry about that later," he answered dismissively. "I've been owed a vacation for years, and I intend on taking it."

"Well said," affirmed Tom, adding an approving nod.

They strolled into the Waterloo Chamber, a stately banquet hall with wood paneled walls, an assortment of 19th century portraits, a barrel-shaped ceiling with arched windows on each side and five chandeliers evenly spaced in the middle.

The room was blazing with activity as servants and staff efficiently worked away. An eighty-foot mahogany table was at the center, polished to perfection and gleaming like a mirror. There were four massive porcelain urns in the middle waiting to be filled with fresh flowers. Each place setting had Royal Doulton bone china plates, surrounded by fifteen distinct pieces of Dixon & Sons silverware and seven different-sized Waterford crystal glasses. Two servants carefully walked along, painstakingly checking each fixture with a ruler. Brass was polished, shelves dusted and oriental carpets cleaned. Everything was perfect.

"It's certainly not like dining at Weatherly," exclaimed Tom, pointing to the table.

"Definitely not," said Sarah, gazing in awe at the magnificent spectacle.

Standing in the center of all the chaos was Philip, giving directions and managing others. He turned and gracefully sauntered over.

"Yes, much better," he said approvingly. "Let's get you something to eat and we can sit down and talk."

"Splendid idea," agreed Hainsworth.

They followed him through the room and into the kitchen area. Tom and Sarah's mouths watered at the prospect of what wonderful delights awaited them.

* * * *

By the time Detective Gowerstone stormed into his Oxford headquarters, it was past 11:00 p.m. A few policemen worked at their desks, while others looked through files or talked on the phone.

"Where have you been, sir?" asked an officer anxiously. "We've tried contacting you several times."

"I was detained by the Prime Minister. He just doesn't understand how important this is," Gowerstone replied resentfully. He then studied a large computer screen showing England and a small dot flashing at Windsor Castle.

Although the detective expected to capture Tom and Sarah in Oxford, he wasn't taking any chances. He had learned that they were both very smart and extremely lucky. He also suspected that they were receiving some form of help or outside assistance, which only complicated matters. Statistically, the longer it took to capture them, the harder it would become. The first twenty-four hours were crucial, but that time had passed. So, after the balloon crashed in Oxford, Gowerstone had one of his technicians place a tracking device in the basket. If for some reason the two children escaped again, he would always know where they were, or at least where the balloon was.

"We've tracked them here, but there's no more movement," said the officer, gesturing to the monitor.

"I see."

"What are they doing at Windsor Castle?"

"I have no idea," he replied irritably. "The way this case is going, I've learned to expect anything." Gowerstone thought for a moment as he looked at his watch. "Is the Queen in residence?"

"No, she's at Buckingham Palace for two days."

"Good. We've got a few loyal contacts at Windsor, correct?"

"Yes, sir."

"Notify them of our situation and have them secure the children until morning." His voice deepened. "Make sure they take every precaution to treat Tom and Sarah kindly. We'll be there first thing to pick them up."

"Why not tonight?"

"I don't want to make a scene, especially at Windsor. We must handle this situation delicately."

"Yes, sir."

"Also, contact the local police and have them positioned around the castle. If Tom and Sarah are there, they'll be locked in for the night."

"I'll take care of everything."

"What have you found out about the man they left with?"

"His name is Dr. Randolph Churchill Hainsworth the third," replied the officer, as he read from a file. "He's been a professor at Trinity College for over thirty years, specializing in physics and mathematics."

"This doesn't make any sense," said the detective as he rubbed his forehead. "How does he know Tom and Sarah? Why is he helping them?"

"I'm not sure. We've searched Hainsworth's rooms but found nothing linking him to the children or Weatherly. Just endless stacks of ungraded papers."

"And the dean of the college?"

"As surprised as you are."

Gowerstone glared out the window, processing the facts. The room went silent. Each officer stopped working and watched the detective with interest.

"So a distinguished and respected professor suddenly leaves his college and runs off in a balloon," he stated with a trace of doubt. "There's got to be more to this."

"Maybe he's a relative?"

"No, he's not," answered Gowerstone assuredly, grabbing the manila envelope from Weatherly.

"There's Sarah's uncle —"

"A worthless, greedy fool," he said sharply, reading through Tom's information again. "Professor Hainsworth shouldn't be involved with this. He has no idea what he's gotten himself into."

* * * *

After finishing a spectacular meal that included shrimp, lobster and steak, Tom and Sarah were led to a small library. Philip and Hainsworth were already sitting in front of a roaring fire chatting about British literature. Both men were holding a snifter of brandy and talking enthusiastically.

"What about the novel *Wuthering Heights*?" Philip inquired. "What if Cathy had married Heathcliff instead of Edgar Linton? Wouldn't that have made an interesting romance?"

"Possibly, but it wouldn't have been as dynamic or tragic, which was Emily Bronte's intention," Hainsworth replied in his scholarly manner. "It's wanting something more than life itself but not being able to obtain it that adds to the drama."

"That's a good point."

"The isolation each sister felt on those Haworth moors profoundly influenced their writings," he added intelligently. "It's that setting that fostered their Gothic novels." He paused to sip his brandy. "Did you know their house was surrounded by a graveyard?"

"No, I didn't," confessed Philip, surprised. "That explains a great deal."

"It certainly does."

"Wasn't Emily writing another book?"

"Yes, but it's never been recovered. Some academics believe her sister Charlotte burned it."

"Now that's tragic."

Hainsworth leisurely savored another sip from his glass. "This brandy is superb. Louis XIII?"

"Yes, well done, Professor."

"Your position does have its advantages."

The two laughed as Tom and Sarah wandered over to the fireplace.

"How was dinner?" inquired Philip.

"Fantastic," answered Tom, plopping down on a gigantic leather chair. "I couldn't eat another bite."

"I didn't know food could taste so good," said Sarah blissfully. "Thank you for everything you've done tonight."

"Yeah, thanks Philip," Tom added quickly.

"First thing in the morning, I'll have your balloon repaired and ready for your travels to London," said Philip thoughtfully, then leaned over. "But may I suggest you take a train."

"I wish we could, but it's not that easy," blurted Tom, followed by a reproachful glare from Sarah.

"Why is that?" he asked inquisitively.

"It's . . . complicated," interrupted the professor. "We'll talk about that later." Quickly changing the subject, he held up his brandy in a gesture of thanks. "To our good friend Philip, whose kindness saved the day."

"Hear, hear," cheered Tom and Sarah.

"It's been my pleasure," said Philip, touched by their gesture.

Following the toast, Hainsworth noticed Tom gazing at the fire, lost in his thoughts.

"What's on your mind, Tom?"

"It's about today," he replied, reflecting on their earlier conversation. "I'm curious what else you know about Britfield."

Hearing the name, Philip's eyes instantly brightened. He shifted in his chair and stared directly at Tom.

"Yes, I almost forgot," admitted Hainsworth, contemplating the question. "As I said before, I haven't heard that name in years. Even scholars don't talk about it anymore."

The professor sat up in his chair as Tom and Sarah moved closer, intrigued.

"What I do know is that the Britfields were one of England's oldest families, going all the way back to Norman times."

"Around the eleven hundreds, right?" asked Tom.

"Yes, very good," he replied, standing up as though he was getting ready to give a lecture. "Through different marriages and relationships, it was said that the Britfields had a strong claim to the English throne, even stronger than other dynasties."

"Dynasties?" inquired Sarah.

"In English terms, a dynasty means a prominent family with a royal connection to the king or queen. Sometimes it's through heredity and other times by marriage. If a claim is strong enough and a family can secure a title or become ruler, that family will hold and maintain power as long as possible."

"Got it," she confirmed.

"The Britfields?" Tom persisted.

"They spent centuries trying to acquire what was rightfully theirs," continued the professor, sipping his brandy and savoring every drop. "But when the Stuarts took power in 1603, the Britfields became unpopular at court."

"Why?" wondered Tom aloud, hanging on every detail.

"It was said that the throne belonged to the Britfields and that they had entitlement over James I, who came from Scotland. A scandal broke out, followed by political deception and fraudulent accusations. Many of the Britfields were arrested on false charges and imprisoned. Some were even killed. Overwhelmed, the Britfields moved to different parts of England while others fled to the Continent."

"You mean Europe?"

"Correct."

"Didn't they fight back?" he asked aggressively, his fists tightening.

"The Britfields were mostly taken by surprise. There were a few skirmishes and battles, but nothing came of it. However, they remained patient, slowly gathering followers and forming a powerful alliance. But as they prepared to take the English crown, the Civil War broke out in 1641. Oliver Cromwell, a successful military leader, took power, established a Commonwealth, abolished royal sovereignty and had King Charles I executed. The country was thrown into chaos."

"Wow," exclaimed Tom and Sarah, finding themselves immersed in English history.

Philip was now on the edge of his chair, watching Tom vigilantly.

"After that," Hainsworth added, "the idea of royal government was unpopular, and the public was divided. Whatever momentum or chance the Britfields had was temporarily lost."

"But what about 1837?" interrupted Sarah. "Why is that date so important?"

"That's the year Victoria became Queen of Great Britain."

"I'm not following," interjected Tom, overwhelmed by information. "What does that have to do with the Britfields?"

"When King George IV, who was part of the Hanover dynasty, died in 1830, Princess Victoria, the only legitimate child, was too young to reign. She was made heiress presumptive after his death, but the law at the time made no special provision for a child monarch. It was also known that the Hanover royal line was mostly German, not English. This was the precise moment the Britfields were waiting for."

"What did they do?"

"The Britfields gathered together from all parts of Europe and once again made claim to the throne, arguing that their family right preceded the current dynasty and any others. They brought in some of the most influential scholars and lawyers of the day, offering countless documents and historical proof."

The professor took a long sip of brandy. Philip became exceedingly tense as he continued to listen. He finished his drink and poured another one, his eyes dancing around wildly.

"What happened?" asked Sarah, engrossed in the story.

"Lord Torrington, one of the Queen's guardians and part of the Hanover dynasty, gathered a group of powerful royals and fought their claims. He was ruthless and deceptive, immediately imprisoning all the scholars and lawyers. Torrington hired mercenaries to hunt down every Britfield and had them murdered. He then burned any legitimate documents or credentials he found, erasing the memory of the Britfields forever."

"Torrington influenced history," Sarah interjected.

"He changed it," Hainsworth expressed bitterly, obviously upset.

"What finally became of the Britfields?"

"A few escaped the persecutions but soon lost their influence and power. Victoria's reign was so popular that nothing could be done. Her years were marked by the expansion of the British Empire. As the country prospered, no one cared about old royal claims. To protect themselves, the Britfields added a "*t*" to their last name, making it *Brittfield,* and vanished into hiding."

"And there's no information since then?" persisted Tom, dismayed.

"From that point on, scholars were discouraged to write about it or even discuss it. Many colleges were forced to remove the name from their curriculum and ignore the truth. If it wasn't recorded, it wasn't taught, and so goes much of history," concluded Hainsworth.

"You must know more, Professor?" asked Sarah.

"My specialties are physics and science, not royal dynasties," he replied with a solemn expression.

Tom slouched back in his chair, disheartened by the conclusion.

Noticing his discouragement, Hainsworth added, "But I do have a colleague at King's College London who specializes in this field. He's usually current with the latest news."

"Can we visit him?" inquired Tom, regaining hope.

"I don't see why not," he answered cheerfully. "He could be very helpful —"

"Why on earth would you bring up this historical *nonsense* tonight?" snapped Philip, his cheeks flushed and tone sharp. "This whole thing is a bunch of rubbish. It's only ancient rumors and ridiculous conspiracy theories."

"My friend Tom has been an orphan his entire life," replied the professor impetuously. "It's not until recently that he was informed his parents may still be alive and was given a slip of paper with the word Britfield on it."

"A piece of paper doesn't mean anything," Philip verbalized defensively. "And there's *nothing* known of the Britfields for the last hundred and fifty years. They vanished, as you said."

"Always the antagonist Philip. I like that about you — taking the opposite side of a debate." Hainsworth sat down, warming his hands in front of the fire. "The piece of paper may indicate nothing. However, it may signify something important. It's definitely worth investigating."

"You're wasting your time with this fantasy," scoffed Philip.

"All I'm doing tonight is providing Tom with some history on a forgotten family."

"Yes, of course," said Philip, drawing back into his chair. "I apologize."

"It's quite all right."

"Do you think there's anything to it, Professor?" asked Sarah as she watched Philip stare at the fire.

"That was a long time ago. I'm just speculating and having a bit of fun jousting with an old student." Hainsworth paused, then turned to Philip. "And you're wrong about any knowledge in the last hundred and fifty years. I simply don't have all the facts, but my colleague in London might."

Philip looked at his watch and stood up. "If you will excuse me, I need to check on something. Make yourselves comfortable. I'll have dessert sent in."

"Take your time, my friend," said the professor, relaxing back into the comfortable chair.

Philip hurried down a corridor to a small office. The room was dimly lit by a Tiffany lamp on a roll-top desk.

He unlocked a drawer and removed a metal box, opening it and fumbling through folders. Finding an old leather address book, he located a name, grabbed the phone and dialed.

"It's me. We may have a problem." He lowered his voice, clearly agitated and upset. "I know it's been a long time, but something important has come up tonight. I need to speak with you immediately. No, not on the phone. We'll have to meet here, in person, tonight. I know it's late. Just get over here as soon as possible."

He slammed the phone down and glanced at a painting of the Queen.

13
BATTLE OF WITS

Thirty minutes later, Tom and Sarah enjoyed a cup of hot chocolate, along with a tray of desserts including Bakewell tarts, Eccles cakes, treacle pudding and crème brûlée. The blazing fire let out a sharp crackle as Hainsworth added another log. The smell of smoky cedar filled the room.

"Don't you think Philip was acting strange, Professor?" Sarah queried.

"Being part of the royal staff carries many unusual requirements," explained Hainsworth calmly. "They live in a world most of us wouldn't understand."

"But his reaction to our conversation about the Britfields was a bit intense," she persisted, discerning something was wrong.

"Think nothing of it," the professor reassured her. "Philip's always been, well, odd."

Tom and Sarah finished their drinks and stared at the dessert tray, indecisive about which delicacy to try next. They nibbled on some cake, but they realized they couldn't eat another bite and reclined in their chairs. Tom let out a deep yawn and stretched his arms. Sarah slowly closed her eyes.

Philip entered the room looking distressed. "I'm sorry for the delay," he said restlessly. "I had to check on the staff."

"I completely understand. Perhaps Tom and Sarah should retire for the night?" said Hainsworth, pouring another glass of brandy and swirling it around in the crystal snifter.

"Good idea," they both murmured, slowly crawling from their chairs and retracing their previous route to the bedrooms.

Philip watched them leave. "I'll have a footman show you —"

"We'll find it — no worries," said Tom confidently.

* * * *

The entire castle was deathly quiet. As Tom and Sarah entered a corridor, a haunting sensation filled the rooms. Their breathing slowed.

"It's sort of spooky, isn't it?" asked Sarah in a subdued whisper.

"Yeah," Tom answered quietly, looking over his shoulder for anything suspicious.

"I couldn't imagine living in a place like this."

"Me neither. It's too big. How would you take care of it?"

"That's what the servants are for," she replied in an aristocratic manner.

"Oh, well, in that case."

The two continued through the antechamber and into the main hallway. Sarah was walking a few paces ahead of Tom when he leaped behind her and grabbed her sides.

"Gotcha!" he said loudly.

She screamed, the sound echoing throughout the room and piercing his ears. Shocked by the noise, he stumbled backwards, disoriented. It was if he'd lit a firecracker and stood too close.

Sarah promptly turned and gave him a scolding look. "Don't do that!" she hissed and shoved him back a few feet.

"I couldn't resist," he snickered, trying to contain his laughter.

Her anger manifested into a combination of frustration and annoyance. "You twit!"

"Sorry."

"Are you?"

"Of course," he replied feebly, a slight smirk still present.

"I doubt it."

"I said I'm —"

She swiftly raised her hand, waving him off. "Grow up, would you?"

He frowned, feeling rebuffed, then followed behind.

They climbed a long flight of stairs, examining ancestral portraits hanging on the walls: centuries of faces looked down somberly, not a smile among them. Their eyes seemed to follow Tom and Sarah's every move.

"Who are all these people?" he asked uncomfortably.

"Relatives, I guess."

"They sure have a big family."

"Yeah, it must be nice."

"I don't like that one," he mumbled, pointing to a grand duke in a purple robe. "He keeps staring at me."

"Then don't look back," she replied offhandedly.

"Fine . . ."

"What do you think about all that stuff the professor talked about?" she asked, searching Tom's face for a reaction.

"It's quite a story," he replied, somewhat impressed. "But I don't see what it has to do with me."

"Maybe you're somehow connected to it."

"I'm just an orphan, Sarah. I always have been. But if my parents are alive, I'd like to find them."

"We can talk to the professor's friend in London. Maybe he knows something."

"I hope so."

After reaching the top, they looked for their bedrooms.

Sarah yawned and rubbed her eyes. "I'm too tired to think any more," she whispered in a scratchy voice. "I'm off to bed, Master Tom."

"Have a good rest."

She entered her room and closed the door. Tom remained for a moment. He had an uneasy sense of being watched.

"Hello? Is that you, Professor?" he asked, noticing a strange figure lurking in the hallway. "Professor?"

A few seconds later, the person disappeared. Tom turned on the spot, rushed to his bedroom and firmly shut the door behind him.

* * * *

It was midnight. The moon broke through the clouds, shining brilliantly over the upper terrace of Windsor Castle. A smoldering fog drifted over the garden and along a pea gravel footpath. Philip stood quietly, speaking to Mr. Coldwell, a middle-aged heavyset man with intense eyes and disheveled black hair.

"Why have you called me here?" Coldwell demanded angrily.

"It's regarding the Britfield incident."

"After all these years, you have the audacity to bring that up now?"

"Keep your voice down," warned Philip, glancing around the courtyard.

Coldwell grumbled, trying to remain calm.

"Something happened tonight," Philip hinted. "It may be nothing, but I'm concerned."

"What is it?" he inquired apprehensively.

"You did take care of that *problem* we had hired you for, correct?" asked Philip with a hint of mistrust.

"That was ten years ago. Why are you asking me now?"

"Did you?"

"Y-yes, of course," replied Coldwell nervously.

Philip paced back and forth, scuffing along the pea gravel. "It's been a very interesting night," he revealed. "I've been sitting inside talking with an old professor of mine and two children."

"What does this have to do with me?" inquired Coldwell.

"The boy looks very familiar, his eyes and facial features — there's something about him," said Philip reflectively, trying to place the image. "He's an orphan, but for some reason he brought up the name *Britfield*. Why?"

Coldwell anxiously lit a cigarette and walked around.

"As I recall, you were paid very well to take care of that situation," stated Philip decisively. "You told us it had been dealt with."

"Yes, and I was promised it would never be brought up again."

"There has never been a reason to." Philip tried to control his temper. He searched the grounds again making sure no one else was listening. "After you kidnapped that child, you disposed of the body, right? Left no traces?"

A long pause followed.

"There was one detail left unfinished," mumbled Coldwell, turning his back.

"What are you telling me?" Philip probed, firmly seizing Coldwell by his shoulder and turned him around.

Coldwell's voice cracked, losing his composure. "I-I couldn't do it. I just couldn't."

"What?!" exclaimed Philip contemptuously, his eyes filling with rage.

"I . . . I grabbed the boy as we p-planned," he stuttered, sweat forming on his forehead.

"And?"

"But I couldn't kill him," he continued uneasily. "I kept the boy for a few days, and then I took him to an orphanage. I paid the woman a generous amount of money to take him in, never to ask any questions and never to contact the authorities."

Philip, stunned by the revelation, turned crimson.

"You careless fool," he vented resentfully. "Do you have any idea the severity of this situation?"

Coldwell looked away, trying to shield himself from Philip's disdain.

"After all these years," Philip scoffed, "and everything we've done, thinking that the *true* royal bloodline was dead."

"For all we know, the child died years ago in the orphanage or ended up in jail like most of them."

"We don't know anything!"

"The secret lies with us. We're the only ones who know the truth."

"Until now."

Philip grabbed Coldwell by his coat. "Your incompetence is unforgivable! When the Committee finds out, it's out of my hands!"

"W-what do you want me to do?" asked Coldwell, desperate to redeem himself and frightened for his own life.

"You need to send your men to that orphanage. Find that child and deal with it!"

"What about them?" Coldwell gestured to the Castle.

Philip looked up toward the bedrooms where Tom and Sarah slept. "I don't want to take any more chances. You'll have to take care of them tomorrow."

* * * *

As the morning sun beamed through the windows, Tom slowly stirred from the best night of rest he'd ever experienced, floating in the middle of a gigantic feather mattress and perfectly sinking in the middle — it was like sleeping on a cloud of cotton.

After the delectable dinner last night, Tom couldn't wait to see what the chef had prepared for breakfast.

He envisioned a grand banquet table with eggs, bacon, sausage, pancakes, waffles, fruit and pitchers of freshly squeezed orange juice.

With great effort, he climbed through the sea of bedding and over the edge, spotting a pair of slippers and a silk robe waiting for him. Unfamiliar with this traditional morning attire, he kicked them aside and dressed in his new clothing. He felt relaxed in his crisp shirt, nice slacks, and comfortable shoes, a wardrobe he thought he could become accustomed to. His only concern was that he'd have to return the items.

He washed his face and combed his tangled hair. Staring at the mirror, Tom remembered last night's conversation by the fire.

"*Thomas Britfield,*" he said out loud and laughed. "Right, that would be the day."

Eager for his delicious breakfast, Tom hurried to the door and tried the knob. It was locked from the outside. He twisted and jiggled it, but it wouldn't open.

"Hey, is anyone out there? The door is stuck," he called softly, giving it a few knocks. "Hello? Anyone there?"

Then he heard the whispers of two men on the opposite side. Tom lightly placed his ear to the door and listened.

"We're supposed to keep them here for another hour. Philip is making arrangements to move the children to a new location where they will be dealt with," said one of the men. "We must keep this to ourselves. Only the inner circle knows."

"What about the professor?" asked the other man.

"He'll be eliminated as well."

"But what if someone finds out?"

"We're the only ones who know they landed here last night. Let's keep it that way."

Tom leaped back from the door, fearful of being near it. The dreamlike experience became a nightmare.

His mind raced with thoughts: *What are these men talking about? Do they work for Gowerstone? Are we being returned to Weatherly? Why do they want the professor? And what do they mean eliminate? Wasn't Philip a friend? No, he's a bloody traitor.*

All Tom knew was that he had to get Sarah and the professor out of Windsor Castle. He examined the room to see if there was another exit. There wasn't, except for the windows.

He rushed over and tugged back the curtains. Looking outside, Tom saw the balloon glimmering in the sunlight. He noticed it had been repaired and readied for takeoff... but why? If they were going to be returned to Weatherly, why fix the balloon? *It doesn't matter*, he thought. He had to escape from this room.

Tom gently opened a window and climbed out onto the ledge, a six-inch stone overhang covered in morning dew.

Cautiously standing up, he edged along the narrow walkway, his leather shoes making it extremely slippery. Knowing Sarah was next door, he carefully moved toward her window. He clung to the building, terrified of bending his body even an inch.

"I hope she's still there," he mumbled to himself. "I hope she's safe."

Tom glanced down and noticed two guards crossing the lawn engaged in conversation. If either one looked up, he was finished.

As he took another step, his foot slipped on the wet surface and threw him off balance.

* * * *

Philip was sitting in his office, listening on the phone. Still dressed in the same clothing from the previous night, he appeared exhausted. Coldwell stood nearby fidgeting with his gun.

"Put that away!" thundered Philip. "I don't want the staff to see it."

Just as Coldwell stuffed the gun in his coat pocket, a servant entered the room. Philip covered the phone's mouthpiece.

"Sir, the balloon has been properly repaired and is ready for flight," said the servant, standing at attention.

"The balloon?" asked Philip, forgetting his previous request.

"You asked last night that everything should be fixed and ready for the morning," replied the servant.

"Yes...that's right," he acknowledged, more concerned about disposing of three bodies than an eighty-foot balloon. "I'll deal with it later."

Noticing his disturbed mood, the servant astutely straightened his tie and fixed his white gloves. "Is there anything else?"

"No. That's all for now."

The servant swiftly left.

Philip spoke into the phone, "Yes, sir, I'm as shocked as you are. I just found out last night." He glared at Coldwell, already planning his punishment. "Yes, I believe the boy has been alive all this time. Well I can't be sure, but the child fits the profile, has similar traits. A blood test would verify it." He took a deep breath, trying to relax. "Sir, all we can do now is resolve the problem, finish what we started. Yes, I understand. I'll take care of it."

After hanging up the phone, he gave Coldwell an icy glare. "They're making the arrangements. A few more minutes and we'll have a location to take them."

"I promise you, I won't fail this time," Coldwell vowed.

"I know you won't."

* * * *

Tom regained his balance by grabbing onto a decorative lion's head protruding from the stone wall. His hands turned white as his body leaned over the edge. He took a deep breath and pulled himself upright, hoping no one had noticed. The guards continued on their route.

After a few minutes, Tom delicately inched his way to Sarah's window. He peeked inside and saw her already dressed and pulling on the bedroom door. It was locked. Frustrated, she kept banging on it.

Tom gently tapped on the glass, relieved to see her.

Sarah looked over, puzzled. She hastened to the window and opened it.

"What're you doing out there?" she asked.

"We've got to leave Windsor," he whispered urgently.

"Why? What's going on?"

"They locked my door, too. I think they want to send us back to Weatherly and do something to the professor," he told her quietly.

"But I thought Philip was helping us."

"So did I."

"Are you sure?"

"He can't be trusted," he replied firmly.

Sarah let out a heavy sigh, a solemn expression on her face. "Why does this keep happening?"

"I don't know."

"I'm tired of running," she complained, the strain visible in her eyes.

"So am I, but we don't have a choice." Tom stared at her. "Are you still afraid of heights?"

"After the balloon — are you kidding me?"

"Good. Let's go."

Not knowing what to think, Sarah climbed onto the ledge and stood next to Tom.

"Where to?" she asked anxiously, the cold morning breeze chilling her legs.

"We should get the professor."

"And after that?"

"Get the heck out of here."

"Agreed," she said, still a bit shaken. "The professor's room is next door."

They cautiously slithered along the overhang, staring straight at the wall, their bodies perfectly erect. Tom kept his hand on Sarah's back, trying to steady her.

"It's slippery," she whispered, finding each step difficult. "And these shoes aren't helping."

"Just take your time."

They finally made it to the window. Hainsworth was gone.

* * * *

A distressed footman entered Philip's office.

"Sir, we just got word that the police are on their way," he announced. "And we're supposed to detain those two children."

"What? How did they find out?" demanded Philip, standing immediately.

"Maybe one of the royal guards. He must have informed Detective Gowerstone. Some of the men here are loyal to him."

"Gowerstone! What does he want with the children?"

The footman nervously cleared his voice. "Supposedly, the two escaped from an orphanage three days ago, and he's been tracking them all over the country."

"What a mess!" shouted Philip, shaking his fist at Coldwell. "If the police take Tom —"

"We've got to act quickly!" exclaimed Coldwell.

"Yes, I know," agreed Philip, calming himself and collecting his thoughts. "Let's bring them from their rooms. I'll stall the detective when he arrives."

"But sir, he already knows the children are here," cautioned the footman.

"Let me worry about that."

Philip walked over to a wall safe hidden behind a cabinet, entered a combination and pulled the latch. He removed three handcuffs and a hypodermic needle, placing them in his coat pocket.

"Let's go retrieve them."

"But why the girl?" Coldwell questioned, a little uneasy.

"She knows too much."

"And the professor?" he continued. "I thought he was a friend —"

"This is beyond friendship," Philip interrupted callously. "You should know that."

"I was just wondering."

"Stop asking stupid questions!"

The three men exited the office and hurried up a back staircase to the bedrooms. Two guards stood by Tom's door.

"Any problems?" asked Philip.

"No sir," answered a guard. "The kids banged on their doors a few times, but nothing else."

"Open it."

The guard removed a key and unlocked the door. No one was there.

"Check the bathroom," Philip asserted, infuriated.

One of the guards investigated.

"It's empty," he declared, searching the rest of the room.

"Where could he be?" asked Coldwell.

Philip then noticed the open window. "Quick! To the girl's room!"

They ran over and burst in. It was abandoned.

"She's gone, too," announced Coldwell, baffled. "How could they have known?"

"I'm not sure," replied Philip skeptically. "Let's grab the professor, and we'll find the kids. They can't be far."

Standing completely exposed on the window ledge, Tom and Sarah watched as the door to Hainsworth's bedroom swung open.

"He's also gone," exclaimed Philip, utterly confounded. He angrily grabbed one of the guards and shook him for an explanation. "How did they escape?"

"I don't know, sir. I locked all three doors last night, just as you ordered."

Suddenly Philip spotted Tom and Sarah peering through the glass.

He smiled and dashed to the window. "Stay there — don't move," he said enticingly. "I'm here to help you."

Startled, Sarah lost her balance and fell backwards. Tom grabbed her and they both plummeted to the ground.

* * * *

Four police cars zipped through the medieval city of Windsor, an affluent suburb nestled by the River Thames. The vibrant streets were filled with fancy shops, quaint restaurants, attractive brick cottages and modern glass buildings. Across the water was Eton, an esteemed prep school shrouded in history.

People leaped out of the way as the vehicles sped around the narrow one-way cobblestone streets. Gowerstone sat in one of the cars, impatient to get to the Castle. They flew down Clarence Boulevard and up Peascod Street, skidding on the wet pavement.

"Are the children still there, Detective?" asked one of the officers.

"All we know is that the balloon is there," he replied bluntly. "Our contacts never responded."

"That's odd."

"Yes, very strange. They may have been compromised."

After a few more reckless turns, the cars approached Windsor Castle's front gate. Towering in the distance was the balloon, firmly anchored to the lawn.

Gowerstone quickly flashed his badge to the security guard.

"Good to see you, sir," the guard remarked with reverence. "It's an honor to have you here."

"Thank you, but we're in a hurry."

"Yes, sir. No problem," he said, waving them through.

The cars continued up the road and parked at the main entrance. Policemen exited their vehicles and raced to the front door.

* * * *

Tom and Sarah fell two stories, landing firmly in a gigantic dogwood bush. Buried deep in the jagged branches, they shifted around, trying to break free.

"You all right?" asked Tom, hoping nothing was broken.

"I'm not sure," she moaned.

"Can you move?"

"I think so."

Tom wiggled free and tumbled to the ground, his hands and legs scratched and covered in twigs. "I'm loose."

"Get me out of here," she insisted, struggling helplessly.

He staggered up and tugged her from the branches, her dress ripping slightly.

"Get them!" yelled Philip, glaring from the window.

The guards followed Coldwell out of the bedroom and descended the back staircase.

"Stay there. It's alright," Philip called down softly. "I just need to speak with you. No one's going to get hurt."

"Sure, I believe you," said Tom under his breath, doubting every word.

Guards quickly rounded both corners, guns unholstered. Realizing they were surrounded, Tom led Sarah to a side door.

"Come on," he said despairingly. "We've got to go back inside."

She nodded tentatively.

Philip watched the two run off, then furiously stomped into the hallway.

"Uh, sir." A footman intercepted him. "Detective Gowerstone is at the front door. He wants to speak with you."

"I'll take care of him," he sighed deeply. "Now find those two children and bring them to my office," he huffed, clenching his fists. "Especially that boy!"

"Yes, sir."

* * * *

Tom and Sarah entered the Queen's Drawing Room, a treasure trove of priceless oil paintings displayed on the walls: Caravaggio, Gainsborough, Rembrandt, Reynolds, Rubens, van Dyck and Vermeer, to name a few.

They crept through an open archway and quietly moved toward the far side of the gallery.

Suddenly the back door crashed open and guards' voices echoed in the chamber.

"Come on, we need to keep moving," Sarah whispered anxiously.

Tom followed Sarah into the King's Dining Room and through the state apartments. Lost in an endless maze of adjoining rooms, they dashed from one to another until they arrived at the Grand Corridor, a long hallway lined with historical artifacts and suits of armor standing at attention. Limestone busts rested on pedestals, and long burgundy drapes hung from the windows.

The rumble of voices approached.

"They're still coming," warned Sarah.

"Where should we hide?"

"Anywhere."

"How about inside one of the suits of armor?"

"Like we have time to climb into one of the knights?"

"Behind it?"

"That'll work."

They rushed over and ducked out of sight. Hearts racing, they nervously waited, pressed against the cold steel of the armor.

Two guards stopped at the other end and searched the passageway.

"Nothing," one of them grumbled. "Let's try another area."

They turned and hurried off in another direction.

"We're completely surrounded," said Sarah, her voice filled with tension. "How are we going to get out of here?"

"Good question."

"Do you have an answer?"

"Not yet."

They continued through the corridor and exited down a flight of granite steps leading into the Albert Memorial Chapel. This sacred sanctuary had an eerie golden hue and a lingering damp smell. The air was frigid. Each wall was illuminated with stained-glass windows vividly depicting famous biblical scenes. The vaulted ceiling was a spider web of ribbed arches projecting out from the plaster. In the middle lay the marble casket of Prince Albert, Queen Victoria's beloved husband.

Aware they had just intruded on a holy shrine, the two stood quietly.

"What is this place?" murmured Sarah.

"It looks like some type of church," Tom answered, observing the colorful windows and ornate woodwork.

"And that?" she wondered aloud, uneasily pointing at the casket.

"Probably just a coffin."

"Wonderful," she mumbled sarcastically. "Now I feel better."

"I'm sure whoever's inside is dead."

"That doesn't help."

Tom leaped on a wooden bench and pulled himself up to a window. He shifted around, trying to peer through the glass.

"Do you see anybody?"

"Two men are coming!"

* * * *

Philip hastened down the stairs and to the front door. Gowerstone waited impatiently, encircled by an army of policemen.

"What can I do for you, Detective?" Philip asked calmly.

"As you well know, I'm here for the two children. Take me to them immediately," he insisted.

"What have they done?" inquired Philip, standing in front of the door and blocking access to the interior.

"None of your concern," replied Gowerstone intolerantly.

"I'm the head butler and superintendent here. I would like to know —"

"You don't need to know anything. Stop stalling."

"Sir, with all due respect, you're on royal property, which supersedes any local jurisdiction —"

"And you're merely a butler interfering with my investigation. Now get out of my way and show me where they are!" demanded Gowerstone as he pushed past Philip and into the foyer.

Philip watched the policemen advancing through the doorway.

"Yes, of course. They're upstairs," he gestured nonchalantly. "Follow me."

The detective motioned four officers to search the

downstairs, two to stay at the door and the rest to follow him.

"Spread out and report to me if you find them," he ordered.

As the group marched upstairs, Gowerstone watched Philip closely. Within seconds of analyzing his expression, he sensed something suspicious. In Gowerstone's brief observation, Philip was far more than an innocent butler humbly serving the Queen.

"How did the children end up at Windsor Castle?" asked Gowerstone, already shifting into interrogation mode. "What possible connection could they have with this place?"

"The whole thing has been quite upsetting," complained Philip, straightening his coat and fiddling with his buttons.

"Humor me with the specifics."

"Well . . . they actually crashed on our front lawn. Those poor kids. I was so worried," he said unpersuasively.

"Why wasn't it reported to the authorities?"

Philip hesitated for a second then answered.

"I knew the gentleman escorting them, Dr. Hainsworth. He was an old professor of mine from Oxford —"

"How convenient," interrupted Gowerstone, unconvinced. "And you let them stay the night?"

"Yes, they were treated as guests. I had no reason to think otherwise."

"I'm sure the Queen would disagree with you. This is her residence, not yours."

They walked to the bedrooms.

"This is where Tom is staying," Philip conveyed.

Expecting the room to be vacant, Gowerstone watched Philip slowly open the door.

"But . . . he's not in here," exclaimed Philip, acting surprised.

Gowerstone stared into Philip's eyes, searching for the truth. He motioned to the policemen. "Check the other rooms."

The officers swung open the doors and searched the rooms thoroughly.

"No one, sir," declared an officer, stepping into the hallway.

"Well, Philip, you have some explaining to do," said Gowerstone harshly. "But for now, let's find Tom and Sarah." He grabbed his radio. "They're gone. Search the entire castle and grounds."

* * * *

Tom and Sarah knelt silently behind a row of old wooden pews as the chapel door creaked open. Two royal guards entered, each carrying a Browning 9 mm handgun.

"I'll search in here," said one of the guards. "Go around the outside and see if you find them."

"Do we shoot on sight?"

"We're supposed to apprehend them but do whatever is necessary."

Tom signaled Sarah to lie on her stomach. They then slid under opposite pews, completely out of sight. Tom could see the guard's shoes approaching their location.

Covered in dust, Sarah grabbed her nose, trying to suppress a sneeze. Desperate to let it out, her eyes began to water. Tom noticed and shook his head, mouthing *no*.

The guard peered down each row then stood directly over their hiding spot, scuffing the ground as he turned.

Scrunching her face and cringing in agony, Sarah struggled to hold it in. Tom closed his eyes in subtle defeat, knowing it was only seconds before she sneezed.

The chapel door opened.

"There's no one out here!" the other guard yelled from the doorway.

"All right, it's all clear in here. We'll search Saint George's Chapel."

He walked to the front and closed the door behind him, making a loud clamor.

"ACHOO!" blasted Sarah, followed rapidly by two more.

The door abruptly swung open again. The guard stood at the doorway, suspiciously looking around.

Tom and Sarah remained frozen.

"What is it?" the other guard asked, peeking in.

"I heard something." He continued to search, carefully listening.

"There's nothing," complained the other guard. "Let's go."

After one last look, the guard slammed the door.

"That was close," whispered Tom, relieved.

Sarah nodded her head and wiped her nose.

Tom slid from under the pew and helped Sarah up. They both brushed off their clothes.

"Where do you think they're hiding the professor?" she asked.

"He could be anywhere," replied Tom glumly, overwhelmed by their predicament.

"You don't think he's involved in all this, do you?"

"No," Tom said. "He's the one who helped us escape from Oxford in the first place. And we could have landed anywhere."

"You're right," she admitted. "It's just this whole thing —"

"I know, but he's been a good friend to us. We've got to find him."

"I agree."

Confirming the coast was clear, Tom and Sarah sneaked out of the chapel. They crawled over an embankment and through the jungle of foliage covering the outside of the castle. Sarah's dress kept getting snagged on the branches.

"Of all the clothes to be wearing," she complained.

"At least the green matches the bushes."

"Very funny," she scoffed, tugging her dress free.

They slowly stumbled along the outer edge of the Round Tower, an ancient, seventy-foot high defensive structure. Sarah watched the grounds as Tom peered through each window, hoping to find the professor.

"See him yet?" she asked worriedly.

"No. What about you?"

"Several guards and a few policemen running back and forth."

"The police are here?" he said tensely, turning to look.

"Yeah."

"That means Detective Gowerstone is with them."

"It's possible."

Tom's spirits plummeted.

"He might not be here," she added, noticing his distress.

"No . . . he's here."

While Tom continued his search, he came upon the small library they had been in the previous night. He then noticed Hainsworth sound asleep slumped back in a leather chair, exactly where they had left him.

"I see the professor," Tom exclaimed. "He's in here."

"Is he all right?"

"I think so."

"What's he doing?"

"Sleeping."

"Sleeping?"

"It looks that way."

Sarah peeked in. "Maybe they knocked him out."

"I hope not."

They dashed around the building until they found a door leading to the room.

"Quickly grab the professor, and I'll watch for any guards," said Tom urgently.

"Okay. I'll be back in a second."

"Be careful."

She hurried inside and over to Hainsworth, gently nudging his shoulder.

"Professor," she whispered loudly. "Wake up."

"Hmm," he mumbled, rubbing his head. "What time is it?" He looked at his watch. "Dear goodness, nine o'clock.

I haven't slept that hard in years." He stretched his arms out, thoroughly satisfied from his rest.

"We have to get out of here," Sarah insisted, tugging his arm.

"I must have fallen asleep after Philip left last night. How silly of me."

"Professor!" she cried out. "We've got to get out of here!"

"Why?" he asked, startled. "What's wrong?"

"It's not safe here," she answered. "Philip can't be trusted!"

"What are you talking about?" he asked, alarmed, noticing her frightened expression.

"He tried to lock us in our rooms," she answered resentfully, lowering her voice to a serious tone. "He wants to do something to us."

"Why would Philip want to do that?"

"I . . . I don't know, but —"

"Where's the boy, Professor?" shouted Coldwell as he entered the room with a gun pointed at Hainsworth.

Sarah froze, shocked into silence.

Hainsworth's eyes filled with indignation. "Who are you?" he asked, slowly rising to his feet. "And why are you pointing a pistol at me?"

"Where is he?" demanded Coldwell.

"I have no idea what you're talking about," he replied crossly.

"The boy — Tom — I want him," continued Coldwell, inching closer.

"I don't appreciate your tone, and I surely wouldn't tell you if I knew. Now put that weapon away!"

Clutching Hainsworth's hand, Sarah slowly moved toward the back door.

"Don't even think about it," growled Coldwell, as he aimed at Sarah.

"Have you lost your head? Pointing a gun at a child!" declared Hainsworth, stepping in front of Sarah.

"I'll do as I wish," he stated arrogantly.

The professor glanced down and noticed his crystal snifter glass, half filled with brandy.

As Tom watched everything from outside, he tapped on the window to cause a distraction.

"There he is," said Coldwell, a sinister smile appearing.

The professor swiftly grabbed the glass and smashed it across Coldwell's face. Hainsworth then stepped forward and threw a punch, knocking Coldwell to the floor. He was out.

"Wow!" gasped Sarah, her eyes wide open.

Shocked, Professor Hainsworth stood over him. "That'll teach you," he announced in a threatening manner.

"Come on, Professor!" yelled Sarah, leading him away.

"Right . . ."

Tom met them at the door. "Nice move —"

"Does someone want to tell me what's going on?" insisted Hainsworth, rubbing his sore knuckles.

"I wish we knew," replied Tom.

* * * *

Gowerstone hurried downstairs, followed by Philip and the other officers.

"Where are they, Philip?" demanded the detective.

"Sir, I'm as surprised as you are —"

"I doubt that," he interrupted, turning at the bottom of the stairs. "Where were they last seen?"

Philip stood there with a blank expression. He hadn't served the Queen for over twenty-five years without mastering this theatrical ability. With all the temperamental guests and egotistical personalities visiting the Castle, he had quickly learned to play his part or face the consequences.

"I have no idea," he replied, overconfident.

"I want those children, now!" demanded Gowerstone and turned to his officers. "Continue searching all the rooms. They're here somewhere."

"Detective, really. This is unprecedented," stated Philip with an air of superiority.

"And so are your lies!"

"I do have my own staff and guards. Surely they could check the —"

"That's enough Philip. You're dismissed."

"The Queen will hear about this!" he roared, walking off in a huff and hoping to locate Tom and Sarah first.

"I'm sure she will," Gowerstone said coldly. "Follow him," he told another officer. "Let me know what you find."

"Yes, sir." The officer closely shadowed Philip out of the room.

Gowerstone knew that he was pushing his luck and jurisdiction by being at Windsor Castle. If the Queen were under attack or in some form of danger, he had the authority to help or intervene, but she wasn't even here. Philip was right about the estate being under royal protection, which is why it had its own trained army of guards. However, this was no ordinary case. Gowerstone knew the stakes were too high, and Philip was deliberately lying. The extent of his involvement was unknown, but he was definitely hiding something.

The detective walked out the front door to survey the property. Several servants were busy polishing exterior light fixtures and sweeping the front steps. A gardener clipped away at the rows of boxwood hedges outlining the gardens. The balloon stood in an open field, glistening magnificently in the morning sunlight and yearning for flight.

Gowerstone grabbed his radio and called in: "I need some officers guarding the balloon."

Static blurted over the receiver, "Sir, we're spread too thin. Not enough men. Should I —"

"I'll watch it myself. Just send a few men and keep me posted."

* * * *

Tom, Sarah and Hainsworth waited by the castle, hiding behind an outcrop of oak trees.

"I don't see anyone," said Sarah quietly.

"What do you think, Professor?" asked Tom anxiously. "Should we try for the balloon?"

Hainsworth hesitated, still baffled by the sudden turn of events, then let out a weary groan. "That may be our only option."

"Good," agreed Tom. "Let's run for it."

All three started with a brisk jog that rapidly turned into an all-out canter. Tom took the lead, followed by Sarah, and then the professor, who hadn't had this much exercise in decades and was lagging behind.

Gowerstone observed the figures bursting from the trees and instantly pursued, cutting across the field to intersect them. He hollered into his radio, ordering everyone to merge on the area.

Tom could see the balloon, now only fifty yards away and getting closer. Everything seemed too easy when suddenly a bullet whizzed by his head and lodged in a nearby tree.

"Someone's shooting at us!" Sarah declared, astonished.

Another bullet flew by, nicking Tom's shirt and piercing his arm. Blood trickled out.

"I'm hit!" he cried, a numbing sensation overtaking his shoulder. He grabbed the wound and kept running, focused on reaching the basket.

Neatly hidden behind a shrub, Coldwell positioned his gun again, aiming for Tom.

"Don't be foolish, you idiot," snarled Philip, walking up behind and jerking Coldwell's arm back. "We'll have *every* police officer in England onto us!"

"But they're getting away," he whined.

"Our guards will take care of them," said Philip confidently. "We just need to get them before the police."

Two royal security vehicles raced toward the balloon, tearing up the grass.

Sarah shook her head, discouraged. "We're not going to make it!"

"Yes we are!" Tom gave her a stern yet comforting look.

He paused for a second as she caught up, then seized her hand and pulled her forward. The area around his shirt was stained red.

"How bad is it?" she asked, fearful.

"It hurts, but I'll be okay."

Hainsworth desperately tried to keep up. He would slow down for a second, catch his breath, run some more, then pause again.

Tom and Sarah jumped into the balloon basket.

"We'll untie the ropes from in here and leave them on the ground!" he yelled, hastily undoing one of the knots.

"Come on, Professor!" screamed Sarah. "Run!"

Hainsworth was now bent over, wheezing. "You kids go on . . ." he said faintly, waving them forward. "Get out of here."

"Don't be ridiculous," she hollered back. "You're coming with us!"

"Sarah, take care of the ropes," said Tom, jumping out of the basket. "I'll get the professor."

The trucks stopped close to the balloon, and the guards dispersed. Each man knew it was his sworn duty to capture the children and protect the crown. Tom and Sarah were no longer guests; they were enemies of the state.

As the guards closed in, Gowerstone took the lead.

Tom helped Hainsworth the last twenty feet but slipped, causing them both to fall. Exhausted, neither could move.

"Get up!" said Sarah frantically.

"I-I can't," moaned Tom, his arm aching and body immobile.

Sarah leaped out and pulled Tom to his feet.

"Help me with the professor," she instructed.

With both of them pushing, they managed to get Hainsworth into the basket. He collapsed on the floor.

They hopped back inside and unhooked the last rope. The balloon soared upward into the midmorning sky.

Gowerstone ran underneath the ascending basket. "Tom . . . wait!"

Leaning over, their eyes met once again.

In unison, the guards raised their rifles.

"NO — ONE — FIRE!" shouted Gowerstone.

From the distance, Coldwell watched the balloon sail through a patch of clouds and disappear from sight.

"Now what do we do?" he grumbled.

"Don't worry," said Philip evenly. "At least the police didn't get them."

"But —"

"They'll be headed to London," he assured him. "I'll alert our associates there. That balloon will be easy to spot."

"London's a huge city. They could go anywhere."

"Yes, but I know where they're likely headed," he added. "The professor talked about a friend at King's College London who specializes in Royal history. Find him, and you'll find the boy. Meanwhile, we'll use our contacts to track them down."

"When I capture them, what do you want me to do?"

"No more mistakes," said Philip sternly. "Get rid of them. All of them!"

14
A TWIST OF FATE

Windsor Castle quickly shrank as the balloon climbed, becoming engulfed in a sea of clouds.

Tom stood on the bench working the funnel, while Sarah controlled the exhaust rope. Hainsworth tried to help but was too fatigued.

Once the balloon was under control, Tom jumped down, holding his sore arm.

"Let me look at that," said Sarah worriedly, removing the pierced fabric to examine the wound.

"I can't believe someone shot me," he said bitterly.

"Neither can I," she added, then firmly held his arm.

"Be careful," he griped, pulling away.

"Of course. Now stop moving."

He frowned.

"It doesn't look too bad," she acknowledged, "just a scratch. I think you'll be okay."

"Easy for you to say," he grumbled.

Sarah released his arm and tore a piece of silk from her outfit.

"What are you doing?" he asked.

"You need a bandage."

"But your dress?"

"Do you think I want to keep anything from those dreadful people?"

"I guess not."

She fastened it securely around his abrasion and tied a knot.

"Is that better?"

"Yeah."

Tom noticed Sarah trembling. He came closer and held her hand.

"I'm scared, Tom, really scared," she confessed.

"So am I . . . but we'll get through this."

"Being chased is one thing, but being shot at is another," she stated, distraught. "I just want it to be over."

She let go and stepped back, looking completely deflated.

"What are your thoughts? What should we do?"

"Get to London, like we planned," he said optimistically. "It shouldn't be more than fifteen miles."

She nodded, revealing a half-felt smile.

Slouched over and rubbing his head, Hainsworth recovered.

"I'm at a loss for words," he admitted, disheartened. "I'm so sorry for what's happened."

"It's not your fault," said Sarah sympathetically. "How could you have known?"

"But I just don't understand," he said resentfully, holding the basket and pulling himself up. "Why would Philip want to harm either of you?" He then hobbled over to Tom and examined his arm.

"We're not sure," she answered with a blank expression.

"And that man with the gun?"

"I've never seen him before."

"It's sickening that this goes on at Windsor Castle."

"It's like you said," interjected Tom, a slight shudder in his voice. "It's another world in there."

"But this is outrageous."

Sarah moved over to comfort the professor. "Everything seemed fine until you were talking about Britfield," she remarked. "Then Philip started acting strange."

"Even angry, if you ask me," added Tom perceptively. "Remember the way he snapped at you, Professor?"

"I thought it was just playful banter, being the devil's advocate. It's a style we teach at Oxford — to take the opposite side of a discussion and form an argument. Philip was always good at that."

"I saw it in his eyes," declared Tom, frightened. "He was serious."

"But everything we talked about was just speculation, ancient history," recalled Hainsworth.

"I think it wasn't ancient history for Philip," Sarah surmised. "He took the subject very seriously."

"Working so closely with the Queen, he would," revealed Hainsworth, now meditating on the subject as his mind searched for answers. "His life has been devoted to protecting the crown."

"But to what extent? Locking us in rooms . . . Tom hearing about us being removed . . . and someone firing at us!" she exclaimed heatedly.

"They mean business, that's for sure," confessed Hainsworth.

There was a moment of stillness while the three

exchanged uncomfortable looks, trying to understand the depth of their dilemma.

"Do you think Philip's working with Detective Gowerstone?" Tom wondered aloud. "I mean, he knew exactly where we were."

"But you said Philip wanted to move us somewhere else," interjected Sarah. "Why would he do that if he knew Gowerstone was coming?"

Tom shrugged, unable to reply.

"Professor, could Tom actually be connected to this?" she wondered aloud. "I mean why all this fuss to send us back to Weatherly?"

"It does seem like a great deal of effort for two orphans." Hainsworth sat down, seriously contemplating the question. "Maybe there's a connection, or at least they think there is," he said theoretically, staring at Tom. "You have no memory of your parents?"

"Not really."

"And no one's ever mentioned anything? References, names, relatives?"

"No," answered Tom despondently. "In fact, they always seemed a bit secretive."

"In what way?" inquired Hainsworth, intrigued.

"Whenever I asked anyone about my family, they always changed the subject, told me to forget it or that it didn't matter," he replied. "If I pursued it, they just got angry and punished me. Finally, I just stopped asking."

"Tell him what you told me," Sarah encouraged him. "About those images you remember."

"There's not much to say, just a few flashes that go through my mind every now and then. It was so long ago I don't even know if they're real."

Captivated, the professor leaned forward. "What images?"

"All I remember is seeing this huge backyard . . . a large house . . . then something covering me . . . feeling scared . . . and suddenly being around strangers," he recalled timidly. "Sometimes when I'm dreaming, I can see it clearly, but when I wake up, it's gone."

"Nothing more?"

"No."

"That's not much to go on. It could mean anything," speculated Hainsworth. "However, it could explain everything."

"Like what?" asked Sarah, her enthusiasm growing.

"The subject is beyond me. I'm not an expert in this field."

"What about your friend in London?"

"Yes, Dr. Beagleswick — a brilliant scholar," he replied with exuberance. "We could pay him a visit and . . ."

Hainsworth's mouth dropped open as he looked out on the horizon.

"What is it?" asked Sarah, noticing his panic.

"I forgot about Heathrow Airport!"

Sarah turned. An enormous 747 four-engine jet was headed right for them.

* * * *

Gowerstone stormed back to Windsor Castle. A few policemen and royal guards followed behind.

In his entire career, Gowerstone had always stayed one step ahead of his opponent. What started as a deduction of facts neatly funneled into a conclusion. It amounted to a hypothesis, analytical reasoning and the ultimate capture of his adversary. Yet this case was far more complex than he had imagined. Gowerstone knew he couldn't trust anyone.

"Find Philip," he told an officer.

"Right away, sir."

Gowerstone went to his car and pulled out a laptop computer. He flipped open the screen which displayed a layout of Great Britain and a small flashing light. Clicking a button, he enlarged the location, showing an object slowly moving toward London. He studied it and then put the computer back in the vehicle.

A minute later, an officer escorted Philip out the front door. As Gowerstone looked up, he noticed Coldwell in the distance entering a pristine four-door sedan and driving away.

"What's this all about?" complained Philip, insulted by his treatment. "Why was I called?"

"Who's that man who just left?" asked Gowerstone.

Philip looked at the car disappearing down the road. "Just a servant. He's running an errand for me."

"In a Mercedes?"

"What other type of car should I send him in?" he answered smugly.

Gowerstone nodded to his men to follow the Mercedes. Two officers ran to their vehicle and took off.

"I heard a gunshot," said the detective angrily. "Who fired?"

"Why are you asking me?" replied Philip innocently.

"You're in charge of these grounds and responsible for everyone's actions. I explicitly said that no one was to harm the children."

"I have no idea who fired, Detective."

Gowerstone moved face to face with Philip, searching his eyes. "You're lying!"

Philip remained silent, unamused by the detective's assumptions.

"What's your involvement with all of this?" asked Gowerstone, his frustration mounting.

"Involvement, Detective?" questioned Philip with a blameless expression.

Gowerstone smiled impersonally, agitated by Philip's evasiveness. "If you continue along this ambiguous path of deceit, I will arrest you for interfering with my investigation," he stated firmly. "Now tell me how Tom and Sarah escaped."

"Perhaps you should stop wasting time questioning me and remove your men from this property," he replied condescendingly. "The children are gone now. You have no reason to be here."

Although Gowerstone was an influential detective, he was still only a servant of the government. Philip's royal connections superseded the government and were far more powerful. In Philip's mind, the detective was only at the surface of something far more complex than he could fathom, and he was already in way over his head. Philip had to keep Gowerstone off track.

"I've already called our royal counsel, Detective. Your actions here today exceed your jurisdiction and authority," claimed Philip. "We'll be filing an official complaint against you and New Scotland Yard."

"Arrest him and put him in the back of my car," ordered Gowerstone. "I will deal with him later."

"You can't arrest me," Philip protested. "I'm . . ."

Before he finished, an officer cuffed Philip's hands, grabbed his shoulder, and stuffed him into the back of a police car. Once inside, Philip started yelling and demanding his release.

"Take him to New Scotland Yard," demanded the detective. "I'll be there in a while."

"Yes, sir," an officer replied. He climbed into the police car and drove off toward Westminster.

Although a few of the royal guards stood by hesitantly, their only obligation was to protect the Royals and Windsor Castle. Most of them respected Detective Gowerstone and felt no need to intervene; in fact, none of them really liked Philip anyway.

"Get all the men together," instructed Gowerstone. "I know where the children are headed."

* * * *

Immobilized by fear, Tom, Sarah and Hainsworth watched the balloon helplessly drift along the path of an oncoming plane. They now realized they were directly over one of the busiest airports in the world. Every altitude had an object flying in a different direction:

single propeller Cessnas, double-propeller cargo planes, passenger jets and double-decker Airbuses.

"W-what do we do?" stammered Sarah. "Tom? Professor?"

Reacting quickly, Tom leaped for the release rope, letting out the air and dropping the balloon straight down. It was the only action he could think of.

The immediate plunge was felt as each one grabbed a side of the basket. Regrettably, the 747 was gaining on them faster than the balloon was descending.

"It's going to hit us!" Sarah shrieked, staring at the plane.

"Hang on tight," warned Hainsworth, fearing the inevitable.

The jet arched upward and blasted over them, just missing the canvas. The powerful turbulence rocked the balloon and shook it senselessly. As they got caught in the airstream, a tidal wave of wind washed over them, blowing the balloon wildly out of control and across the sky.

All three were thrown back, toppling over each other.

Tom struggled to his feet only to see an A380, four-engine, double-decker Airbus approaching.

"T-there's another one coming," he sputtered.

The professor jumped into action. He helped Sarah up, then all three frantically worked together, pulling the ropes and moving the funnel. They rolled and tossed from side to side, desperately aiming for anywhere out of the flight pattern.

After being whipped through the air from one jet stream to another, they were able to descend 1500 feet and maneuver across the busy M25, a massive gridlocked highway encircling the outer towns of London.

The Airbus rocketed by, vibrating the balloon and soaring over the countryside.

"That was close," said Tom breathlessly, glancing at the others.

"Too close," gasped Sarah, her heart beating rapidly.

"Good work, you two," acknowledged Hainsworth admiringly. "That was quick thinking."

They rested for a moment, mouths parched, palms sweaty and nerves on edge.

Tom sat on the bench, rattled by the near-death experience. Sarah collapsed next to him, pulling her disheveled hair back and refastening it with her ribbon. She yearned for solid ground again.

"So in the future, no more airports," jested Tom, trying to lighten the mood.

"Yes, brilliant deduction, Thomas," said Sarah coldly.

He gave her hair a tug.

She pushed him back.

They crossed their arms and frowned at each other, holding their ground until the other shied away.

"Look, I can see the outline of London," said the professor, observing the approaching city.

In the hazy distance, a silhouette of towering skyscrapers and ancient structures magically appeared as the morning mist burned away.

Tom rushed to the side. "It's fantastic."

"I told you so," said Sarah. "Wait until we're closer."

Catching an east wind, the balloon blew across a variety of small villages until it was directly over

Richmond, a historical town situated by the Thames. Victorian mansions lined the riverfront, and colorful boats sailed back and forth. Centered in the neighborhood square were stately homes surrounded by narrow streets cluttered with art galleries, coffee houses and antique shops. A patch of lawn bustled with activity as locals played cricket.

"Any idea where we are?" inquired Sarah.

Tom searched his map, now wrinkled and torn.

"Richmond," answered Hainsworth promptly, a hint of melancholy in his voice. "I know it well."

"Really?" said Sarah, finding it hard to imagine the professor anywhere but Oxford.

"Yes, it's one of the nicest towns outside of London," he said reflectively.

"You sound like you miss it," she noticed, now interested.

"I suppose I do," he laughed. "I haven't been back for quite some time."

"Why's that?"

"It's a long story," he replied dismissively.

"I see," she continued, skillfully reading his reaction. "It's about a girl, right?"

Hainsworth paused, uneasy about the query.

"Well?" she motioned, raising her hands and demanding an answer.

"As I said, it was a long time ago."

"And?"

"I haven't spoken to her for years," he admitted regretfully. "Let's leave it at that."

"I knew it," she exclaimed triumphantly, her feminine instinct prevailing.

"Why not?" asked Tom, now curious.

"It's very complicated."

"It usually is," said Sarah understandingly.

Hainsworth hesitated, pondering his past. "She moved to France four years ago. Can you imagine that? France?"

"Isn't that our sworn rival?" interjected Tom.

"Figuratively speaking."

"Have you talked to her since?" persisted Sarah.

"No!"

"Why not?"

Hainsworth felt uncomfortable with the continuing inquiry.

"Were you going to get married?" asked Sarah delicately, a romantic tone in her voice.

"I think that's enough for now," replied Hainsworth, flustered.

Sarah threw Tom a smirk.

The professor quickly changed the subject, shifting into educational mode and pointing to historical sites. Tom and Sarah looked on with interest.

The balloon slowly glided over Richmond Park, its vast acres covered with green pastures and patches of trees. Small pathways filled with people cut across the landscape as hundreds of wild deer ran freely among the hills.

"So you think your friend in London can help us, Professor?" asked Sarah. "You know, about Britfield and any current information."

"I believe he can," answered Hainsworth, hopeful. "He's one of the most brilliant minds I've ever met."

As Tom reached inside the bench to grab the water jug, he noticed a small black object attached to the bottom of the basket. He curiously picked it up and handed it to Hainsworth.

"Professor, what is this?" he inquired.

Hainsworth scrutinized it closely. "It looks like a tracking device," he replied suspiciously. "I suppose that's how Detective Gowerstone has been following us."

"He must have put it in the balloon when we were at Oxford," said Tom, frustrated he hadn't found it sooner.

"And it explains how he knew we were at Windsor Castle," concluded Sarah.

"More than likely," agreed the professor, realizing just how clever Gowerstone was.

"What should we do with it?" Tom asked inquisitively.

Hainsworth observed the object again. "Get rid of it — quickly." He leaned over the side and dropped it into some passing trees.

Although Tom and Sarah smiled, knowing they had outsmarted the detective, Hainsworth didn't share their joy.

"What's wrong, Professor?" inquired Tom, noticing his concern.

"Why is this detective so intent on capturing you?"

* * * *

Coldwell hastily drove through the town of Windsor and onto the M4 headed for London. He knew once he arrived at King's College, he would find the professor of Royal Studies and set a trap. If Philip was right, Coldwell could eliminate Tom, Sarah and Hainsworth all at once.

After all these years, he couldn't help thinking that his past had come back to haunt him. *How could I have been so careless, so weak, so foolish not to finish the job I was hired for?* he thought. Regardless, he would never make that mistake again. Whether Tom was connected to the real royal bloodline or not, Coldwell would get rid of him.

Continuing along the highway, he noticed a police car strategically hidden a few vehicles back. Trying to lose it, Coldwell quickly accelerated. He couldn't afford to get pulled over and questioned, or worse, arrested.

Suddenly, the police car turned on its flashing lights and sped up.

Coldwell increased his speed to over 100 miles an hour, recklessly darting in and out of traffic. What started as a simple drive to London soon escalated into a dangerous chase.

Coldwell abruptly pulled off the M4 and into the town of Hammersmith, a small suburb of London. He raced through the congested streets, running stoplights and causing other vehicles to collide.

One of the officers called Gowerstone, conveying their location and asking for backup. It was obvious this was no servant on an errand. It also proved Philip was lying.

Desperate to lose the police, Coldwell veered down an alley and onto a one-way street going the opposite direction. Cars swerved to the sides, toppling onto the sidewalks and knocking over trashcans. Pedestrians frantically leaped for safety.

Coldwell then shot through a busy intersection. Cars skidded to a stop, smashing into one another. A delivery van flipped on its side and a truck rammed into a passing bus. Shattered glass and twisted metal covered the road.

Coldwell was frantic. He turned left, then right, then down another street. After a few more turns, he noticed the police car had vanished. He'd lost them.

Relieved, he took a deep breath and continued.

* * * *

The balloon rapidly approached London, its majestic outline growing with every passing second. Hainsworth sat down, mulling over everything that had transpired, then turned to Tom and Sarah.

"What are your plans once you get to London?" he wondered.

"We don't really know, but anything's better than Weatherly," replied Sarah straightforwardly.

"I figured I could find a job and learn something useful," Tom added. "I don't mind working. I'd just like to get paid for it."

"Yeah," she continued, "and not having to work all the time."

"And be able to go out and see things."

"Like a museum —"

"Or a movie —"

"An art gallery or theater —"

"Play in the park —"

"Have new clothes —"

"Eat what you want —"

"As much as you want —"

"Whenever you want —"

"And have some fun growing up," concluded Tom.

The professor laughed cheerfully. He had forgotten about the simple pleasures of life and what it was like to be young. For him, it was hard to fathom what Tom and Sarah had gone through: never having a family or enjoying holidays and birthdays; not getting presents or playing with friends; and never going to school to learn something new. They had missed all the things that made life worth living.

Peering out of the basket, Tom and Sarah were excited as they glimpsed London. They could see the grand townhouses of Kensington and Notting Hill; Holland Park buzzing with activity; Piccadilly Circus crowded with tourists; the splendor of Buckingham Palace and Westminster Abbey; the Thames flowing by the House of Parliament; Big Ben soaring into the sky; Tower Bridge crossing the river; black cabs and red double-decker buses dashing everywhere.

Tom had a wide grin on his face, his eyes bouncing back and forth from one thing to another. After all those years of dreaming and planning, he was finally here. His spirits soared, and his heart raced with anticipation.

"It's brilliant," he said, astounded.

"Was it worth the wait, Tom?" asked Hainsworth, grinning.

"Absolutely."

"And was I right?" Sarah inquired with a smirk.

"Yes, you were right, Sarah."

"Where do you think we should land, Professor?" wondered Sarah, the problem now apparent.

It was a question Hainsworth hadn't thought about. Landing a balloon in the middle of London was extremely dangerous, considering the populace and densely packed buildings.

"We'll have to find an open field," he answered reluctantly, leaning over the basket and searching the city.

The balloon flew above the tiled rooftops of Chelsea and onto Hyde Park, its beautiful grass fields and winding walkways scattered throughout six hundred acres. People were relaxing outside, cycling along the paths and playing a variety of sports. Others walked along the Serpentine, a three-mile lake used for boating and water activities.

People looked up and pointed, trying to figure out what it was.

A patrolling officer caught sight and hastily contacted headquarters.

Driving along, Coldwell saw the balloon and quickly parked. He rushed towards the site, pushing his way through a growing crowd.

Making inquiries all over London, Speckle watched from a distance as the enormous object approached. He was well-informed about the stolen balloon from Yorkshire, and now he knew where it was. His inside contacts had paid off. Speckle scribbled something in his notebook and hurried towards the park entrance.

"We need to find an open spot," said Sarah anxiously.

"We can't land on the grass. It's too crowded!" warned Tom, now panicked.

Not knowing what else to do, Tom aimed for the lake. He gave the release rope a solid tug and the balloon swiftly descended.

"Tom!" Sarah shouted fearfully, glaring at him white-faced and petrified. "I can't swim!"

It was too late. The balloon splashed into the Serpentine Lake, tipping over the basket and dumping everyone out.

Submerged, Tom quickly swam to the surface looking for Sarah. Hainsworth floundered around, trying to help.

"Where is she?" gasped Tom, turning his head left, right, then back again. "I don't see her!"

"Keep looking!" yelled the professor. "She's here somewhere."

Tom dove down and swam under the balloon, searching through the murky water and moving his hands from side to side hoping to grab something. The professor did the same as they both scoured the area.

Tom popped back to the surface, a scared look on his face.

"I can't find her!"

* * * *

Gowerstone and his men rushed toward the town of Richmond, their police cars racing down the crowded streets.

"Make sure all the exits are thoroughly covered," ordered the detective into his radio. "Give each officer a description of the children and the professor. Make sure to apprehend them gently."

After navigating the jam-packed roads, they entered Richmond Park.

Studying the laptop screen, an officer in the backseat gave directions: "Turn right . . . keep going straight . . . go left up this street . . ."

The lead vehicle veered off the main boulevard and onto a grassy field, bouncing along the uneven ground. A parade of police cars followed in a cloud of dust, scattering the deer and disrupting the otherwise quiet countryside.

As they approached a clump of trees, it didn't take long to realize there was no balloon.

"Something must be wrong with the device," exclaimed the officer, fidgeting with the laptop.

"No, there's nothing wrong with the device," Gowerstone stated bluntly. "It's just no longer in the balloon."

The cars screeched to a stop.

Doors rapidly opened and closed.

The detective grabbed the laptop, which was making a distinct beeping noise, and walked around the trees. Coming across a small black object, he leaned over and seized it.

"Very clever," he sighed to himself. "Someone tossed it over the side."

"Sir, a balloon just crashed in Hyde Park!" an officer cried out as he got off the radio. "What would you like to do?"

"We'll head to London," he said with urgency. "I already have a few agents on their way."

"I'll get the men ready."

Gowerstone pulled out his cell phone and dialed. "Are you there yet? Good, I should be in London in thirty minutes. Keep me posted."

* * * *

Although only a few officers ran toward the balloon, other authorities had been contacted. It wouldn't be long before the park was crawling with an army of policemen, firemen, paramedics and news reporters.

Terrified, Tom continued to search. He couldn't imagine losing Sarah. His imagination ran wild with fear as he dove down again, hoping to see her. He kicked his feet around, swimming blindly from one side to the other.

Hainsworth scouted the water's surface, looking for any sign of movement.

"Sarah!" he yelled, his voiced strained. "Sarah!"

Tourists eagerly gathered at the Serpentine's edge, mumbling among themselves and speculating about what was happening.

Diving in another section, Tom desperately tried to keep his eyes open in the cloudy water. Then suddenly ahead of him, he saw an emerald dress silently floating. He knew what it was and prayed it wasn't too late.

As he got closer, he could see Sarah submerged three feet below the surface helplessly moving her arms. He was relieved to find her — he knew every second counted.

Grabbing her waist, Tom swiftly pulled her to the surface, lifting her head above the water. She gasped for air.

Hainsworth swam over and helped guide them to the shore. A few bystanders waded into the lake and gently tugged Sarah out, her face pale and eyes shut.

Half conscious, she lay on the ground, coughing up water. Tom firmly held her and gently patted her back. She gagged, struggling to breathe and spit up more water.

The professor leaned down, clearing her long hair from her face. "That's it, keep breathing," he comforted her. "It's okay now; you'll be all right."

Taking a deep breath, she opened her eyes. She glared at Tom.

"I *told* you I couldn't swim," she scolded him.

Tom was taken aback by her sharp reaction. "Y-you scared the life out of me," he stuttered. "I . . . I thought you were gone."

"So . . . (*cough*) did . . . (*cough*) I," she mumbled.

Hainsworth carefully lifted her up and walked her to a bench.

She slouched over, still wheezing and lightheaded, and moved her hair to one side. Her normal breathing slowly returned.

"Do you feel okay?" asked Hainsworth, trying to calm her.

"I think so . . ."

"Is there anything I can do?"

"No, I'll . . . I'll be fine."

"I hate to rush you, but it looks like our old friends

are coming," said Tom apprehensively, pointing to the approaching police.

"I haven't gone through all of this to get caught now," she said between coughs, slowly rising to her feet.

"Are you sure you can move?" questioned the professor.

"Let's go," she replied bravely.

Hiding among the spectators, Coldwell tried to follow but stopped when he heard the police sirens. He knew the entire area was crawling with officers, so his only option was to find King's College. He turned and left.

Tom and Hainsworth helped Sarah along as they disappeared through the crowd and into the park. They scurried over a hill and toward a small groundskeeper's cottage with a maintenance van parked out front.

Tom tested the front door, but it was locked.

Hainsworth wandered around to the backdoor only to find it bolted.

Eager to get out of sight, Sarah tried a few windows until one nudged open.

"Over here," she whispered loudly.

All three haphazardly muscled through the gap, tumbled inside and closed it behind them. The room was cold and musty, with landscaping equipment and several chairs strewn about.

Sarah sat down, still coughing and shivering in her drenched clothing.

"We should get her to a hospital," suggested Tom, worried.

"Don't be crazy!" she snapped. "I'm fine."

"Professor?" he asked, wondering what they should do.

"Well, we need to get out of these wet clothes and somewhere safe."

"I suppose this is more than you bargained for, Professor." Sarah sighed, feeling guilty for everything he'd endured.

"Yeah, I mean, you don't have to stay with us anymore," Tom added precariously. "We would understand."

"Are you kidding?" Hainsworth laughed. "Aside from Sarah almost drowning, this is the best time I've had in years." He sat down, collecting his thoughts. "Anyway, I'm intrigued to find out what Philip is hiding and if Tom is somehow connected to the Britfields."

"But you got us to London like you promised."

"No buts. Let's see this thing through to the end."

A variety of sirens blared outside.

Tom moved to a dusty window and peered out. Hyde Park was animated with activity and swarming with police. Some were on horses searching the grounds, while others questioned the onlookers. People dramatically recounted what had happened, all pointing in different directions. Service workers floated in boats, struggling to remove the balloon from the lake. Several news vehicles pulled up with anxious reporters looking for a story. It was total mayhem.

Tom turned to Hainsworth. "How are we ever going to get out of —"

"Wha da ya think ya doin' in here?" a sharp cockney voice pierced the room. "Dis place is off limits!" complained the groundskeeper. An old, weathered man with straggly hair, stained baggy pants and Wellingtons up to his knees stood in the doorway. "I'm callin' da authorities!" he said resentfully, walking toward the phone.

"Sir, please . . ." interrupted Sarah, cold and trembling. "You can't do that."

"And why's dat?" grumbled the groundskeeper, clearly agitated by their illegal entrance.

Sarah swiftly looked at Tom for an answer.

"Because you must help us, sir," pleaded Tom, playing his innocent look for all it's worth.

The man laughed hoarsely, "I don't have ta da anything." He paused and then looked out the window. "Can't believe da chaos out dare? Some nuts crashed dare stinking balloon right into da lake. Now wha kind of idiot would . . ."

He turned, now noticing everyone's wet hair and clothing.

"Da ya have something ta da with dis mess?" asked the groundskeeper, distrustful.

They all nodded their heads with an uneasy *yes*.

The man scratched his salt-and-pepper colored beard and contemplated the situation. "Wha were ya doing in a balloon ta begin with?"

"It's a long story, sir," replied Tom resignedly.

"And I suppose ya don't hav da time ta tell it?"

"Umm, not really," he replied candidly.

The groundskeeper turned to Professor Hainsworth. "How'd ya get dem into dis mess?"

"I've just been along for the ride, you know, chaperoning," he answered understatedly.

"Hmm," grunted the groundskeeper, taking a long

breath as he squinted at Tom and Sarah through his beady eyes. "I could lose ma job."

"You might," replied Hainsworth honestly. "But these children need your help."

The minutes crept by as Tom exchanged worried looks with the others.

"Oh, wha da heck," grumbled the groundskeeper. "Dis city hasn't given me a raise in ten years, anyway." He walked to the door. "Ya can hide in da back of da van, but I can only drive ya ta da edge of da park."

"That would be great, sir," exclaimed Tom. Sarah and Hainsworth smiled, giving the man a nod.

"Wait here," he said, as he opened the door. "I'll back it up."

He walked outside and started the van, then drove it to the front door. "Hurry up! I dan't have all day!"

* * * *

Gowerstone drove up Exhibition Road and parked on the bridge overlooking the Serpentine Lake. He got out of the car and gazed down at the chaotic site: police cars, fire engines and medical vehicles were everywhere. People came from all over to view the spectacle and watch the balloon being retrieved from the water.

For the detective, the fact that Tom and Sarah had made it to London only complicated the matter. In such a busy metropolis with thousands of buildings and millions of people, the odds of locating them were slim. Gowerstone was anxious to get over to New Scotland Yard and question Philip, but for now, finding Tom and Sarah was paramount. He was soon met by one of his agents.

"Anything?" inquired Gowerstone.

"No, sir. No sight of them."

"Stay on it and report directly to me. We must find those two."

"Understood."

The agent made a phone call, got in his vehicle and drove away.

Gowerstone went back to his car and grabbed a pair of binoculars. He stood on the bridge and carefully surveyed the perimeter of the lake, stopping and focusing on each child—nothing. He continued to search, scouting up the paths, around the trees and over the grassy hills. With so many people moving, it was impossible to view everyone, but he was patient. He slowly moved in one direction, saw something, stopped, then moved on. After ten minutes of thoroughly examining the entire area, he saw a van parked on the North Side. He watched a man walk to the back door and let three people out.

As Hainsworth, Tom, and Sarah exited Hyde Park, Gowerstone grabbed his radio. "Get all available officers to Mayfair!"

* * * *

Tom, Sarah and the professor hurried through a tunnel under Park Lane and up Mount Street past Scott's restaurant, its seductive aroma reminding them of their hunger. Located on the corner was the Connaught

Hotel, its ever-present doorman standing by the iconic entrance. Dressed in his familiar tan topcoat, dark blue hat and white gloves, he was a stylish symbol of this quintessential British establishment. He looked over and gave a friendly wave as they hurried by.

"What part of London is this?" asked Sarah.

"Mayfair, one of the most civilized sections," answered Hainsworth, a glimmer of nostalgia in his eyes.

"You've been here before?"

"Many times."

"We should find a place to hide, don't you think?" said Tom impatiently, hearing sirens getting closer.

"First we need to find a clothing shop," he said rather calmly.

"Now?"

"The entire city will be looking for a girl in an emerald dress, and these wet clothes are a dead giveaway," replied Hainsworth frankly.

"Good point," acknowledged Tom, lowering his voice. "Umm, Professor, we don't have any money. I have ten pounds, but, well, we've learned that doesn't really get us very far."

"Don't worry, Tom. While we're in London, it's my treat," Hainsworth assured him. "Now let's make haste."

Sensing a familiar presence, Tom looked behind him.

"What's wrong?" inquired Sarah, noticing his behavior.

"I have a weird feeling someone is following us."

"Everyone's following us."

"No, I mean . . ." He glanced back again.

"What is it?"

"It's nothing ... forget it," he said dismissively, troubled by an uncomfortable sensation in his gut.

Two blocks back, hidden behind a building, Speckle watched intently. He stepped into the road to follow but was nearly hit by a speeding black cab and tumbled to the ground.

"Blasted," he cursed, then swiftly got to his feet. "Bloody cab!"

He brushed himself off and looked over. They had disappeared.

Angered, Speckle quickly continued his pursuit, hoping to catch them before anyone else did.

Tom, Sarah and Hainsworth crossed Berkeley Square, walked up Burton Road and over to Old Bond Street, an opulent cascade of luxurious shops and cafés. Taking its name from the developer Sir Thomas Bond, this boulevard is the Rodeo Drive of London. Every well-known clothier and brand-name store is represented: Asprey, Burberrys, Cartier, Harry Winston, Hermes, Mulberry, Ralph Lauren, Smythson, Sotheby's, Tiffany & Co., among many others.

Hainsworth spotted his favorite clothing store, England's oldest, and confidently walked in.

None of the salesmen moved, aghast at what they saw.

Finally, an attendant reluctantly walked over, examining Sarah's torn dress and the green bandage wrapped around Tom's arm.

"Can I . . . help you?" asked the snobbish salesman condescendingly.

"Yes, my friends and I need new clothes," Hainsworth answered assertively.

"Perhaps you're in the wrong store, sir," he continued

in an arrogant tone.

"Maybe you'd like a new job, clerk," countered Hainsworth, now perturbed by the man's flagrant disrespect.

"I beg your pardon?"

"Is Sir Reynolds here?"

The man's overconfidence melted away into mortal panic. "Y-you mean t-the owner?"

"Is there another Sir Reynolds?"

"No, I mean . . . yes, no, r-right away, sir. I'll, um . . . get him for you," stuttered the attendant, clumsily scrambling up the stairs.

Hainsworth gave Tom and Sarah a reassuring nod as they perused all the exquisite merchandise: cashmere scarves, woolen sweaters, silk ties, leather shoes, custom-made suits, tailored coats, hunting jackets, Bowler hats, silver cufflinks . . .

Moments later a dapperly dressed elderly man walked into the room. Sir Reynolds' sour face instantly blossomed into a charismatic grin when he saw Professor Hainsworth. Although he noticed his drenched appearance, he remained silent: an old-school creed of showing respect and never stating the obvious.

"My good fellow, Dr. Hainsworth," said Sir Reynolds spiritedly. "What a delightful surprise. It's been —"

"Years," interjected Hainsworth, his eyes brightening.

"Yes, too many. How is Oxford?"

"How I left it, cold and stuffy."

Sir Reynolds laughed as the two men shook hands and embraced.

"How's Anna?" inquired Sir Reynolds.

Hainsworth's face turned solemn. "I haven't spoken to her for a while."

"I see."

Tom curiously whispered to Sarah, "Anna?"

"Probably his old girlfriend," she replied with a nod.

"Oh, got it."

The awkward tension was broken by the clap of Sir Reynolds' hands. The attendants responded instantly.

"Well, let's get you suited up," announced Sir Reynolds merrily.

"Indeed," replied Hainsworth, "and we could use some disinfectant and a few bandages for my friend."

"As you wish."

Thirty minutes later, all three left the shop. Dressed in what would be considered classic yet conservative attire, they looked like a picture straight out of *Town & Country* magazine. Sporting a rugby sweater and blazer, Tom appeared more suited for an exclusive prep school than an ominous stroll through the back streets of London. Sarah was dressed in a cashmere cardigan and a Black Watch pleated skirt, her hair pulled back into a ponytail. And Hainsworth was wearing a crisp, grey pinstriped suit, as if ready for a heated debate in the House of Parliament.

They searched the area for policemen and cautiously proceeded down Bond Street.

Tom's stomach gave a kick, followed by an angry rumble.

"Sorry," he said, embarrassed.

"We should have a cup of tea and something to eat," proposed Hainsworth, noticing their weary faces.

"Perhaps get out of sight and plan our strategy."

"You sure love your tea, Professor," said Sarah observantly.

"That's an understatement," he replied dryly.

"What would you do without it?"

"Hmm," he laughed. "Probably leave the country in search of a substitute."

"You're a bit . . . addicted, aren't you?"

"I wouldn't call it an addiction, but merely a pleasurable comfort of life."

"That's one way to put it."

"Can we get some food or what?" Tom grumbled.

"Yes, of course," replied Hainsworth.

"What about that café over there?" he inquired, hoping to hastily satisfy his hunger.

"No, that won't do. There's only one place in Mayfair for tea: Brown's Hotel," replied the professor adamantly.

"That's fine with me," Tom agreed enthusiastically.

Appearing on the opposite side of the street, a group of officers were looking in stores and questioning nearby shoppers.

"Let's go, quickly," urged Hainsworth, leading the way to Albemarle Street.

They ducked inside the famous hotel and sat at the first available table.

Established by James Brown in 1837, the English Tea Room, with its cherry paneled walls and white coffered ceiling, was a favorite destination among London's sophisticated elite.

* * * *

Determined to thoroughly interrogate Philip, Gowerstone drove over to New Scotland Yard, 10 Broadway, Westminster. While his men systematically searched Mayfair, he hoped to find out what the butler was hiding.

After parking in front of the modern, steel and glass high-rise, Gowerstone stormed through the main entrance and down to the holding cell two floors underground. He had called ahead to make sure Philip was prepped: handcuffed and sitting in an isolated room with a table and two chairs.

As the detective entered, Philip maliciously glared at him.

"This is outrageous!" he complained, hysterical. "I demand to be —"

"Quiet," insisted Gowerstone, his patience running thin. He then moved closer to Philip. "Why don't we start at the beginning and you tell me what's going on."

"I don't know what you're talking —"

"Why you lied to me, who you're protecting, and where Tom and Sarah are," he demanded, staring deeply into Philip's deceitful eyes.

Philip awkwardly smiled, trying to resurrect his confidence. "You're way out of your league . . . and pay scale, Detective. You have no idea what you're getting yourself into."

"Then enlighten me."

"I don't have to tell you anything," he scoffed.

Gowerstone firmly grabbed Philip and raised him to his feet. "You're going to tell me *everything*!"

This rattled Philip, causing his phony facade and arrogant demeanor to quickly crumble.

"You can't treat me like this," he said defensively. "You're . . . you're insane!"

"Maybe," replied Gowerstone, slamming Philip back into his chair. "But I do know one thing. This can be the easiest hour or the worst day of your life. You decide." Gowerstone took off his jacket and loosened his tie.

"But —"

"I want to know where Tom and Sarah are, now!" he roared, approaching Philip with his arm raised as if to strike him. This was not the detective's normal style, but he was running out of time and he was tired of verbally fencing with this obstinate butler.

He grabbed Philip once again and threw him against the wall.

"I — don't — know!" yelled Philip, now scared for his life. "They, they mentioned something about . . . about seeing a professor . . . at King's College."

"WHAT'S HIS NAME?"

"I'm, I'm not sure . . ."

The door unexpectedly swung open. An officer walked in.

"D-detective Gowerstone, I'm s-sorry to interrupt, but Philip has just been . . . released," he stuttered timidly, head bowed.

"What?!" shouted Gowerstone. "I haven't even *started* with him!"

The Chief of Police followed behind and motioned the detective out of the room.

"What's going on?" asked Gowerstone, impatiently walking into the hallway.

"We have to let him go."

"On whose authority?"

"I'm not at liberty to say."

"Not even to me?"

"No," replied the chief uncomfortably. "It's completely out of my hands."

"Who has this kind of power?"

"Who do you think?" The chief gave him an odd but telling look.

"You're letting a dangerous and calculating criminal go," exclaimed Gowerstone, shocked by the audacity.

The chief remained silent, powerless to do anything.

Gowerstone shook his head in disgust as he watched Philip escorted from the room and down the hallway, soon to be set free.

* * * *

Finishing up a feast of finger sandwiches and pastries, Tom and Sarah leaned back in their cozy chairs. Nothing remained on the silver trays except a few crumbs. This short break from their turbulent day was thoroughly welcomed.

"More tea?" asked a waiter politely.

"Sure," they answered simultaneously.

The waiter gracefully poured tea from a steaming pot through a silver strainer into each china cup.

"What's the plan, Professor?" Sarah wondered aloud.

"First we need to find a place to stay." Hainsworth glanced at his watch. "It's now two o'clock. I'll call Dr. Beagleswick to see if we can meet him later. Perhaps he'll know what this whole thing's about."

"Why don't we stay here?" asked Tom, surveying the room and lobby.

"If the police start calling the hotels, it could cause a problem. We should also leave Mayfair." He continued thinking. "But there's one place in St. James that might be perfect, at least for now."

"Whatever you believe is best, but we should leave soon," said Tom anxiously, pointing to an officer walking by a window.

Without hesitation, they sprang to their feet. The professor hastily paid the bill, and all three left by the back entrance onto Dover Street.

Mayfair was now a beehive of police activity, teeming with officers and law enforcement personnel.

Although Tom, Sarah and Hainsworth had changed their clothes, they were still conspicuous: a boy, a girl, and a tall older man walking together.

Realizing the obvious, they carefully sneaked along side roads and quickly crossed Piccadilly Street. They passed the Ritz Hotel and hurried down St. James Street to one of the oldest areas of London. The main avenue was dominated by historic buildings, upscale restaurants and a variety of prominent shirt-makers.

"Professor, are we close yet?" Sarah asked despairingly, a slight limp in her step.

"Just around the corner," he replied, endeavoring to find his bearings.

"Thank goodness," murmured Tom. "My feet are killing me."

"Yours are?" stated Sarah adamantly. "Try walking in *these* shoes!"

"Not on your life."

"Then stop your complaining unless you want to trade."

They scurried past a collection of Georgian flats and down a secluded alleyway. Inconspicuously situated at the end of the cul-de-sac was Dukes Hotel, a quaint four-story brick building with oversized sash windows, white stone details and a distinctive wrought-iron entryway. A British flag proudly hung above the front door.

"Welcome to Dukes," announced the doorman. "Do you have any bags I may attend to?"

Comically glancing at each other, they answered in unison, "No."

"Well then, right this way."

Hainsworth walked to the reception counter where a young lady eagerly waited to help.

"I'll take two adjoining rooms, one with a king bed and the other with two twins," he requested with a sense of urgency.

"Yes, sir," she replied, happily taking his credit card.

"Is your manager, Brandon, here?"

"Why yes," she answered pleasantly, then walked to the back office.

A minute later, a distinguished man, late thirties and neatly dressed, approached.

"Professor," exclaimed Brandon, somewhat perplexed.

"Hello, Brandon," Hainsworth said in a scholarly fashion. "You look well."

"Thank you," he smiled, strolling around the counter and shaking the professor's hand. "I haven't seen you for quite some time. You look good, Professor. I hope they're not working you too hard at Oxford."

"That's one of the reasons I'm here." Hainsworth leaned closer and whispered, "We'll be staying for a few nights and don't want to be disturbed if anyone particular comes asking. Pretend we're not here."

"Yes, I quite understand."

"I'll explain later."

Brandon knew well that this was a common request of his discerning clients and demanding guests, who always appreciated their privacy. It was also the professor's only safeguard against the police.

"Let me get your room keys, Professor," Brandon said cordially. "Best in the house."

"Splendid," said Hainsworth then turned to Tom and Sarah. "Brandon was another student of mine. He's a good lad, honest and trustworthy."

"He sure knows a lot of people," Tom whispered to Sarah.

"Yeah but remember what happened with the *last* student he knew," she replied apprehensively, referring to Philip.

"Hopefully this one's not crazy."

They were shown to their bedrooms. Hainsworth had a suite, and Tom and Sarah shared a smaller one next door.

Their room was exquisitely furnished: luxurious Berber carpet; comfy leather chairs with woolen blankets draped over the side; artful prints of the English countryside; decorative royal blue cushions embroidered with crowns; and a large bay window with a built-in seat.

After a moment, the adjoining door opened and the professor sauntered in.

"This is perfect," exclaimed Tom, surveying his elegant surroundings.

"And more than we could have hoped for," added Sarah earnestly.

"I'm glad you approve," said Hainsworth, now appearing fatigued from his long day. "We should be safe here, at least for the moment."

He walked to the phone.

"Let me call my friend and see if he's available."

After speaking with an operator, the professor got through to King's College:

"Dr. Beagleswick, this is Dr. Hainsworth from Oxford. Yes, yes, it has been a while . . . It's good to hear your voice, too. Yes, probably ten years. Funny you should remember that." He started laughing about an inside joke. "Look, I'm in London for a few days and was hoping to come by and see you. It's regarding an important area of your expertise." There was a brief pause. "Six o'clock tonight, that would be excellent. All right, just give me one minute." He grabbed a nearby pencil and a scrap of paper. "Main campus, Surrey Street, Strand Building, room K-8 — perfect . . . I look forward to seeing you again." He hung up the phone.

Tom and Sarah looked over, encouraged by the conversation.

"Do you think he'll know about Britfield, and maybe even Tom?" asked Sarah.

"Hard to say, but if anyone knows, it will be Dr. Beagleswick," he replied assertively, moving toward the adjoining door. "We have some time before we leave. I think I'll wash up and rest for a bit."

"That sounds like a good idea," said Tom, plopping down on his plush bed.

Sarah collapsed next to him, taking the pillow from under his head and using it for herself.

"Hey," he exclaimed, "give me that."

"Get another one," she said playfully, then put both hands behind her head.

"What kind of girl takes a boy's only pillow?"

"One that's tired."

"Where are your manners?"

"I left them downstairs," she replied teasingly. "Anyway, a gentleman always relinquishes his pillow to a lady."

"Says who?"

"It's just an unquestionable law of life."

"Whatever . . ." Tom threw Sarah a cold look, grabbed another pillow, and turned his back.

Hainsworth watched with amusement, then disappeared into his bedroom.

While Tom and Sarah drifted off to sleep, two policemen marched into the hotel's lobby.

* * * *

After circling Hyde Park, Coldwell headed to King's College, desperate to find the professor of Royal Studies.

He stopped on a desolate road and quickly switched the car's license plates. After his reckless chase through Hammersmith, he couldn't take any chance that he might be identified.

Surveying his map, Coldwell located the main campus five miles away.

He drove along Constitution Hill, darted up The Mall and turned onto the Strand, a busy boulevard packed with cars and pedestrians.

Spotting the college, Coldwell parked nearby.

He then searched the grounds for the school directory, discovering that the only professor specializing in Royal Studies was Dr. Beagleswick. He jotted down the information.

Coldwell got back in his car and drove around the corner to Temple Place, parking close to Beagleswick's second story office at the South West Building. He could see a figure in the window, confirming the professor was in.

Coldwell pulled out his gun and screwed on a short black silencer to muffle any gunshots. He wouldn't approach Dr. Beagleswick yet. Coldwell would simply wait until the others arrived, then head inside to eliminate all of them.

* * * *

Back at the Dukes Hotel, two policemen were questioning the front attendant when Brandon immediately intercepted them.

"May I help you?" he asked calmly.

"Yes, we're looking for two children, Tom and Sarah, and an older man, Dr. Hainsworth," said one officer, handing Brandon a printed sketch perfectly depicting all three. "They crashed a balloon in Hyde Park a few hours ago and have been on the run ever since."

This last sentence startled Brandon: *"crashed a balloon in Hyde Park . . . on the run ever since."* In all the years he had studied under Dr. Hainsworth, he never imagined the professor had such a rebellious side; it was exhilarating to picture.

"Hmm," mumbled Brandon, curiously looking at the picture. "No, I don't think I can help you. It's been very quiet here today."

"Keep a lookout and let us know if you see anything." The officer handed him a card with a phone number. "Don't hesitate to contact us."

"Yes, Officer," replied Brandon, seemingly indifferent.

Once the policemen left, Brandon called Hainsworth to notify him of his unwanted visitors. They chatted for a minute as the professor tried to explain the situation, leaving out most of the details.

* * * *

Gowerstone was not only stunned that Philip had been released, but also that someone had challenged his authority. Nothing like that had ever happened — well, only once before. Someone had interfered with his investigation, but that was almost a decade ago. For now, finding Tom and Sarah was all that mattered. Just having the name of a school wasn't much of a lead, considering King's College had five separate campuses spread out over half of London. However, it was better than nothing. He had dispatched police cars to the different locations, knowing he would eventually have to investigate each one himself.

Although his men continued searching Mayfair, they failed to turn up any relevant information. The officers had checked every store, café, pub, park and hotel, yet couldn't find a single clue or reliable witness. He also contacted the Transport Authorities, which operated more than 20,000 CCTV surveillance cameras, but they hadn't identified anyone fitting the descriptions. Gowerstone even posted plainclothes officers at key locations, but London was just too big a city. Tom and Sarah could be anywhere.

Before leaving New Scotland Yard, Gowerstone gathered a team of officers to accompany him to the first college campus. His mind raced like a computer, mulling over all the information. *Who released Philip and why? What was Tom and Sarah's next move? Who's at King's College? What connection did that have to Professor Hainsworth? And why haven't I caught these two orphans?*

This last question troubled him the most. Even with all his experience and a nearly flawless record, those two children kept slipping through his fingers.

* * * *

An hour later, Tom, Sarah and Hainsworth appeared in the lobby ready to leave. Cinnamon cookies and hot apple cider sat on the counter. They paused to indulge in these holiday treats.

The doorman walked out and flagged down a passing black cab. Known as a Hackney carriage, with its high interior ceiling and beetle-shaped body, it was a distinctive trademark of Britain.

The cab pulled up.

"Where to, sir?" asked the doorman.

"King's College, the Strand Building," answered the professor, a slight apprehension in his voice.

The doorman repeated the address to the driver.

All three entered the cab and took off.

Although it was dangerous to leave the hotel or to be seen in London, they were determined to find out what Dr. Beagleswick knew.

Tom and Sarah shifted around the inside, eagerly peering through the windows. The dark landscape offered a carnival of illumination, giving each building a magical appearance.

The cab rushed down St. James Street and onto Pall Mall, passing St. James Palace, a Tudor style brick building with octangular turrets and mock battlements. Two Grenadier guards were posted by the entrance, confidently wearing their familiar bright red coats and tall black caps.

They continued by the Institute of Directors, a grand four-story limestone building, and entered Trafalgar

Square. The atmosphere was a spectacle of lights. Towering in the center was a 151-foot granite column atop which stood a statue of Admiral Horatio Nelson, one of the country's greatest heroes. Two enormous lions sat at the bottom, surrounded by sparkling fountains dancing in the air. Tom and Sarah were mesmerized by the circus of activity. This was London, and it was amazing.

The cab continued up the Strand, passing the Savoy Hotel and Somerset House, then whipped around the corner onto Surrey Street, parking next to King's College.

Tom and Sarah hopped out as Hainsworth paid the driver. The campus was quiet.

All three walked around until they located a school map. The professor surveyed the diagram and found Dr. Beagleswick's office.

* * * *

Gowerstone had covered the colleges of St. Thomas, Guy's, Waterloo and Denmark Hill. He explored each campus looking for anything suspicious. Professors were questioned, buildings searched and police posted at every imaginable location. However, there was no sign of Tom, Sarah or Dr. Hainsworth.

The only remaining campus was on the other side of the River Thames. The detective rounded up ten officers and headed toward the last college on his list.

* * * *

When Tom, Sarah and Hainsworth entered the Strand Building, it was empty. Each felt a sense of uneasiness and tension.

They mounted the stairs to the second floor and were suddenly engulfed in darkness. A lonely light flickered at room K-8. As they walked down a long corridor, the sound of their footsteps echoed off the walls.

Hainsworth approached the office and gave the door a gentle knock. It was silent for a moment, followed by the noise of shuffling papers and banging drawers.

The professor cautiously stepped back, throwing Tom and Sarah an uncertain look. They glanced behind them to make sure it was clear if they had to run.

Movement came closer to the door.

A figure appeared behind the frosted glass.

The handle twisted.

The door slowly squeaked opened.

A feeble little man appeared, scarcely five feet tall. He seemed too old to be a teacher, and as if the years had been neither kind nor gentle. The man had a long, crooked nose, narrow spectacles and a tiny patch of grey hair on each side of his balding head.

Looking at Tom, he grumbled, "Yes, yes, what is it?"

"Dr. Beagleswick?" he wondered, almost standing eye level.

"Correct. What do you want?"

Hainsworth appeared from behind the door, towering over the tiny professor. "My good friend and colleague," he said kindly.

The man's eyes glimmered with excitement. "Oh, Dr. Hainsworth. Brilliant, brilliant, come in, come in."

They entered the room, making their way through an overwhelming clutter of books, maps and file cabinets.

"Do all professors live like this?" Tom whispered to Sarah, referring to the mess.

"I guess so. Perhaps it's an occupational hazard."

After the proper introductions, Hainsworth and Dr. Beagleswick chatted away while Tom and Sarah investigated all the fascinating pictures and lineage charts covering the walls. The diagrams looked like tree roots that started at the top with a royal name and branched out at every new name, then split off again, and again and again — it was dizzying. There were different maps of England in the 1400s, 1500s, 1600s and so on. Hanging in another area was an illustration of English history that showed all the ruling dynasties. An old portrait of Queen Elizabeth I hung on one side of the room, and there was a picture of Queen Victoria on the other. Tom and Sarah concluded that they were certainly in the right place. After a few minutes, everyone found a chair and sat down.

Meanwhile, peering through binoculars, Coldwell watched their shadows cast distinct images on the window shade. He put his gun in his coat pocket and left the car.

15
LOST IN LONDON

Tom, Sarah, Hainsworth and Dr. Beagleswick sat in a circle on an assortment of mismatched chairs.

"What can I do for you, Professor?" asked Dr. Beagleswick in a direct, academic manner.

Hainsworth gave him a serious, penetrating stare. "We're interested in finding out any recent information regarding the Britfield Dynasty."

The words hung in the room like an unwelcome guest.

Alarmed, Dr. Beagleswick became uncomfortable. He gazed at Hainsworth, wondering if there had been a mistake with his question, but there obviously wasn't. After an uneasy minute, the silence was broken.

"Britfield . . . hmm . . . well . . . that's an odd request," mumbled Dr. Beagleswick, anxiously glancing around the office. "That's a name that can cause a lot of trouble. Not talked about in universities today."

"I know it's a delicate subject. However, it's not an area of my expertise or knowledge," continued Hainsworth.

"It's no one's expertise," warned Dr. Beagleswick. "And it's best left that way!"

"You must know *something*," Tom interrupted.

"What does this have to do with you?" snapped Dr. Beagleswick, feeling cornered and pressured.

Hainsworth leaned forward. "We think that Tom may somehow be connected to the family."

"Impossible! There's no one left," stated Dr. Beagleswick defensively, although still intrigued by the notion.

Silence fell over the room again. The professor's last comment had shocked Tom and Sarah. Dr. Beagleswick glanced at Tom, carefully scrutinizing his every detail.

"I understand it's a sensitive topic," said Hainsworth firmly, "but you're our only hope of finding the truth."

Dr. Beagleswick's face contorted as he mulled over what to do. His breathing became shallow and his eyes were distant, like he was in some kind of trance. He removed his glasses and cleaned them with a handkerchief, then carefully replaced them on his face.

"Well, there might be someone left," he said hesitantly, peering up from his spectacles.

"Anything would be helpful, sir," urged Sarah.

Dr. Beagleswick let out a grunt, then eased off his chair and walked over to a file cabinet. He just stood there, staring at it.

Hainsworth nodded encouragingly to Tom and Sarah.

Dr. Beagleswick pulled out a set of keys from the depths of his pocket and unlocked the bottom drawer. He tugged it open, rummaged through some files and grabbed a large discolored folder with a royal crest on its front.

"I've been collecting information for years," he said warily, then crept back to his chair and plopped down.

The anticipation in the room felt like Christmas, and the largest present was just about to be opened.

"I find it a *shame* that such things are not allowed in

academic circles," he murmured, the tension in his voice growing. "Not right, you know, to suppress the past. History is history and should be taught as such."

"I agree," interjected Tom, feeling he needed to say something.

"Britfield . . . Britfield," he said, flipping through the pages. "Now you know the name was changed in 1837."

"Yes!" everyone answered together.

This both surprised and impressed Dr. Beagleswick. Few living people knew this information. "Good. Now, where to begin?"

"Perhaps with Queen Victoria's reign," Hainsworth suggested. "I've already explained to Tom and Sarah about Lord Torrington, his brutality, and the banishing of the Britfields —"

"*Nasty* business that was," reproached Dr. Beagleswick, shaking his head with repugnance. "A low point in our long and illustrious history. Few know of it . . . not many documents left."

"What happened then?" asked Tom, leaning in closer.

Dr. Beagleswick straightened up, as though ready to give a lecture.

"Queen Victoria's reign was a long and powerful one, the longest in our history. Because of her popularity, nothing could be done to challenge her claim to the throne, so the Britfields waited patiently." He paused and raised a finger to Tom. "Not many of them left by then, mind you, but still, they waited."

"Where?" inquired Sarah.

His voice became deeper as he cleared his throat.

"Those who didn't leave Britain moved to southern England and hid in isolated manors along the coast."

"Why did they stay at all, knowing they could be killed?" questioned Tom.

"This was *their* country! They had every right to be here and they didn't like being told otherwise!" he stated with conviction. "Stubborn people those Britfields, but strong-minded and unwavering."

Sarah smirked at Tom to acknowledge the similar traits.

"Then what?" continued Tom, grasping his hands tensely.

"Queen Victoria died in 1901 and was succeeded by her son, Edward VII, bringing in the House of Saxe-Coburg-Gotha, another *German* affiliation, but that only lasted nine years. His son, George V, took over the monarchy and changed their last name to the House of Windsor —"

"Our current dynasty," interrupted Sarah.

"Exactly! Now, around this time, the Britfields hoped to once again reclaim the throne. They tried to unite support, but World War I broke out in 1914 . . . almost conveniently."

"Why does that matter?" asked Tom.

Dr. Beagleswick let out a sorrowful sigh. "Because the war involved everyone. It was long and brutal. So many innocent lives were lost. When it was finally over in 1918, it took Britain years to recover."

"Then what happened?"

"Two decades later was World War II, even longer and costlier. But the country rallied, especially behind their

King. People were proud of their British heritage. Although we finally won in 1945, the country was devastated. No one wanted any more fighting or controversy, especially over old claims about legal heirs."

"But that's not fair," protested Tom, as if he had a personal interest in it.

"Life is usually like that, my young friend," said Dr. Beagleswick sympathetically.

After a moment of reflection, he resumed. "Still, the current dynasty never felt safe or secure having usurped the Britfield's rightful claim to the throne, so they searched for any remaining Britfields. Their lands were confiscated, their houses ransacked and their priceless artwork stolen. Anyone found alive was dealt with severely."

"Severely?" Sarah wondered aloud.

"Murdered," answered Beagleswick harshly, his voice growing intense. "The last remaining family moved to a secret location in Kent, close to the channel and the European continent. Decades passed with no further trouble until one day the Britfields were *betrayed* by a close friend. Their house was found and their only child, a son, was taken. This ended any hope to the future of Britfield." Dr. Beagleswick leaned back in his chair, exhausted and distressed from recounting such a terrible story. "That happened almost a decade ago."

"How do you know all this?" inquired Tom.

He was silent for a moment, hesitating with the answer. "A trusted acquaintance," he replied cautiously.

"Did they ever find the child?" asked Sarah, glaring over at Tom.

"No," he mumbled sadly. "The Britfields stayed for a few years, hiding in different places and hoping their son would be recovered, but he was never found. Devastated and in fear for their own lives, they left England forever. But where . . . or even if they're still alive, no one really knows."

Tom slouched in his chair, crushed by the news.

Hainsworth moved forward. "This *acquaintance*, is it possible for us to speak to him —"

"No! It's too dangerous!" snapped Dr. Beagleswick, springing forward and waving his hands wildly.

"Professor," Hainsworth said sternly, "I appreciate your caution regarding this subject, but I also know your passion for the truth. If there's any link between Tom and the Britfields, it *must* be investigated."

"It's too risky. Much too risky."

Dr. Beagleswick edged out of his chair, walked over to the file cabinet, and put the file back inside, locking it securely.

"Please," pleaded Sarah.

Although he felt pressured, Dr. Beagleswick knew they were right. He looked over at Tom, who suddenly perked up and smiled.

"It will put you in more danger."

"We understand," acknowledged Hainsworth.

Dr. Beagleswick sighed heavily, distressed. "The Archbishop of Canterbury. He was their closest friend and confidant. If anyone knows where the last Britfields are, he does."

"Then we'll find him," stated Hainsworth as he got ready to leave.

"Wait! There's one more thing I must tell you. Someone else who's involved in all this. The one who betrayed the Britfields..."

A noise came from the hallway.

"Lock the door," exclaimed Dr. Beagleswick, frightened for his life.

Tom leaped up and rushed over, turning an old rusty key protruding from the lock.

Dr. Beagleswick gave Hainsworth a harsh glare as if to say, *We should never have talked about this!*

The door handle jiggled.

No one moved or spoke a word.

The handle shook again, followed by violent pounding.

"We need to get out of here," announced Tom, frantically pulling up the shade and opening the window.

"He's right," agreed Hainsworth.

Tom nodded to Sarah, who glanced down at the ten-foot drop.

"You want me to jump?" she asked pointedly.

"Just hang onto the side, stretch your arms down and let go," he stated as though it were a matter of ease.

She hesitated.

The door continued to rattle.

Tom motioned her closer. "We don't have time —"

"All right!" she replied loudly, mounting the window sill.

Tom helped her over the ledge and she lowered herself down.

"You'll be okay," he assured her.

Sarah let go, dropping the last four feet and rolling on the grass. Hainsworth went next, landing by her side.

"Come on, Professor!" Tom shouted to Dr. Beagleswick, who stood in shock. "Professor, we've got to . . ."

The door smashed open. Coldwell rushed in and knocked Dr. Beagleswick to the ground.

Tom jumped on the ledge but felt a hand forcefully grasp his blazer.

"You're not going anywhere," stated Coldwell, fuming with rage.

Dazed, Dr. Beagleswick slowly got up. He grabbed a heavy book and threw it at Coldwell, smacking his head and causing him to lose his grip. Tom fell from the window, landing firmly on the grass.

"You stupid little man!" roared Coldwell, striking Dr. Beagleswick again and knocking him unconscious.

Tom, Sarah and Hainsworth quickly took off down Temple Place Road. Watching the figures swiftly vanish, Coldwell pulled out his gun and aimed from the window.

A flash of light.

Muffled gunshot.

A steel blue haze of smoke.

A bullet whizzed by Hainsworth, causing a nearby car window to shatter.

"He's shooting at us!" exclaimed Tom.

"Keep your heads down and run for the embankment!" yelled Hainsworth, glancing back toward the campus.

Another bullet flew by.

Ducking their heads, they made their way to Victoria Embankment, a main road paralleling the River Thames. Approaching police cars were visible in the distance, lights flashing. Not knowing which was worse, Coldwell or getting arrested, they decided to avoid both.

Running a few more blocks, they hid in an alleyway to catch their breath.

Tom and Sarah stood still, scared and expressionless.

"T-that's the guy from Windsor," declared Tom, clearly shaken.

"Yes. And he means to finish us this time," said Hainsworth angrily.

"How did he know where we were?"

"Philip," answered the professor without hesitation.

"But why is he still chasing us?" asked Sarah, dismayed.

"And shooting at us!" continued Tom.

Hainsworth looked profoundly worried. "I have no idea. This whole thing is beyond me . . ." his voice trailed off as he became lost in thought.

Little by little things were becoming clearer to the professor: Philip's odd behavior at Windsor Castle, Tom's possible connection to Britfield and this crazy man's relentless pursuit. Was Tom actually the lost prince? Perhaps he was.

"Professor, what about Dr. Beagleswick?" wondered Sarah, concerned for the safety of their new ally.

"The police are already on their way —"

"Look!" she screamed, pointing at Coldwell running toward them.

Another shot was fired.

* * * *

Gowerstone was driving straight to the Strand Building when he saw three figures sprinting down the road, followed by a man.

He instantly got on the radio and alerted police units to merge on the area, then accelerated after them.

* * * *

A bullet flew by, ricocheting off a wall.

Tom, Sarah and the professor hastily scurried up Black Friars Lane, a dodgy maze of interconnecting alleys. They hit two dead-ends and quickly backtracked, finally crossing Fleet Street, a busy avenue through the City of London.

Lit by towering skyscrapers, the atmosphere was alive with activity: vehicles zipped back and forth; colorful lights flashed in storefronts; Christmas music blared from cafés; and people hustled about shopping for gifts.

Police cars soon raced from every direction.

"Where should we hide?" asked Tom frantically.

"What about in there?" suggested Sarah, indicating St. Paul's Cathedral, its 365-foot dome dominating the urban skyline.

"Good idea, but it might be closing," acknowledged Hainsworth, glancing at his watch. "Let's make haste."

As they sprinted toward the colossal structure, tourists filed out of the front entrance.

Coldwell spotted them and staggered behind. Slowed by exhaustion, he tried to keep up.

Avoiding the front, Tom checked one of the side doors. It opened. He motioned Sarah and Hainsworth in, while attendants cleared the remaining visitors.

Tilting their heads back, Tom and Sarah stood in awe. The dome soared overhead, shimmering in splendor. Biblical frescos exploded with vibrant colors: cobalt, crimson, indigo and gold.

"We can admire it later," Hainsworth expressed bluntly. "Let's find somewhere to hide."

Snapping out of his trance, Tom quickly surveyed their options.

"Through here," he said quietly.

They followed his lead up a staircase and into the *Whispering Gallery*, an enormous circular terrace overlooking the marble floor below. The dome was suspended above, magnifying every sound and projecting their voices throughout the church.

Glancing over the railing, Sarah noticed Coldwell hobble in, his clothes soaked in sweat. He looked around wildly.

Sarah whispered, "Professor, should we try to go down the other . . ."

Before she finished, each word loudly bounced off the walls. Coldwell looked up, just catching her surprised face pulling back.

"He saw me," she gasped.

"Got them!" he declared, running to the nearest staircase.

Halfway there an attendant yelled over. "Hey, buddy! We're closed! No one's allowed in here!"

Unfazed, Coldwell continued onward.

Not knowing what else to do, Tom, Sarah and Hainsworth ran to the stairs and climbed up into the mighty dome. Floor by floor they mounted the steps, each one getting steeper and narrower, the walls curving inward. The interior cavern became damp and dark. A cold breeze rushed through, chilling their bodies.

After tremendous effort, they emerged on top of The Golden Gallery, an outside platform offering a panoramic vista of the entire city: London was blazing with lights. The brisk night air whipped around, almost knocking them off balance.

Looking down to the street, they saw a parade of police cars parked in front, the familiar red and blue lights flashing.

"We're trapped," declared Sarah, overwhelmed with fright.

"It looks that way," replied Hainsworth candidly.

"There's got to be another exit," said Tom stubbornly. He then rushed around the circular deck and reappeared a few seconds later, defeated. "Nothing," he reported.

Footsteps could be heard climbing the staircase.

They waited quietly for what felt like their impending doom.

"Now what?" asked Sarah, gripping Tom's arm.

Hainsworth braced himself. "Confront him if we have to," he answered bravely, clenching his fists.

The footsteps began to slow: Coldwell was running out of breath. He had also heard the sirens outside and was aware the police had arrived. Concerned for his own safety, he turned and clumsily descended.

"He's leaving," exclaimed Sarah, feeling a mixed sensation of relief and uncertainty.

"He doesn't want to get caught," concluded Hainsworth.

"Neither do I," said Tom restlessly, moving for the exit. He was abruptly stopped by Hainsworth.

"Wait till he's gone," he said firmly, holding him back.

* * * *

Gowerstone parked next to St. Paul's Cathedral and got out. He was surveying the situation when an officer approached.

"A couple of policemen reported seeing two kids and an older man run inside," the officer stated.

"Anything else?"

"Some attendant claims that a man ran up the stairs to the dome."

"The professor?"

"He said he was heavyset, with dark hair."

"Who could be chasing them?" Gowerstone murmured to himself. He abruptly turned to the officer. "Seal off all the exits around the cathedral."

"We don't have enough men —"

"Then get more!" he said sharply.

The detective walked up to the West entrance. Standing by two massive wooden doors, he nodded to six officers who then followed him inside.

* * * *

After a few moments, Tom, Sarah and Hainsworth carefully descended the stairs, vigilantly watching for Coldwell. They could hear the police below shouting and running in different directions.

"How are we going to get out of here, Professor?" inquired Tom, discouraged by the seemingly hopeless situation.

"Through the Crypt," replied Hainsworth, undaunted.

"The Crypt?"

"Trust me."

They made it to the main level and ducked into a hidden alcove as officers walked by, then continued their descent into the belly of the church.

The Crypt, or burial chamber, was a catacomb of marble caskets, low arched ceilings and rows of slender alabaster columns.

All three cautiously entered.

The air was frosty and stale, the lighting faint and sporadic, the stone floor pitted and uneven. Policemen's footsteps shuffled overhead, their voices echoing.

Sarah clutched Tom's hand, her eyes widening.

"I-I've got a b-bad feeling about this," she stammered, her teeth chattering as a chill ran up her neck.

"It's not so bad . . . if you're dead," Tom said dryly.

"Thanks, you're a real help."

"Through here," said Hainsworth, confidently leading the way.

"W-what's that, Professor?" she stuttered, now standing in front of a large black sarcophagus six feet off the ground.

"Lord Nelson's tomb," he answered reverently in a soft whisper. "One of history's finest admirals."

"Is he . . . is he still in there?"

"I hope so," he replied offhandedly, then proceeded onward.

Moving her head back and forth, Sarah was now aware of being surrounded by *coffins* of famous artists, scientists and noblemen. The Duke of Wellington was on one side, and the poet William Blake was on the other. This revelation only added to her uneasiness.

"There are b-bodies in all these coffins?"

"Most of them," answered the professor evenly. "Some are buried elsewhere."

Sarah squeezed Tom's hand tighter.

"Ouch," he mumbled, releasing himself from her hold.

"Sorry . . . a bit nervous."

Quietly moving through the unsettling darkness, they reached a set of stairs leading up to an exit.

Hainsworth ascended the steps to a metal door.

"This heads outside, but . . ."

"But what?" asked Tom impatiently.

"It may have an alarm."

Hainsworth gently pushed the handle.

The door popped open — no sound, no alarm. He eased it forward, looking through the gap and viewing the deserted churchyard.

"It appears safe," he announced reassuringly.

Each of them stepped out of the crypt and onto the grass. A blast of fresh air filled their lungs.

"Let's head over to that structure," suggested Hainsworth, motioning to an apartment complex across the street. "We can —"

"Stop right there!" an officer yelled as he and his partner sprinted over.

Hainsworth turned to Tom. "Get Sarah out of here and keep her safe."

"But what about you —"

"Run, Tom! Run!"

With that, Hainsworth intercepted the officers, grappling with them for a brief second and making the greatest sacrifice he could, himself.

Stunned, Tom and Sarah bolted across the street, looking back as the professor was wrestled to the ground and handcuffed.

Tom stopped. "We've got to help him!"

"It's too late!" Sarah pulled him forward as they hurried toward the buildings.

Gowerstone rounded the corner just in time to see Tom and Sarah advance down Watling Road and onto Cannon Street. He continued after them, signaling other officers to follow.

The detective quickly gained.

He was close behind when Tom and Sarah ran right in front of a double-decker bus.

Gowerstone froze, inches from hitting it.

As the bus whisked by, they vanished into a crowd of people. Frustrated, Gowerstone motioned two police cars to pursue while four officers continued on foot.

* * * *

Barely escaping from the Cathedral, Coldwell hid in a nearby café. He watched the police activity from a safe distance, waiting to see if Tom, Sarah or Hainsworth would be caught.

Thirty minutes later, he saw the professor brought to

a police car and hauled away. This was a serious problem and only complicated matters, given that Hainsworth knew way too much. However, neither Tom nor Sarah was accounted for. Coldwell concluded that they must have escaped. He decided to head back to King's College and interrogate Dr. Beagleswick.

By the time Coldwell arrived at the campus, the Strand Building was swarming with policemen. Kneeling behind a bush, he observed an officer escorting Dr. Beagleswick outside to a waiting car, either for questioning, protection or both.

After a paramedic attended to the professor's injuries, he was whisked away to New Scotland Yard. Out of options, Coldwell carefully sneaked back to his vehicle and left the area.

* * * *

Skillfully evading the police, Tom and Sarah ran to a neighborhood park and hid in some overgrown shrubs. Nearby, the Tower Bridge hovered over the Thames, its two gigantic towers overshadowing the river. It was late, damp and cold. Three miles from St. James and their hotel, they had no idea what to do.

Tom and Sarah both felt responsible for Hainsworth's capture. What started as an escape from Weatherly and a journey to London had escalated into a crisis, and their newfound friend had been arrested.

"I can't believe he's gone," said Sarah despondently, a tear trickling down her cheek.

"He sacrificed everything just so we could get away," added Tom, overcome by guilt.

"What's going to happen to him?"

"Once Gowerstone gets his hands on him, who knows?"

"He'll tell him everything."

"Maybe," Tom speculated. "But the professor's pretty smart."

"That he is." Sarah wiped her eyes. "What should we do now?"

"We can head back to the hotel, at least for the night."

"But the police might be there."

"No one knows where we're staying except the professor."

"What if he . . ." She caught herself in mid-sentence. "No, he won't tell. I know we can trust him."

"I agree," said Tom confidently. "Anyway, it's a risk we'll have to take."

"Perhaps they'll let him go," she added optimistically. "It's not like he broke any laws. We're the ones the police want, not him."

"I hope you're right."

Staying close to the buildings and keeping out of sight, they tried to find the Dukes Hotel. At least the room was dry, and the beds were warm. From their experience, they had no reason to doubt the professor. He was a trustworthy ally.

Sarah turned in a circle. "What direction should we head?"

"Not a clue . . ."

* * * *

About two hours later, Tom and Sarah were still wandering around London, completely lost. What seemed like the right direction only brought them back full-circle. The problem was, none of the streets were straight or laid out in any kind of comprehensible manner. Instead of the traditional square grid of modern cities, London was a maze of mismatched roads and twisting boulevards.

After asking directions five times for the Dukes Hotel, they finally bought a map with Tom's ten-pound note, leaving him six pounds. They figured out their location and made their way back to Victoria Embankment, using the river as a guide. Across the Thames was The London Eye, a magnificent white Ferris wheel brightly illuminated and slowly turning. It was a welcome landmark they had seen before.

"I've never walked so much in my entire life," Sarah moaned, her face emotionless and her arms drooping by her side.

"Neither have I," agreed Tom despairingly.

"Are we close?"

Tom glanced at the map again. "Somewhat . . . I think. We'll have to cut through there."

He pointed toward the Houses of Parliament, an enormous 19th century Neo-Gothic building washed in fluorescent lights. Its haunting steeples soared into the midnight sky. Attached to one side was Big Ben, a 316-foot clock tower chiming 12:00 a.m.

"It's late," she said, rubbing her weary eyes.

"The hotel must be close." Tom spun around and searched the area. "If *Big Ben* is here . . . and the *Thames* is there . . . then we should head in *that* direction," he motioned towards St. James.

"I trust you," she sighed deeply, "since you have the map."

"Thanks," he mumbled halfheartedly, not sure if it was a compliment or a criticism.

They cut across Parliament Square and walked by Westminster Abbey, a French-Gothic cathedral with flying buttresses supporting the outer walls. An enormous rose window reflected the moonlight.

Tom paused and stared at the Abbey. "It's beautiful, don't you think?"

"It's kind of eerie, if you ask me. Let's find our hotel and go to sleep," she said impatiently, yanking his arm. "We'll sightsee another time."

"Fine . . ." he said, dejected.

After trudging through St. James Park, they safely made it to the hotel. Too exhausted to care, they marched in, got their key and went directly upstairs.

Tom tapped on the professor's door, hoping against hope that he was in. There was no answer.

"Maybe he'll be here tomorrow," suggested Sarah, her tone encouraging yet mixed with doubt.

"He better be."

* * * *

Early the next morning, Gowerstone drove back to 10 Downing Street. Although he needed to get over to

New Scotland Yard and thoroughly question Professor Hainsworth and Dr. Beagleswick, the Prime Minister demanded to speak with him.

After going through security, the detective walked into the office. The Prime Minster was fuming.

"Sit," he said tensely, pacing the room.

"Yes, sir."

"I heard about last night."

"We apprehended Dr. Hainsworth —"

"And the orphans escaped again."

"Yes," said Gowerstone regrettably. "But once I talk to —"

"This whole fiasco has got to stop!" yelled the Prime Minister. "It's gone too far!"

"But I just need a few more —"

"I'm shutting your operation down."

"What?"

"A balloon crashing in Hyde Park . . . news reporters everywhere . . . policemen frantically rushing around London . . . colleges ransacked . . . and our beloved St. Paul's Cathedral turned into a circus!"

"Prime Minister, I'm close to completing this case."

"Just as close as you were three days ago?"

The sarcastic remark was an insulting slap to Gowerstone.

"There have been complications," he said irritably, his eyes drifting toward the Queen's portrait. "This whole thing goes deeper than I imagined."

"Explain it to me."

"I can't . . . not yet," he replied cautiously, looking back at the Prime Minister. "But I had a key witness released yesterday."

"I know. I released him."

The detective stood from his chair. "*You* released him?"

"Of course I did," he snapped. "Arresting the *Queen's* superintendent!" The Prime Minister threw up his hands. "Are you out of your mind?"

"But he's involved."

"I was on the phone for an hour yesterday with the royal counsel. The Queen is furious!"

"He's hiding something."

"It doesn't matter, Detective. You crossed the line."

"I've done exactly what I had to."

"You mean you've done your best," the Prime Minister said condescendingly.

Gowerstone's face tightened. It was a spiteful comment, implying that he had failed.

"I want you off this case. I'll have someone else handle it." The Prime Minister's voice lowered, almost sympathetically. "In fact, I need to suspend you, just for now."

Gowerstone stared in disbelief: twenty-five years of devotion and dedication suddenly evaporated into thin air.

"Look," said the Prime Minister persuasively, putting his hand on Gowerstone's shoulder, "take a couple of weeks off and let this case go. When you come back, we'll see what we can do about getting you reinstated."

Speechless, Gowerstone shook off the Prime Minister's

hand and abruptly left his office. He exited the building, thinking about what had just happened. *Maybe the Prime Minister was correct. Maybe I have gone too far this time.*

No, something in his gut told him he was right, that his instinct about this case was correct. Ignoring the Prime Minister's order, Gowerstone decided he would risk everything to find Tom and Sarah.

Knowing that Professor Hainsworth might have the answers, Gowerstone headed back to New Scotland Yard.

* * * *

Sound asleep, Sarah and Tom were abruptly awakened by a tapping on the door. It soon escalated into a proper knock.

Tom defensively sprung to his feet as Sarah ran to the window, ready for a hasty escape. This had become second nature.

Trying to look through the peephole, all Tom could see was a man dressed in a dark uniform.

"Who is it?" whispered Sarah.

"I don't know."

"We're *three* flights up with no outside ledge. We can't get out this way."

Tom chained the door and cautiously cracked it open.

"Room service," announced the attendant.

Peeking out, Tom saw a young man dressed in a butler's outfit next to a rolling table: the delicious smell of breakfast engulfed his senses.

Relieved, Tom unchained the lock and the attendant

carried in a tray of scrambled eggs, bacon, sausage, pancakes, fruit and freshly squeezed orange juice.

"Compliments of the manager," said the attendant cheerfully.

"Is the professor back?"

"Dr. Hainsworth? I'm not sure," he replied, setting the tray down. "I'm headed to his room right now."

Sarah scurried over and opened the adjoining door. No one was there, and the bed was still made.

"He's not back. Any ideas?"

Tom contemplated for less than a second. "Eat," he smiled. "Then we'll figure out our next step."

"Always thinking with your stomach," she chuckled, then dug into the feast as the attendant bowed his head and left.

* * * *

Hoping to locate Tom and Sarah, Coldwell called all his contacts in London, but nothing materialized. Although his associates knew the importance of finding the two orphans, no one had seen or heard anything. Coldwell was desperate to silence Professor Hainsworth before he got a chance to talk, but the last place he wanted to go was New Scotland Yard. With his problems intensifying and time running out, he had only one choice left — to contact Philip.

He grabbed a quick coffee at a nearby café and made the dreaded phone call.

"P-Philip, it's Coldwell," he stuttered nervously.

"Did you take care of them?"

There was a long pause.

"Not yet. There's been a . . . *complication*."

"What happened?" his voice bellowed through the phone.

Coldwell was startled, spilling his coffee.

"They got away."

"You idiot! How could you be so stupid?"

"There were policemen everywhere . . . and Professor Hainsworth was . . . was arrested. *Someone* must have told them where the children were headed."

Philip knew he was the one who divulged this information to Detective Gowerstone. His voice quieted as he tried to restrain his mounting anger.

"Tell me the details."

"They met with a Dr. Beagleswick."

"That lunatic. That was Hainsworth's contact?"

"You know of him?"

"Yes. He's been babbling on about lost dynasties and conspiracy theories for decades. No one takes him seriously. Still, we should have silenced him years ago."

"He was also taken into custody before I could question him."

"It doesn't matter," grumbled Philip. "The police will just think he's a crazy old man."

"What does he know?"

"If they talked to Beagleswick, he probably mentioned Canterbury. It was the last known location of the Britfields."

"What do you want me to do?"

"Get to Canterbury Cathedral," ordered Philip. "There's an Archbishop there who knew the Britfields. We questioned him many times, but he's a stubborn man, adamant he knows nothing."

"Why wasn't he eliminated?"

"He's an Archbishop — there are limits. Anyway, he's no threat to the Crown."

"What about London?"

"We've got enough people looking already. If Tom and Sarah are still in the city, we'll find them."

"And when I locate the Archbishop?"

"Do whatever you have to, but get rid of those kids, especially Tom."

16
THE WISE ARCHBISHOP

After finishing breakfast, Tom and Sarah decided to wait for Hainsworth. They wandered down to the lobby and asked Brandon if he had heard from the professor or received any messages. He said no. Brandon realized there must be something going on, but his loyalty to Hainsworth was unwavering: an Oxford creed practiced among the graduates.

Tom and Sarah stayed in their room for another hour but began to lose hope. They both felt it was only a matter of time before someone found them at the hotel, and it was too risky to stay in the city any longer. Although London had always been their main objective, things had drastically changed over the last few days.

"We can't wait here forever," said Sarah apprehensively, staring out the window.

"What do you think the professor would want us to do?" asked Tom, pondering the question himself.

She thought for a moment. "Probably continue on. He's helped us this far. We can make it on our own the rest of the way."

"You mean to Canterbury?"

"Yes."

"But aren't you worried . . . or even scared?"

"Of course I am," she replied in a serious tone. "But we've managed on our own before, and we're still together."

Tom smiled, amazed at her resolve. "Okay, how do we get there?"

"By train."

Tom pulled out the remaining six pounds from his pocket. "With this?"

"We'll sneak on and avoid the ticket collectors, then move from cabin to cabin if we see them," she replied in a way that suggested past experience.

"And when we run out of cabins?"

"We'll deal with it."

"You're as devious as I am," he said admiringly.

"You've *just* noticed?" she teased, then twirled around and grabbed an apple from the table.

"It won't be easy," warned Tom.

"Has anything been easy?"

"No, not really," he answered reflectively. He opened his map and spread it on the bed. "So what train station?"

She pointed to a location. "Waterloo — it's the most direct route."

Tom glanced down. "That's almost two miles away."

"Then we'll take the underground. Your six pounds should be enough for the tickets."

He threw her a bewildered look. "Take the what?"

"The tube, silly," she goaded him, chomping on her fruit. "A train . . . the underground."

"How do you know all these things?"

"I told you. I wasn't always in an orphanage."

Twenty minutes later, Tom and Sarah walked out the main entrance where the morning doorman stood at attention.

"Where are you two headed?" he asked with a suspicious undertone.

"We're off to Waterloo Station," replied Tom.

"You should take the tube — much faster. Go through Green Park. There's an entrance at the other end of the street."

"Will do, thanks."

As they left, the doorman immediately got on his cell phone and made a call.

"Yes, it's me. I just spotted them. They've been staying at the Dukes Hotel," he said urgently, watching Tom and Sarah disappear around the corner. "How was I supposed to know they were here? I just started my shift an hour ago. Yeah, they're headed to Waterloo Station, probably be there in twenty minutes. I understand, but don't forget to pay me this time."

The doorman glanced at the lobby to see if anyone noticed that he'd been talking on his phone, then causally returned to his post.

Eager to stay off the main roads, Tom and Sarah entered Green Park, a sprawling area of meadows and wild flowers. They hurried along a gravel pathway covered in leaves dampened by a passing shower. The late morning air was brisk and fresh, promising a better day. After last night, even walking a few blocks was painful. Their feet were sore, and their legs cramped.

As they approached Piccadilly Circus tube station, they noticed an officer posted at the entrance. He was a burly man with an angry scowl across his face.

Tom and Sarah waited until he turned his head, then hustled down the stairs with the rest of the crowd.

Two stories underground, the subway station was a chaotic jungle. Kindness was forgotten, and proper etiquette abandoned as obnoxious people bumped into one another rushing to catch their trains.

"Let's figure out which one goes to Waterloo!" Sarah hollered over the loud noise.

"Good idea!" Tom yelled back, feeling intimidated by the maze of subterranean corridors.

They reviewed a map displaying various train routes, a colorful zigzag of intersecting lines.

"It looks like the only way to Waterloo is to take the Blue Line to Leicester Square, get off, then get back on the Black Line," said Sarah confidently.

"Why doesn't it just go straight there?"

"Because it's London!"

"It seems like a lot of effort for a couple of miles."

"Welcome to city life," she added with a flare of sophistication.

After purchasing their tickets for five pounds, they searched for the correct train. They ran up one flight of steps, crossed over a track, came down the other side and waited. People were tightly bunched together, each one desperate to get on first and claim any vacant seats. Most of the time everyone just ended up standing.

Over the loud speaker a repetitive voice kept mumbling: "*Mind* the gap . . . *Mind* the gap . . ."

"Why does he keep saying that?" inquired Tom, irritated by the repetitive announcement.

Sarah motioned to the ground. "It's the gap between the train and the platform. They don't want anyone to fall in."

"I'll remember that," he murmured, suddenly envisioning what that might look like and shivering at the thought.

A long silver train screeched to a stop. Multiple doors flung open, and a stampede of passengers tumbled out.

Sarah took Tom's hand and fought through the swarm, finally getting inside. They stood in the jam-packed crowd, waiting by the door and hoping to get off first.

The train bolted forward. People shifted backwards then settled. The odd routine and experience reminded Tom of the orphanage: cramped quarters, stale smell and an unfriendly atmosphere. The compartment shook and rattled as the train motored along, then abruptly stopped: Leicester Square.

Still clutching Tom's hand, Sarah pulled him forward. "Come on. Let's get off."

The doors slid open and they struggled free, running toward their connecting train. A flood of people followed.

Finding the Black Line, they waited impatiently. A police officer occasionally walked by, prompting Tom and Sarah to look away and bury their heads in their map — so far it had worked.

When the next train stopped, a torrent of exiting passengers knocked Tom back while Sarah was carried into the compartment with the crowd.

The doors closed. Sarah was locked inside.

Tom smacked the window, hoping the doors would open — they didn't.

As the trained started moving, Tom ran along the outside platform waving his arms in a feeble attempt to make it stop. Sarah was glued to the window silently mouthing, "Tom! Tom!" The train disappeared down the track and into a dark tunnel.

Tom stood there in shock. He pulled Sarah's locket from his pocket and held it tightly in his hand, then turned to a bystander reading the morning newspaper.

"Sir, I've got to get to Waterloo Station. When does the next train come?"

"I'm not sure."

"I've got to get there right now! She's all alone!"

"Who?"

"My friend Sarah," exclaimed Tom, frantically looking around for other options. "What am I going to do?"

"Take a cab."

"Right . . . a cab. That's a brilliant idea. Thanks, mister."

"Don't mention it," he nodded, feeling his good deed for the day was done.

Tom sprinted up the stairs to the street exit. He looked back and forth for a black cab.

He frantically flagged one down and it pulled over.

"I need to get to Waterloo Station right away!"

The driver looked at him oddly. "All by yourself?"

"Look, I have money," said Tom defensively, showing the driver his one pound.

"That wouldn't get you halfway up the block, my friend," laughed the driver.

Feeling defeated, Tom bowed his head.

The driver exhaled heavily, shaking his head.

"Here," he said somewhat grudgingly, motioning to the backseat. "Get in."

"Really?" exclaimed Tom, his spirits lifted.

"Why not?" he sighed. "You look like you could use a break."

"I could," agreed Tom as he jumped in.

The driver cranked the cab into drive and sped down St. Martin's Lane.

* * * *

Sarah glared out the window wondering what to do: *Should I get off at the next stop and make it back to Tom or hope he gets to Waterloo?* She didn't know.

The one thing they always had going for them was that they were together, but now they were apart. Her mind was seized with anxiety. *What if he's not there? What if I lose him? What if I never see him again? What if . . .*

The train slowed at the next stop, Charing Cross. The passengers pushed forward and tumbled out.

Standing by the door, Sarah decided to step off the train.

* * * *

The cab jerked left and right as the driver shot down one street and up another. Tom haphazardly slid around the backseat while nervously chatting with the driver.

"You lost your friend on the tube?" asked the man, concerned.

"My best friend." Tom was fast to correct him.

"Ah . . . well . . . that's just rubbish. No worries though, I'll get you to Waterloo as fast as possible."

"Cheers," he said, grabbing the safety straps and firmly holding on.

They whipped around a corner and came to Seven Dials, a merging intersection of seven different streets.

Just missing the approaching cars, the cab entered the roundabout, swirled in a circle and dashed up Earlham Road.

Tom peered out the window while the cab miraculously came within inches of the parked cars. He marveled at the driver's precision and mastery of his vehicle.

They hurried down Neal Street past The Royal Opera House and through Covent Garden, a large enclosed Piazza with an assortment of boutique shops and coffee bars. A thirty-foot Christmas tree stood in front, swaying in the wind. Shoppers hurried about carrying wrapped packages and bags filled with gifts.

It's such a fascinating city, Tom thought, *it's a shame we must leave it.*

* * * *

As the doors started to close, Sarah leaped back onto the train. If she knew Tom at all, he'd be heading to Waterloo station.

"I know he'll be there," she assured herself.

She anxiously stood, grasping onto a rail as the train pulled forward and onto the next stop.

* * * *

The driver handled his cab with the finesse of a seasoned jockey. Traveling at breakneck speed, he had a relaxed rhythm to his style, casually turning the wheel one way and back the other, barely avoiding oncoming traffic. An occasional toot of the horn gave pedestrians a split second to move aside as he raced down the narrow streets. If driving was this exciting, Tom couldn't wait to have his own car.

Maneuvering onto Waterloo Bridge, the cab quickly crossed over the Thames. The river glistened in the afternoon sunlight as people enjoyed a leisurely walk along the embankment. Barges and small boats bustled up and down the waterway. The London Eye was once again in view.

The driver took a sharp left and stopped at Victory Arch, the main entrance leading into the train station.

As a token of appreciation, Tom handed the man his last pound.

"The fare is on me, my little friend," said the driver cheerfully.

"It's a tip. That was the best driving I've ever seen."

The driver chuckled, admiring the coin. "I'll keep it with me as a reminder of our meeting."

Tom waved goodbye and ran up the stairs to the terminal.

* * * *

Lodged against the door, Sarah restlessly waited for the train to stop. Each passing second felt like an hour, her heart racing. The train finally screeched to a halt and the doors slid open.

She dashed up the escalator two steps at a time and emerged on the ground floor.

The interior of Waterloo Station resembled a covered shopping mall with restaurants and stores lining each side. Towering overhead, a web of metal trusses supported the glass rooftop, and an enormous four-sided clock hung from a girder, showing 2:20. Around the outer borders was a network of platforms with railways heading all over Britain. People hurried back and forth as one train arrived and another left.

Sarah didn't know where to begin. She ran over to every boy who resembled Tom only to have the child give her a puzzled look. After countless attempts to find him, she spotted a British Transport policewoman scouting the area and quickly moved behind a postcard stand. It didn't take Sarah long to remember that half of London was looking for them.

Meanwhile, at the other end of the terminal, Tom desperately hunted for Sarah. Keeping clear of the authorities, he filtered through the crowd and scurried in and out of the shops. While he tried to stay optimistic, he was worried he might never see her again.

Suddenly he spotted a familiar figure in the distance and sprinted toward her. As she turned, he lunged forward and hugged her.

"Thank goodness," he gasped, his anxiety turning to relief.

She squeezed him back, laughing and sniffling at the same time.

"How on earth did you get here?" she asked, perplexed.

"A cab."

"With only a pound?"

"I got lucky."

"I . . . I was so —"

"I know . . ."

"I thought I'd never —"

"Me too."

She let out a lengthy sigh and gave him a playful shove. "How *dare* you leave me on the train all alone."

"But . . . I . . . sorry."

She smirked and clutched his hand. "Let's find our train and get out of here."

While locating the platform to Canterbury, they exchanged stories about their recent escapade. Tom's adventure through the streets of London was far more exciting.

After they had waited ten minutes, the train arrived. It had fifteen separate boxcars, each one sixty feet long and separated by two sliding doors at each end.

As they walked toward a passenger door, a figure ran out from behind and snatched Sarah.

"Going somewhere?" exclaimed Speckle, wrapping his bony arm around her waist and lifting her off the ground.

Filled with terror, Sarah screamed at the top of her lungs. She desperately struggled to free herself, but his grip was too strong.

Speckle then grabbed Tom's jacket and yanked him closer.

"It's about time I found you two," he said in an angry murmur. "But we'll soon get everything sorted out."

"Help!" cried Sarah, frantically squirming. "Help!"

A few bystanders looked over, wondering what all the commotion was about.

"Tom, do something!" she gasped.

Reacting quickly, Tom hit Speckle's hand with his

fists and broke free. He then spotted a fire extinguisher hanging on the wall and grabbed it.

"Let her go!" demanded Tom, pointing the opening at Speckle.

"Don't even think about it," growled Speckle in a threatening tone.

"Do it, Tom!" yelled Sarah, ducking her head to one side.

"I said, don't even think . . ."

Tom pulled the trigger. A white chalky substance blasted out, covering Speckle's face and stinging his eyes. He immediately dropped Sarah and wiped his face, cursing and moaning. Sarah stomped on his foot.

"Ouch!" he shrieked, leaning over. "You . . . rotten . . . little . . ."

Tom then took the extinguisher and whacked Speckle across the head, knocking him to the ground and causing his cell phone to fall free.

Sarah crushed it under her foot.

"Come on," hollered Tom, grabbing her hand and running for the train as it pulled out from the station.

They got to a passenger door, jerked it open and jumped in.

Speckle slowly rose, disheveled and trembling with rage. His head was cut, and blood trickled down his cheek. He wiped it off and limped toward the train. Tom and Sarah anxiously watched from the window.

"He's going to catch us!" she exclaimed.

"He'll never make it."

Determined, Speckle reached the window and slapped the glass, smearing it with blood.

Startled, Sarah and Tom fell backwards.

Speckle took a few more steps, grabbed his head in pain, and tumbled to the pavement. He looked up with a cold, calculating stare.

Tom and Sarah shook in horror, eyes wide open. Rubbing her bruised waist, she could still smell Speckle's stink.

"You all right?" inquired Tom warily.

"No," she answered miserably, her eyes tearing.

"It's okay, Speckle's gone," he said comfortingly.

"How did that freak find us?"

"I wish I knew, but we should be safe now."

"We'll never be safe."

She hugged Tom, holding him for a long moment.

"I wish that psycho would leave us alone," she said bitterly.

"Yes . . . he's definitely a psycho." Tom couldn't help but chuckle, perhaps feeling relieved they were safe or perhaps because of the way Sarah said *psycho.*

"It's not funny!" she snapped, smacking his shoulder. "He could have hurt me."

"I know, I know," he admitted.

She gave him a hard stare followed by a push. After a tense moment, she let out a faint giggle.

"You really nailed him with the fire extinguisher," she said admiringly. "That had to hurt."

"Yeah, and nice job with the phone. He won't be making any calls soon."

"What if he follows us to Canterbury?"

"We'll just have to be extra careful," Tom answered. "Anyway, we have a head start."

They soon found two empty seats toward the middle

section and sat. Still rattled from the experience, Sarah watched the skyline disappear in the distance.

"It's sad we're leaving London," she said, disheartened.

"We'll be back someday," he insisted, trying to encourage her.

"What do you think will happen to the professor?"

"Hopefully Gowerstone will release him."

"What if he doesn't?"

Tom shook his head in frustration. "I'm not sure, but there's nothing we can do."

"I already miss him," she said fondly, reflecting on all his kindness.

"He's a great friend, isn't he?"

"The best of friends."

"Do you think we'll ever see him again?"

"I know we will."

After settling into their seats, they actually felt safe for the first time in days. There was a calm serenity as the train rumbled southeast toward Canterbury.

Tom rested, and Sarah watched the scenery rush by the window: a crumbling castle perched on a hilltop, an old abbey weathered by time and lonely cottages scattered throughout the countryside. There were tiny canals crisscrossing the landscape; emerald meadows surrounded by marshlands; cows and other animals grazing in the open fields.

Thirty minutes later, the train crossed the River Medway and flew by the seaport of Rochester, its impressive Norman fortress still guarding the nearby harbor.

Looking up, Sarah noticed a ticket collector gathering fares from the passengers.

"Come on." She nudged Tom, pulling him off his seat.

"What?" he garbled, half awake.

"We've got to go."

"Now?"

"Yes."

Opening the interconnecting doors, they quickly dashed through one compartment and into the next.

"We're going to run out of train," he mumbled.

"Just keep moving."

They hurried through each passenger car until they reached the first-class section, a secluded area with a narrow aisle on one side and separate compartments on the other.

Sarah slid open a door and yanked Tom inside a private room. Nestling in the cozy chairs, they tried to relax.

"Don't worry," she reassured him, "the ticket collectors hardly ever come back to this area."

A moment later the door opened.

"Tickets," barked a woman. About sixty years old, she had rosy cheeks and a round plump body. Her weary expression suggested long hours and little pay.

Startled, all Tom offered was a blank expression.

Sarah picked up a newspaper and covered her face as if hiding behind it somehow made her invisible.

The woman snatched the newspaper. "Come on kids, I don't have all day," she grumbled. "Where're your tickets?"

"Hmm . . ." Sarah's face crinkled as she searched her pocket-less skirt. "Where did we put them, Tom?"

"I'm . . . I'm not sure?" He began rummaging around the seat.

"Let me guess," the woman scoffed, putting her hands on her waist. "You misplaced them."

"It appears that way," answered Sarah frankly then paused. "Actually, we don't have any tickets."

"Well, at least you're honest." The woman pulled out a leather booklet. "You can purchase tickets for forty-two pounds, each."

"Eighty-four pounds," exclaimed Sarah, rolling her eyes. "You've got to be kidding! We don't have that kind of money!"

"How much do you have?"

They both stared at the ground.

"It figures. And aren't you cheeky," she laughed, "sitting in first class."

Tom and Sarah stood, ready to leave.

"We'll go," said Tom in a dismal voice.

The woman looked down the deserted corridor. "Hold on," she exhaled, exasperated. "You can stay here. Just remember, I *never* saw you," she added with a whisper and closed the door behind her.

"Wow. What a stroke of luck," said Tom, stunned by her generosity.

"I told you."

"Told me what?"

"Not to worry."

* * * *

Around 5:00 p.m. the train eased into Canterbury station and slowed to a stop. Tom and Sarah left their compartment and exited with the other passengers. While they walked up Dunstan Street, lampposts flickered on as the sun slowly dipped below the horizon.

Named *Durovernum Cantiacorum* by the Romans in the first century AD, the ancient town of Canterbury has been an ecclesiastical pilgrimage site for religious travelers ever since Archbishop Thomas Becket was murdered in the cathedral in 1170 by four of King Henry II's knights.

Surrounded by distinctive centuries of architecture, the entire town conveyed a transcendent feeling of going back in time: old Roman fortifications and defense walls around the perimeter (*200-300s*); a Norman Castle situated in the center of town (*1200s*); Gothic church spires reaching to the heavens (*1300s*); half-timbered Elizabethan homes (*1500s*); Victorian shops with large display windows and colorful facades (*1800s*); and modern concrete and steel buildings. Small rowboats skimmed along the River Stour, running under bridges and cutting through the town.

Tom and Sarah entered through the West Gate and walked up St. Peter's Street.

"Look, that's got to be it," said Tom excitedly, gesturing to an enormous cathedral rising over the rooftops.

"Do you think the Archbishop will be there?"

"If he isn't, I'm all out of ideas."

Glancing around, Sarah noticed people rushing back and forth carrying presents and holiday gifts.

"I almost forgot, it's Christmas Eve."

Tom stopped for moment, moved by the comment.

"This will be my first Christmas out of an orphanage," he said reflectively.

Sarah grinned. "I'm glad to be spending it with you."

"Me too."

"Now let's get there before it closes."

"I didn't know churches closed . . ."

Before he finished, Sarah took off up one of the streets. Vowing never to be beaten by a girl, he trailed closely behind.

Designed in the shape of a Latin cross, with a long nave and an intersecting transept, Canterbury Cathedral was awe-inspiring. Its three square towers and multifaceted pinnacles pierced the sky. The setting sun transformed the rustic, windswept stone into an angelic glow of pinks and reds. The greenish copper roof shimmered, and the stained-glass windows came to life.

Tom and Sarah cautiously entered.

The church was cold and empty. Rows of pews neatly lined the nave. The smell of incense filled the entire chamber with an almost hypnotic sensation. An endless sea of candles danced in the cool breeze. Slender alabaster pillars climbed the walls, securing the massive arches and ribbed vaults overhead.

While Tom and Sarah curiously investigated, a bishop strolled over, hands clasped in front of him.

"May I help you?" he inquired humbly.

"Yes," said Tom, barely able to hold his words back. "We're looking for the Archbishop."

"Do you have an *appointment*?"

"No," he replied flatly. "But we must see —"

"I apologize, but you'll have to call the main office and schedule a time. He's usually booked months in advance."

"But we need to talk to him now!"

"That won't be possible." The bishop smiled tightly, more perturbed than helpful. "But you're welcome to view the church. We'll be closing soon to set up for our Christmas Eve service tonight."

He gave a gentle bow and turned to walk away.

"Tell him that Dr. Beagleswick sent us," said Sarah firmly. "It's *very* important."

The name resonated for a moment as the bishop slowly turned back, a deadly silence lingering. The candles flickered. An uneasy feeling crept over Tom and Sarah.

"Wait here," ordered the bishop, now more serious than pleasant.

After twenty apprehensive minutes, Tom and Sarah heard a door creaking open. In the background, they saw a shadowy figure emerge. Back slightly bent, the man led with his left leg, slowly dragging the right; every step looked painful. An occasional glimmer of candlelight jumped across his elderly face.

Sarah grabbed Tom's hand, frightened by what they had released from the inner walls of this saintly sanctuary. Yet as the man gradually approached, there was a tranquil and peaceful manner about him. Dressed in a black robe with a purple sash around his waist, he was an impressive figure, old but wise. A simple gold cross dangled from his neck.

When Tom and Sarah peered into his radiant eyes, they both felt a comfortable familiarity that neither could explain.

"My children, what can I do for you?" he asked in a low, reverent voice.

Sarah leaned forward, remembering the proper protocol from earlier childhood. "Your Grace."

"Please, call me Alexander. I don't care for titles, only what one does with one's life and who one serves."

"Alexander," she said calmly, "we've come to speak to you about —"

"Britfield!" blurted Tom.

The Archbishop's eyes widened as his gaze drifted around the church, checking to see if there were others close by. He breathed a heavy sigh, then motioned Tom and Sarah down an aisle.

"We should speak in my office."

They followed him into a secluded room, small but cozy. It was pristine, with religious artifacts and books filling the space.

"Please, sit down," he urged them as he sat on a cushioned chair. "You're interested in the Britfields?"

"Yes," said Tom eagerly.

"What makes you believe I can assist you?" inquired the Archbishop suspiciously, his words cautious and guarded.

"Dr. Beagleswick recommended that we find you," interjected Sarah, hoping to pass the formality and get to the point.

"Ah yes, Dr. Beagleswick, a *fine* professor. I've known him for over forty years." The Archbishop eased forward in his chair. "What exactly did he tell you?"

"Everything," said Tom bluntly.

"*Except* where they are now," added Sarah.

"But why does this concern either of you?" inquired the Archbishop.

Tom hesitated for a second. "I may be their son," he said delicately, finally accepting the possibility.

The Archbishop was clearly surprised and slightly shaken. He gently grabbed his cross, as though he was searching for strength and guidance. His eyes glistened as he stared directly at Tom.

"Tell me how you've come to know this," he asked.

Tom spent the next ten minutes explaining everything that had happened to him: his vague memories, the different orphanages, Weatherly and the secret file, his escape with Sarah, meeting Hainsworth, Windsor Castle, London, Dr. Beagleswick and their journey to Canterbury.

After Tom finished, the Archbishop leaned back in his chair, lost in contemplation.

"Your story is compelling, Tom," he said with a heavy heart, then glanced at Sarah, "and both your lives have been *very* difficult. I'm truly sorry you've had to endure so much at such a young age."

His compassionate words glided over Tom and Sarah's hearts like a warm breeze, remarkably easing some of their hurt and sorrow.

The Archbishop gave Tom a fatherly look. "You have the Britfield eyes," he smiled, "their manner, their fortitude, but I'm no expert. It could merely be a coincidence. Only *they* would know for sure."

"Then it's true," exclaimed Sarah. "You knew them."

"Yes, I knew the last Britfields," he sighed. "Magnificent people with the strength of lions and unwavering faith in destiny."

"Are you familiar with the *whole* story — the history?" inquired Tom.

"I'm familiar."

"All of it?"

"Yes," he confirmed sadly, "from their beginning until their end." He closed his eyes as his voice wavered. "I was present ten years ago when they lost their only child. Terrible time . . . heart wrenching. They suffered grief beyond anything I've ever seen. I counseled them the best I could, spent time with them waiting for their son to be found, but . . ." He paused, lost in grief.

"But he wasn't found," added Sarah.

"It destroyed them . . . and their *faith*. They lost all hope, belief in everything and everyone."

The room became still. They all sat in silence for what seemed like an eternity.

"What if Tom is their son?" Sarah asked pointedly.

The Archbishop suddenly beamed intensely. "Then it would be one of the greatest miracles I've ever witnessed and an answer to many prayers."

"Then we need to find them," she insisted.

"I don't know," he said, hesitating and glancing toward the ceiling. "They've already been through so much."

"Don't you think it's important for them to know that maybe —"

"It's too treacherous to get involved any further," cautioned the Archbishop as he raised his hand. "Sometimes there are things we never understand, that are best left alone."

Tom looked at Sarah for confirmation; she nodded yes. It was if they had developed their own unspoken language and knew the other's thoughts.

"Alexander, we're aware of the dangers, but it doesn't frighten us. It's worth any risk to find the truth," said Tom with conviction. "I don't care about titles either. I just want to find my parents if they're still alive."

"You have a good heart and your determination is worthy, but you're both only . . ."

"Children," said Sarah.

"Yes. I can't be responsible for sending either of you into something that could jeopardize your lives any further."

Tom stood up. "We may be young, but after what we've gone through, we're also wise," he said boldly. "We know what's important. Many spend a lifetime and never learn that. If my parents are out there, I'd like to find them."

"Well spoken, Tom," said Alexander in a soft, caring voice.

Tom turned to Sarah. "Sarah is my *best* friend in the world and the only family I have. I've learned that's more important to me than anything."

Deeply moved, she reached over and tenderly touched his arm.

The Archbishop slowly rose from his seat and walked over to them, his movement unhurried and seemingly difficult.

"Would you allow me some time to consider it?" he asked.

"We're kind of in a hurry," responded Sarah, rising quickly and standing next to Tom.

"I see." Alexander pondered for a moment, searching for the proper answers and direction to offer. "Then grant me a few minutes in private and wait for me in the outside hallway."

"Okay, Alexander," said Tom, encouraged. "We'll wait for your decision."

They left the room and closed the door behind them. As they wandered around the corridor, Sarah approached Tom.

"Thank you for what you said," she whispered affectionately.

"I meant it."

"I know you did."

The quiet tranquility was suddenly broken by the sound of distant footsteps echoing across the stone floor. Searching the open cathedral, neither Sarah nor Tom could see anyone.

"Probably just some visitors," she whispered unconvincingly.

"Yeah . . . it's nothing," he added with suspicion, knowing the church was now closed.

"Do you think Alexander will help us?" she inquired, trying to change the subject.

"I suppose he'll do whatever he believes is right."

After a few moments, the door opened.

The Archbishop calmly stepped forward, filled with confidence and assurance. He handed Tom a folded paper.

"Everything you need to know is written on this. Guard it safely."

"I will," said Tom courageously. "You have my word."

"The Britfields moved to France seven years ago and are staying at the royal Château de Chambord in the Loire River Valley." Alexander's voice became serious and tense. "I *can't* emphasize enough how dangerous this is, but it's not my place to judge, only to offer guidance. If there's hope to be given, then I will not stand in the way."

Sarah was filled with a mixture of anticipation and fear. While she was excited about the news, France seemed like a world away.

Tom carefully put the paper in his pocket. "Thank you, Alexander . . . for trusting us."

"If you need any help or get in trouble, contact Archbishop Filberte at Notre Dame in Paris. He's a good friend. His information is also on the paper I gave you."

"Understood, Archbishop Filberte in Paris," Tom repeated.

"Why don't you stay here tonight, and I will arrange your passage in the morning. We have a few rooms in a nearby abbey that should be suitable. Wait at the entrance for Bishop Carmichael to escort you there."

They each hugged the Archbishop and bid him farewell, then headed along the nave toward the front.

The wind rustled outside, causing the windows to rattle. A draft circulated through the interior, making some of the candles flicker and extinguishing others. A moment later they heard the sharp patter of footsteps again.

Tom whipped around and saw a silhouette approaching. "It's just the bishop, right?" he tried to assure himself.

"I hope so," replied Sarah, her voice quivering.

Now deeply worried, she stepped behind Tom for protection.

He looked again, but the figure disappeared. "Bishop Carmichael . . ."

There was the sudden sound of a thud, like someone had fallen to the ground.

"What was that?" exclaimed Sarah, more nervous than ever.

Tom could feel her shaking as she brushed against him. She became silent, her eyes widening and mouth slightly open.

They steadily inched toward the front entrance thirty feet away.

The movement continued, followed by the distinct sound of a door being latched.

"I have a really bad feeling about this," mumbled Sarah.

Sensing an unwelcome presence, they turned.

Coldwell's devilish eyes peered down, a menacing smile across his face. Close by lay Bishop Carmichael, unconscious.

"You've caused me nothing but trouble!" exclaimed Coldwell resentfully.

Horror-struck, Tom and Sarah went limp, a paralyzing chill running through their bodies.

"W-what do you want?" stuttered Tom, trying to muster his courage and strength.

"To *finish* what I started," answered Coldwell, a heartless indifference in his tone.

"Why can't you just leave us alone?" said Sarah, both frightened and angry.

"Because the monarchy is counting on me." Coldwell reached into his trench coat and removed his pistol.

"You don't have to do this," pleaded Sarah.

"Yes I do."

"But we haven't done anything!"

Coldwell slowly aimed. "I'm sorry, but I *must* do my duty."

Two gunshots rang out, rumbling through the church.

One bullet pierced Coldwell's arm, throwing him to the ground; the other hit a candelabra, knocking it onto a long velvet curtain. A bluish-orange flame instantly engulfed the drape and rapidly climbed upward.

Disoriented, Coldwell squirmed on the limestone floor reaching for his weapon, a trail of smoke snaking from the barrel.

"Stay where you are!" shouted Detective Gowerstone, emerging from behind one of the pillars.

Although relieved, Tom and Sarah's hearts sank. They knew they'd be arrested and returned to Weatherly.

"Tom! Sarah! Step away from him!" ordered Gowerstone as he marched over to Coldwell.

"Do it! Finish it!" provoked Coldwell, ready to die to protect the Crown's secrets.

Gowerstone lowered his weapon. "No, you have too many questions to answer and a long jail sentence to serve."

The flames continued to spread, quickly consuming everything in their path. There was the distinct crackle of burning cloth as hazy black smoke filled the air.

A group of policemen burst through the front door, yanking Coldwell up and handcuffing him.

"Help me get this fire out!" yelled Gowerstone. He hurried to the blazing curtain and tugged it to the ground.

A few officers ran over and frantically stamped on the fire, the smoldering drape sparking and hissing. The flames were soon extinguished.

In the distance, the Archbishop staggered out of his office.

"What's going on out here?" he demanded, then looked over and recognized Gowerstone. "You?"

"Everything is under control," said Gowerstone forcefully. "Just wait there."

During all the confusion, Tom grabbed Sarah and took off down a row of pews toward an exit.

Gowerstone coolly watched as he mumbled something into his radio. He turned to the other officers. "See to the prisoner's gunshot wound and put him in the back of one of the cars. Wait for my instructions."

"Yes, sir," replied a policeman, dragging Coldwell out of the cathedral.

Tom and Sarah pushed their way through a side door and into the freezing night. They hadn't gone more than a few paces when a familiar hand grasped their arms. They tried to struggle free, but it was useless.

"Where do you think you're going?" scoffed Speckle, his face expressionless, his eyes stoic, his head bandaged.

Tom and Sarah's mouths dropped open. They attempted to yell but were paralyzed by fear.

It can't be, thought Tom. *It just can't* . . .

"Come with me," demanded Speckle, escorting them back inside the church and over to a small room, his grip surprisingly gentler than usual.

"Wait here," he said decisively, locking the door behind him.

"Speckle!" uttered Tom. "That rat!"

"Oh Tom," murmured Sarah, wiping her eyes. "This can't be happening. Not after everything we've been through."

Tom felt his hope vanish. Now he understood what it was like to lose his faith.

"Just a little more time and we would have been free," he mumbled to himself. "We were so close, so close, so close . . ."

Sarah collapsed onto a wooden chair, her spirit crushed.

"I can't believe Speckle works for Gowerstone," she stated, her sorrow turning to anger. "I hate that man! I hate them both!"

Tom bowed his head unable to offer any comfort.

"We've got to escape from here," she insisted, searching the windowless room for an exit.

"We'll figure something out." Tom gently held her hand, trying to console her. "At least we're together."

"What if they separate us?"

He hadn't considered that. "Then I'll find you, wherever you are."

A few minutes later, the door clicked open and Gowerstone walked in, the smell of smoke trailing behind.

"You *wretched* man," snapped Sarah. "Why are you doing this?"

"I understand how you must feel," said Gowerstone sympathetically.

Sarah leaped from her chair, her resentment growing. "You don't understand anything!"

"More than you realize."

"How did you know we were here?" asked Tom adamantly.

"Dr. Hainsworth informed me this afternoon."

"You didn't hurt him, did you?" inquired Sarah in a protective manner.

"Of course not," he answered firmly.

Tom and Sarah couldn't help feeling betrayed. However, they didn't blame the professor; they assumed he had no choice.

"He didn't do anything wrong. You can't punish him!" she exclaimed, once again ready to lunge toward the detective.

"I'm not going to," said Gowerstone reassuringly.

"Where is he now?" asked Tom pointedly.

Gowerstone hesitated. "In my protective custody, at least for the moment."

"Why?"

"His life is in danger, just as yours are."

The last comment struck Tom as odd, but his thought was interrupted when Speckle entered the room and stood by the door.

"Speckle works for you?" said Tom spitefully. "You're all part of this."

"Yes, he works for me," answered Gowerstone evenly, "but —"

"And now you're sending us back to Weatherly. Back to that horrible place!"

"You misunderstand me, Tom," said Gowerstone empathetically, his tone becoming gentler. "I haven't been chasing you all over England, so I can arrest you. I want to *help* you."

17
THE ENGLISH CHANNEL

Tom and Sarah stared at Gowerstone, dumbfounded.

"What?" they gasped together.

"Let me explain," replied the detective, approaching the question in his methodical way. "Speckle does work for me, but not in the capacity that you believe."

Not trusting a single word, Tom and Sarah rushed for the door and shook the knob. It was locked.

Gowerstone calmly motioned them to sit down, trying to control the situation. They grudgingly turned and took a seat, defeated.

"As I was saying," continued Gowerstone, "Speckle is one of my agents assigned to investigate Weatherly. We were getting ready to shut down the orphanage and arrest Mr. and Mrs. Grievous when you two escaped."

An awkward moment of silence ensued as Tom and Sarah traded confused glances.

Speckle stepped forward. "I'm sorry I was so hard on everyone," he said sincerely. "I couldn't afford to be exposed..."

"No — no — no," interrupted Sarah, shaking her head in disbelief, "there's no way someone as wicked as you could be good. Nope, no way. I don't buy it."

"Neither do I," added Tom bitterly.

"It was vital for me to be as convincing as possible," continued Speckle firmly. "I had to stay in character all the time."

"You played your role *extremely* well!" stated Sarah resentfully, still harboring hostile feelings.

"As I had to," he retorted, defending his actions. "The Grievouses are clever people. I couldn't take the risk of letting them know who I was or why I was there."

"You're a hurtful man who should go to jail," she continued unrelentingly. "Along with the rest of the criminals!"

Speckle threw up his hands in frustration and looked to Gowerstone for help.

"That's enough," interjected the detective.

"So you've known about Weatherly?" Tom asked Gowerstone.

"Yes, for quite a while, but there was *nothing* we could do until we gathered enough evidence." Gowerstone paced the room as he explained. "It's not just that orphanage, Tom, but a chain of them from Cornwall to Edinburgh. They're all involved in fraudulent and despicable activities: stealing money from the government and using it for their own ends, providing horrible substandard conditions and using children as labor," he said angrily. "Weatherly is at the center of it."

"And quite a dreadful center," Speckle added succinctly.

"You're not sending us back there?" Tom tried to confirm, finally feeling a sliver of hope.

"No — never."

"Then why not let us go?" inquired Sarah as she eased toward the door.

"Because . . ." Gowerstone paused as he composed his thoughts. "When I read Tom's file and saw the name Britfield, his picture, his assumed age of twelve, everything became clear to me."

"I don't understand," said Tom, his head spinning.

"I was the detective in charge of finding the Britfield's lost child ten years ago."

Sarah's mouth dropped open. She squeezed Tom's arm and shot him an astonished look.

"It was the *only* case I ever failed to solve," continued Gowerstone reflectively, a trace of resentment in his voice.

Tom rubbed his head, trying to make sense of the information. "You've been chasing us all over England —"

"To apprehend you for your own protection. If you are who I believe you are, then there are others who want you —"

"We know!" Tom and Sarah exclaimed in unison.

There was another moment of silence.

"What happened ten years ago?" asked Sarah, eager to solve the puzzle.

"It was a disaster," replied Gowerstone, his eyes wandering as he recalled the incident.

"Why?"

"Every time I got close to finding a clue or a connection, someone interfered and sabotaged my work. Important documents were stolen, and witnesses vanished. I had never seen anything like it!" he recalled with animosity. "After two hard years of investigation, I was forced by my superiors to let it go."

"And?"

"But I never did, and I *never* forgot."

"Then you think Tom is their son?"

The detective carefully contemplated the question, then nodded his head vigorously. "Yes, I believe he is."

"Wow," she gasped, overwhelmed by the revelation.

"Wow indeed."

Sarah stared at Tom. He was motionless, not sure what to think or how to react.

Gowerstone walked closer to them. "I was afraid for your lives and wanted to protect you."

"Then Tom might be the rightful *heir* to the throne of Great Britain?" she interrupted, trying to cut to the point.

"I'm no historian, but if it's true, then he's in grave danger and so are you. After speaking to Dr. Hainsworth, I knew there was more to it, that my suspicion about Philip was correct. This whole thing goes deeper than anyone can imagine, and there's more to it than I wanted to believe."

"This entire time you were just trying to help us?" asked Tom, now realizing the irony of everything they went through.

"Correct." Gowerstone faintly laughed to himself. "But you two. You gave me the hardest chase of my career, from Yorkshire to Canterbury."

"Sorry," blurted Sarah. "We thought you were trying to —"

"I know."

"Now what?" asked Tom directly as a whirlwind of emotions raced through his mind.

"We need to get you back to London. I can explain everything to the Prime Minister, and we'll get to the bottom of this. I'll personally see to your safety."

"But what about after that?"

"I promise things will be better, for both of you."

"And my family?"

"I'll help you find them."

Sarah leaned over to Gowerstone, suddenly realizing everything he'd done. "Thank you for saving us from that — killer."

"Yeah," added Tom quickly, his tension easing. "That was close. We owe you."

"That's my job," said Gowerstone proudly. "You owe me nothing."

While Speckle motioned them out of the room, Sarah glared at him again.

"Don't worry about Speckle," Gowerstone reassured her, "he's one of my best agents."

"Somehow I find that hard to believe," she said bluntly, not quite ready to relinquish her animosity.

They marched into the main cathedral. A thin layer of smoke lingered.

The detective walked over to the Archbishop, who had been patiently waiting and wondering what was going on in his church. They shook hands and talked for a moment, both recognizing each other from a decade earlier.

As Gowerstone explained the situation, the Archbishop nodded his head in agreement and smiled at Tom and Sarah, once again bidding them a heartfelt farewell.

Tom and Sarah followed Gowerstone outside where a small gathering of curious spectators milled around. Five police vehicles were parked in the street, along with a fire truck and paramedics.

Professor Hainsworth quickly got out of a police car and hurried over.

"What's he doing here?" Gowerstone asked a senior officer.

"He insisted on coming down. Said he had to speak with Tom and Sarah."

"Make it quick."

Sarah instantly ran up and hugged the professor, holding him close. Tom joined in.

"It's so good to see you both safe," said Hainsworth cheerfully. "I was terribly worried."

"We were too," confessed Sarah, grateful to be reunited. "We . . . we didn't know if we'd ever see you again."

"I hope you're not upset that I told Detective Gowerstone about Canterbury, but after speaking with him, I knew he was on our side . . . perhaps our best ally."

Tom shook his head in disbelief. "Gowerstone . . ." he mumbled. "It's still hard to believe."

"Don't worry, Professor, we understand," said Sarah. "He wants to take us back to London to speak with the Prime Minister."

Hainsworth's smile melted away.

"You *can't* do that!" he declared, then motioned the detective over to his side.

"Why not?" wondered Tom.

"Because . . ." he hesitated, lowering his voice, "the Prime Minister is involved in this whole thing."

"That's absurd!" exclaimed Gowerstone, stunned by the accusation.

"Unfortunately, it's not," acknowledged Hainsworth, his voice deadly serious. "When I was detained last night at New Scotland Yard, I had a chance to speak with Dr. Beagleswick again. He told me the Prime Minister has spent the last twelve years protecting the crown . . . at all costs."

"That's his job — to serve the queen," said Gowerstone.

"Not the way he's been doing it." Hainsworth paused for a moment, aware of the effect this disclosure had on the detective. "He's closely connected with the Royals and a clandestine group called the Committee. That's how he got his position in the first place, more out of privilege than hard work or lawful elections."

"I just can't believe that."

"He was also connected with the kidnapping ten years ago."

"You have proof?"

"Dr. Beagleswick has everything. He has just been afraid to come forward."

Gowerstone was more distressed than anyone. He stepped back, unsure what to think. Nevertheless, things suddenly made sense: The Prime Minister's ease through Oxford, although he was a poor student; his quick rise in politics, although he was inexperienced; his overwhelming wealth, although he came from a poor family; all the controversy surrounding his elections; and his evasiveness with this entire case.

"I should have known," he whispered to himself. "I allowed friendship to replace instinct."

"Sometimes we're so close to something, we fail to see it for what it is," said Hainsworth philosophically.

"I've spent my entire life defending the truth, but it's all been a lie, a cover-up, a conspiracy." For the first time in his career, Detective Gowerstone felt completely lost, his internal world destroyed. "I'll have to resign from the force."

"Why?" interrupted Hainsworth. "The Prime Minister is still unaware you know — keep it that way. Use his own tactics against him and get to the bottom of this thing."

Gowerstone was surprised by the professor's shrewdness. "You're a pretty smart man, Professor," he admitted, suddenly encouraged by this insight. "Perhaps you're right."

Tom signaled Hainsworth to lean over.

"Professor," he said softly. "We know where the Britfields are."

"The Archbishop told you?"

"Yes," he whispered in Hainsworth's ear, "they moved to France seven years ago. I have the exact location."

"What is it?" inquired Gowerstone.

"Tom knows the location of his . . . *possible* family."

"The Britfields? Where?"

The professor glanced at Tom for approval. He nodded yes, affirming that he trusted Gowerstone.

"They may be in France," answered Hainsworth quietly, his words guarded.

"And you think Tom and Sarah should go there?"

"Yes."

"It's impossible. I can't let them out of my sight, not now."

"But we don't know who to trust . . . England isn't safe anymore."

The detective looked around at each officer, then the bystanders, the cathedral, and the surrounding buildings. It was apparent he didn't know what to think or who to believe.

"What about you?" he asked Hainsworth. "You can't go back to Oxford — they'll find you. You know too much."

"I wasn't planning on going back. That part of my life is finished."

Gowerstone gazed at Tom and Sarah, searching for an answer. "Just let these children go . . . on their own?" He paused for a moment. "Never."

"Look how well they've done so far," smiled Hainsworth, resting a hand on each of their shoulders.

"That's true," said the detective. "Maybe I should go with —"

"No, your work lies here. Finish what you've started. Shut down those orphanages, find homes for the children and expose this conspiracy. Tom and Sarah are free now. They have their *own* lives to live."

Gowerstone shook his head. "I'm sorry, but I can't let them go — not on their own."

"You won't have to," said Hainsworth confidently, realizing the importance of his statement. "I'll go with them."

"You?"

"Why not? They'll need my help. I can get them safely to France," he persisted fervently.

"But once you're there, then what?

"I have a . . . friend at the Sorbonne in Paris. She can help us when we arrive."

"All of you will be in constant danger," affirmed Gowerstone, reluctant to agree.

"We're used to it," interjected Tom.

The detective thought for a moment, as though having an argument with himself, his expression forceful, his concentration fierce. He paced along the steps, rubbing his forehead and contemplating the circumstances.

"I'll let them go," he announced, "but on one condition." He pulled out two cards and wrote a name and phone number on the back. "I have a contact in France. Her name is Inspector Fontaine, and she works with Interpol. She's an excellent agent and extremely trustworthy. I'll contact her and have her meet you at the Port de Calais, France. She can help you. Do whatever she instructs."

He handed one card to Tom and one to Hainsworth, who nodded his head in agreement.

Gowerstone looked at them sternly. "I want to know everything that happens. Contact me with anything you find out."

"We will," said the professor, tucking the card safely in his coat pocket.

"And I need to speak with Tom and Sarah for a moment. I want to hear about their experience at Weatherly and any other details that might be useful."

"No problem," agreed Tom and Sarah, relieved to finally help the orphans.

They spent the next hour telling the detective all about the orphanage and their experience since they left. It felt good to expose the Grievouses and the horrible place they had created for the orphans. Their descriptions were vivid, leaving nothing out. A policeman wrote down the details, desperately trying to keep up with the rapid conversation.

When Tom and Sarah finished, they waited next to the professor.

"It's best to leave now, take a ship from Dover," Gowerstone stated urgently.

"Yes, of course," agreed Hainsworth.

"If things are as bad as you say, there's no time to pack or say good-bye."

"I understand."

"I'll drive you personally," he insisted, and walked over to his officers, who were patiently waiting for their instructions.

Although there were only a few policemen the detective could trust, the ones he brought to Canterbury were his best. He briefly spoke to each one about the situation, not going into any detail, and sent them back to London. Coldwell would receive further medical attention and be taken to New Scotland Yard for questioning.

Glancing over, Speckle nodded to Tom and Sarah, a slight smile visible on his face. He got into his vehicle and left. They watched him drive away, feeling a combination of resentment and admiration for what he had done.

Gowerstone motioned Sarah, Tom and Hainsworth into his car and they swiftly took off.

They raced through the picturesque villages along the southeastern coast of England until they entered Dover, a busy seaport filled with cargo ships and passenger ferries. The ocean surrounded the harbor, the surf smashing against the coast.

The car pulled up to a ferry terminal, the distinct smell of salt filling the air.

Everyone exited the vehicle, and Hainsworth went to purchase tickets. After Gowerstone cautiously looked around, he turned to Tom and Sarah, firmly shaking their hands. It was an odd moment to share an embrace with this brilliant adversary who was now a friend.

"Thank you for helping us through all this," said Tom earnestly.

"It's not over yet," warned the detective.

"What do you mean?"

"I fear it's just begun," he replied candidly with a sense of foreboding. "But the professor's right. England is not safe."

These words were sobering to Tom yet gave him a greater sense of purpose and determination.

"Remember, stay with Professor Hainsworth at all times," continued Gowerstone. "And always be on your guard."

"Yes, sir," they both nodded.

The detective gave them a serious look. "Trust no one!" he added firmly.

"We understand," said Tom, drifting to another thought. "And you'll help the orphans? I gave them my word."

"Yes, everything will be taken care of."

Hainsworth walked back. "Pier two, right over there," he said, pointing to the dock. "It's the last one leaving tonight—we have fifteen minutes."

Gowerstone let out a long sigh and smiled. "Godspeed Tom, Sarah."

They stared at him, lost for words.

"You'll guard Dr. Beagleswick?" asked Hainsworth. "They'll be after him now."

"He'll be protected," answered Gowerstone.

"Then we should go."

All three headed down the dock and climbed up a gangplank to a large red and white hydrofoil gently rocking with the current. A few late-night travelers hurried on with brightly wrapped packages, including one man carrying a briefcase. When the last passenger boarded, a loud horn blew.

As the boat pulled out of the harbor, Tom and Sarah watched Gowerstone's faint silhouette disappear in the mist. His help and kindness would never be forgotten.

The boat chugged along, picking up speed as it headed to the Port de Calais, France. The weather was rough as a storm brewed in the distance.

Hainsworth sat down on an outside bench, pleased with his decision. Never in his life had he been so happy or certain about his destiny. He wasn't just responsible for his two friends; he was protecting his newfound family.

He glanced at his watch then looked up at Tom and Sarah.

"It's twelve-ten," he said keenly. "Happy Christmas."

"Happy Christmas, Professor," said Tom and Sarah joyfully.

"This has been the best holiday I've ever had, thanks to you two."

"You're right, Professor," agreed Tom soulfully. "The best ever."

Hainsworth stood and they gave him a hug, knowing his sacrifice and love were undeniable.

"May it be the first in many great ones to come."

After a moment Tom and Sarah moved to the back of the boat and watched the magnificent white cliffs of Dover fade in the distance.

"I've never left England before," said Sarah, somewhat reflective.

"Neither have I."

"It's sort of exciting . . . but scary, don't you think?"

"Yeah." His gaze drifted down to the swirling water, thinking about everything they had gone through.

Smiling warmly, Sarah gave Tom a long look.

"Don't worry, Tom, it'll all work out," she assured him, rubbing his shoulder.

"I'm not worried," he smiled and grabbed her hand. "We're together and that's all that matters."

* * * *

Shortly after Canterbury, Detective Gowerstone gathered a force of policemen and headed to Weatherly. He arrested Mr. and Mrs. Grievous, who were each sentenced to thirty years in prison. Although they showed little remorse, their despicable enterprise was shut down and the orphanage closed forever. After that, Gowerstone worked relentlessly to find each orphan a safe home and loving family.

Patrick was adopted by a wealthy couple in the South of France where he works at their automobile factory test driving race cars and living life to its fullest. Richie moved in with a prominent family in Glasgow and helps run their enormous estate, along with watching over their younger children. Bertie lives with a couple in Devon and helps design toys for their popular stores along the coast. Trevor was adopted by a lovely American family and is enjoying his sunny days on a beach in California. Danika and Daylen moved in with an Italian couple who run a fancy bistro in Mayfair. The two girls have become renowned pastry chefs, and the restaurant is one of the hottest places in London. Mr. Picketers now works at The Savoy Hotel as head chef, serving film stars and wealthy patrons. And Dr. Beagleswick retired to an island somewhere in the South Pacific, exact location unknown. The rest of the orphans found warm homes and caring families.

They all stayed in touch, either by email, over the phone or with visits during school vacations. Everyone was grateful to Tom and Sarah, knowing that they had helped in some way. Although no one knew where they were, a part of them remained with the other orphans, for the children would always be connected. They shared a special bond that nothing could ever break.

"Fide et Amore"
(By Faith and Love)

THE END

As for Tom and Sarah, their adventure continues in
BRITFIELD & THE RISE OF THE LION, BOOK II.

Continuing the series, **Britfield & the Rise of the Lion** will be released in July 2021. Taking place throughout France, Tom and Sarah face an entirely new enemy, a nefarious and clandestine group with unlimited resources. With their ultimate destination as the castle Chambord, Tom and Sarah must first navigate through Paris streets and over rooftops, Notre Dame, the Eiffel Tower, and the Louvre, chased by an assassin determined to wipe out any potential threat to the British throne. Including old friends and new allies, Tom and Sarah's intense adventure is filled with twists and turns, unexpected betrayals and lifechanging revelations.

Born in Newport Beach, California, **C. R. Stewart** has 20 years of experience in writing fiction, non-fiction and movie screenplays. He is an international consultant, creativity specialist, producer and prolific writer. Founder of prestigious Devonfield, an innovative company dedicated to the highest quality in film production, publishing and education, Chad is an expert in the areas of global strategy, film and media production, and global marketing. He received a Bachelor of Arts in British Literature and European History from Brown University; earned an M.B.A. from Boston College; and is pursuing a Master of Science in Advanced Management and a PhD in Strategy at Peter F. Drucker and Masatoshi Ito Graduate School of Management, Claremont Graduate University. Chad has traveled throughout the world and spent two years in England for education and research. Now based in San Diego, he is a strong supporter of education and the arts. Chad enjoys world travel, reading, riding, swimming, sailing, tennis and writing.

We'd love to hear what you thought of BRITFIELD & THE LOST CROWN. Please feel free to email us at Britfield@DevonfieldPublishing.com

1) What was your impression of *Britfield & the Lost Crown*?

2) What was your favorite scene and why?

3) Who was your favorite character?

4) Any other comments about *Britfield & the Lost Crown*?

**Don't forget to explore *The World of Britfield*
www.Britfield.com**